**Praise for Brenda Gates Smith's
extraordinary debut,
*Secrets of the Ancient Goddess***

"Brenda Gates Smith has created an
absorbing story filled with ritual, romance,
adventure, and magic. This is a highly
entertaining novel that bears witness to
the importance and enduring power of
female spirituality."
—Mary Mackey, author of
The Year the Horses Came

"A fascinating and compelling novel."
—Joan Wolf, author of
The Daughter of the Red Deer

"The action-packed story line brings
antiquity to life through the wonderful
tales of two intrepid human beings. . . .
Brenda Gates Smith paints a vivid,
magical place that seems very plausible . . .
one of the sub-genre's most entertaining
novels of the year."
—Painted Rock Reviews

Goddess of the Mountain Harvest

Brenda Gates Smith

AN ONYX BOOK

For my sons
Both wonderful gifts
The best gifts of this life

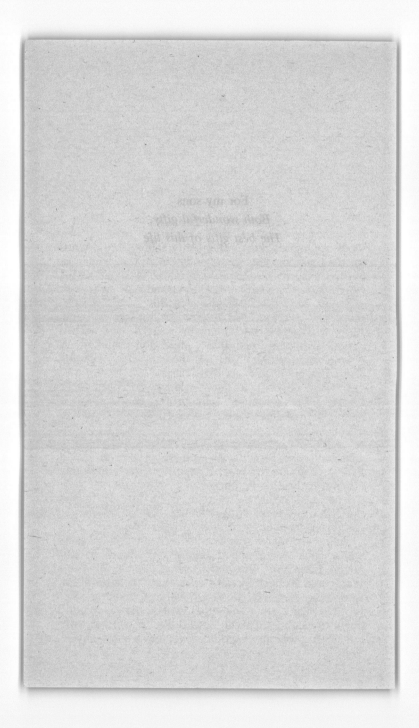

ACKNOWLEDGMENTS

Once again I'd like to thank my family and friends for their support and encouragement. I want to particularly thank my mother, Judith Gates. I am positive I would have been lost without Grandma's help with the boys during the last phase of this novel. Thanks, Mom, and you, too, Dad, for sharing her. My husband, Judd, what can I say? I am blessed to have such a patient, supportive man in my life. I don't think many people could put up with all the characters running around in my head on a daily basis.

I'd especially like to acknowledge my agent, Jean Naggar, and her staff. All are professional, dedicated people with smiles in their voices every time I call the office. Thank you.

I'd like to thank my editor, Hilary Ross, for her comments and insights, as well as all the people at Penguin Putnam for supporting my efforts, and seeing this novel through its phases of production.

I am grateful to my reading group for assisting in the editing process: Megan Pence, Cathy d'Almeida, Katharine Rumbaugh, and Stephanie Wong.

There are many researchers, writers, and thinkers whose ideas have added breath and depth to this novel. Elizabeth Wayland Barber's book *Women's Work*, and Robert Ekvall's case study in cultural anthropology *Fields on the Hoof*, were particularly helpful. There are so many other works that I couldn't begin to catalog them all, but I'd like to say that without others, this novel would never have come alive.

Prologue

Yana wasn't sure if her eyes were open or closed but a steady glow of light fought the darkness of the cave around her. It would not go away. She was drawn to the light. She wanted to dance with it, play with it. The light was so separate from the spirits of potential around her. She sensed the amusement of the Goddess, indulgent laughter, the sound a mother makes when her child discovers something new. "Go ahead," the laugh said. "Go play with the defining light if you want to."

Yana reached out and found the light was wet. For some reason this delighted her. She reached deeper into the wetness following the light, melting into the dark pool of the cavern, allowing her body to become the water. She was completely drawn, completely absorbed by the desire of the light. *What are we choosing now, Goddess?* her spirit asked.

The light became brighter. She swam deeper and deeper, following the underground river. Occasionally her body demanded she come up for air and her head bumped the top of the tunnel, but there was always just enough room to inhale. The flow filled the widening tunnel; the current forced her deeper. The light was above her now. She struggled against the current, swimming for the brightness. Her head broke the surface and small waves rippled around her. Soft morning sunlight greeted her eyes.

A woman dropped the pot she had just lifted from

the water, shattering it, screeching and running away.
Yana wanted to stop her—tell her there was nothing
to fear. She climbed out of the water and onto the
stone slabs leading down to the pool. The warm stone
felt wonderful on her skin and she sat for a moment
basking in the sun, then stood slowly, ascending the
steps.

People gathered around the pool. They stepped
back, shock and wonder on their faces. Yana's heart
filled with joy. *I did it,* she thought elatedly. *I belong.
The Mother Goddess has found me worthy to be
adopted into this village. I have a home now!*

From the surprise on the faces around her, Yana
realized that most of the people of the village had not
expected her to survive the cave of the Goddess,
where one could easily get lost in the labyrinth of
tunnels. Most of the passages were too narrow to
squeeze through. Fortunately the Goddess had shown
Yana that she could escape by swimming to the pool
in the center of the village.

An old man with a twisted foot dropped to his
knees, making the sign of the Goddess and burying
his face in the dirt. Yana went to him, caught him
under the arms, and lifted him. How could she explain
that he did not need to be afraid? How could she tell
him not to make that choice?

Yana turned around, surveying the people. She saw
Tern, the man she hoped would someday be her
hearth mate. His face was alight with joy, but she also
saw apprehension in his eyes. *Do I look as different
as I feel?* she wondered. *He knows I've changed, but
he must know we will find each other again.* She smiled
warmly. He smiled tentatively in return. Then Yana's
eyes rested on Galea, the woman she would now call
Mother for the rest of her life. Her adoptive mother
was crying happily. Little Atum strained in her arms,
reaching for Yana. She went to her son. Galea placed
the boy in her arms reverently, as if bestowing a valuable gift. Atum looked at her and curiously patted her

wet hair. "I will be more careful of my choices," she promised him. "We have so much more to learn together."

An aged priestess, her misshapen arm tucked in a wool shawl, approached Yana. The elder saw new strength in Yana, new calm as she stood naked, glistening wet with Atum in her arms. The young woman had emerged from the sacred cave and waters of the Goddess, radiating beauty and acceptance. The High Priestess's eyes were shining. She reached out her good hand to share the priestess touch. Yana placed her palm under the palm of the elder woman.

"We share the priestess touch, Daughter," Telna said, her voice cracking with emotion. "You have experienced the ancient darkness of the Goddess and are now adopted into the people. Not only have you escaped the cave of Her darkness, you have come through Her sacred waters. This has never been done before. Her ways are a mystery, but She has found you worthy. You shall be the Mother Priestess of the people when I go to Her womb in death."

Loud gasps and murmurs ran through the crowd of onlookers.

A figure appeared on a distant hill. Yana pointed. The people turned at once, like one body. Descending the hill was a heavily pregnant woman on the back of a horse, escorted by traders from a distant village. The red highlights of her hair glimmered in the sunlight as the woman sat proudly on her mount.

Seeing her true daughter alive, Galea let out a joyful scream. "Henne," she shrieked, running toward the hill. The older woman ran with the agility of a child, her skirt fluttering in the breeze.

A surprised rumble passed through the crowd as they watched the horse cautiously make its way down the hill with the precious load it carried. They had heard of barbarians who rode horses, but had never seen it done, and amazingly this horse carried one of their own. Henne had somehow escaped the horsemen, returning home with a child filling her womb.

The people parted in awe as Henne passed, but up close the young woman seemed flushed, less certain. A glaze of sweat and dust covered her face and arms. She suddenly paled, dropped the reins, and groaned, doubling over while holding the mound of her belly.

PART 1

The Descent

1

Ancient Turkey, 5700 BC

The low, husky groan grew to a growl of pain. Yana watched as people froze at their tasks, waiting for the growl to recede. Their silence amplified the sound, lifting it beyond the walls of the mud brick house. It hovered in the courtyard, settling into anxiety on the faces of the villagers: a worried crease here, a stiff jaw there, a dropping of the eyes. As the groan faded, the chanting began, the fire's sizzle was heard, and the hustle of wind through the grasses, felt once more.

It was early evening. The groans, growing all day, came from a house at the far end of the courtyard. Yana looked up as the deer hide curtain covering the door was tossed aside. Lamplight cut through the shadows, and the rotund form of the High Priestess filled the doorway. The old woman scanned the faces in the courtyard until her eyes found Yana.

"Come, Yana," she hissed urgently, gesturing with her stunted arm. "Your mother needs you. It is almost time to sing the birthing song for your sister and the child."

Startled, Yana dropped the small bone needle and limestone beads she was using to decorate the hem of her skirt. Her mother needed her. Her mother! Now that the ordeal of the adoption was over, she had a family that wanted her. Yana's heart swelled in gratitude. Galea was her mother now, and Henne, her sister. Her family expected the power of her prayers to the Goddess. They wanted her to sing!

She stumbled to a stand, her weak legs shaking. The adoption ritual had been rigorous, but her new sister deserved all her remaining strength. Yana took a deep breath, struggling not to sway on her feet, but shadows and people wavered as she made her way across the courtyard. She paused before the door of the mud brick house, then pushed the door flap aside.

The air in the room was humid, sticky with the smells of labored breath, birthing fluid, and sweat. Yellow light from the oil lamps fluttered on the soot-smudged ceiling and plastered walls. Henne lay on her back near the east wall of the house, the place where the Sun Goddess gave birth each morning.

Henne's eyes grew wide. Her face contorted. She screamed, her body lifting from the matted sheepskin rug. A priestess with long bleached hair leaned against her feet, giving leverage as she bore down. An old healing woman, Ninka, waved the young priestess away. The elder's arms and neck were tattooed with the black swirling symbols of fertility. When she stooped to knead Henne's belly, the tattoos danced rhythmically along the muscles of her arms.

Henne's eyes squeezed shut, then flew open again. A gasp came from the back of her throat, guttural, more urgent this time. The small black crown of the baby's head protruded, then receded.

"It is time," Ninka said gruffly. With the help of two priestesses, the healer pulled the laboring woman to a squatting position.

Yana moved closer, her stomach knotted with worry. This birth was different. New life was sacred to the people, but this was Henne bearing her first child—Henne, the daughter who had been stolen, captured by northern barbaric invaders. Earth Goddess had gone through a full cycle of seasons since she had been taken. The wonder of Henne's return was too new, too fresh in the minds of the villagers, making it hard to cope with the travails of birth. For many it was as if Henne had just returned from the dead, only to fight death again as she labored.

Seated near the door, the bulky figure of the High Priestess prayed in a pulsing drone, protecting the entrance from harmful spirits. Telna stopped chanting. "Galea, Yana," her scraping voice commanded. "It's time to sing for your kinswoman. The baby must be welcomed with the songs of the ancestors."

Yana felt a wave of dizziness as her adopted mother reached for her hand, turning her to the east. She echoed Galea's words as together they raised their arms, singing to the place where the yolk of the Goddess rises in the morning. Slowly they circled west, where light descends into darkness, calling for the child's long life and fertility. As they sang, Yana's eyes watered. Things in the room lost their edges, blurred. She was unsteady on her feet. Galea supported her by leaning close as they chanted.

Henne's tightly stretched belly rippled with the life inside it. Sweat trailed her neck and face. Grimacing, she grunted and strained hard. Bit by bit the baby's head protruded. The healing woman stepped between Henne's blood-smeared thighs and cupped the infant's head, gently moving it side to side, urging Henne to push harder. A shoulder appeared and a tiny fist. Galea gasped. Her fingers dug into Yana's wrist as the rest of the baby's body slipped into the healer's arms. Henne collapsed back onto the sheepskin rug.

"Welcome, little mother," the healing woman said, her voice husky with emotion. "Galea, you have a granddaughter." She turned to the priestesses. "Kara," she said, nodding to the priestess with bleached hair, "release the child from the snake of the Mother." Kara stepped forward, severing the umbilical cord with a flint knife.

Yana moved closer. Her breath caught in her chest. The baby's skin color—it was too dark, almost blue!

The healing woman massaged Henne's belly until

the afterbirth passed. She put this in a clay bowl and covered it with a small piece of hide, handing the bowl to Galea, who scurried out of the room to bury it in the fields. Ninka turned and hastily pushed past Yana. She took the child in her arms and crossed the room to the hearth, where a large bowl of sand was being warmed. With one hand she dumped the sand into a mound on the ground, then checked the temperature of the sand before smoothing it flat with the back of her arm, making an indentation for the child's head and buttocks.

"The Earth Goddess holds you, little one," the healer said the ritual words as she lay the infant on the cradle of sand and began moving its arms outward and above the head. She manipulated the small chest, then lifted the baby's arms again.

"Her sacred breath must come," Yana whispered the prayer.

Ninka nodded curtly. She put her mouth over the tiny nostrils, sucking out mucus and birthing fluid, spitting it on the floor. She pinched the infant's nose and began blowing into her mouth. The High Priestess seated near the door began to chant louder as if her words alone could command the death away.

Henne lifted herself on her elbows. "Where is the voice of my daughter? Where is her cry?" she demanded.

Galea entered the room, taking in the situation. She went to Henne, smoothing back the sweat-drenched hair on her forehead. "Sometimes we must wait for the breath of the Goddess, Daughter," she tried to reassure her. "It is early yet."

It was as if Henne did not hear her mother. "Sing to the Goddess, Daughter!" she demanded, her voice rising. "Cry!"

"She is trying," a young priestess snapped, obviously upset.

Yana turned to the child. It was true. The infant's mouth was opening and closing like a minnow in water, but no sound came out. Its tiny fists were flailing at the air, but the silence was smothering, thick, covering everything. Then she heard it. In the distance Grandmother Frog was croaking, calling—

The room began to shift. A flush of heat rose to Yana's cheeks, then she was cold, so cold. Her long limbs went numb. Her eyes lost focus. Light and sound faded. Desperately she reached for the last dwindling sound, the croaking drone of distant frogs calling to the night shadows. She lost control of her trembling legs, sinking to a seated position, shoulders hunched, dark hair hanging over her face.

The High Priestess saw Yana crumple to the floor. Telna stopped chanting and struggled to stand, cursing at the slowness of aged legs. She took a deep breath and steadied herself on the door frame. Yana sat so still, her face pale. Could the young woman be in a trance? Telna lumbered across the room, squatting down. With gnarled fingers she lifted the younger woman's chin. Her aged, watery eyes peered into Yana's fevered ones.

"What is it, child?" she whispered.

Yana's head lolled to one side. "Can't you hear it, Honored One?" she mumbled. "Grandmother Frog calls—calls my sister's little girl. Her womb will travel far."

The elder shivered. A prophecy?

"She must leave the liquid of the womb," Yana whispered, clasping the old one's hand, her eyes wild, desperate. "This child must live."

And then the High Priestess heard it, the loud croaking of the Frog Goddess. That was it, the child had fluid in her lungs!

The old one pushed to a stand, elbowing her way past Kara and Galea. The healer was still patiently blowing into the child's mouth while massaging its chest. Telna interrupted, taking the child in her arms. At first the High Priestess looked uncertain. Instinctively she lifted the infant, patting her back while pressing just below the tiny ribs. Fluid dribbled, then gushed from the baby's mouth. The infant took a deep breath, bawling lustily. Henne, who had risen to a hunched stand, sobbed with relief, and collapsed against the nearby wall. Kara hastened to her side, helping the new mother back into a reclining position.

A grin spread across Galea's face as the child's color took on a healthy pink glow. She went to the door, announcing the birth of her granddaughter to the people. Laughter and cheering could be heard from the courtyard. She reentered the room and the child was again put on the warm sand. An ear of barley was placed at the infant's head, wheat at her side. The chanting began again. A smile crackled in the voice of the High Priestess.

"The Earth Goddess holds you, little one
The gifts of Her womb are yours.
From Her soil the Great Bull rises
On the staff of life-giving barley
Barley is hardy when drought is in the land.
May you stand strong in the dry season."

She picked up an ear of wheat and crushed it in her palm, sprinkling seeds over the baby's stomach. The smell of summer baked grasses permeated the room.

"As wheat fills the belly in times of abundance,
May your life be abundant and long,
May your seed spread on the wind
Finding rich soil until the Mother Goddess
Holds you once again in Her sacred womb."

The elder motioned the healer to bring a small bowl of white ash from the fire. Together they sprinkled ashes over the baby, rubbing hard to remove the birthing fluid and the waxy film coating her skin. The yowling protests of the infant brought indulgent smiles from the onlookers. The healer took a mouthful of tepid juniper tea, spitting it on the little girl's face and labia, massaging both deeply. A burst of laughter erupted when the arch of the child's warm urine sprayed the hands of the healer.

Yana felt as if she had just awakened to a wondrous dream. Although her skin was clammy, the nausea plaguing her seemed to recede into small, tolerable waves. She leaned against the rough plaster wall, her eyes caressing each face: her adoptive mother, Galea, her new sister, Henne, the young priestess, Kara, and Ninka, the healer. They were all connected in this happiness; each one lit up from within. The face of the High Priestess became radiant as she proudly picked up the infant for all in the room to see. How different it was from Yana's own experience birthing her son, Atum. She had been so alone then, cursed because of her son's twisted foot. She pushed the sad thought away. Bad luck no longer followed her. Now she had a mother, a sister, a village family. Finally she was part of something large, whole, like the Goddess. If only her bones didn't ache. If only she wasn't weary, dizzy, and cold. . . .

2

Henne lifted the damp hair clinging to her neck, pulling it over her shoulder before relaxing into the fresh blankets and cushions laid out for her by Kara. She absentmindedly raked fingers through tangled russet hair. Someone brought a marble bowl of warm juniper tea, but she was too distracted to drink it. She waited impatiently as Ninka and the High Priestess finished the ritual washing of her baby. Finally the High Priestess lifted the clean infant from the sand, wrapping her in a roughly woven linen cloth before whispering a blessing in the child's ear and kissing her forehead. Telna crossed the room to where Henne lay. The new mother eagerly lifted her arms, reaching for her daughter.

Henne gathered the little one close and turned back the cloth to look at her. She gasped. The newborn's tiny raised fist was next to her cheek. How often had she seen Ralic with his fist raised just so when sleeping? Ralic, the man she had hated, then loved—the barbarian who had almost destroyed her sanity. My daughter must have been positioned in the womb with her fist next to her cheek, Henne reasoned. But then the little one also had Ralic's brooding brow, his firm jaw and mass of dark curls, somehow made beautiful in tiny feminine features. The baby shifted, mewling in her sleep. A fierce possessiveness clutched at Henne's heart. She didn't know what she had expected after the long months of waiting with this child kicking in her womb. She hadn't expected a person so vitally alive, separate from herself, someone she would have to learn to know.

Galea leaned over Henne's shoulder, admiring her sleeping grandchild. "I think she is going to have your eyes, Daughter," she said in a hushed voice. "She seems strong. Our ancestors are proud. Can you feel it?"

Henne nodded, her eyes welling with tears. *Not just our ancestors, Mother,* she thought. *Ralic would be celebrating if he were alive, feasting and dancing if he could see the power in his little girl's face—although he had wished for a boy.*

The High Priestess crossed the room and helped Yana to stand, escorting her back to the small family group. "Henne," she said gravely, her stance slightly formal, "the baby needs your sister's welcome. Yana must bless the child before your daughter is named."

Henne's green eyes darted between Galea and the High Priestess, brows furrowing a question. "Sister? I have no sister," she said.

Galea's strong fingers closed around Yana's hand; she drew her close. Her wide mouth opened to say something, but closed again. Her gray-flecked brows pulled together, looking to Telna for help, but the High Priestess remained sternly silent. Galea took a deep breath, realizing she must explain to Henne why she had adopted another daughter in her absence. She let go of Yana's hand and dropped to a kneeling position, reverently touching her daughter's face.

"When I was told of your capture by the barbarians," she whispered, "the pain of it was like a deep wound in my chest, an ache that never went away. There were days when I could not face the yolk of the morning sun. I turned my back on the Goddess, staying in my sleeping blankets." Galea reached for Yana's hand again, inviting her to sit beside them. "Yana and her son were the only ones who could ease the pain," she continued. "It was understood she

didn't try. But when
the adoption cere-
d daughter."

throat. "Your return
We didn't have time
—your birthing pains
to be made . . ."

"So much has hap-
given you back to
have a granddaugh-
adopted by our peo-
r. "Yana is not only
ter's moon sister."
Goddess," Telna said
alea's words. "Yana

Yana's face was too
pallor. Her dark hair
eyes were shadowed

"But you must first learn to swim between the dark and light places, just as the frog travels between water and air. These are my words and my blessing." She kissed the child on the forehead.

Galea reached for the infant, also whispering her blessing before handing the infant back to Henne.

"Henne and the baby must rest now," the High Priestess asserted. "We all must rest. I will not wait another moon to name this child. The child has proved her willingness to live, and her moon day has had many good omens. I will name the baby tonight, when the Goddess of the Night Sky rises. The priestesses will inform the elders and the people, but we must sleep until then."

Galea nodded. Yana stood up, swaying slightly, intending to leave with the High Priestess. Telna looked at her sharply. "You especially need sleep, Yana," she observed. "The adoption ritual took your strength. Stay here in your mother's house. It is your home now. I will have your brother Dagron bring a sleeping mat and your blankets."

"But what of my son? I have not seen Atum since—"

"Atum is well," the High Priestess interrupted. "Nachen is caring for him. Your son can wait. You must rest now."

Tern sat in the doorway trying to catch the last light of the sun before it sank into the mountains beyond the valley. It took everything in his power to concentrate on the work in his lap. He squinted over an obsidian sickle blade that had come loose from its gazelle bone shaft. He pushed a sandy lock of hair out of his eyes. Occasionally he looked up, covertly watching the door of Galea's house, hoping for a glimpse of Yana. He shook his head in wonder. It still didn't feel real. Yana had endured the adoption ritual, a ritual most thought only children could survive.

He still remembered the night Yana was sent on a

he womb of the Goddess,
d ritual dances and meet-
d then. When she didn't
ening of the tunnel at the
ht she was dead. He had
Yana escaped the cave by
derground river emptying
e people. This had never
Priestess took it as a sign
omen, confirmed shortly
seen riding into the valley.
other resin-smeared blade
l been given a chance to
n anything, he wanted to
was alive into the curl of
ely since his hearth mate,
was one of the people, it
would allow them to be-

he High Priestess ducked
a's house. His long fingers
his hands. But only the
ved the elder as she hob-
ward the Goddess's shrine.
ent. Yana must have de-
e others, and he couldn't
ment of the day, she had

ame. Yana heard but her
dn't want to open them.
calling her name again.
It is almost time for the

caused Yana to drag her
it in her adopted mother's
ed once more. Galea's face
lished the older woman's
rooked nose, and the pro-

truding chin softening with age. Course strings of gray escaped charred braids, braids wound and fastened on the top of her head like a cap. This woman was her mother now. Did she sense the importance of it also?

"Daughter," Galea said softly, as if to answer, "I have brought a fresh wrap and combs for your hair. Shall I braid it for you?"

Yana sat up. Searing pain shot through her left breast. She tried not to wince as she reached out. "You have other things to do, Galea. I can dress myself," she said, taking the bone combs and brown wool dress.

Galea nodded and stood to leave, but hesitated at the door. "Daughter," she said deliberately. "Your home is here now. It would be better if you addressed me as Mother."

Yana's eyes grew moist. "Thank you . . . Mother. I will try to remember."

Galea smiled warmly, nodding with approval before leaving.

Without getting up, Yana shrugged off the dress she had been sleeping in. Her fever was worse. Her head throbbed as she braided her hair, and each movement brought pain. Her breasts were heavy, hot. A swelling knot had formed in the left one, tender to the touch. *I am sick, very sick.* The thought should have startled her, but it didn't. Since her adoption, it was as if part of her was numb, unbelieving. Life seemed to float around her while inside she was very still. She decided the sickness must stay concealed until the ceremony was over. She did not want to bring bad luck to the child's naming day. She finished dressing, tying a brightly woven sash around her waist.

The priestess Kara pushed aside the deer hide curtain. Yana looked up. She thought Kara's large, round eyes at odds with her narrow face, although her looks had a strange kind of allure. The young woman's straight hair, bleached with limestone paste, hung from a fine skull, adding length to features that already seemed long.

h

vered. A stream of
down the neck of
nket, covering her-
torso.

" Kara exclaimed,
m to escort you to
ss wishes to include

y stand. How could
mony? "Kara," she
can."

er pale brows knit
squatted, bleached
ut her.

"This is not only a
lso the new moon,
ting."

dropping her eyes.
ink I can stand for
aten and . . ." Her
vously, not wanting

's face, noting for

through the courtyard, Yana leaning on Kara for support, glad that the priestess didn't expect her to speak. It took all her strength just to walk.

The courtyard was empty, the working hearth's abandoned coals burning in lava hills surrounded by rocks. They passed the large clay bins where the people stored their grain. Near the bins, belly-shaped ovens used for baking bread sat in hunched mounds. Overhead, countless stars speckled the sky. The moon was curved like a sickle blade, but the outline of its full shadow belied its true shape. The cedar trees beyond the village stood tall and silent while Grandmother Frog still pumped a hoarse croak.

At first Yana did not know where Kara was taking her, but soon realized they were headed for the shrine and Sacred Waters of the Goddess; the same waters she had swam through during the adoption ritual. As they rounded the corner of the last house, she could hear the murmuring of the people near the spring.

"You are to sit over there," Kara whispered, pointing to the place where the elders were gathered. "Do you think you can make it alone? I need to speak to the High Priestess before the ceremony begins."

Yana took a deep breath, squaring her shoulders to steady herself. "I will be all right as long as I can sit down."

Kara disappeared into the Goddess's shrine as Yana carefully made her way through the throng of people waiting by the spring. Her eyes focused on the welcoming face of old man Heth, the knife maker. He moved over, making a place for her. Yana sank to the ground, wiping away the cold sweat gathering on her forehead. She shivered and pulled the heavy woolen blanket close while hugging her knees to her body, toes curling into the dirt for warmth. She suspected her chill was the result of the fast. How long had it been? Had a handspan of days really passed? She shook her head. That is what Galea had told her, but it didn't seem possible. Strange. She wasn't hungry—just cold.

Her son was playing a short distance away with Nachen's granddaughter, Isha. The two babies were pulling the seeds from pinecones they'd discovered. Atum caught sight of Yana and dropped his. He pushed himself up, rump first, steadying his small feet before waddling toward his mother. Yana smiled at how fast her son was changing. He was much surer on his feet, and her heart expanded with gratitude. When Atum was an infant, the people of this village showed her how to straighten his leg with a brace of sticks. She shook her head with amazement. Now her son was walking, walking like any other child his age. Atum gained momentum as he came closer, careening into her arms, gnawing on her face with wet kisses before nuzzling into her blanket to nurse.

Yana's breasts ached when Atum tugged on them. She yelped in surprised pain as the milk let down. Her body wanted to feed him, but it hurt. Nothing came out. She sucked in a cheek as her little boy struggled to draw milk. He pulled on her nipples. One cracked and began to bleed. Had she been gone too long? Was she unable to nurse? Atum tried once more then gave a frustrated grunt. He caught sight of Isha, who was pulling on the ears of a half-grown puppy. He pumped his little body, laughing, then pushed out of Yana's lap, crawling toward the other child. She smiled wanly after him. Apparently Atum was more interested in the dog than eating.

Two priestesses in long black robes left the shrine, carrying oil lamps. With great ceremony they lit large torches stationed around the rim of the sacred pool. When finished, they returned to the shrine. Gold light splashed on the black water, water that trembled in the breeze.

Yana inhaled cool evening air tinged with the taste of wood smoke. The elder who had been sitting beside Yana stirred, leaning closer, his prickly brows lifting with inquiry. "I'm told you were at the birth," he said in gravelly tones. "The first birth is always hardest. I am not a woman, but I understand the body fights the transformation. Going from maid to mother is a great honor."

Yana wondered if the old man was speaking of Henne or her own rebirth journey through the cave of the Goddess. His voice dropped and Yana had to bend close to hear.

"I wonder what it is like to feel your youth slip into another body, to be born outside. It must be hard to let it go. This has been in my thoughts. I am a man— an old man. Only now do I see the youth I have expelled in things outside. I want to pull it all close, pull it back, hold it." He sighed wistfully.

Yana turned, offering a weary smile. The old man's eyes gleamed with the love for new life. Yana understood the elder was only talking to her intimately because of her recent spiritual quest. She put a hand on his lame knee. "The baby is beautiful," she said quietly. "And Henne has returned to us safely. Her journey is over."

The old man fingered a worn cowry shell that hung from a thong of leather around his neck. He sat thinking, then grunted. "Yes, what you say is true," he said. "I was thinking of my own journey away from home. I wonder what would have happened if I had returned." He lifted the shell for her to inspect. "It was a gift from my father the last day we fished together . . ."

Yana knew the cowry shell represented the abundant womb of the Goddess and she sensed a story building on the old man's thin, freckled lips. She waited respectfully for him to continue. Across the crowd Tern's impatient eyes caught hers. They hadn't had a chance to be alone together since Henne was seen riding into the village, and he was not allowed to approach the elder's circle without invitation. Clearly he expected Yana to come to him. She inclined her head toward the elder, trying to convey the impossibility of this with her eyes.

The old one was silent for a long time. Yana began to wonder if he was dozing. Her head ached. The trill of crickets and the hollow croak of frogs thudded in her temple. Why was it all so uncomfortably loud? Grandmother Frog seemed to be everywhere tonight. The elder beside her finally cleared his throat and began to speak, but she had to focus all of her attention just to listen.

"I lived in a small village near the Great Waters of the Goddess," he began, speaking slowly. "My mother died. Soon afterward my father took a new mate. At first I thought my new mother cared for me, but as she became large with child, her eyes became round with fear every time I approached her."

He hesitated for a moment, rubbing his lame leg as if it pained him. "The day she went to the birthing hut," he continued, "my father took me to our small fishing boat. He gave me a pack of dried meat, flat cakes, and this cowry shell. He told me to follow the coastline south until I saw an island on the horizon. I was to go to the people of the island—trade my shell for something beautiful for my mother. He told me to stay away until the baby had been named. "I . . . I never saw him again."

Yana tilted her head sympathetically toward his leg. "The woman was afraid for her child," she said, stating the obvious. "She was afraid of your luck."

"The people here taught me it was ignorance to fear my twisted leg. They welcomed me because they had too few healthy children. That was long ago. The blood of the people is strong now. The children here are born healthy, but it was not always that way."

"Did you ever make it to the island?"

He ran his tongue over his teeth. "There was a storm in the night. My boat was overcome with the Waters of the Goddess. Somehow I made it to shore, but I was starving when traders found me. They sold me to other traders and that is how I came to live here."

And now, old man, you are a respected elder, Yana thought as the frogs croaked in the distance. The Goddess of Wandering had brought a stranger to a place where he was accepted, and now she had found the same home.

"I often dream of that island." His voice quavered. "Sometimes, when the morning mist settles in the valley and the distant hills peak above, I can almost see it. I always thought I'd make the journey someday, but a man with a bent leg does not make a good traveler." The thin skin of his lips stretched into a crooked grin.

Somewhere, a child giggled. A dog slouching nearby scooted forward, nose inching for a friendly pat. Tern's face was angled away, but Yana could feel his awareness of her, his need to be with her like the pressure building in her skull. She wanted to go to him, but her curdling stomach objected. Her head felt loose on her shoulders. She was not at all sure she could stand. Yana rested her forehead on her knees.

"My words must not sadden you, Daughter," the old one said in concern, misunderstanding her distress. "I have been very happy here. I have sons and daughters who honor me. You will have this too. The island was a dream."

Yana's head felt thick as she lifted it. "It is not your dream that disturbs my stomach, honored one," was her hushed reply. "I am afraid I have not completely recovered from the adoption ritual."

Heth sat thinking for a moment, then nodded abruptly as if he had come to a conclusion. "Ah then, your journey is not yet finished," he responded gravely, looking Yana in the eye.

Tern frowned, the crescents around his mouth cut into his closely cropped beard as he realized that Yana would not be able to come to him. He tried to pull

Isha into his arms, cuddle her, but she would have none of it; his daughter was too busy with Atum and the puppy. He sighed. Isha seemed to want him less and less since living with her grandmother, and this was to be expected. Isha belonged with Nachen now; it was the women of the village who passed on the lineage of family. Dala has been gone almost two harvest seasons, he reminded himself, and the elders would expect him to take another mate, raising children with someone new, but his little girl would always hold a special place in his heart.

He glanced at Yana, sitting in a place of honor with the elders. Yana knew what it was to feel alone, discarded, but now that she had a mother, a home, would she want him as she had before? If only she would look at him. If only she would stop talking with old man Heth, come to him, sit down, touch his hand.

The High Priestess emerged from the shrine, followed by four priestesses. Everyone stood. The crowd parted for them at a place where wide, flat-hewn rocks descended to the womb-shaped pool fed by an underground river. The priestesses took their places on the marble steps next to the torches. Telna stood in the middle. The young priestesses lifted their arms in unison, a gesture to quiet the people. The High Priestess glanced sharply at Yana, studying the strength in the younger woman's features before telling everyone to sit. Yana exhaled in relief and sank to the ground.

Henne, leaning on Galea for support, was escorted from the shrine, and room was made for them on a stone directly opposite Yana. Yana smiled tentatively in their direction. Galea took the baby from Henne's arms and offered the newborn to the closest priestess before taking her seat.

The High Priestess surveyed the assembly until she was satisfied that everyone was present. She was dressed in a long gray robe made of woven plant fiber, decorated with meandering zigzag lines in saffron, blue, and red. Water symbols, Yana realized. The aged woman lifted her head, her voice throbbing in a vibrant chant.

From the waters of the womb, the child is given,
From the watered earth womb, the plant rises
From the tears of the sky, life is restored.

She paused, voice dropping, but still loud enough to be heard clearly. "A short time ago a young woman came to us," she said. "Yana dared to face the darkness of the cave to become our sister and daughter." The old one pointed a draped arm to the glistening wetness behind her. "Today at dawn, Yana emerged from these sacred waters to be reborn to our people. At the moment of her rebirth," the priestess continued solemnly, "Henne was seen entering our valley on the back of a horse, ripe with the seed of the Goddess in her womb. As the sun set, another daughter was born to our people."

The elder turned to the priestess beside her and gathered Henne's baby in the crook of her draped arm. She smiled tenderly at the infant, walking to where Yana was seated. The elders moved aside. The priestess placed her good hand on Yana's head. She cleared her throat to speak, lifting the infant in the crook of her arm.

"At the time of this little one's birth," she said, "the child could not speak. But Yana gave words to our small daughter's mouth."

Henne's head jerked in surprise.

"Yana was in a trance. She told me that Grandmother Frog was calling. I listened and it was true." The High Priestess raised her hand against the rumbling questions of the people. She hesitated, allowing a moment of stillness. Nothing was heard except the croaking frogs in the distance and the gurgling of the spring.

"Grandmother Frog was singing, telling her daughter it was time to leave the liquid of the womb. With the help of the Goddess I pushed the water from her breathing place. If Yana had not been listening to Grandmother Frog . . ." The old one shook her head gravely, letting her words dwindle to silence.

The people began to whisper in awe. Henne's heart thumped in her chest. Was it true? Had Yana really saved her daughter?

Telna turned to Yana, her eyes kind. "Someday, Yana, you will take my place as High Priestess of the people. The Goddess walks in you. You listen to Her voice. This child," she said, stooping to place the infant in Yana's arms, "was born the day of your rebirth. I name her Enyana, water sister of Yana."

Yana's pale face shone like the moon in darkness, her eyes wide and luminous.

Henne stared at Yana in disbelief. Her daughter had another woman's name. And how did a stranger become the High Priestess of the people? How dare she! Did Yana have any priestess training at all? She leaned toward Galea. "Mother, I don't understand," she hissed, but Galea was gazing raptly at Yana and her grandchild. She patted Henne's arm without looking at her. "It is a long story," she whispered. "I will explain later.

Yana rubbed the back of her hand along the downy cheek of the infant. The baby made smacking sounds as she sucked sleepily on the dimpled knuckle still closed in a fist. *The name is a good one,* Yana thought. The two of them would always be connected because of it, always be of the same family. She felt a wave of gratitude toward the little one. She glanced at Henne and Galea. Galea's eyes spoke her pride, but Henne was frowning, her eyes clouded. Yana felt a stab of apprehension. What was wrong? Where was her adoptive sister's smile?

Telna bent to pick up the baby, returning her to Galea before joining the priestesses still gathered on the steps. With a sweeping gesture, she motioned all the priestesses but Kara to sit. One by one the priestesses found places along the border of the stone slabs, leaving a wedge-shaped path to the water's edge. The High Priestess murmured something in Kara's ear then stepped aside so the younger woman could address the people.

Kara stood in the middle of the marble steps, her bleached tresses glowing like a halo against the gleaming black waters. Her wrists were covered with carved bone bracelets. From her ears, copper pendants swung. A rope of amber birthstones girdled her waist. Her lips, painted dark as bruised berries, parted slightly. Her soft voice slithered among the people.

"The moon has risen." She sighed into the night breeze. "Grandmother Frog tells us it is time for spring planting to begin. Her children spawn in the trenches of our fields. Where Her tail was, legs grow. Arms spring from Her back. She lifts Her nose from the waters, breathing the spring air, croaking triumph, yet stays mysterious, hiding in moist shadows. In the dry season She disappears, only to return with the rains. Grandmother Frog is found in all the land during the time of rebirth. She is the Womb That Travels Far."

Kara lifted her arms and voice. The sleeves of her black robe fell back, revealing tattoos of chevrons and spirals above the elbows and on her shoulders. "Grandmother Frog is everywhere in things unborn. She is the unspoken thought that forces words to come. She is the urge between a man and a woman. She is in the carver's hand and the potter's eye. She is the Goddess of Becoming, the Mistress of the Waters."

Kara turned to the High Priestess. The elder removed the girdle of red birthstones from around the younger woman's waist. Yana knew the yellow-red stones represented blood, life, and motherhood. She watched with enormous eyes as the ritual continued.

"Why, Grandmother, have you taken my birthing girdle?" Kara asked, acting confused and surprised.

"Enter, my daughter. This is the sacred law of the Mistress of the Waters."

Kara descended the next step, where another priestess waited to strip her bone bracelets; the white of the bone symbolizing the Goddess of Death and Regeneration.

"Why, Sister, have you taken my bracelets?"

"Enter, my sister," the priestess droned. "This is the sacred law of the Mistress of the Waters."

Yana realized she was watching the reenactment of Maiden Goddess's descent into the womb of rebirth. She shivered in anticipation. With each step downward another article of clothing was removed. Kara's earrings, necklaces, and finally the cover of her robe were taken; black representing the color of fertility and rich soil. The tattoos winding along Kara's arms and narrow shoulder blades stood starkly against her pale skin and hair. Her legs were long, spindly, her body jutting curves. The young woman stood naked before the dark waters, stripped of everything defining her, slowly entering the pool, taking deep breaths before submerging. Her white limbs separated, moving like Grandmother Frog as she dove, the flash of her pale body rippling in the deep water.

The world around Yana pulsed with light and dark shadows as she remembered her own experience in the womb of the Goddess. A strange humming started in her ears, and it took a moment before she realized the people were whispering a chant, begging the Goddess to return to them. Kara stayed underwater for what seemed to be an unendurable length of time. In the endless waiting, Yana's sickness rose like a serpent. It curled itself along her spine and limbs, squeezing. She became aware of everything in her body that ached. Her throat closed, her face burned. Sweat gathered at her temple. The stone she sat on cut into her hip. Even the cool night air felt abrasive on her skin.

Kara's head broke the surface of the water, and a release of bated breath hissed through the crowd as the villagers murmured a greeting. The young woman crawled out on the lowest step, water streaming from her small breasts and hair. Kara stood, chin set, holding in her left hand a water skin.

The priestess waiting on the lowest step approached and bowed, returning Kara's robe, helping her dress. Kara faced the priestess.

"Why have you given me this robe?" she demanded, her eyes flashing.

The priestess bowed again. "To give your body form, Honored One."

Kara climbed the steps one by one. Her garments were returned, followed by the rehearsed response of those dressing her. Finally she reached the High Priestess holding aloft the birthstone girdle.

"Why have you given me this girdle?" Kara asked with the voice of an impertinent goddess.

The High Priestess fastened the belt to hang low on Kara's hips, then bowed. "I have returned your birthstone girdle so you will remember the fertility of the people, Honored One."

Kara lifted the plain water bag she had been carrying and gave it to Telna. She waved her hand over the villagers. "Sprinkle them with the Water of Life. My sacrifice is my tears as I give birth. This is womb water falling as rain, my gift to the people." Kara abruptly turned to leave. The crowd of onlookers moved aside as she walked to the Goddess's shrine.

The High Priestess first sprinkled Yana and the baby. Yana barely felt the spattering of droplets on her hot skin before the elder moved on through the crowd. The symbolism was evident. The Goddess gave life and water. In return, the people were to follow her example, giving water to the crops during the hot season, feeding and watering the grain and sheep. As the people received the water they began to disperse. Yana sighed. Now perhaps, she could rest.

3

Atum's pudgy fingers poked at Yana's face. He pulled at an eyelid. "Mam, Mam, Mam," he droned persistently, trying to wake her. Yana groaned and rolled away, facing the wall. He climbed over their sleeping blankets to get at her face again. He pouted, patting her cheek, pulling on her hair. Something was wrong. Mammar would not open her eyes, would not smile at him. A tear tumbled to his lower lip, a sad whimper escaped his mouth.

Galea, working near the hearth, heard Atum's whimper. It had been a late night, but Yana should be up by now. Her son was hungry. Morning had stretched into afternoon. Even Henne was awake and nursing her newborn. It wasn't like Yana to sleep so long.

"Come now, Atum," Galea cooed, reaching for him. "It will be all right. Grandmother will waken Mammar."

Atum crawled over Yana's sleeping back and let Galea pick him up. With a free hand she stooped to shake the younger woman's shoulder. "Yana," she said loudly. "It is late. Everyone is up. Atum is hungry!"

Yana did not respond. Galea reached out to shake her again, but noticed that Yana's hair was wet, sticky. Startled, she pulled Yana over until she was flat on her back. "Oh, Goddess," she whispered, placing a hand over her mouth. She put Atum down. "Oh, no. Not my Yana."

Yana's face was a mask of white. Drool pooled, draining down her chin. The imprint of the blanket pressed the lower half of her cheek, and damp hair plastered her skull. Her sleeping blankets were musty with the smell of sweat, wet wool, and sickness. Galea reached for Yana's forehead, feeling the heat. A small moan of dismay rose from her chest. She jumped to her feet, groping toward the hearth and the large clay urn standing next to it. Her hands shook as she dipped a gopher wood bowl into the water.

"Mother, what is it?" Henne asked.

"Yana has the burning sickness," Galea responded brusquely, returning to Yana without looking at Henne. She knelt next to Yana, tried to pour water into her mouth. Yana convulsed, sputtering, but the water did not rouse her.

"Yana, you must wake up," Galea insisted.

Henne heard fear in her mother's voice. She instinctively covered her daughter with a blanket, hiding her. High fever in an adult was a bad sign, unlucky. And everyone knew fevers could spread from bed to bed like a malign spirit searching for nourishment, consuming life's sacred breath. Her brother, Dagron, a trader, had once told her of a whole village that had been struck down by a fever accompanied with sores of rotting skin. She had to get up, take little Enyana away before it was too late!

The door flap made a scraping sound as it was pushed aside. Dagron had to duck his large head and shoulders to enter his mother's house. He brought a pair of leather leggings and a wool tunic to be mended. He knew Galea would scowl at him for not washing them first, but since his father's death, Dagron suspected she enjoyed doing for a man once in a while. He also knew that with the return of Henne and her baby, Galea would soon be too busy to attend his needs, and he hoped to get his things to her before she realized this. He was surprised to see his Henne up and moving about after yesterday's hard labor. He opened his mouth to tell her so when Henne interrupted him.

"Dagron, you must help me with my things," she said hurriedly, barely giving the burly man a sideways glance. "Enyana and I must leave. Mother should leave also. Yana has the burning sickness."

Dagron strode quickly across the room to Galea, who was bent over Yana. "Yana is sick?" he asked. Galea sat back on her heals, shaking her head, her face pinched with anxiety. Yana moaned, tossing in her blankets. Dagron could see for himself the pale mask of death in Yana's face.

"She won't drink," Galea said, fear rising in her voice. "You must go for Ninka. Yana needs a healer's touch."

"But Dagron must help with Enyana and our things," objected Henne. "Someone else can go!"

"She's right, Mother," Dagron agreed, glancing once more at Yana's pale face. "You and the children must leave. The priestesses and the healing woman are the only ones who can fight this sickness."

Atum whimpered louder, sensing the anxiety in the room. Galea picked him up, handing the child to Dagron. "Take your sister and the children to Nachen. She will care for them until Yana is well. Find Tern. Send him to get Ninka. Tell him to hurry!"

"But, Mother, you must come," said Henne. "The smell of rottenness is here and—"

Galea interrupted by lifting a hand, casting a warning glance at Henne. "There will be no such talk in this house while Yana still fights to breathe! She has a very strong spirit, Henne," she admonished. "You have no idea what she has been through. I am her mother now. I will stay with her!"

Henne stepped back from the harshness in her mother's voice. It startled her, hurt her. *You have no idea what I have been through,* she wanted to retaliate,

*how badly I needed to see my mother's face, hear your
voice, when all I heard was the harsh tongue of the
nomads. Who was there to wash my face when I had
the burning sickness and my body was covered with
the bruises of rape? And now that I am home, you risk
yourself for another who is not even your true daughter.* She glared at Galea's bent back, biting back the
words, but her mother took no notice as she readied
the hearth to heat some water.

Dagron took Henne's arm. "Leave her," he said
quietly. "I'm sure the High Priestess will talk sense
into her. Let's take the children to Nachen. I will come
back for the things you need."

Word spread quickly. Even with Ninka's help, Yana
was not getting better. Rarely had the people seen
their High Priestess in such a state of agitation as she
shuffled across the courtyard. Telna even forgot to
cover the arm she usually hid in a shawl. The old
woman clutched at her skirt with the deformed hand,
pulling her skirt up so she could move faster. The
people moved uneasily about their tasks, sharing troubled glances, afraid to give form to the questions rising
in their minds. Was Yana unworthy, unlucky? Was
she too old to be adopted into the people? Would
they all be punished, and the crops wither?

Sitting in his doorway, Tern could see the people
whispering, wondering. *No,* he wanted to shout at
them. *It's my bad luck, not hers!*

Tern's greenstone chisel slipped, cutting too deeply
into the wooden box he was carving. He cursed, tossing the tool to the rock floor. It clattered as it
dropped. The box was a surprise gift for Yana. Now
the lid would not fit snugly, and the box would have
to be reworked. He stood up, ran long fingers through
his sandy hair, rubbing the back of his neck as he
moved restlessly about the house.

Long ago he had helped build this house for his first
wife, Dala, and he had come to hope that Yana would

someday share it with him. Like others in the settlement, the house had a raised rock foundation to keep
out dampness. It had plastered mud brick walls and a
storage loft that kept supplies dry and away from rodents. Two of the walls were still decorated with the
wool tapestries Dala had made. The tapestries were
woven with the dyed wool from long-haired sheep in
sacred geometric symbols representing life and fertility. He sighed remembering how diligently his hearth
mate had worked, how she had prayed over those
tapestries.

Dala wanted a child so much. Unfortunately, after
three harvest seasons together, her womb never woke
from its slumber. The elders urged her to join the
priestesses and Tern join with another. To avoid being
separated, the couple volunteered to be a part of a
trading group. The trading expedition seemed the perfect opportunity to find a child to raise, a child no one
else wanted. Surprisingly, a few months into the long
walk, life stirred in Dala's womb. Her moon flow
stopped altogether. The going was much slower, but
everyone was happy for the couple. Baby Isha was
born in a cave overlooking a lake so clear and blue
the clouds overhead swam in its reflection. Unfortunately, a moonspan later, all their good luck changed.

Tern frowned. The bad luck happened soon after
Isha was born. The group, traveling through desertlike
mountains, stopped to rest. Dala climbed on an outcropping of rocks, settling down to nurse Isha when a
venomous snake bit her. She died shortly afterward.
Tern went crazy with grief. To make matters worse,
Isha became sick. She was too young to be weaned
and began to starve without her mother's milk. That
is when they happened upon Yana's village.

Yana was an outcast in her village, considered unlucky because her son had been born with a twisted
foot, but when he thought of it, it still seemed a mira-
cle that she consented to leave her home to travel
with strangers. She offered her services as nursemaid

to Isha, saving his infant daughter's life while nursing her own son.

After a long year of traveling together, Tern grew to love the woman who was willing to give so much of herself. He took comfort in the thought that Yana knew what it was like to be alone without her reflection in a loved one's eyes. He did not have to hide his pain from her. They bent toward each other like two trees whose trunks are joined. When they returned to his homeland, he hoped the elders would allow Yana to become his hearth mate.

He should have known better. Now Yana was sick, possibly dying. He picked up a flat wheat cake, chewing slowly, but it was tasteless in his mouth. The world appeared as pale as the gray-white walls of his house. He tossed the bread aside. The rooms he had helped build seemed to mock him. Would he ever have a family of his own? Would bad luck always follow him?

Yana's eyes were glassy, unseeing. An oily sheen covered her face. The healing woman gently folded back her blankets and reached to release the bone clasp at the shoulder of Yana's woolen dress. She pulled the dress down, unveiling her chest and abdomen.

Yana had the full breasts of a mother suckling a child, but now they were bloodless, white as hard marble, except the left breast where a web of veins the color of deep wine spread like an angry claw. Ninka probed the sore area with stiff fingers, her worn, tattooed hands contrasting starkly with Yana's smooth skin. She felt around the hard knot that had formed in the left breast. Yana flinched, moaned, but didn't open her eyes.

"It is the milk sickness," she said with certainty, sitting back on her haunches. "Yana has gone too long without nursing Atum. The milk has turned to poison in her breasts. Yana should have done her duty as mother. The spirits are angry."

The High Priestess heard the accusation in the woman's voice. She gave the healer a sharp sideways glance. Ninka's face was blank, unreadable, and the High Priestess cursed under her breath. The elders of the village had been against the adoption ritual—a ritual meant only for children, taking days to accomplish, but Telna had been persuasive. She had grown fond of Yana. She glanced down at her withered hand. Yana did not shrink from touching what the High Priestess had always kept hidden from outsiders. But now the young woman was sick, possibly dying, inviting bad luck to all the people. *Ninka has every right to blame me.*

The healer placed her hands on other parts of Yana's body, probing, prodding for the illness. Occasionally she closed her eyes after massaging an area, letting her weathered hands rest while breathing deeply, touching with the healing energy of the Goddess. Satisfied that she had thoroughly examined Yana, the old woman moved toward the hearth, picking up a small box with engravings of dark triangles, circles and wavy lines. She removed the lid and took something out, tossing it on the fire. The herb ignited, smoldering, filling the air with a sweet woodsy smoke. The healer reached again into her box and removed an inner scraping of willow bark, dropping it in a stone grinding bowl. With hard twisting motions she ground the bark to a grainy paste, spitting moisture into the bowl as she worked. When finished she carried the mixture to Yana, forcing the sick woman's mouth open. The healer dipped the crook of her finger into the pulp and rubbed it into Yana's gums, then dipped her finger in again to line Yana's mouth with a thicker film of the medicine. She gestured to Kara, indicating she should bring a bowl of water. Ninka patiently dribbled the tepid liquid into Yana's mouth, watching anxiously as the young woman swallowed.

"We must pray now," she declared to the High

Priestess, nodding resolutely as she spoke. "The medicine should help, but it is for the spirits to decide."

Telna motioned to the rest of her priestesses to resume chanting. Deep into the night they sang prayers to the Goddess. Occasionally the healer administered more medicine, but Yana's fever refused to break. Her breathing became shallow. She tossed. Creamy spittle foamed at the corners of her mouth.

"Yana is dying," Ninka whispered to the High Priestess. "It is time to prepare the people . . . they must sing her to the ancestors."

Yana's eyes rolled back in her head.

The withered hand of the Head Priestess went to her throat. She swallowed hard, nodding mutely. A great despondency overtook her. It was true then. She was to lose Yana. The Priestess shook her head. It didn't make sense. All the omens had been positive, and as High Priestess, she recognized the goodness in Yana. Yana walked with the Goddess. Why then was she leaving them for the company of the ancestors? She searched the faces in the room, grasping for an answer. She had been so sure about Yana, especially since the adoption ritual, and yet the others had doubted. . . .

Kara passed by with fresh blankets in her arms. Telna grabbed the young priestess above the elbow.

"What is it, Honored One?" Kara asked, slowing her step, staring at the hand holding her elbow. The withered hand shook with more than the tremors of age; Telna seemed very upset.

"Leave the blankets," the old one said gruffly. She turned to the other priestesses in the room. "Leave! All of you. Wake the elders and the people. Everyone must meet at the Goddess's shrine!"

"But we can't leave Yana," Kara objected. "We must sing her spirit—"

"We've already left Yana," the elder spat impatiently.

Kara's eyes glazed with confusion.

"I haven't time to explain. Go, all of you!"

One by one the priestesses shuffled out the door, looking back fearfully. The High Priestess was asking them to abandon Yana when she needed the protection of their chants. It didn't make sense.

The High Priestess slowly walked across the room. She stood before the healer, suddenly hesitant. "Ninka," she said with downcast eyes, adding, "Old friend. This is not Yana's fault. I must make the people understand. I must speak with them. Will you stay with her?" she asked, tilting her head toward Yana's bed. "If her spirit leaves, will you pray her to the path of the ancestors?" Telna knew she was asking a lot of Ninka. Strange things were known to happen when a person passed to the realm of spirits. Ninka wasn't a priestess, but she was strong, wise, and wore the charms of the Goddess.

Ninka nodded slowly. She had been against Yana's adoption. The elders had conferred for many days, but the High Priestess had convinced them. If Yana died, they all shared the blame. The healer sighed deeply. "I will stay with the girl." The elder reached in her box for more willow bark.

The High Priestess stilled Ninka's arm. "And you will sing prayers?"

"I will pray."

The large room was full, but not all the villagers could fit in the Goddess's shrine. Many huddled outside in the cold, relying on others to relay the message of the High Priestess. Children shivered, having been pulled from their warm sleeping blankets. Parents held them protectively in their laps, drawing strength from their youth, trying to quiet their own inner tremblings. Something must be terribly wrong. The priestesses rarely called the entire village out of a slumber to meet in the sacred shrine.

Henne sat next to Dagron and Galea just inside the door. Tern sat a short distance away, his face pensive.

Henne straightened her spine, lifting her head to peer above those sitting in front of her. The elders were seated near the wooden idol of the Goddess, their faces sober. Reluctantly Henne's eyes went to the fig-shaped statue. The idol's neck was elongated, like a bird's. It's eyes were two slits that resembled kernels of grain. Hands extended straight from the waist, palms up to receive the priestess touch and the offering of the people. The statue towered over a rock dish with a fire crackling in its depths, but the flames of the fire and oil lamps couldn't dispel the gloom in the room. The people sat in strained silence, waiting.

The High Priestess stepped out from behind the statue, her stunted hand clutching a dark cloak over her breasts, visibly flushed even in the dim light. Out of her cloak she pulled a skull. Its face had been molded with plaster, resembling flesh, and painted a soft yellow with saffron. Two cowry shells embedded the eyes; braided hair wound around the crown. She lifted it for all to see. Her voice was grave as she spoke.

"Our ancestors came from a far place and settled in this valley, planting their seeds," she said. "Their spirits dwell within our houses. Their bones, like seeds, rest beneath our floors. Here the spirits of the ancestors live and breathe." The old woman coughed, clearing her throat. "There comes a time when all priestesses must ask for the strength of the Goddess living in the people."

She lifted the skull again. "Yana came from a far land also, but her father was one of ours. Derk now walks with the ancestors, but I have seen the strength of our ancestors in Yana's face. She has the ability to become a great priestess, to lead the people when I go to sleep in the womb of death. Yana has survived our adoption ceremony—has proven her will to live with us, but have we proven our willingness to accept her?" The elder quieted, her words resting heavily on the people as she waited for their response.

"Yana is sick," a voice barked from the back of the room. "The Goddess doesn't want her here."

"She is a stranger to our land. She was too old to be adopted," another added. "She'll bring bad luck to the crops."

"She is too weak to lead."

Henne's eyes darted to the man seated across from her who had spoken her own thoughts. *It is true,* she thought. *Yana does not have the spirit of a leader and they all know it.*

The High Priestess pulled on her chin, saying nothing. The people grew restless. She tilted her head toward the skull, whispered something into its ear, then paused as if to listen. A dark look shadowed the lines of her face.

"No wonder Yana is ill," she responded in low, admonishing tones. "What do you think a leader is?" She paused for emphasis. "Above all, a true priestess is a servant to the people," she continued. "Yana has a servant's heart. Can't any of you see the strength in this? The ancestors say you test her with your doubts. No one can thrive in a family that doubts them."

The room quieted with guilty silence. Henne bit her lip.

The High Priestess moved closer to the idol of the Goddess. From somewhere above a small gust of wind blew her words back in an echo of whispers. *Above all, a priestess is a servant of the people.* The words chilled her. Telna could almost hear a dry chuckle from the idol beside her. The fixed smile on the skull in her hand appeared to widen, mocking her. She flushed with embarrassment. Her stooped shoulders slumped even more. *This old priestess still has much to learn,* she thought.

Telna's voice rasped over the lump in her throat. "Perhaps I was wrong to choose an outsider as your next High Priestess. I should have consulted with the elders. Do not hold this against Yana—another choice can be made." She sighed deeply, the ache in her hip suddenly unbearable. "But Yana has been adopted. She is one of us now. She needs the commitment of your hearts if she is to live among us." She paused, adding quietly, "Sing to our ancestors this night—talk to them. Pray for Yana. Open yourselves to her. The priestesses and elders will guide your chants."

Little Enyana stirred in Henne's cloak. Henne looked down on her downy head of curls. Her child was alive because of Yana. Perhaps her newly adopted sister would bring luck to the people after all. She glanced at her mother, whose eyes were wide with unshed tears. The muscles in Dagron's face were stiff against his emotions. Her family loved Yana. Was it too much to ask?

Yes. I will pray, Henne thought.

Yana tossed, moaned. Her cheeks were numb, plaster cold. Stones seemed to hold her eyelids shut. She tried to lift her head, see past the stones, but her neck was weak, her head too heavy. She called for help, but the sound coming from her throat was only a wisp of air. She was trapped, unable to escape. Phantom hands clawed at the empty air. She called out again, but no one heard, no one came. They had left her again.

Darkness breathed about her. Fear entered the openings of her skull, pulling her down in a current of black. The darkness swirled around her, pressing inward, the breath of spirit beings surging to consume her. Large ancient animals came at her, whirling about in a primitive dance: a bull with a painted slash of horns: two black stags bellowed as they clashed antlers: a predatory cat watched with yellow, hungry eyes. She cried out in despair. "Goddess. Your womb. I don't understand. Why must I face this again!"

The High Priestess placed her ear near Yana's mouth. Was the young woman trying to say something? A mumbled groan hissed from between Yana's teeth, bringing the stink of sickness, but nothing more.

Telna stood and placed a hand on her hip, stretching. She glanced uneasily around the room, feeling the gathering of ancestors, almost seeing their distorted faces in the twisting shadows on the walls. She recognized some of them. Mother, of course, and her brother, Roan, who had been the people's Hunting Priest. In the corner she thought she saw the shadow of his spear and the silhouette of the vulture skull he wore on a thong about his neck. Her eyes turned worriedly back to Yana and the healer.

Ninka stooped to give Yana water, but the liquid dribbled from her mouth and down the sides of her neck, dampening her hair and blankets. The healing woman shook her head sadly, lines of resignation in her face. She gave the High Priestess a hopeless look. "Honored One," she said heavily. "I feel the sacred breath of the ancestors. They come for Yana."

The High Priestess rubbed her stunted arm. "Yes, yes. I have felt them too." She sighed. "You have done all you can, Ninka. You must join the others at the shrine. Pray for me. Pray for Yana."

The healer nodded reluctantly and stood to walk toward the door.

"Have Kara bring food," Telna added. "The ancestors will expect to eat."

Ninka dropped her chin and quickly left. A few moments later Kara entered with food folded in her skirt, and carrying a large basket containing three skulls. She carefully placed the skulls in varied positions on a small wooden table, the family altar that stood near the hearth next to the ritual pottery urn used for washing. In front of the skulls, Kara placed pistachio nuts, cooked snails, acorns, barley bread, and dates. She poured a small bowl of precious olive oil for dipping the bread.

Kara knew she would not actually see the ancestors consume the food. Everyone understood the ancestors ate only the spirit of the bread, just as the people consume the spirits of trees and plants in the fruits and nuts they ate. After the ritual feast, the food offering would be burned slowly in the hearth so its essence could be returned to the Mother Goddess. Kara stood and brushed the crumbs from her hands and dress before checking once more to see if everything was set out correctly. She approached the High Priestess, seated on a deep pile of furs, eyes closed, and humming. Kara waited silently for the elder to acknowledge her.

Telna eventually cocked her head, opening her rheumy eyes, allowing them to drift past the young priestess to the altar and the prepared food. The elder nodded slowly. "Everything is well, Daughter," she said quietly. "You may go now. Return to the people. Help them sing for Yana."

"But I should stay here. I wish to help *you* sing," Kara objected. "You should not face the spirits alone."

The old one almost snapped at her, but saw the earnestness in Kara's eyes. She reached with her good arm, palm up to receive the priestess touch. Kara grasped the loose flesh of the wrinkled hand.

"You are with me when you sing, Daughter. Yana is new to our people," she explained. "The ancestors do not know her. I must sing her life to them, sing what I know of her spirit. It would be better if I did this alone." The old woman dropped her hand, unable to say what was in her heart, unable to say how painful it was going to be to let Yana go.

Kara seemed to understand. "I will sing your strength, Grandmother," she murmured, glancing despondently at Yana. She took a deep breath, nodding. "And hers also." She stepped backward and bowed to the altar out of respect for the ancestors before leaving the room.

The dark thoughts returned. Tern tried to push them away, but they loomed large and angry anyway. Yana was dying. All his women died. The bad luck of his youth still haunted him. Tern could still see the dark face of the elder who had cursed him, sending him from his village.

He had been a boy, barely ten harvest seasons when it happened. The old one believed him responsible for the fire that had consumed two houses, one where his parents and grandparents slept. For many moons he hid in the forest nearby, only to come out at night to root in the refuse, hoping to find a small marrow-filled bone, or a chunk of moldy bread. If the trader hadn't passed through his village and offered to buy him as a slave, he probably would have starved.

The trader gave an amber bowl and a hunk of raw obsidian for him. Tern still remembered the day the big man had squatted down, eye level, and whispered he was to be his son, not a slave. Secretly, Tern had thought the trader was making a big mistake. Who would want a child cursed with bad luck? Though his new father was kind, guilt plagued him. He shuffled slowly behind the trader toward his new homeland, chin down, bare feet scraping puffs of dirt as he walked; he had been a lonely, troubled child.

All that changed when he married Dala. She brought laughter to his heart and a hopeful future filled with children whom he would never abandon. He almost forgot the bad luck of his childhood . . . and then she died. Tern rubbed his forehead. And now Yana was dying too. All the people were singing for her. Yana, whose touch was salve to his torn heart. Yana, whose deep, gold-brown eyes soothed him like pools of oil. There was no end to her understanding. It wasn't her laughter that healed him; it was something more, something quiet and certain.

Tern's throat was raw as he sang the chant for her. It was an ancient chant. With each hollow boom of the clay drum, he forced the sounds past his lips, not hearing the words. Deep inside, he begged the Goddess.

Her breathing slowed, stalled, and began again. The High Priestess barely felt Yana's sacred breath on her leathery palm. It was time to speak with the ancestors, argue for the young woman's life.

The elder approached the hearth, a hitch in her gait. She added dried dung to the fire, crossed her legs, grunting as she settled down on a mat before the altar. She reached into her robe for the snakeskin pouch tucked between sagging breasts. She removed a fistful of seeds and sprinkled them on the altar for the ancestors to eat, then took out another small handful and put it in her mouth. She mulled the seeds over missing teeth and loose gums, softening them with saliva. The seeds were from a sacred mother plant that had wide, serrated leaves. As she chewed, she hummed, the sounds vibrating the few teeth she had left. Slowly, the familiar aching in her joints began to dissipate.

The priestess took another handful from the pouch. Her lips felt thick as she pushed the seeds once more past her gums. Little things about the room intensified in significance. Her eyes fell to the bone needle sitting on top of a man's tunic, then moved on to the coiled patterns of the Snake Goddess in a basket's weave. The skulls sitting opposite her seemed to be gazing around too. One had a ragged crack along the jawbone. Its empty eyes drew her inward. Telna became aware that the essence of living things mixed with death breathed everywhere, in everything. All had spirit. All were waiting.

The ancestors gathered in the shadows. Her head swarmed with their murmurings. They were singing the old stories, stories she had heard as a child. They sang of the long journey from the north, of traveling to this valley, staying because of the spring of living water that bubbled through all the seasons. Two men began to argue. One insisted that he had been the first to find the sacred cave of the Goddess; the ancestor with the cracked jaw remembered it differently.

He sang of a hunt and a mother bear's bloody struggle to protect her cub. He sang of a spear in her eye and throat. His partner skinned the bear while he followed the bawling cub into its mother's winter cave. What he found deep inside stopped him in his tracks. He knew he could go no further without the permission of the elders.

His song quieted as he remembered. He had been frightened by the majesty of the living paintings on the cave walls; the large staring bull, the fighting stags, and running horses. The Mother's Womb was a great and terrible place.

The High Priestess listened to all this. She knew the stories and joined in the chanting. Something flitted at the corner of her eye—or was it the shadow of her mother's hand reaching for a loaf of bread. The old one lifted her arm and saw her mother's frail fingers superimposed on her own, and suddenly her gnarled paw was a precious thing. She held it midair, and gazed at its withered beauty. Telna felt her eyes mist. Sometimes it wasn't enough to know her mother was close.

The ancestors stopped telling the old stories as they ate. Instead they began to boast about the feats of their children and their children's children. This one could braid strong ropes like his grandfather. That one had the sweet voice of her mother. His son made strong pots that held the womb water of the Goddess. Her great granddaughter was carrying twins. The priestess listened to their chattering until she began to feel the lull of sleep.

Yana whimpered—a child's call in the night. The old one started, shaking her head to clear the drowsiness. Yana. She had forgotten about Yana.

The High Priestess forced her aching legs to unfold, and stood. She hobbled across the room to kneel next to Yana's bedding, the hard rock floor cutting into her knees. She heard the rustle of spirits moving in the shadows as the ancestors knelt with her.

In the distance the steady throb of the drums spoke, waking the ancients to the prayers of their people. The spirits hovered around the sick girl. The High

Priestess sensed their intense curiosity. They pressured her with silent questions. *Who is the girl? Why is she sick?* Telna turned down the blankets, revealing Yana's breasts so the ancestors could see for themselves her sickness. She bent over her face; the young woman's breath was faint. Was it too late? No. It couldn't be. She had to explain—had to sing Yana's spirit to the ancestors so they would know her, welcome her. The old one sat back, rocking as she hummed.

> *A young mother came to us—a stranger*
> *Claiming to be our own*
> *Her son has the look of Derk.*

The High Priestess felt the spirits move aside as if the name of Derk had summoned a change, adding the whisper of another. Would he claim Yana or disown her? She hurried on with her chant.

> *Yana braved the Cave of the Ancestors*
> *The Womb of the Bear Goddess*
> *Fighting the narrow tunnels of adoption*
> *She was too large to squeeze through the tunnels of*
>   *rebirth*
> *But Yana listened to the voice of Goddess*
> *Swimming through the living womb water*
> *And was reborn to us.*

The excited buzzing of the ancestors turned to a ringing in the old one's ears. The priestess felt the swell of spirits converge, wrestling over the sick woman. She had the impression some thought Yana too powerful, believing evil spirits would be drawn to her strength. Others were sure the people needed Yana. Her coming symbolized a great change, a rebirth of the people as a whole.

Telna could do nothing but hunch over the sick girl, protect her from their bantering. She found herself

trying to push past their confusion while earnestly en-
treating the Goddess. In broken whispers she admitted
the real reason she wanted Yana to live. Telna whispered her pain to the Goddess—the pain of a life lived
with a deformed arm. She had never allowed a child
to grow in her womb or suckle at her breasts because
of it. Over the years, emptiness had eaten at her, leaving her feeling empty, hollow inside. But the unafraid
touch of a young woman, a stranger, eased the pain.
Yana was the daughter she had always wished for, and
now the young woman was dying.

The room stilled. A dispassionate peace settled over
the High Priestess. She felt her mother near. She saw
the tremor of her mother's aged hands as they wiped
Yana's breasts with a cloth. She watched her white
head bend over the sick girl, placing loose lips over
Yana's left breast, working her jaw, suckling, manipu-
lating the crusty sore nipple to softness. And then the
poison came. Yana's body lurched. The young woman
cried out. The ancient one continued to spit the drawn
poison into a clay bowl beside the bed until sweet
milk replaced the sickness.

Telna sat back, her filmy eyes drooping with sleep,
wondering about the vision she'd seen. As she nodded
off, she could almost taste the saltiness of Yana's skin,
feel the sour pus of sickness filtering over empty gums,
and the dribble of spit on her own chin.

Yana dreamed.

She was in a dark place but Atum was hungry, tugging on her breast. He cried for her. His cry made her
realize she was no longer alone. Another voice was
added to his, and another. Suddenly it was as if a
hundred children were crying for her, hungry for her,
waiting to consume what she had to offer. Could she
really feed them all? Was she willing? She lifted her
breasts in offering, feeling a burning ache in her chest
as they swelled with milk.

4

Little Enyana continued her hungry bleat. Henne hoped she'd go back to sleep but it appeared her daughter was in no mood to cooperate. The young mother blindly reached across her sleeping blankets, feeling around in the dark for the squalling bundle, pulling the little one close. She adjusted her shift and guided the infant's mouth to her tender nipple.

The baby attacked her breast with enthusiasm. Henne had to stifle a yelp of pain. She took a quick breath, scraping her lower lip with her teeth. Her nipple was chapped, sore from her daughter's determined sucking. Who would have thought such a small mouth could be so strong. Galea had told her nursing would hurt at first, assuring her the nipple would toughen over time. Henne wasn't so sure.

Mothering was much harder than Henne had anticipated. She had never been fascinated with tiny infants and toddlers like other young women of the village. As a girl, she never carried a straw doll in her sling, pretending to be a mother. She preferred racing, playing stick games, sporting with the animals in the corrals, or joining the young men on hunts. Yet she had always thought that someday the Goddess would bless her with a child; motherhood was supposed to bring one closer to wisdom. Didn't the priestesses say it was the highest honor? Didn't one learn about the sacrifices of the Goddess through bearing children? But Henne began to suspect that the Goddess sometimes resented her needy children. Of course she loved little Enyana, but why couldn't her daughter sleep a little longer?

Henne frowned. Nothing about her homecoming had gone as expected. She had expected a celebration, a feast in her honor, but Yana had gotten sick and somehow the feast forgotten. And where were the welcoming gifts for her and the baby? She scowled, knowing very well the answer as she listened for the steady breathing of her newly adopted sister sleeping nearby.

Henne supposed she should feel sorry for her. Yana's fever had left her unable to speak, and she was still weak, but Galea worried over her too much, and Henne suspected her new sister liked it that way. To make matters worse, the steady stream of people coming to acknowledge the baby seemed to spend most of their time near Yana's sleeping blankets. They gave her sister gifts. Old man Heth gave Yana a finely carved flint knife. Jozer, the potter, made her a new oil lamp. Ninka brought her a finely crafted basket filled with hazelnuts. Henne knew why. They were sorry for not accepting her after the adoption ceremony, and Henne understood it was too much to expect the villagers to donate more gifts to her mother's household. After all, didn't the women of the same home share their wealth?

Henne shifted the baby to the other breast and winced once more as the little one took hold. As Priestess of the Herd she had been given slaves, even a horse. Anything in the camp she wished to take was hers since she was the first wife of the headman. Henne thought of the day she arrived home. She had imagined the people would be awestruck over her ability to ride a horse, but the villagers had already heard about horses from traders. Their interest had been short-lived. Now Moon was corralled with the other domesticated animals, and she would have to wait until her birthing place healed before experiencing the exhilaration of riding again.

Henne shook her head to dispel arrogant thoughts. What was wrong with her? She was happy to be home. She was finally back with her people who revered life in the Goddess. How could she be thinking wistfully of a people whose way of life was carnage, death, and stealing from the Goddess in order to survive?

Enyana tugged on her nipple and Henne felt a surge of guilt. Of course she loved the little one. She would easily give her life for her. But her daughter's suckling made her feel tied to the Goddess in ways she never thought possible. Nothing felt right. Home was not the same—she was not the same. The people here could never comprehend leaving the boundaries of their homeland. They had never wandered under an open summer sky, not knowing what the next day would bring. They did not understand the driving purpose of the God of the Shining Sky and the freedom of his horse. Henne swallowed hard, thankful for the cloak of darkness as a tear slipped from her eye. She was home. She should be happy. But where was her welcoming feast?

Once again, Galea roused a grumbling Dagron from his sleeping blankets, instructing him to carry Yana to a working hearth in the courtyard. Galea insisted her new daughter welcome each dawn by greeting the yolk of the Sun Goddess, inhaling the air of rebirth until she was completely recovered from her illness.

Yana had not spoken since her fever. Some thought she couldn't, others were not so sure. Yana herself didn't know. It was as if something inside would not let her. Every time she opened her mouth to speak, revulsion clawed at her throat and she'd snap her lips shut again. Life in the Goddess was profound. Words would only diminished it.

This morning Yana vigorously shook her head, trying to convey to Dagron that she did not want to be carried. Pushing up from her sleeping blankets, she took an unsteady step toward the door. Dagron placed his body in her way, arms crossed, stubbornly refusing to let her pass. Yana frowned impatiently. He didn't move. She tried to push past him but he swept her up in his arms. She thought about struggling, but then decided against it. Dagron was one of the most stubborn men she knew, and there was no reasoning with him when his mind was set.

It was hard for Yana to get used to the idea that the bull of a man towering over her was now her brother. A year ago he had been a stranger, a trader traveling through her homeland with Tern and a handful of others. At that time she had mistaken his gruff manner for arrogance, but after months of traveling with him, she learned that Dagron's abrasive personality hid a loyal spirit. True, he was somewhat dominating, but if he was gruff, it was usually because he was worried and didn't know how to express it.

Dagron cradled her in his arms, shouldering aside the hide curtain, carrying her out the door. His eyes avoided hers. He didn't want her to see his concern. He was a man used to repairing things, but Yana's voice was not something he could fix. He wondered if she would ever speak again, hoping so for Tern's sake. As he gently set her on the reed mat, she tried to gesture her thanks, but her gratitude only made him more uncomfortable. He ducked his head, mumbling excuses, and departed.

Yana looked around. Silver light began to replace the darkness. Morning dew touched everything with a damp finger. The village was asleep. Even the goats and pigs still slumbered in their corrals. A black mutt loped over and sniffed at Yana's hand, nose nuzzling for a scratch behind the ears. She ruffled the dog's matted fur. The mongrel pushed up next to her for warmth, forcing her to share the mat.

The dawn horizon yawned blue and gold. Clouds furrowed the sky with bellies burnt the same russet color as the clay jug near the fire. Below the clouds, the terraced hills of the valley were rich and dark, a lumpy blanket of overturned soil, recently planted with wheat, barley, peas, lentils, and crucifers. A shallow river meandered in the heart of the valley, disappearing behind a distant mound. Yana remembered being told the river dried to a trickle during hot season.

Her eyes rested on an isolated house on a far hill. The house had been her home, the place she had lived before the adoption ceremony. She spent the winter there, alone. The customs of the people forbade a stranger to live in the village; the elders were afraid bad luck would visit them if an outsider brought strange gods and customs to their homeland. Yana thought her old house looked sad now, in need of company. She decided she must visit it as soon as she was strong enough. Many of the items she had made during the winter remained inside.

A handful of elders were up moving about the settlement. They smiled at Yana with warm eyes, acknowledging her with quiet nods, not wanting to break the magic of predawn silence. Old man Heth passed by, then returned to adjust the blanket around her shoulders. He didn't say a word, but gently squeezed her shoulder before heading toward the sacred spring. Yana began to suspect age brought with it the pleasures of silence in the Goddess. Lately, this was something she could understand.

In her silence, she saw things she would have missed otherwise. Everything around her seemed to have a message, patterning something more than itself. A man's thumbprint had engraved swirls, wavy lines in a clay pot near the fire, symbols of the water that had been baked out of it—water the jug now held. Yana reached down and absentmindedly scratched the hard bone of the dog's head as she watched a grandmother and her grandchild lug a basket of dung from the corrals to a grassy stretch beside their house. The two dipped their hands in the fresh dung, smoothing it on the grass so it would dry into a thin crust they could break up and store for fuel later. Yana couldn't hear what the child was talking about, but the young one was certainly excited about something. Nearby a squirrel chattered on a tree stump, mimicking the chubby-cheeked child. Nobody saw. Nobody heard. Only Yana saw the Goddess's laughter, the reflections inside the reflection. Somehow she knew that if she talked, if she woke up from this dream, she would never see this way again. Her words would create different patterns. No. It was best to be quiet, watch and listen.

Galea emerged from the door of her house, holding a bowl of steaming blood broth. She hesitated, gazing out over the sunrise, then nodded briskly as if to tell the day it was starting out well. She crossed the courtyard and extended the bowl to Yana. Yana took the bowl, offering a smile of thanks. Galea smiled in return, but frown lines cornered her eyes. Another day and Yana still would not speak her gratitude.

Yana wanted to tell Galea about the silence of the Goddess, but she was not sure her new mother would understand. There was a busyness in Galea's body when she moved about the hearth making barley cakes or tea. Galea wasn't one to sit and savor the Goddess.

A baby cried. The pigs in the corral began to snort for food. The village stirred. Children left their blankets to relieve themselves as mothers leaned over storage bins to gather seeds and flour for the morning meal. Henne called to Galea from inside the house. Yana took a sip of broth, and Henne called again.

Galea turned to Yana. "I'm afraid mothering does not come easily to your sister," she said, keeping her voice low so that others would not hear. "I will have Dagron bring you a bowl of grain and nuts as soon as it has been warmed and softened. Can I get you anything else?"

Yana took her mother's hand, tugging on it gently, indicating she would like the older woman to sit and share her company. From inside, Henne voiced her impatience. Little Enyana joined her mother, crying vigorously. Galea lifted her shoulder in an apologetic shrug, and Yana grudgingly gave up her mother's hand, lifting the marble bowl to her mouth, her eyes and nose warmed by the steaming broth and the sight of Galea bustling back across the courtyard. The dog beside her uncurled and stretched its paws forward, rump high, then shook out its back legs and ambled toward one of the houses. Yana heard the crunching sounds of footsteps behind her. She twisted her head in time to see Tern approach. He gestured to the spot the dog had just vacated. Yana nodded, inviting him to sit beside her, patting the ground, a smile playing on her lips. Again she saw into the patterns of things. The warmth of one body replacing another. The nurturing aspects of the Goddess were everywhere if one just looked for them.

Tern folded his lanky legs and sank down. She silently offered him a sip of broth. His long fingers clasped the marble bowl. He swished the meaty broth over his teeth and tongue before swallowing. He handed the bowl back, fingers brushing hers, eyes speaking his need for her.

Tern's touch caused the skin to tingle along her arms. Yana knew she was not thinking clearly, but this morning every movement, every thought seemed significant. She looked into Tern's face, and a great tenderness rose in her. She examined the freckles on his narrow nose and the way his wide gentle mouth curled downward into his cropped beard. She wanted to smooth with her thumbs the sun-beaten lines of his forehead, push in place a wayward lock of sandy hair, and more, much more. But now was not the time. They must wait for the consent of the elders.

Tern saw the desire in her eyes and leaned close to

her ear, whispering. "I know of a way we can be to-gether," he said.

Alarmed, Yana pulled back. Everyone knew that they had feelings for each other, but still, they *must* wait. She was newly adopted by the village and could not risk displeasing the elders. Didn't he know this?

"Yana," Tern said quickly, seeing the fear in her eyes. "I know the elders will allow us to be together. As soon as you are able to speak again, we will ap-proach them about a marriage ceremony, but the mat-ing ceremonies take place after the spring rains are over and the houses have been plastered again. I don't think I can wait that long."

Yana heard the urgency in his voice but still couldn't believe he was asking her to risk her status for his need. There were priestesses in the village who would gladly help him relieve his passions, not that she wanted him to go to them, but she couldn't chance the anger of the elders. She put the bowl down and frowned.

Tern reached to twine his fingers through hers. He wished she would speak to him. He couldn't tell what she was thinking, he only knew that she was dis-pleased. Was he wrong? Perhaps he shouldn't ask her to share with him the Night of Waking Fields.

"Yana." He hesitated then began again. "I know it is not customary for a man to ask a woman to share the night the Goddess kisses the wombs of women as they dance in Her fields. It is the woman who chooses. But since you can't speak . . . I thought . . ."

Relief flooded Yana's features. She almost laughed she was so pleased. Tern wasn't asking her to risk the wrath of the elders. He only wanted her to share with him the stimulating power of the Goddess, the night when the fields were awakened by the ritual matings of the people. She nodded happily. This would be a way for them to be together with the blessings of the elders in their ears.

Tern's relieved smile matched her own. He grinned

like a pleased boy. "You must get well quickly," he said, picking up the bowl of broth and shoving it toward her hands. "The moon is almost right for Night of Waking Fields. You will need all your strength." He leaned closer and growled seductively into her ear. "I plan on keeping you awake very late. Perhaps by then you will be able to whisper your passion to me."

5

like a pleased boy. "You must get well quickly," he said, picking up the bodkne cloth and showing it toward her hands. The rite is almost right for Night of Waking Fields. You must send all your strength." He leaned closer and growled seductively into her ear. "I plan on keeping you awake, very late. Perhaps as then you will be able to whimper your passion to me."

"**Y**our sister's beauty alone could waken the Earth Goddess," Galea said over her shoulder. "Don't you agree?"

Henne sat in the corner twirling damp hemp fibers into a long thread. She nodded, trying to keep the resentment out of her face as she watched Galea fasten a hip belt and short string skirt around Yana's waist. The skirt had once belonged to Henne, but Galea had insisted that Yana wear it since Henne would not be able to take part in the fertility ritual of the Night of Waking Fields. It was against custom for a new mother to take part in the ceremonies.

Henne wanted to be happy for Yana. Her sister looked especially lovely tonight. Yana's healthy complexion had returned, her gaunt cheeks had begun to fill out, and her eyes sparkled with anticipation and excitement. The short string skirt swung seductively low on Yana's hips, barely covering the tops of her thighs, showing glimpses of bronzed skin beneath. The bottoms of the strings were twined by spacing cord to keep them straight, and ornamented with heavy knots. The skirt swung sensually when she walked, drawing the observer's eyes to her woman's place. Galea added two necklaces of shells and painted red beads, looping each one over and under a naked breast. The older woman stood back, clucking appreciation at her handiwork.

"I hope Tern will be able to keep the sap of his

manhood from spilling at the sight of you." Galea laughed huskily. "Such beauty should be enjoyed for a long, long time."

A blush of warmth spread from Yana's neck to her cheeks. She wanted to inform her mother that Tern was not the sort of man who disappointed a woman with his lovemaking, but her mouth still would not open and speak.

Galea read her look and snorted a laugh. "I'm sure Tern will not disappoint the Maiden Goddess of Desire," she said, the teasing glimmer still in her eyes. "If he spills his sap, I'm sure he will find more where that came from. Tonight the Goddess will sing in ecstasy."

Yana's face became eager, trusting. Henne dropped her head, ashamed of her envious thoughts, thoughts she couldn't seem to push away. How long had it been since she had quivered beneath the thrust of Ralic's manhood? When would she ever feel love's fingers on her skin again? Her eyes grew moist. *And Yana is wearing* my *string skirt—the skirt I wore at my first mating.* She cocked her head and looked at Yana once more. *How dare she.*

A stick underneath his foot cracked. The doe's head snapped up. She froze, instinctively attempting to blend with the browns and tans of the forest. The fawn beside her did the same. Tern squatted in the underbrush, an arrow notched in his bow, not daring to breathe; she was still too far away. Sweat gathered at the nape of his neck and trickled down his back. The doe didn't move. She seemed to be staring right into his hiding place. He waited. In his waiting he thought of Yana. She reminded him of this doe, gentle-eyed, but wary.

After a long while, the deer flicked an ear and lowered her long neck to resume grazing. The tension went out of Tern's fingers. Unfortunately, at that moment a flurry of movement caught his eye. He stood, taking aim, but the doe and her fawn bounded off, tails high, over a log and into the thickness of the trees.

Dagron emerged from the other side of the clearing.

"You were supposed to chase them this way," Tern accused loudly.

"I thought you were over there," he responded as he approached, pointing to a clump of aspen.

The men glared, then exchanged a sheepish grin. Their minds had not truly been on the hunt. Dagron bent to pick up Tern's quiver, handing it to him. "Do you think it will happen tonight?" he asked.

Tern took the offered strap and slung it over his arm and back. "The moon is right. The nights seem warm enough."

Dagron anxiously looked up with his thick brows drawn together, willing the few tattered clouds out of the sky. If it rained they would have to wait until next moon for the Night of Waking Fields.

"I haven't slept for a handspan of days," he complained. "I wake in the night thinking I'm hearing the rustle of Niam's string skirt when it is only the sounds of night breeze. Why does it all have to be so secretive?"

Tern slapped Dagron on the back, his tone mocking, a teasing glint in his eyes. "You know the stories as well as I do. The Goddess must remain hidden until the time of Her unfolding. Her ways are a mystery, never to be completely understood," he chided.

Dagron groaned. "You're never going to let me forget that night," he said, speaking of an escapade they had tried to pull off when much younger.

"It wasn't my idea to spy on the women's secret dances."

"As I recall, you were more than willing to go along, but I'm the one who got the beating."

"I was new to the village. The Hunting Priest knew you talked me into it, and I believe he also knew that the story he told us later scared me into never trying it again."

For a moment they both remembered the story the Hunting Priest had told them about a boy who disguised himself as a girl then went to the sacred dances. When the Goddess discovered the boy's duplicity, she bit off his genitals and fed them to the women. For the rest of his life he lived as a woman with the priestesses. Now, Tern doubted the truth of the story, but he had been convinced as a child. He shuddered. "I like my manhood," he said.

"I still wonder what they do at those dances," Dagron mused.

Tern's mouth dipped in a crooked grin. "They can keep their secrets, as long as Yana comes for me . . ."

The moon glowed like a pregnant woman, belly round and high, its brightness dimming the stars. Everything, swathed in cold moonlight, cast a blue shadow. Yana quickly followed Galea's shadow as they made their way around the courtyard through a narrow alley between the brick buildings. They tried to be as quiet as possible. The women had put a sleeping herb into the evening tea, careful not to drink it themselves, but there was no guarantee that someone wasn't awake and watching as they headed toward a secret place in the forest just beyond the edge of the fields.

Galea moved quickly through the trees, following a trail only she seemed able to see. They pressed deeper into the woods. Moments later, Yana thought she heard the excited murmur of women, and the twittering of young nervous girls who would choose a man this night for the first time.

Galea stopped abruptly. Yana bumped into her, panting, perspiring, and slightly out of breath. They were standing on the edge of a clearing. In the middle a large bonfire crackled, sending bug-sized sparks into the blackness. Radiant faces, glowing red from the fire's heat, surrounded the fire.

Galea frowned worriedly at the sheen on Yana's

forehead. "Are you sure you can dance tonight, Yana? The High Priestess said that if you were not well enough—"

Yana shook her head and pleaded with her eyes, trying to convey how very much she wanted to take part in the ritual. Galea nodded slowly. "You are my daughter now. Normally I would say you need more time to recover, but our people need to begin to see you as one of us." She gave Yana a stern look. "But do not exert yourself too much."

A young girl with long dark hair and twinkling eyes skipped over and pulled on Yana's hand. "Yana." She laughed. "I want my friends to meet my new sister. Will you come?"

"Niam," Galea admonished, "you must wait another moon to call Yana Sister, and the elders may change their minds if you are presumptuous. Dagron may change his mind."

"Not after tonight." Niam giggled, jiggling her pert, bare breasts. "He wouldn't dare."

Galea rolled her eyes and waved them away.

Niam, only fourteen harvest seasons, chattered gaily as they walked around the fire. Many said that Niam looked like a younger version of Yana. They could easily pass for sisters. But where Yana was gentle-spirited and soft-spoken, Niam was known to be assertive, headstrong. The girl's one saving grace was the perpetual laugh on her lips.

Yana learned all about Niam from Galea. Although Galea spoke of Niam with disapproval in her voice, Yana knew she was fond of the girl because her mother's face became soft when Niam was near. Yana discovered that Niam had always been enamored of Dagron. Even as a child she followed the big man everywhere, informing everyone that someday she would take him as hearth mate. Dagron tolerated her adoration, giving her small gifts, thinking she'd eventually outgrow her infatuation. Trading took him away from the village for long periods of time, often many years. For this reason none of the other women chose him for a husband. Niam's exuberance when he returned home after the long trading journeys was endearing, but he had never really meant to encourage her.

One season while he was away, Niam became a woman. She waited two harvest seasons for him, refusing to even consider another mate. The elders grew impatient. They were about to choose a man for her when Dagron returned with Yana and the others from his most recent trading expedition. He decided to settle down, agreeing to satisfy himself with local trade for the sake of Niam. The people of the village were amused at how the older man doted on the girl once the decision had been made.

Yana was drawn into a group of young girls who cooed over her shell necklaces. Niam introduced her to everyone, speaking for her if someone asked a question. For the first time in a long time Yana wished she could talk so she could tell the young women how lovely they were, but one girl, a little older than the rest, with wispy brown hair and tiny childlike features, hung back, her small mouth and nose pulled together in disapproval.

Kara clapped her hands to get everyone's attention.

Yana's cheeks warmed with excitement. Galea found her way to Yana's side and reached to feel the heat of her daughter's flushed face. Yana knew her new mother was being too protective, but welcomed Galea's concern. She took her mother's hand and rubbed it reassuringly.

Kara cleared her throat and lifted her sharp chin, speaking in a loud voice. "First we toss the stones, then we will drink the milk of the Goddess." She threw up her arms. "Then we dance!"

The women huddled in a seated circle. The couplings this night were important. Most of the choices were known ahead of time. Very few conflicts arose. But if two women spoke for the same man, the stones were tossed and the Goddess decided who would mate and who must choose another.

The selection of men moved quickly as each woman stood and stated her choice. Finally it was Yana's turn. Galea stood up in her place.

"Yana can not speak yet, due to her illness," Galea stated. "But my daughter has indicated to me that she has chosen Tern to wake her womb this night."

The young woman Yana had seen earlier with the small heart-shaped mouth slowly rose from her seated position. "I would also like to mate with Tern," she said firmly in a voice that seemed too strong for her small features.

Whispers flew.

Niam, who was sitting behind Yana, leaned forward and hissed in her ear. "That is Tamuz. She is mated to Appa, the man who makes ropes. They have been together for two harvest seasons and she still hasn't conceived."

Yana's eyes became round, uncomprehending. *Why? Why Tern? Why take this from me?*

The girl tossed her head. "I hear your whispers," she said, her eyes brushing the crowd, settling boldly on Yana. "I know it is Yana's first time and I should be considerate of her. But this is the Night of Waking Fields, the only night I may choose a man other than my mate. My womb has been empty. I don't know if my husband will ever wake it." She planted her fists in her waist, elbows out, her face determined as she eyed the priestesses. "Tern's mate, Dala—her womb was empty—remember. It took them three harvest seasons, but finally Dala conceived. Isha is a beautiful little girl. If anyone can wake my womb, Tern can." She flipped her head in Yana's direction. "She already has a son."

The High Priestess motioned the young woman to come closer. "Your reasoning is good, Tamuz," the elder said with a nod. "The stones will be tossed. The Goddess will decide."

The small handful of pebbles were highly polished, green on one side and white on the other. They gleamed in the moonlight. The stones were to be thrown into a wide circle drawn in the dirt that represented the womb of the Goddess. The one who threw the most stones with the green side up was believed to have the Goddess's blessing. Tamuz went first since she was already mated.

Yana held her breath as the stones flew through the air, tumbling onto the dirt. She blinked. More than half of the stones lay green side up.

Kara gathered the stones and carefully stepped around the circle, handing them to Yana with a sympathetic smile. The stones were cool on Yana's palm. She let them sit there for a moment, absorbing her warmth. They were different shapes and sizes, each unique. For a brief second she felt connected to them. Would they give her what she asked? She glanced at Tamuz, who was chewing a length of hair. The young woman's face was fixed yearningly on the stones in Yana's hand. A thought crossed Yana's mind. *Do I want Tern as badly as Tamuz wants a child?* A current of air breathed through the trees, as if a whisper. *Toss the stones—it is not good to hold on to anything too strongly.*

Yana smiled. *You choose, Goddess,* her spirit responded as she cast the stones.

Tern tossed the wool blankets off, unable to sleep. The night was too warm. There had been a nervous energy in the village that evening, veiled looks, secret smiles. Although it was taboo to speak of it, everyone knew tonight was the Night of Waking Fields. But it was still early. The women wouldn't come until the sacred dark hours just before dawn. He was beginning to wish that he'd partaken of the sleeping drink and suspected that many of the other young men were thinking the same thing. It was an important part of the ritual that the men were found asleep when the women came for them.

Dagron, snoring in his own blankets on the other side of the room, snorted and mumbled something unintelligible. Tern smirked at his sleeping companion. After so many restless nights, Dagron was finally sleeping now that he knew Niam would be coming soon. Tern shook his head at the mysterious ways of the Goddess. He determinedly closed his eyes again, trying to clear his thoughts. Out of the darkness an image of Yana rose in his mind. Her mouth was slightly open, her generous lips inviting. Her skin, the soft hue of slightly roasted wheat grain, covered pliant breasts waiting to be suckled. And eyes. No one had eyes like Yana: warm, tender, wise.

Tern moaned as his member began to stiffen. "No," he whispered to himself. "I must wait." He rolled over and sat up. Perhaps the evening tea was still in the warming jug near the courtyard fires. He went outside, found the jug, and drank deeply.

The stones spilled over each other into the dirt.

The High Priestess leaned forward, thoughtfully pulling a coarse hair on her chin. Was there an image in the pattern, the outline of the Frog Goddess? No. It was her imagination. Still—

Kara's bleached hair hung over her face as she bent to count the pebbles. The young priestess sat back on her heels. "Yana has thrown one more green stone than Tamuz," she said decisively. "Tern will wake her womb this night."

Yana didn't realize she was holding her breath. She exhaled slowly, her glance slipping over Tamuz's face. Tamuz nodded blandly to the woman beside her as if the decision was unimportant, but Yana sensed she was covering her disappointment. The rest of the men were chosen without incident. Afterward the priestesses picked up their instruments and began to play.

One began a skipping rhythm on a clay drum. Another lifted a flute made of bird bone, its hollow sound soaring above the thump of the drum. Kara shook a string of shells in a clattering rhythm. She began singing, her vibrant soprano voice strong. She sang of sun-lengthened days that woke the Earth Mother. She called to the bees in their hives, inviting them to work over the fields of wildflowers, lifting her clear voice to the rutting deer, to birds with nesting twigs in their beaks. She sang of flowers shaped like cups, drinking the golden yolk of the Sun Goddess in their orange petals.

As Kara sang, the High Priestess passed a clay ceremonial bowl shaped like a doe lying in the grass. She made sure each woman drank deeply of the filmy liquid inside. The liquid had been cut with goat's milk, but Yana noted the acrid taste of poppy extract. She took only a little sip of the juice, knowing she should be careful. Ceremonies affected her strangely. Haunting songs and visions welled deep from within when she swallowed deeply of the sacred drinks. Her real mother had been a priestess and Yana suspected that the calling ran in her blood, but this was not the time or place to be different. More than anything, Yana wanted to be accepted by these people.

Telna noticed her small sip and frowned. She continued to hold out the bowl, insisting Yana drink more. Yana worriedly chewed on the inside of her cheek, hesitating, but then took the offered bowl and drank until the High Priestess's eyes lost their disapproval. She wiped her mouth with the back of her hand as the elder moved on around the circle.

Galea leaned close. "Now for the dances," she breathed in an almost seductive whisper.

The older women, those no longer of childbearing years, lined an inner circle around the fire. Yana and the younger women arranged themselves facing the elders of their households. As Yana stood, a languor seeped into her bones. A stupefying smile spread on her lips. She turned her head slowly and found the same smile on other faces, as if she were gazing at different sizes and shapes of herself. They were all so comical. Her cheeks burned from smiling hard.

The older women started chanting to their daughters and granddaughters, provocatively gesturing toward their sagging breasts and wombs. They spoke of the wisdom of the Goddess, how it was stored in their wombs now that their moon flows had ceased. The elders hinted at sharing this wisdom. They turned away and reached toward something hidden beneath their skirts. Yana thought she saw a small pouch in Galea's fist. And then her mother was touching her! Touching her woman's place! Yana looked down and saw Galea's hand beneath her string skirt. Her mother removed her hand and laughed at the look on Yana's shocked face.

"It is not only the man who wakes your womb, Daughter," she cackled. "He gives his rising energy, but the Goddess gives desire."

Stinging warmth spread through Yana's moisture, crawling up into her birthing place. Soon the stinging dissipated and was replaced by a tingling sensation. She felt the muscles inside relax—unfold like an opening flower. And then desire, yearning need uncoiled in a spasm up her spine. She gasped, becoming aware that the throbbing drums pulsed with the want of her birthing place.

Galea took her hand and they danced, slowly at first, the languor of their bodies moving like wavering flames. Yana felt the earth beneath her bare feet, between her toes, rise to meet each thump of the drum. Goddess Earth is here, dancing with me, she thought. She lifted her arms and twirled with the joy of it. Other women were spinning, laughing, their eyes glimmering as the stars overhead, their long tresses loosening from thick braids.

The drums changed, gaining tempo, chanting a new rhythm. The dancing became frenzied. Yana did not see who started it, but the young women began to spin away from the fire. They laughed, gesturing at each other to come as they ran toward the woods in the direction of the fields. Galea shoved her, indicating she should go with the others.

Yana ran. She became a prancing deer, dancing up over a tree limb, around a berry bramble, past a flower. Her muscles were alive—connected to everything, yet her thoughts were detached. *It's easy to move between things when they are not thought of as obstacles,* she mused.

The women ran through the newly plowed fields. They laughed, squatting, kissing the dark earth with the lips of their woman's places. Yana did as the others. The moist ground felt cool, alive beneath her. And then, as if of one mind, the women turned toward the village. It was time to wake the men. Time to add their energy to the fertility of the fields.

Niam caught up with Yana and wordlessly took her hand. Together they flew through the darkness, connected in sisterhood. Something in Yana swelled with joy, a feeling of union and belonging. *This is what it is like to have family,* she thought. The two of them silently ran around the houses toward the place where Tern and Dagron slept. Niam's eyes twinkled in mischief as they stood outside, listening to Dagron's steady snore. They dropped hands. Niam put a shushing finger to her lips and pushed away the hide covering the door. They slowly crept inside.

The young women stood quietly in the darkness, letting their eyes adjust. Moonbeams cast a slant of light through an open window. Yana could barely make out the shadowed shapes of baskets, pots, and the humped forms of the two men sleeping on opposite sides of the room.

Dagron snorted in his sleep and Niam giggled. She ran toward his blankets, flinging herself on his prostrate body, mauling him with kisses like a wild kitten. Dagron woke with a start, bellowing in surprise, but soon growled in pleasure, rolling Niam over and returning her kisses.

The commotion woke Tern. He sat up, groggily rubbing his face. Yana approached him slowly, reaching out a hand invitingly. Was this his dream? He stood, taking her offered palm. They shared a long silent look, then he enveloped her with an embrace. His mouth sought her lips and tongue. Yana's body sang as his body strained to find her, explore her.

Niam jumped up with a bubbling laugh, shoving a sleeping blanket in Dagron's arms and darted out of the house. Dagron took after her like a young boy. Yana shook her head in amazement. Her brother changed around Niam. It was as if the serious, tongue-tied man became more alive, something more than himself.

Tern bent to pick up a sleeping blanket and pointed toward the door. Arm in arm they slowly strolled toward the newly plowed fields, enjoying the luminous moon as they walked. Occasionally he ran a hand through the strings of Yana's skirt, exploring the hardened curves of her backside, moaning his need into the cup of her neck.

Soon they came to the fields. Dotted across landscape of newly turned soil, the shadowed forms of couples raised over each other in anticipation, or locked in tight embraces, added sizzle to the sweet night air. Yana and Tern found their own place, separate from the pleasurable moans of the others by the rise of a small knoll near the edge of the forest.

Tern spread his blanket and pulled her down next to him. He feather-kissed the edges of her lips, eyes, and chin. He gazed into her wide, brown-gold eyes, noting the pearly moon reflecting in their depths. He planted his mouth over hers, sucking in her breath, running his hands over the contours of her body as he ran his tongue over the inside of her mouth. Yana felt the pulsing response of her need. She reached for the stalk of his manhood. Their touching became insistent, urgent. He took her hands in his, palm to palm, placing them above her head, gazing into the fertile depths of her eyes as he burrowed to wake her womb.

Henne stood in the corral with baby Enyana asleep in a sling next to her breast. She absentmindedly petted her mare's mane while looking out over the fields of embracing couples. She knew she should be sleeping, but she was restless. Sadness weighed in her chest as she lifted her face to the moon.

The full moon had always called to her. Even as a child she had been unable to sleep when the nights were loud with light. Often she had wandered the village, trying to lure other children out to play. For this reason, the High Priestess decided Henne needed to be trained as a priestess. Everyone knew the power of the Goddess was strongest when the night glowed like shadowed daylight. It seemed Henne had the calling.

Henne's mare snorted, interrupting her thoughts, its wet nose pushing for the small dried crab apple in her palm. After feeding the horse, Henne lifted her hand to whisk away a clump of hair in her eyes. She caught the scent of horse on her fingers. It was the smell of the People of the Herd—of Ralic. She leaned her head against the muscled neck of her mare, Ralic's daughter between her and the horse, breathing the scent.

Ralic was dead now, gone to his underworld of night shadows, never to touch her again, never to rub his manhood against her thigh. Luckily, Henne's priestess training had saved her from living as a slave after being captured by the barbarians. The headman saw the power of the Goddess in her dancing and made her his wife. Ralic had been a hard, but passionate man. She had grown to love him, admire him, despite his brutish ways. Henne's throat grew tight with sadness. Would any man be able to quench the passion for life that Ralic had awakened in her? Could a man

of the Goddess ever understand her needs? She was
tainted with the ways of the Horse People. Large tears
formed in her eyes. She threw her arms around her
mare's thick neck, choking back sobs for the void she
felt inside.

Yana raised herself on an elbow and gazed down
on Tern's sleeping features. Her lover had worn himself out pleasing her. She tenderly traced the curve of
his jaw with a finger. His nose twitched at her touch.
She bent to kiss the corner of his mouth when the
sound of someone crying stopped her. She straightened, listening. It seemed to be coming from the other
side of the knoll.

She stood, bending to gather Tern's discarded cloak,
tossing it around her shoulders for warmth, wondering
who was crying on such a splendid night. As she
climbed, she thought she saw the huddled form of a
woman on the top of the hill. She quickened her pace,
but once on top, she discovered that the woman had
disappeared. Yana waited for a moment, confused,
wondering which direction the woman had gone. From
her vantage the entire valley, the village, and the corrals could be seen. Henne's pale mare stood out in
the moonlight. The horse nickered, but the sobbing
woman was gone. How could she have disappeared so
quickly? Yana sank to the ground, folding her legs
beneath her. Despondency still hung in the air like
the heavy dew that was beginning to settle on the
overturned earth. She saw something glint in the
moonlight next to her hand. She dug it out of the soil.
It was a belly-shaped shard of pottery. *Someone must
have dropped it here long ago,* Yana decided. She
rubbed her thumb over its pitted surface as a story
came to her mind.

Yana wasn't sure where she had heard the story.
Probably one of the priestesses in her home village
had told it to her when she was a child, but why was
she thinking of it now? She tilted her head toward the

moon, noting the bright rings surrounding its ample girth. The tale was about First Mother and the pregnancy of First Daughter. As the story unfolded in Yana's mind, she wished she could speak the words—wished she could sing the beauty of the pictures that pulled at her heart.

PART 2

Seasons
of Growth

6

One by one the heavy hides and reed curtains that kept the wind and rain out were removed from the doorways of the village houses. The sun beat steady warmth on the little mud brick buildings, a sure sign that spring had come to stay.

Niam burst through the entrance of Galea's house, breathing hard from a fast run, toppling little Atum in her haste. She stooped to brush him off, making sure he wasn't hurt, before grabbing Galea's worn hands, spinning the older woman around the room.

"Galea is a grandmother, Grandmother Galea," she sang breathlessly.

Galea shook her hands loose, her eyes smoldering with impatience. "Of course I'm a . . ." Slowly a hand went to her mouth, her eyes widened. She put the other hand on Niam's shoulder, hoping to still the girl's wiggling. "You're with child?" she asked in a disbelieving whisper. "The Night of Waking Fields?"

Niam nodded vigorously. "My mother and the High Priestess just confirmed it." Her eyes twinkled. She puffed out her chest proudly. "My breasts are swollen and my bleeding has stopped. Dagron certainly helped to wake my womb on the Night of Waking Fields. The High Priestess says this is a very good omen. Soon I will be a mother and you will be a grandmother again!" Niam reached to take Galea's hands, eager to return to her gay dance, but the older woman would have none of it.

"I am too old to go hopping about this house like a young rabbit," she said firmly, but her eyes smiled happiness as she gave Niam a quick hug.

The girl turned to Yana, who was seated on her sleeping blankets sewing a tunic for Atum. "You dance with me," Niam insisted, pulling Yana up from her seated position.

The two young women danced about the room, mirror images of happiness. Galea walked to where Henne was nursing Enyana. She squatted down next to her daughter. She caressed her granddaughter's cheek with the back of a finger.

"It seems our family is growing," she commented, "and soon this little one will have a playmate."

Henne wanted to speak out, tell her mother she wasn't ready, she needed more time to adjust. Why couldn't everything stay the same? Why was their family changing so fast?

Galea saw the uncertainty in her face and misread Henne's apprehension. "Enyana will always be the first granddaughter of this household, Henne," she said, her voice slightly admonishing. "Dagron will move to Niam's mother's home soon and I will only be second grandmother to their child."

Henne's eyes burned with shame. A lump formed in her throat. "It is not Enyana's place I'm worried about," she mumbled. "It is just that everything is so different now. Nothing is the same . . ."

Galea watched the two young women frolicking around the room and smiled at their youthful exuberance. The older woman didn't appear to hear the pain in her daughter's voice.

"Yes, things change," Galea agreed. "It is the way of the Goddess."

7

The moon had gone through its cycle twice since the Night of Waking Fields. Breathing deeply, the High Priestess could almost taste the hot breath of summer on the edge of her tongue. She gazed over the fields that were certainly wide awake and thriving. Green crops of barley and wheat were calf high. The outbursts of spring rain were a rare occurrence now, and the small river that ran through their valley was shrinking in its banks. Often, especially late afternoon, the green smells of spring were replaced by the scent of baked soil, languid grasses, and animals sweating in their corrals. In a handspan of days they would plaster and whitewash the houses, hearth mates would be chosen. The Earth Goddess was transforming, soon to lose Her sprightly maiden form to the laden opulence of the Fertile Mother. Everything looked prosperous, promising. Why then the feeling of foreboding?

The High Priestess licked her dry lips. She turned toward Galea's house, knowing the others had already gathered and were waiting. Henne was to speak soon, telling of her abduction and time spent with the barbarians. The elders had waited until the young mother's birthing place was completely healed, wanting Henne to feel strong when she told of her experience. But the day had brought evidence Henne was already strong enough to tell of her abduction.

That morning, the whole village had watched as Henne rode through the valley on the back of her white

mare, her spine erect, head thrown back, a look of rap-
ture on her face. The coppery highlights in Henne's
unbraided hair caught the sun, and it flowed with the
shimmering mane of her horse. The animal's hooves
gouged deep ruts in the dark soil as they galloped
along the bank of the small river. The sight was unsettling, foreign. It was time for Henne to tell her story.

The High Priestess stepped into Galea's house. The
people fell silent. Her aged eyes wandered the room.
The elders were present as well as all the people who
had been on the trading expedition: Dagron, Tern,
Yana, broad-faced Lolim and her hearth mate, Dak.
The old one sighed as she thought of those not here,
those now walking with the ancestors because of the
attack by the raiders. The bones of beautiful Napore
and her strong husband, Sente, would soon be taken
from their leather wrappings. They would be buried
under the floor in the houses of their families when it
was time to whitewash and repair the buildings of the
village. What kind of men brutally attacked defenseless villagers? The old one turned to Henne. The
young woman knew the answers. It was hidden behind
Henne's eyes, a foreign knowledge, a foreign strength.

The elders had saved a place for the High Priestess
near the cooking hearth. She gratefully sank down on
a leather cushion stuffed with the wool of long-haired
sheep. She waved her hand in Dagron's direction as
she settled. "Dagron, since you were leader of the
trading expedition, you begin."

Dagron sputtered. "But, Honored One, you've
heard all this before. I've already told you what I
know."

"Yes, yes. But Henne wasn't present. We must remember together once more if she is to tell us her
story."

"I do not like remembering," Lolim objected under
her breath.

The High Priestess snorted frustration. "I saw the
fear in your eyes, Lolim, when Henne galloped back

to the village this morning. You were remembering then. You will remember every time Henne rides her horse. We must not let this fear spread through the village."

Lolim's head dropped and Henne felt a rush of heat in her cheeks.

"The horse is not like other animals," Dak said, reaching to take his mate's square hand, giving it a comforting squeeze. "The horse is too strong, too powerful."

Dagron also came to Lolim's defense. "Lolim was with the women on the beach when the barbarians attacked the Leopard People," he explained. "She was there when Napore was killed. She saw children run through with spears—heard their screams. She witnessed men forcing themselves on women, not waiting to share the Mother's gift—"

The High Priestess lifted her hand. "Start at the beginning," she said firmly.

Dagron did not like speaking before groups. He preferred the easy banter of traders and craftsmen. It took too much work to make words come out right, creating the sounds of a story. His broad, square fingers nervously scratched at his prickly beard. He hesitated, looked around, then began to talk slowly.

"The homeland of the Leopard People was our last trading destination. As most of you know, the Leopard People live in a great city overlooking a grassy plain. The people enter their houses from the rooftops. They work on the roofs under the shade of reed awnings, and a man can walk across the entire city by stepping from one roof ladder to the next. They have a nice view of their crops and the river that flows by the city." He paused as if unsure how to continue, his forehead wrinkled in concentration.

The eyes of the High Priestess betrayed her impatience.

"I was talking to another man, trading a flint blade for a bag of salt when we heard screaming coming from the women's bathing area," he continued hurriedly. "At first we thought someone was caught in the current, but then we saw the horses and strange-looking men with greased skin, wearing nothing but loincloths of animal skins. They were attacking the women on the beach." Dagron shook his head. His tongue felt swollen from trying to make the words sound right.

The High Priestess must have sensed his unwillingness to speak further. She shifted her eyes to Tern and waved at him to continue the story.

Tern sat straighter, eyes narrowing as he remembered, anger pumping in his voice. "We grabbed anything that could be used to fight the barbarians, sickles, hoes, digging tools. The city's hunters grabbed bows and spears, the craftsmen brought knives. Men and women jumped from the roofs with weapons in their hands and ran toward the beach. We surrounded the barbarians, outnumbered them, but they had horses. We couldn't stop them from taking some of the women. Henne was one of those abducted.

"Why?" Lolim asked, agitated. She searched Henne's face. "Why did they kill children? Why take the women—the life-givers of the city? Do they hate the Goddess? What kind of men—"

"We are all wondering these things," Heth interrupted, absentmindedly rubbing his twisted leg. "It is hard to believe they are men at all. Perhaps they are angry spirits somehow trapped in the skins of men."

Henne's heart sank. The People of the Herd were only too real. She wondered how she was going to explain the driving purpose of such a people? The God of the Shining Sky lived only for the light of day and the glory of the moment. Life was to be taken, fought for, just as the strongest stallion took all the mares. Henne frowned. She could not deny the strength of this, she had seen too much.

The High Priestess noticed Henne's hesitation. She

sniffed, lifting her chin in the younger woman's direction. "Begin with what you first remember," she said.

Henne sat quietly for a moment, head down. As priestess of the People of the Herd she had learned how to act for a crowd, and automatically did this now. The elders leaned forward, waiting for her words. Henne slowly raised her green-flecked eyes to the expectant faces around her.

"I was in the river bathing when I heard the screams," she began in the whiskey tones of a storyteller. "I swam as fast as I could, hoping to at least save some of the children. I grabbed a spear that one of the men had dropped." She paused and shuddered. "I don't know much of what happened next. When I woke I was lying on my back in the dust. Someone was pouring warm, dirty water over my head. My body ached. Horsehair clung to my skin—under my nails. The stink of horse was everywhere. I must have fainted again."

Henne hesitated dramatically, then plunged on. "I don't know how long I was in the Mother's darkness, but when I woke I was in the tent of the captured women. A man of the Goddess, captured also, convinced me to use my priestess training to gain power in the camp of the barbarians. He told me that if I did not, I would become a slave for life.

The people gasped. Slavery was not unheard of among the peoples of the Goddess, but it was usually for only a short time, until the person could pay off a debt or infraction. Henne continued by telling how she gained favor with the headman. He had been curious about the Goddess's power. She became a priestess, instructing the barbarians in the ways of the Goddess. Ralic made her his mate and she was allowed many privileges. She was given a mare and the right to ride it, something most women of the Herd were not allowed. At this point Henne grew silent, waiting for the people to absorb the impact of her words. Would they understand the power she had had as Priestess of the Herd?

The elders sat quietly, contemplating. Ninka leaned forward. "What happened to the other captured women?" the old healer asked slowly.

Henne's heart skipped a beat. The question she feared the most had been asked. Her initial composure began to unravel. She put her palms up in almost a pleading gesture. "I did not have control over the women," she said in a tight voice, trying not to sound defensive. "My power was dependent on the status of my mate. I'm sure if I had stayed longer—"

"Nobody's blaming you," the High Priestess interjected. "I am sure you did all you could for the women. Go on with your story."

Henne flushed guiltily. Could she have done more? Had she been so wrapped up in her power as priestess that she enjoyed the subservience of the women? She pushed the awful thought away.

"In order to survive, I had to learn the ways of the God of the Shining Sky and His horse. The horse is swift like the mother leopard, strong. It can travel great distances without tiring. I can only compare it to the ride on the back of the bull during the domestication games, but instead of the force of life dying to be reborn from the blood of the bull, the life-giving energy of the horse goes on and on. The Herders have a word for this strength. *Power.*" Henne's face was eager, hopeful. "We could capture many horses, and be as strong as the Herders. I am willing to teach the people about this power."

The room fell silent.

"No," Yana said.

The first word Yana had spoken since her illness came out much harder than she intended. It was strong in her mouth, sounding absolute and infinite. She felt worlds converge, change as she uttered it. "No," she said again. The late afternoon shadows pulsed as the sound of her voice reverberated around the room.

The faces around Yana registered shock. Tern's

mouth dropped. Lolim and Dak wore the same blank expression of surprise. Niam rested her hand on Dagron's sleeve, her eyes wide. The shriveled hand of the High Priestess went to her throat. They were waiting for more words. Yana could see it in their faces, in the tension of their bodies as they leaned toward her. She opened her mouth to say more, but the words weren't there.

Galea took her hand. "What is it, Daughter?" she whispered. "What is it you object to?"

Yana didn't know why she was so angry. She trembled with a rage she didn't understand. How could she tell them that learning the words of the Herders, learning their ways would change the people forever? Tears of frustration formed in her eyes, spilling down her cheeks. She wanted to speak—say something to make them understand. Her fist curled and slammed the ground. And then it came to her, the story she remembered of First Mother pounding the dark earth over her daughter's grave. She now knew what to speak.

"You . . . will . . . remember this story; it is about words . . . and change." The sounds coming out of her mouth were awkward, harsh, grating like sand between her teeth, a statement that demanded attention. Yana's eyes roved the room, locking for a brief moment on each face.

There was a time when people did not speak
Their eyes spoke, their ears heard differently,
But words had not yet been uttered
Instead, life had the freedom to change in the light it
*   was seen.*

Yana thrust out her jaw. The rough words quickly gave way to the smoothness of a chant. The people saw anger in Yana's eyes as she spoke, and something more. It reminded them of the power of the Goddess. Yana was no longer timid, sweet-tempered. She was

strong, sure of herself. Indignation furrowed her brow
as her voice rang out.

*Before people talked, the oak was many things: She
    Who Stands Tall,*
*She Who Lifts Her Arms to the Sun, She Who Gives
    Rest and Shade*
*The doe was She of Soft Eyes, She of Warm Hides,
    She of Silence*

This was very long ago
When people slept in the womb cave of the Goddess
When the dreams of life were not diminished by words.

Yana went on to tell the story of how the Goddess
pushed her children from her womb, out of the cave
of dreams to the bounty of her body. The days grew
warm. The milk of the earth flowed. The people wandered, harvesting the seeds of fields and the fruit of
trees, learning the cries of their voices. As the people
wandered, First Daughter grew to be a beautiful
woman with hair the color of ripening wheat, and her
pregnant womb grew with her. Yana made with her
hands in the air the mounded shape of a belly.

As First Daughter's belly expanded,
She became tired of wandering,
She missed the cool dream cave of the Goddess
Mother and infant gave up their sacred breath
Returning to the place of dreams.

Yana's words slowed, labored with sadness.

*The children of First Mother buried the bones of
    First Daughter*
They scattered seeds in her grave
Something for First Daughter to eat
While sleeping in the Cave of Dreams
And again the people wandered.

Yana explained that the next harvest season the people returned to the place where First Daughter dreamed, finding a great abundance of barley growing on her grave. The people harvested the barley, bringing it as a gift to First Mother, and still First Mother could not be comforted. She missed her daughter with hair the color of ripe grain, and lay on the grave, where the barley had been harvested, pounding the earth with sad fists. First Mother would not leave her daughter's dreaming place.

Yana's voice rose with wonder.

A great mother swallow told the people to build a nest
A dream cave of mud, and straw around First Mother,
First Mother stayed in her cave, suffering through the
    winter
Resting on the bones of her daughter.

Yana lifted her hands and her voice lightened.

Eventually, warmth came once more to the land.
The people left their caves of mud
Spring wheat and barley grew in the fields
The cry of a newborn daughter was on the breeze
Some said the child had the eyes of First Daughter

First Mother stood in the doorway of her mud cave
Letting her eyes wander over the land where the bone
    seeds of her daughter slept
She saw her daughter's smile in the rays of the sun
Her hair in the ripening grain
She listened to her new daughter's cry
And woke from her sad dream.

Everything changed when First Mother
Spoke a word never heard before . . .
Home.

The word "home" trailed into the silence. Yana closed her mouth. She was done. The story had been told. Her anger disappeared with the passion of the words. It was as if some spirit had left her, had said its piece. She felt slightly deflated at its passing.

Niam was crying. Everyone was stunned, touched. The words were so sweet, so true. Of course they knew this story, or some version of it, but where had they heard it before? Henne's eyes were wide. She looked at Yana as if she had never seen her before.

The High Priestess took a deep breath. Her hands were clammy, shaking. "Yana," she said quietly. "Who told you this story?"

Yana flushed. "I don't know, Honored One," she said in a half whisper. "I must have heard it as a child," she reasoned. "I remembered it on the Night of Waking Fields." She blushed deeper, nodding toward Tern. "He had just fallen asleep. I took a walk. The pregnant moon made everything clear—beautiful. I came to a small mound in the field and thought I heard a woman crying. But when I reached the top, no one was there. I sat down on a wide flat rock, looking at the moon, when the story came to me."

The High Priestess tried to still her trembling hands by folding them in her shawl. Very few knew the secrets of the sacred mound. She exchanged a glance with Ninka, who also knew what was hidden in the soil beneath the grass. Her friend nodded sagely. They were in the presence of a great priestess and the people in this room did not know it. Yana had the power to create change. Is this what the ancestors had argued about when Yana had the burning sickness?

"Yana," she said quietly, almost humbly. "What do you think the story means?"

Yana shook her head, obviously confused. "It is a story, Honored One. The meaning is for the listener to find . . ." Her voice dropped with embarrassment.

"But you were angry when you told it," Heth pressed.

Some of Yana's vehemence returned. "I was angry at the barbarians. I was there. I saw them kill Napore. I don't care about their power. They have no place in the Goddess. I do not want to learn their words. I do not want to learn their ways—" Her voice broke off.

Henne's face went flat, but not before Yana had seen a look of betrayal cross her features. Her sister's chin was up, but her eye slid past Yana as if not seeing her. Yana clutched at her skirt. She had said too much.

"I agree with Yana," Lolim said. "Who knows what will become of us if we learn the ways of the barbarians. Nothing will be the same."

Ninka leaned forward. "They are not a people who have learned the word 'home.' "

"They are still wandering," Jozer the potter added. "The bones of the ancestors do not call to them. They do not suckle from the breast of the land."

The High Priestess nodded slowly, pulling on her chin. "The ways of the Horse People are strange," she agreed. "We must think on the story Yana has told, share it with the rest of the village. Meanwhile, Henne will refrain from riding her horse. The sight is too disrupting."

Telna's words hit Henne like a blow, taking her wind. Not ride? That was like asking her not to breathe or think. It was too painful to contemplate. Her mare was more than a horse. She was a friend who understood the need to run and be free. Henne's unhappiness must have shown because everyone was looking at her with varying levels of sympathy on their faces. Henne became angry. *I do not need this. I don't need their pity.*

Yana saw the anger flash in her sister's eyes. She hurried to speak before Henne could let her anger be known. "Honored One," she blurted, gesturing toward the High Priestess. "Henne has done nothing wrong. It is not the horse's fault that it was captured and raised by barbarians. Henne obviously enjoys riding.

Can't she ride her mare somewhere as long as it doesn't disturb the village?''

Henne cocked her head toward Yana, genuinely confused. Yana was looking at her, apologizing with her eyes. At one moment her sister seemed to be condemning her, and the next, protecting. Which was it?

The High Priestess frowned disapprovingly. It was not proper for a young person to question an elder's decision, but perhaps customs were different where Yana came from. Still, this was the young woman's home now. If Yana was to be a powerful priestess someday, she must learn that such rudeness could not be tolerated. Telna's eyes swept the room, gliding past Yana as if she were nothing.

"Sometimes a *child* doesn't hear her mother's words," the elder said to the group. "A mother should not have to repeat herself if the child is in the same room."

Yana's cheeks burned with shame. To be called a child in front of family and friends was the highest form of humiliation. A verbal apology to the elders now would only make matters worse. No. She would have to prove her sincerity by doing small things over a long period of time to win their approval again. She hung her head.

Henne felt her heart go out to Yana, realizing she should be the one sitting slump-shouldered. She had been angry, for a moment forgetting she was not a priestess anymore. She would have spoken against the decision of the High Priestess if Yana hadn't spoken first, only her words would have been much harsher. Yana had saved her from the disapproval of the elders. She shook her head. Who was this woman who told strange stories, accepting humiliation in order to protect others?

One by one the elders stood to leave, shuffling out the door. The others stood to follow. That is, all but Yana, who sat quietly, chin down, gazing at her lap and folded hands.

8

The bent woman reached into the grave, moving aside the bones of her ancestors to make room for the skull of her daughter. Oma had aged in the year Yana had known her. Sorrow left deep crags in her forehead and around her mouth. Usually the woman hid her pain for the sake of her children, but not today. Today tears ran freely as she lovingly placed the ochre-stained skull of Napore into the communal grave beneath the floor of her house.

Napore had been a member of the small trading group traveling with Yana when the barbarians from the north attacked. She died trying to protect a child from the spear of one of the Herdsmen. The raiders left as quickly as they came, fleeing the arrows of the Leopard People, leaving sorrow in their wake. The following day the Leopard People erected large scaffolds, placing the headless bodies of their loved ones where the sacred vultures could easily consume their flesh. After the ceremonies of excarnation, Dagron carefully placed Napore's skull in a leather wrap to bring home to Oma for the second burial.

Yana's throat was raw with emotion as she sang the dreaming song of death and rebirth. The ritual of second burial was the same in her former homeland. The people believed the cranium held the kernel of a person's essence. After death, the skull rested on an altar near the hearth until the next burial season. It was a year of saying good-bye. Sometimes the skull was plastered with the clay of the Earth Goddess, molded to resemble the person's flesh. It was talked to and fed the sacrifices of wheat cakes and incense. Everyone understood the spirit of a loved one did not settle into the unseen world at once. Often the departed returned through dreams and memories. If the person had been angry before dying, injustices were addressed through rituals to insure bad luck would not visit the household. The next spring, when the houses were white-washed and repaired, the skull was given back to the Earth Goddess.

The family of the dead was now ready to look toward the future. The cranium was prepared for planting, painted the blood color of rebirth, and put in the grave with the bones of the rest of the ancestors. But like Oma, Yana could not find it in her heart to let go. Napore had been closer than a sister, her first true friend. Yana's sadness solidified into a core as hard as the skull being placed in the dirt, and buried just as deep. The barbarians took that away. She would never forgive them that cruelty.

She reached to wipe away an angry tear hanging from her lashes as the floor of the house was repacked with clay and sand. Finally the stones tiling the floor were put back in place. Oma's brightly woven sleeping blankets and cushions were again placed over the grave. Napore would live on in the dreams and the couplings of future generations living within the womb walls of her mother's house, breathing in them, light-ing the smiles they gave to one another. Perhaps a part of her spirit would be reborn to the people.

The singing over, the mourners retreated to the courtyard. Yana was glad to escape the gloom of the house and her resentful thoughts. The sun momen-tarily blinded her, beating warmth into her upturned cheeks. Atum toddled over. She hoisted him to her hip. His dimpled face and hands were smudged with dirt. His fingers pried into her shift, looking to nurse. Yana pushed away his hands.

"Atum, you know we're done with that," she admonished.

Atum pouted. Yana regretted the severe sound of her words, but the healer had insisted she wean him; she could not risk getting the milk sickness again. Yana adjusted the tight band around her breasts, remembering that she'd forgotten to drink the tea that morning that Ninka had given to help dry her breast milk. Atum tugged on the band, letting her know he was determined to nurse. Yana couldn't blame him. She too missed the closeness of their time together sharing the sacred gift of the Goddess. She squeezed him close, grateful to be part of the seen world after sending Napore to the unseen world. She resolutely pushed away the thoughts of the barbarians and their savagery, and smiled into her son's eyes. Hopefully she'd never have to face the Herdsmen again, but now it was time to think of other things, time to get to work.

Directly after the second burials, the people whitewashed and repaired the houses. Repairing and painting the houses was sacred work. The home, regarded as the womb of the family, had to be carefully tended. It was considered alive, the abode of the ancestors as well as the living. Within the walls, life and death dwelt side by side. Each year the women of the village painted a new skin of plaster on the houses, symbolizing the rebirth of life and prosperity in the Goddess. At the base of each dwelling a band of red paint connected the home to the Earth Mother. Many prayers were needed to keep the houses healthy and evil spirits away.

By midmorning Yana was hard at work. She slapped another glob of the wet plaster on the east outer wall of Galea's house, then smoothed it with the flat side of her spatula. The hot sun on her neck made it hard to concentrate on her prayers as she labored.

Henne worked on the shaded side of Galea's house since the intense heat of the sun side was too much for little Enyana. Yana discretely glanced at her own son sitting a short distance away next to Dagron and Tern. Atum's small fist curled around a rock, his little face determined as he tried to imitate the older men, who were crushing limestone into a chalk.

Yana heard her sister call for more plaster. She looked down into her trough, realizing that it too was almost empty. She leaned against a section of wall she hadn't plastered yet, reaching with the back of her arm to swipe the sweat trickling down the side of her face. Tern, who had been scooping up the chalky dust into a large basket, grinned in her direction. Yana waved at him, indicating she needed more of the limestone mixture. Nodding, he stooped to drag one of the chalk-filled baskets toward her. He hesitated near a pile of sand and Yana's urn, checking to see if she had enough water for mixing. Yana joined him, dragging the trough to where they would mix the paste.

Yana was a mess. Her braids were loose. Flyaway hair clung to her heat-flushed face. Drying plaster splotched her legs, caking her hands to the elbows. Her brows were chalky clumps where she'd inadvertently wiped the perspiration from her forehead. Tern thought she'd never looked lovelier and he couldn't help telling her so as they bent to fill the trough with limestone, sand, and water.

"If we were hearth mates," he growled seductively, "I'd convince you to take a real break. I'm sure the Earth Mother wouldn't mind if we shared her gift in the cool of the house while the yolk of the Sun Goddess burns hottest."

"We are not hearth mates yet." Yana's eyes twinkled back. "And Galea is determined to have this house done by nightfall."

Tern's face lost its humor. "Don't you think it's time we talked to the elders, Yana?"

Yana dropped her eyes. She hunkered over the trough, stirring the mixture with a firm hand. "The

High Priestess may still be angry with me," she mumbled.

Tern stilled her arm. "Yana, I'm sure the Honored One has forgiven you by now. You were only trying to protect Henne. Everyone knows that."

Yana lifted her gaze to the warmth in his eyes. She suspected Tern was right. Just that morning the High Priestess had smiled in her direction. The smile held no shadow of reprisal behind it. No, her hesitation had to do with something more.

Yana glanced across the courtyard at Atum. Galea had taken Tern's place, squatting beside her grandson. The older woman offered Atum a drink of water from a gopherwood bowl. Yana had to shade her eyes against the brutal sun. Her heart squeezed with gratitude as she saw Atum drink deeply. Galea was a thoughtful grandmother. The time with her had been incredibly short. As second daughter, she would have to move from her mother's house when she took a hearth mate. Eventually Henne would inherit Galea's goods and household.

Tern followed Yana's eyes to where Galea sat. He sensed her uncertainty. "Yana," he said gently, "Galea has Henne now. You and I must make a home of our own. Dagron and Niam will soon be mated." His voice lowered. The back of his fingers grazed her cheek. "The elders may choose another mate for me if you do not take me to your hearth," he chided gently.

Yana sat back on her heels. Her lips parted in surprise. She hadn't thought of that. Then she remembered Tamuz, how the young woman had wanted to mate with Tern. Her eyes ran the length of his sinewy arms and strong thighs. She loved the way his sandy hair flopped into his eyes. She suddenly realized there were sure to be others who desired him. As much as she loved being close to her new mother, losing Tern was not worth the risk.

"We will talk to the elders soon," she promised.

9

A plan began to form in Henne's mind. Somehow she must make the people understand that they need not fear the power of the horse. She had to show them how gentle her mare could be. She yanked a coarse handful of the horse's mane, knotting strands in the way of the people of the herd, patting the mare while talking softly.

"The elders will soon see how beautiful you are," she said in low tones, running her palm along the hair of the mare's thick neck. "You serve the Goddess now. They will see that you no longer run with the People of the Herd."

Henne knew that if she wanted to ride again she must convince the High Priestess. If the elder conceded that Moon was safe, others would follow. But it had to be soon. Her horse needed the exercise, and she needed the escape—it was getting impossible to live in the same house with Yana.

Yana wasn't the same person Henne had known when they had traveled together. Then Yana had been independent, self-supporting, but now the opposite was true. Her sister acted as if she were helpless, and sought Galea's advice about everything. She couldn't mend a skirt or make a meal without her mother's input. She asked questions about the ancestors, memorizing their names and escapades aloud, purposely making them her own stories. Annoyingly, Galea seemed to revel in the storytelling. Even worse, their mother made the two sisters mend, cook, and clean together. It appeared she was determined her daughters would become friends. When Henne tried to explain her frustrations, Galea waved her complaints away, admonishing her. Henne had wanted to scream. Somehow she had to find a way to get away from the smothering presence of her new sister.

Twisting her wrist, Henne finished the last knot of Moon's mane. "There," she said, scratching the horse's nose, "that will keep the heat off your neck."

She turned around, searching the ground for the bone comb she had set down. Instead she found Ninka's grandson, a lanky boy named Shem who spent most of his time in the foothills of the mountains herding sheep and cattle. He was draped over the top rail of the holding pen, raptly watching her groom the horse. Henne smiled. Everyone knew Shem loved animals. The large nut brown dog that hung close to his heels was proof of this.

"Would you like to feed her?" Henne asked. "I have extra apples."

Shem's face lit up. The dog's tail slapped the dirt. The boy threw a long leg over the fence, dropped to the ground, and confidently strode toward the mare. He barely looked at Henne.

"How old is she?" he asked, taking the shriveled crab apple from her hand. Before she had a chance to answer he pelted her with another question. "Was she raised from a foal, or captured and then trained?"

The boy spoke with the authority of a man. Henne was surprised to see that he innately knew how to feed Moon. He didn't shy away from the mare's large teeth and reaching lips. He confidently offered the apple from an open palm, then scratched the bone of the mare's forehead and nose as Henne had done.

"I think she's four harvest seasons," Henne answered, enjoying his interest. "I believe she was captured as a foal, but I'm not sure."

"How long did it take you to learn to ride?"

"Not long. I used to enjoy the bull games," she explained, speaking of the harvest domestication rituals. "Riding a horse is much easier than riding a bull." She paused, adding, "And safer." She tenderly stroked the bow of the mare's neck. "It is not a fight to overcome wild nature of the Goddess. Our muscles move together." Riding Moon was more than that, Henne thought. It was like flinging herself at the Goddess. The tireless rhythm of life churning beneath the mare's hooves chased the unattainable edges of things where life and death met. She felt invincible. She wasn't sure anyone could understand her addiction to the chase, its seduction.

"I wish I could ride her." Shem sighed wistfully, lifting his hand from the dog to reverently run it along Moon's hard flank.

Henne glanced at Shem's yearning face. The dog strained toward his fingers as he absentmindedly kneaded a floppy ear. The boy seemed to hang on her every word. He had a deep love for animals, and they for him. It was possible he was the only person in the settlement who understood her relationship with Moon. If only the others in the village could see the mare with his eyes.

Henne took a deep breath. The plan chewing at her mind found form. Ideas fell into place, solidifying. Of course. Why hadn't she thought of it before? Shem was young . . . unafraid. "Perhaps someday you can ride her," Henne replied thoughtfully. "But first you must help me with the other children."

Yana and Tern sat side by side before the elders, their faces expectant as they waited.

The High Priestess fingered her chin, musing. So, the couple wanted to take part in the upcoming mating ceremonies. Telna had anticipated this and had voiced her concerns to Ninka. She couldn't help believing the young woman was destined for another life. Yana's mother had been a priestess, and Yana had shown evidence of the same calling. Usually when one was distracted by the tasks of raising a family, the call of the Goddess became dormant, weak, like an unused muscle. Would Yana be saddened when the call dimmed in her life, wishing she'd made other choices? The High Priestess glanced discreetly at Ninka. Ninka returned a barely perceptible nod before lifting her chin to Yana.

"Are you sure you're ready, Yana?" the healer asked purposefully. "You have only been in Galea's household a short while. You haven't had time to make the things you'll need, and with Henne's return, Galea won't have much to share."

Yana felt a sudden sense of loss as Galea's name was mentioned. She searched Tern's face. He squeezed her hand reassuringly. She took a determined breath before addressing the elders. "I was alone most of the winter," she reminded them. "I spent my time making baskets, mats . . . a few blankets. Most of them are still stored in the house on the hill."

Tern smiled, proud of her accomplishments. "And Dagron and I spent last fall and winter hunting," he said. "I have saved the best of my winter pelts. I can trade them for whatever we need."

The High Priestess tucked the shawl about her crippled arm, stalling for time. Tern's face was so eager. It wasn't going to be easy to withstand the disappointment in his eyes. She lifted her eyes to Jozer the potter, her voice grave as she spoke. "Do you think Yana has learned all the ways of our people?" she asked him carefully.

The old man appeared taken aback by the question. "She hasn't had time," he spouted.

Yana's heart stilled. She paled and dropped her eyes. So, the old woman hadn't forgiven her.

Telna noted Yana's discomfort and wished she could simply say what was in her heart. The Goddess demanded complete devotion. Yana needed to know the strength of her spirit, realize who she could become, without pressure from Tern.

"I'm sure she'll learn the customs of our people quickly," Heth interjected on Yana's behalf.

The High Priestess cocked her head. "And how long did it take you, old friend, to learn?"

Heth licked his freckled lips. "I was a boy, that was long ago—"

Telna noted a flicker of movement from Ninka's eyes—a silent message. "Yana came from a far place," the healer interjected kindly, lifting her painted arms. "She doesn't know the medicine plants here. I would be happy to teach her."

The High Priestess heard a plan in Ninka's words. If Yana spent time with the priestesses, she might come around to realize her place in the Goddess. It was a good plan. It might work. She tapped her mouth, nodding slowly. "Yes. And Kara can teach her the sacred songs and rituals," the High Priestess added. "Heth, you can teach her the stories." The old one straightened decisively. "By next spring she will know everything there is to know about the customs of our people. If Tern and Yana wish to be mated then, I'm sure there will be no objection."

Yana fixed her gaze on her folded hands. "You are still angry with me," she said quietly.

The priestess snorted impatiently, dismissing Yana's words with a wave of her stunted hand.

Tern's face remained controlled, but his nostrils flared. "Yana is adopted. She is no longer a danger to the people. She can live with me while learning the customs of the people. We are ready to be together."

Heth, the elder closest to Yana, leaned over and patted her knee with an age-spotted hand. "What do you say, Daughter? What do you want?"

Yana's dark brows pulled together indecisively. The High Priestess was still angry with her. Clearly the elder wanted Yana to learn more of the customs of the people. Did she dare defy her again? And what about Galea? She glanced at Tern. He was waiting for her to speak for him, and she wanted to, but all her life she had longed for family, a heritage of her own. She opened her mouth to say so, but then closed it again. How could she explain her needs simply?

Heth saw her hesitation. He cleared his throat. "I say Yana and Tern should wait," he said decisively.

The elders nodded their agreement.

Tern knew there was no arguing once the elders were in agreement. He nodded stiffly, eyes hooded in disappointment. He glanced at Yana, who looked away. Why hadn't she spoken for him? Now they would have to wait a year to be together. It didn't make sense.

Later, after everyone had left the Goddess's shrine, only Ninka remained with the High Priestess. She kept her eyes on her work, weaving the thick fibrous reeds into a basket. Her worn voice cracked as she spoke. "Telna," she said quietly, "their hearts will suffer."

The High Priestess lifted her chin. Her old friend rarely used her childhood name. Like the others in the village, Ninka addressed her as Honored One or Sister. Hearing the name of her youth on the healer's lips brought the heaviness of years binding them. Ninka had been there when she was a laughing girl. Very few knew her as Telna anymore, but somewhere deep in her spirit Telna was there, waiting to be released from the burdens of life's decisions.

"Children suffer," the High Priestess asserted.

"But to be the instrument of that suffering—"

"Yes. The Goddess can be indifferent to the cries of her children." She paused, idly wondering, then decided to speak her thoughts aloud. "Are we being indifferent because we wish Yana to explore all sides of herself?"

Ninka responded with an even gaze. "Yana would have come to us anyway," she said quietly.

The High Priestess returned the look, unflinching

and determined. "Time is short, old friend. She has much to learn."

"There are others, Telna."

The priestess's forehead wrinkled in thought. "I suppose Kara has the presence of a High Priestess, but I do not believe she has the calling. And Henne has changed. I fear the Herdsmen wounded her spirit. I do not trust her with the heart of the people." She hesitated. Her watery eyes became distant. "Yana is still unformed. And I need to know . . ."

Ninka's hands went back to her work. She was a healer. She had seen her friend trying to hide the pain in her back and hip for many seasons now. The High Priestess was right. Time was short. "They will suffer," she repeated, sorrow muffling her voice.

The High Priestess nodded in agreement. She remembered a saying her mother had taught her when she was a little girl, something about how the wind-whipped tree learned to withstand the storm. She cleared her throat. "We will teach her," she said curtly.

"Let me do it," the little girl crowding Henne's elbow begged. Henne stood aside, allowing Mere to work the hyacinth and daisies into Moon's braided mane.

During the hottest part of the day, when the adults were inside working or resting, Henne hobbled Moon under the shade of the old oak tree at the edge of the village. There the children gathered to watch her groom and feed her horse. They were naturally very curious about the horse. The young ones had been brought up to think of horses as food, wild animals to be hunted. Henne's mare was obviously not wild, yet it didn't behave like the other domesticated animals in the settlement. It didn't ram at the wooden gate like the goats and sheep, bleating for food. The horse was gentle. The children laughed, clapping when Moon nuzzled Henne's hair or bumped her gently, begging for a treat or to be petted. More importantly, the mare appeared to listen when Henne talked to her. Niam's youngest sister, a child of four harvest seasons, was especially fascinated.

"When my sister takes Dagron as mate, Moon will also belong to our household," she proudly told the other children.

"No, Mere," Henne corrected. "The man does not take the goods of his family to begin a new home, the woman does. Moon is my horse. She will stay with me."

Mere's lower lip jutted out. Tears threatened to spill down her plump cheeks. "But Niam said our houses will be joined when Dagron becomes her hearth mate. You and Yana are supposed to become my new sisters. And Moon—"

Henne squatted until she was eye level with Mere. "Our houses will be joined," she agreed. "The children of Niam and Dagron will always be welcome in our home, and that goes for all the people who live in their womb circle." Henne lifted Mere's chin with a finger. "And as for Moon," she said gently, "as long as I am with you, you may visit her anytime, little sister."

Mere braved a watery smile. "Do you think Moon would let me sit on her back like Shem does?" she asked shyly, glancing at the tall boy standing at the back of the small gathering.

Henne showered Shem with a brilliant smile. Her plan was beginning to work. "I don't think Moon will mind at all," she said casually. The important question was, would the High Priestess mind?

Henne put the riding blanket on Moon before helping the girl up. When Mere was safely seated, she bent down to untie the horse, taking the leather reins, slowly leading the horse through the village. All the children followed.

The High Priestess stood in the doorway of her house, her good hand knotted in a ball, digging into the ache of her hip. Henne walked her mare to the middle of the courtyard. The horse was dressed in beautiful flowers. Mere sat high on the mare's back, her chubby cheeks spread in a wide grin, and Telna couldn't help thinking of the youngster as an added bright flower of the Goddess. Mere obviously enjoyed being the center of attention.

The people of the village milled about, curiously eyeing the horse, occasionally glancing discreetly at the High Priestess, waiting for her reaction. A few brave souls did not wait for her approval, but ventured forward to pet the proud beast. A bemused smile cornered the priestess's mouth. Henne was obviously using the curiosity of the people to win them over. How could one fear an animal that was gentle with children? For the first time the elder realized how deeply Henne had changed since becoming priestess of the barbarians. The old Henne would never have challenged her in such a way. The young woman was certainly bolder than she had been before, more defiant. But truthfully, Henne had been the only one restricted from riding. The High Priestess pushed her fist deeper into her hip. There was a place for a daring heart in the scheme of nature. Often the Goddess gave even the most timid creatures the spirit of boldness when protecting their young. Henne had showed her boldness in a constructive way. Telna would have to think on this.

10

If Yana had only spoken up, Tern thought glumly, he would be choosing a pig for her, instead of assisting Dagron to choose one for Niam.

"How about this one?" Dagron said, lifting a squealing bundle that almost wiggled out of his hands.

Tern pushed himself away from the fence, ambling over to examine the animal, but his heart wasn't in it. If he'd looked closer, he might have seen the film over the pig's eyes.

"Seems strong enough," Tern agreed. "And he's bigger than the others. Niam's mother will be pleased."

Dagron nodded brusquely, hefting the animal under an arm to take to the small holding pen where two other piglets also waited to be sacrificed.

Yana saw them in the distance and waved vigorously. Dagron ducked his chin. A flush of embarrassment crept up his large neck, and Yana couldn't help thinking how difficult this day was going to be for her shy brother. She sought Tern's face. He smiled briefly, but the smile died in his eyes. His shoulders slumped as he looked away. *It's not my fault,* she wanted to scream at his back. *It was the elders' decision, not mine!*

But Yana knew it was more than that. Secretly she felt the elders were right. She did not grow up in this village, the spirits here were new to her. She had more to learn about these people if she was to make her home among them. Many of their traditions, such as reading the entrails, were foreign to her. Her brows came together in a contemplative line. What meaning would the priestesses find when the pigs were gutted?

Yana walked toward the holding pen. Two of the fleshly animals grunted and ran toward her. They bunted each other, trying to get close, thinking she brought food. Another stood apart, distancing itself. Yana thought its behavior curious. She slowly walked around the pen, the other two following, squealing their demands. She squatted, peering between the rough planks of wood. She shoved away the pigs pushing their noses through, blocking her view. As she leaned closer, the lone one grudgingly lifted its head. There was a dull sheen in its eyes. *That one is not well!* Yana thought, alarmed. *We would not offer that pig to the Goddess in my old village. I wonder if the priestesses know?*

Yana looked around for one of the priestesses. A short distance away Kara sat cross-legged in the shade of a house, showing a child how to use the spinning stick to make thread. The youngster gazed raptly at Kara, obviously more entranced with her instructor than the job in front of her.

Yana hesitated as she drew near. She didn't know Kara well. At first impression, Kara seemed aloof, but the children of the village appeared to admire her. More often than not Yana had seen the priestess in the company of one or two youngsters, playing counting games with sticks, or instructing them in the ways of the Goddess. Yana wondered why Kara bleached her hair with limestone paste, wearing the white hair of the Goddess of Death when obviously she was drawn to the young life of the village.

"Honored One," Yana said quietly as she approached.

Kara looked up, a flicker of impatience in her odd, round eyes. Yana rubbed her hands on the outside of her wrap. "I must speak with you before the betrothal ceremony."

Kara waited in silence for Yana to continue, and

Yana felt her annoyance building. Kara was a priest-ess. The woman should be more approachable. She lifted her chin. "Could we speak where there are no ears to listen?" she asked briskly.

Kara frowned. She reluctantly stood, giving the girl beside her a nod to continue spinning. They began to walk. Yana tilted her head toward the temporary holding pen.

"I was taught that only the best animals are sacri-ficed," she began, sounding confused. "Only the strong ones can pass through the Goddess's womb to be reborn as strength in the people. Why would your people"—she paused and corrected herself—"why would *our* people offer a sick animal to the Goddess?"

Kara stopped walking, reaching to grasp Yana's forearm. "Are you saying the pigs fight an evil spirit?" she asked, her voice rising in alarm.

"Not all of them," Yana said hurriedly. "Only one."

Kara released her grip and scurried toward the hold-ing pen. In the short time it had taken to walk across the courtyard and back, the pigs had fallen asleep in a huddled mound in the shade. Flies lazily circled above. The two women leaned against the fence.

"Which one?" Kara asked.

Yana pointed to the large one sleeping a short dis-tance from the others. "His eyes are not clear," she explained quietly. "And when I came near, it acted different, as if its spirit was heavy . . ."

Kara gave her a strange look. Yana chewed her lip. Perhaps she had used the wrong words, but it was the only way to explain what she instinctively knew—that pig was sick!

"Do you know who chose it?"

Yana's heart stilled as she recalled Dagron's flushed face. Had he chosen the animal? Would he lose his luck if his sacrifice to the Goddess became sick? She couldn't be sure which pig he had chosen; her thoughts had been on Tern. She looked into Kara's eyes, fear for Dagron on her face. "I don't know," she breathed.

Kara pursed her lips thoughtfully. Resolutely she lifted her short skirt and stepped over the low railing of the pen. She nudged the pigs awake with a sandled foot. They woke squealing and grunting, throwing dirt with their snouts. The largest one did seem quieter than the others. Kara bent to examine its eyes. She frowned, bending to pick it up. The piglet suddenly came alive, thrashing in her hands. She put the squally bundle down and walked back toward Yana.

"There may be something to what you say, Yana," she said gravely, nodding her head in the pig's direction. "There's a dullness in that one's eyes, but he is very strong, vigorous when disturbed. Still, to be safe the priestesses will have another animal ready, a healthy one, but these animals have been chosen, and the omens must be read. Hopefully, this animal is not sick and the omens will be good."

Yana nodded and stepped away from holding pen. She gazed across the courtyard at Niam, who was standing in the shade under a reed-covered veranda with three other women. She silently whispered a prayer to the Goddess. The day must go well for Dagron and Niam; the couple deserved to be happy. Yana sighed. If things had gone differently, she would have been one of the women waiting for the mating ceremony to begin. She watched enviously as Niam cupped a hand over her mouth, giggling a whisper to one of her companions.

Niam's face was outlined in a black ring with a dot under her nose. The painted symbols depicted the seed within the womb of the Goddess. Bright sun pushed through the overhead lattice of leaves, leaving leopard spots of light on each of the women's richly oiled skin. Ropes of red and yellow poppies were tied in their hip-length hair. Bare breasts, painted the blood color of the goddess, peeked through cascades of blossoms. The women wore betrothal aprons, small flaps of beaded cloth that barely covered their woman's place, leaving the buttocks bare. Amber birthing belts swung below their navels. Niam was only two moon cycles pregnant, but her belly already protruded in a small mound. Yana repressed a smile, suspecting the young woman was probably deliberately distending her belly.

Yana scanned the gathering for Tern. Immediately after the meeting with the elders she had tried to convey her reasons for not speaking up for him, explaining that the High Priestess was obviously still displeased. At the time he had seemed to understand, but as the mating ceremony drew closer, he began to avoid her, drifting further and further away.

Kara covertly watched Yana's yearning face, wondering about her. Yana's words had been strange. *Its spirit is heavy?* Not many would have questioned the selection of the sacrifices to the Goddess, but if the pig was sick, Yana may have just saved the marriage of one of the couples now waiting for the ceremonies to begin. One ill omen could be overlooked, but not two. I must hurry and tell the High Priestess, Kara thought. Another pig must be chosen—a healthy one.

The first part of the ceremony began in silence. The people of the village sat in the courtyard, staring at the couples under the veranda for a hot finger's length of sun time. The staring ritual was a public proclamation of the couples' intent to be joined, and the acknowledged acceptance of the village. Tern tried to push away the envy building in his chest as he stared, waving away a fly drawn to the sweat of his forehead.

The men wore leopard skin caps and leggings. Trifold spots of the predatory cat, indicating the three faces of the Goddess, were painted on their chests, arms, and faces. Each man carried a marriage stick he would eventually give to the woman of his choice. As the sun beat heat onto the heads of the people, it grew unbearable for those not sitting under the shade. Finally the High Priestess nodded.

Tern craned his neck to see Dagron and Niam.

Niam gave her betrothed a sweet smile as he stood. She ceremoniously handed him the marriage stick that had been lying between them. Tern wished Yana would smile like that at him; her looks had been so guarded lately.

The marriage sticks were arm-sized lengths of bone or wood, carved with the symbols of the Goddess. Some had swirling water symbols, or the meandering images of life uncoiling from the seed. Others had more definite lines, carvings of the Goddess in her many forms such as bears, birds, bees, and deer.

The men walked a short distance away and used their sticks to draw separate circles the width of large trees, the pillars of life. In unison, they laid the sticks down, one end touching the rim of the circle, the other end pointing to its center.

Tern let his breath out slowly. The placing of the sticks was a sacred act. It had multiple meanings. The stick pointing inward depicted the cave of the vulva pointing into the womb of the Goddess. It was the full moon and its phases, the slit of the seed from which the pillar of life unfolded, and the symbol of a man's life force as it entered the maiden, stimulating the life of the Goddess.

After the sticks were placed, the priestesses took up reed instruments and clay drums. The men danced around the circles they had drawn, pouncing, bobbing up and down, swiping at the air with imaginary claws. The men sang. The people echoed.

Enter, Daughter, the protection of the Goddess
The heart of the leopard will guard your young
The heart of the leopard will hunt for you, plow for you
Feeding your womb till your birthing days are done.

Their feet pounded into the earth with the rhythmic thud of a heartbeat. Puffs of dirt swirled around their ankles.

Enter, Daughter, the protection of the leopard
The sap of his sweetness is for you
For you his blood waters the fields
For you he dances, for you he pleases.

One by one the women ducked past the frenzied
dancing, stepping into the circles their men had drawn,
standing on one side of the marriage sticks. The drums
and the music suddenly stilled. Tern's heart stilled, it
was time for the turning of the skirts.

He chanced a glance at Yana. She was sitting near
Galea with Atum nestled in her lap, her hair freshly
washed, loose instead of braided. Perspiration curled
small hairs at her forehead. Her low-cut dress revealed
the curve of full breasts. The wrap had been freshly
stamped with the honeycomb pattern of the Goddess,
accentuating her darkly painted eyes and hair. He
never wanted her more than he did at that moment.
He fought the feeling of resentment building in his
chest. Yana should be standing in a circle with poppies
in her hair. He should be presenting her with the marriage stick, instead of sitting here in the dust, watching
others act out the ritual.

Yana turned her head and caught Tern staring at
her. He flushed guiltily and looked away, but not before she saw the bitterness in his eyes. Yana decided
she wasn't going to let Tern's disappointment spoil the
day for her. Her brother was joining Niam as her
hearth mate. It should be a joyous time. Tern had
been moping for a moonspan now and she was getting
tired of it. She resolutely lifted her chin, focusing again
on the young couples to be mated.

Dagron stepped inside the circle with Niam, standing on the opposite side of the marriage stick. Niam
motioned him to bend down and she whispered something in his ear as she grappled behind her back with
the string holding up the flap of skirt. Apparently
Niam was having trouble untying her string. She giggled and flipped around, brandishing her hard, naked

buttocks, arching her back, playfully presenting herself
as he helped untie the holding string. People snick-
ered. Dagron's cheeks flamed. His thick fingers fum-
bled with the cords. Finally the leather thongs came
loose, but he almost dropped the skirt. The laughing
onlookers gasped, then bellowed louder. Galea
clucked her tongue, but smiled as she did. Niam was
certainly gregarious, but Dagron was often too serious,
and Galea liked the change she saw in her son when
the girl was near.

The skirts were turned, unveiling the pubic triangle
in front, covering the buttocks behind. No longer were
the garments maiden cloths, they were now birthing
girdles to be worn under or over other clothes until
the delivery of the woman's first child.

The High Priestess carried a marble bowl with the
smoke of myrrh twirling above it. She stood before
each couple and blew the smoke into their faces. She
slowly walked the perimeter of each circle, chanting.

> *May the wisdom of agreement speak in your mouths*
> *May the ancestors dance in your womb ring*
> *From death, life is restored*
> *May the breath of the Goddess blow in your womb*
>   *circle.*

The young men caught up the marriage sticks. They
resolutely walked to the holding pen, jumping the low
fence. Each man swung his stick like a club. The pigs
ran, squealed, kicking up dust, and then were silent.
The men brought their sacrifices back to the circles.
They handed the sticks back to the women. The stick
was now hers forever. It symbolized his willingness to
provide and share his life with her. If either party
died, or wished to separate, the sacred stick was
burned before the whole village.

Tern thought of the marriage stick he had made for
Yana. He had covered it with fertility symbols. On
one side he had carved the great bull, the crescent

horns representing the moon, the measure of life, the length of the bull's snout was the image of a woman's womb. On the other side he had carved the Bear Goddess. The mother bear was the greatest of all mothers. Tern's eyes returned to Yana, lingering for a long moment on her face. Atum had fallen asleep in her lap, his plump brown cheek pressed to her chest. Yana was a good mother. He could not wait to have children with her. How he wished he could lie in her arms, bury his face between her breasts, listening to the steady beat of her heart. He sighed. Next spring.

The three men stood to one side in their circles as the hunting priest of the village slit the animals down the middle and pulled out their entrails, spreading the gory mess across the circle. The people waited breathlessly as the priestesses moved from place to place, reading the snakelike intestines, the heart, and liver. Flies and bees swirled above the carcasses, landing in the drying blood.

Yana prayed to the Goddess as the elders and priestesses approached Dagron and Niam's circle. Her heart felt as if it were pushing up into her throat. She had seen the pig her brother had slain, the large swine with dullness in its eyes. *But Dagron and Niam belong together,* she reasoned. A child grew from their union. *The omens must go well!*

People stood, craning their necks to hear the verdict of the Honored Ones. Yana pushed up awkwardly, standing with sleepy Atum in her arms. She pressed through the crowd to her brother's drawn womb circle just in time to see the High Priestess rub her wrinkled chin and frown. "Oh, Goddess, no," she whispered silently. *I shouldn't have said anything. I shouldn't have alerted the priestesses. The Honored One must not see something bad for Niam and Dagron.*

The High Priestess squatted, bending over the carcass. She flicked at the liver with a gnarled finger. The liver had a faint greenish sheen. The elder motioned to one of her priestesses, who helped her to stand.

She cleared her throat, flipping her wrist at Dagron. "Bring another sacrifice," she croaked.

Dagron paled. Niam's eyes grew wide with panic. Dagron reached out and squeezed Niam's arm in comfort. He set his shoulders and strode down the alley between the houses to his mother's holding pen, and was surprised to find Kara waiting for him with a piglet in her arms. His brows lifted, questioning.

"Yana was upset," Kara explained. "She didn't know who the pig belonged to, but she thought it might be sick. When I saw which one you chose, I hurried here to help you choose another, just in case the omens did not go well. You are very lucky to have Yana as a sister—she has the rare gift of insight."

Dagron's eyes did not lose their worried expression, but he did manage a smile. He thoughtfully rubbed the inside corner of his mouth with a thumb. "Are you sure this one does not fight evil spirits?"

Kara lifted her chin. "I have examined him," she asserted. "I think the Goddess will be pleased."

Dagron reached for the piglet, ignoring its grunting protests as he turned it over in his large hands. He nodded reluctantly. It was not as big as the other, but its gut was firm and fleshy, its beady eyes were bright. Kara had made a good choice.

The two walked quickly back to the gathering. Dagron's heart squeezed with remorse when he saw Niam's stricken face. He should have been more careful—spent more time examining his offering to the Goddess.

The old entrails were shoved aside as the new pig was dropped into the womb circle. A blow to the head and it was silent. Dagron seemed especially vicious in his attack and everyone sensed the tension in the man. Warm blood spurted in an arch as the Hunting Priest slit the animal open.

The High Priestess and the Hunting Priest walked slowly around the ring, scrutinizing the ropes of intestines. The priestess bent down and squeezed a pale slithery-looking tube between two fingers. She straightened awkwardly.

"The Goddess is satisfied," she said.

The crowd murmured relief.

She held up a bloody finger to silence them. "But She has shown that the couple will have difficulties to overcome," she cautioned. The elder appraised Dagron and Niam. "Are you willing to face these obstacles?"

Dagron nodded quickly.

Niam's wide eyes were polished with unshed tears. For once the girl was serious. She took Dagron's hand. "I will do anything," she said in a hoarse whisper.

The people of the village were silent before Niam's declaration. All were taught from childhood that love was the movement of life, a thing to be reveled in, enjoyed, as one danced through the womb rings of experience. But the humble slump in Niam's shoulders, the shattered confidence of her face, reminded them of the pain of love. Here was love's true form, vulnerable, trusting, believing in the future.

Telna raised the hand not hidden in her shawl. "So be it," she said quietly. She turned to include the other couples to be mated. "The Goddess has seen the birth of your future together."

She nodded once more. The feasting and dancing began.

11

Later that day, the sun hung low in the sky like a huge pomegranate wanting to be plucked, casting a rosy melon glow over the valley. The people of the village lounged in the shade of their mud brick houses, allowing time for the food in their swollen bellies to digest as they waited for the second round of feasting and dancing to begin. Others left to take care of chores that could not be put off; feeding and watering the animals could not wait.

Henne rested with Galea and Yana under the marriage veranda in a special place set aside for the families of the mated couples. The shade was hot with the lazy hum of insects. Henne felt rooted to the earth as she closed her eyes and leaned against a pole supporting the lattice of leaves overhead. Baby Enyana stirred in her arms, head bobbing, looking to nurse. Henne opened her eyes, resolutely pushing away her shift. Enyana gummed her nipple. Henne's body responded. A rush of milk from some deep, unseen well filled her breasts until they were taut with the fluid of the Goddess. It no longer hurt to nurse her daughter. The tug of the little one's lips and her pleasurable smacking sounds satisfied something deep in Henne's spirit. The lids of her eyes drooped once more. Mothering does change one, she mused, fingering one of her daughter's damp curls. Something slow and savoring happened, connecting, forcing her inward. When Enyana's little hands and mouth kneaded her breasts, she was quiet inside.

The sound of shouting startled Henne out of her reverie. Her back straightened. She sat up, dislodging Enyana from her breast. The infant howled in protest. Shem, on a distant hill, raced along the terraced edges of the crops in an effort to reach the village. Something was wrong. Henne could see it in the tense way his body moved. She quickly handed Enyana to Galea, jumped up, and hiked up her skirt to run and meet the boy. Others followed.

Shem, breathing hard, could hardly speak when they reached him. He was bent double, hands on his knees, panting. "Leopard," he stuttered, "got a lamb . . . chased Ryle . . . slipped over the edge into the ravine."

Henne thought of Ryle, Shem's younger brother, a square-faced boy with Shem's bright eyes. Her heart froze. "Is he hurt?" she asked in urgent tones. "Could he talk to you? Would he hear me if I called to him?"

Shem nodded and gulped in air, unfolding his body as he took another breath. "He's on a narrow ledge, hanging on the root of a tree. His arm is badly hurt. I don't know how long he can hang on."

Without thinking, Henne ran toward Moon, tethered in the usual place under the oak tree at the edge of the village. Shem realized Henne's plan and raced after her, stopping just long enough to grab a rope. He yelled at Henne, waving the rope in the air. She mounted, reined the mare in his direction, and trotted up next to him.

"Take me with you," Shem gasped, handing her the rope. "I know where he is."

Henne nodded briskly and reached down, pulling the boy up behind her.

Henne and Shem galloped swiftly through the valley. Henne, bent over Moon's long neck, urged the horse faster while Shem's lanky body cupped hers. The people of the village stood immobilized, mouths gaping. The sight brought something wild and beauti-

ful to the people, a feeling of hope as the horse's
hooves ate up the land. Some prayed to the Goddess
for the boy, others prayed for the wild power they
were witnessing. For Yana, the racing horse unleashed
memories of the wanton destruction of the barbarians,
and she was afraid.

Tern saw Yana pale and shudder. He stepped next
to her and placed an arm about her waist. "Henne
will do all she can for the boy," he whispered in an
effort to comfort both of them. "Shem will help her."
They watched the riding couple disappear over a distant hill.

Rocks flew beneath the mare's hooves. Shem held
tightly to Henne. Her new mother's belly flesh was
soft, contrasting with the hard muscles of her thighs
riding against his. The long cord of her back braced
his chest, their sweat mingled. It had a good smell,
uniting them in panic for Ryle, tying them to the excitement of the thundering ride, and something
more—something that caused his breath to move shal-
lowly in his chest. As they closed in on the scene of
the accident, he spotted tufts of wool caught on the
brambly underbrush, evidence of the scared and scattered sheep. A ewe with her lamb tried to hide behind
a tree. Another was tucked under a bush. Shem
pointed past two limestone boulders, and Henne urged
her horse in that direction. He motioned her to stop
and slid off, running toward the edge of the ravine,
falling on his belly, inching his head over the side.

"Ryle," he yelled. "I brought help!"

Shem waited. No response. Panic crept into his
voice. "Ryle, answer me!"

Henne heard the low whimpering of a frightened
child. A responding sob of relief caught in her throat.
He was still there, still alive. She jumped off the horse
with the rope in her hands. She quickly tied a loop in
one end. As she approached, Shem motioned her to
lie down. She scooted forward.

"The ground here is very unstable," he explained

in a rushed whisper as a shower of gravel tumbled into the void below.

Henne looked over the rim of the ravine. All she could see was the top of the boy's dark head. "Ryle," she called. The boy looked up. His face was dirt-smudged, his eyes round with fear and pain. "Ryle," she called again. "We have a rope. Slip the loop over your head and under your arms. We'll pull you up!"

She fed him the rope made of long twisted hemp fibers. The noose dangled above the boy's head. He did not reach for it.

"The rope is strong," Henne said in a patient, controlled voice. Appa made it. You know his ropes are the best."

"Ryle, take the rope!" Shem demanded.

Henne laid a calming hand on the younger man's arm, quieting him.

"Ryle," she coaxed, "I know your arm hurts, but you must do this. You must slip the rope over your shoulders and under your arms. Shem and I can't come down and help you. The ground up here is about to give way."

They heard the boy sniffling. Henne's horse snorted. She looked back. Moon was edgy. For the first time she thought of the leopard. Did her mare sense the big cat's presence? She turned back to the boy, more determined.

"Ryle," she said evenly, "the Goddess has given you a second chance, but you must show Her you want the life she offers. Take the rope. Trust us. We won't let you go!"

Henne breathed a sigh of relief as she saw the boy tentatively reach for the rope. "That's right," she encouraged. "Over your shoulders and under—"

Ryle seemed to be having a little difficulty with his injured arm but finally he looked up and nodded, his face working against the tears glistening in his eyes.

"All right. We're going to pull you up now," Shem

called, "but we've got to get away from the edge to do it. We will signal you when we're ready."

They backed up slowly. Henne began to think. If the bank gave way, the two of them might lose their balance, falling, the rope slipping from their hands. Apparently Shem had the same thought. They shared a look of concern then his eyes lit up. "What about Moon?" he asked quietly. "Can she help us?"

Moon. Why hadn't she thought of that? "I'll get her," Henne said.

Henne led her mare as close as she dared to the edge of the cliff. The rope didn't quite reach around the horse's thick neck. Shem's face showed his disappointment.

"We'll have to use the reins," Henne said, already untying them as she spoke. We'll use the leather thongs to extend the rope."

"But how will you lead her?

"She will follow me," Henne said confidently, looping one end of the reins around Moon's neck, cinching the other end to the rope with a secure knot. "And you will help her pull."

Shem's nod was decisive as he turned to his task. He yanked on the rope to let Ryle know they were ready to pull. Henne couldn't help admiring the young man. The boy was self-assured, steady. They worked well together. He was nothing like the men of the Herd who considered a woman's opinion as worthless.

Henne urged Moon forward. "Go slowly, girl," she said in soothing tones as the horse took its first tentative steps. "You must not move fast. Ryle has been hurt enough."

The horse seemed to understand Henne's words. Shem was amazed at the smooth, even tug Moon exerted on the rope. He barely helped pull at all. His chest expanded in admiration for the mare and the woman leading her. Soon Ryle would be safe. The rope snagged something. Shem's head jerked in fear. Moon balked at the resistance, sidestepping and snorting. The bank near the edge of the cliff began to crumble. The knuckles of Shem's hands went white as he held on to the rope. The scuttling sounds of rocks cascaded into the canyon below, then all was quiet.

"Ryle!" Shem yelled.

The boy coughed. Shem closed his eyes in relief, leaning his head against the sweaty haunch of the horse's flank, thankful the mare had anchored the rope. His younger brother had gotten a faceful of dust and rocks, but the sound of his hacking meant Ryle was alive, conscious.

Moon stood firm, but tossed her head in nervousness. Henne smoothed the coarse hair on her neck, coaxing the mare forward again. Moments later the top of Ryle's dark head poked above the edge of the cliff. Shem resisted the urge to run to his brother. The bank was still unstable. It would be better to wait until Ryle was on solid ground.

When Henne thought it was safe, she told Moon to halt and ran back to help Shem with Ryle. The boy's dark hair was powdered with dust, his body was scraped and bruised. The broken left arm hung at an awkward angle below the elbow. The child's eyes were dark with pain and exhaustion. Henne wanted to hold him, whispering comfort into his ear, but sensed Ryle would not welcome her embrace. The youngster was trying so hard to be brave. His jaw was clenched against tears hidden behind his eyes. Instead Henne patted him on the knee, commending him for his courage. She made a sling for his arm with the scarf belting the waist of her tunic. Then, with the help of Shem, she helped Ryle onto her horse and swung up behind him.

Shem untied the rope and reins, putting the bone bit back in Moon's mouth. His gaze lingered for a moment on his young brother's worn features. The boy began to nod off. Shem gave Henne the reins, and squeezed her hand gratefully. They shared a moment with their eyes, both knowing they would never forget this day. "My mother's house thanks you," he said quietly.

Henne nodded stiffly. Saying anything more would diminish the power of his words.

Shem cleared his throat. "I must gather the sheep. Tell the others I will be late returning to the celebration."

"But the leopard . . ." Henne objected.

Shem's chest puffed out slightly as he spoke. "Ryle was defenseless against her claws, but I doubt the leopard would attack me," he said with emphasis. "Besides, she has gotten her kill for the day, and I have my sling for protection," he reached for the weapon belted to his waist.

Henne appraised him slowly. The sinewy muscles of long arms and gangly legs proved Shem more man than boy. The cat would think twice before attacking him. Ryle groaned groggily. Henne pulled the child closer. It was time to get him back. The healing woman and priestesses must see to his arm, convincing the angry spirits to take their wrath elsewhere.

On the return ride, Henne passed a large oak. The bloody carcass of the lamb dangled high in the branches of the tree where the leopard had carried it to feast on later. The elders would have to be informed. It had been many harvest seasons since a young leopard had resided so close to the settlement. Perhaps it had come in response to the leopard dance. Whatever the reason, the threat to the goats and sheep of the village, not to mention the children, must be removed.

Halfway back, Henne met the men of the village striding up the hill. At first they showed confusion, surprise at seeing Ryle, but then relieved grins erupted on their faces. Henne pulled up close to them.

"Shem is over the next rise trying to round up the sheep. He could use some help," she suggested. "I need to take this one"—she tilted her head toward Ryle—"to the healing woman. His arm is broken."

One or two of the men nodded solemnly. A few of the younger ones separated themselves from the others and headed up the hill. The older men turned back toward the village.

Henne kicked her horse to a trot. Ryle slept deeply. As she crested the next hill, the valley of terraced fields spread out below her. The top-heavy stalks of grain nodded in the slight breeze, bringing the musty smell of warm earth and the green scent of grasses. Everything around her rustled quietly. She inhaled deeply, her heart swelling in gratitude at the steady breath of the boy in her arms.

Beyond the fields, on the other side of the valley, her village sat on a slight incline. The neat white-washed houses looked like small bright boxes, each packaging something precious, fragile and vulnerable. It was a good place, full of loving people. From her perch, her recent frustrations seemed small. For the first time since she had been abducted, she felt like she was coming home. An image shadowed her thoughts. For an instant she couldn't help seeing the village through the eyes of a person of the Herd—the bright little boxes blatantly seductive, waiting to be ravished. "I will protect you," she vowed. "The People of the Herd will never trample you into the dust with the hooves of their horses." Suddenly she was in a hurry to be home among her friends, with her mother.

Telna stood under the mating veranda, holding a wooden pole for support. She watched Henne ride carefully along the rim of the terraced fields with Ryle nestled in her arms. The way the horse picked its way reminded her of the day when Henne first rode into the valley after her capture. She had been pregnant, swollen with the abundance of the Mother. Something about the scene was compelling—a young woman seated on a strong animal, the horse considerate of the burden it carried. Here was restrained power bringing Ryle, a son of the people, back to his mother's arms. She shook her head. The day had been filled with omens, good and bad. The unseen world was testing again, the balance of power dancing in the shadows. A change was coming, and the spirits were preparing them. Everyone knew the flexibility of and strength of an arm muscle expanded with the added weight of working an ax. The High Priestess looked once more upon the restrained gentleness of the horse. Perhaps Henne should be allowed to ride her horse.

12

Yana followed Ninka's short, sturdy legs as she climbed a slight incline toward a stand of tall oaks. Grasshoppers escaped her feet in a crisp whir of startled wings. Lengths of grass and twigs caught between her toes and in the flap of her sandals as she strode to keep up with the older woman. Not for the first time she wished she'd put on the laced leather walking boots, the boots she had worn while traveling with Dagron and the others, but they were stiff from disuse, the soles thin and polished black with wear. Yana supposed pride caused her to choose her new sandals instead, and now she must accept the consequences.

This was the first day of her lessons with Ninka, who was to teach her about the land in which she now lived by showing her the sacred groves, sharing her expertise on gathering the medicinal plants. Already Yana had learned how to scrape the inside yellow bark of a curious shrub, a plant foreign in her former homeland. The plant's power was used to relieve constipation and to clear the sinuses.

"And you must never take the mother plant," the healer had insisted, pointing to the largest shrub. "She is usually in the middle of many others at the heart of her children, content in herself. After you find her sacred circle of offspring, protect it. Always be aware of how it is doing before taking from it. The younger plants crave attention, like all children. Find the one that is willing, soft, and pliant, or the one that is daring, willing to become part of the people. If a plant shows too much resistance, it is not ready to be harvested."

"But how will I know?"

The old woman squeezed a leaf of the plant in her tattooed hand, motioning Yana to do the same, then closed her eyes. For a long moment there was only the complacent sigh of breezes skimming the surface of grasses and leaves.

"Does this child have male or female power in its leaves," the healer asked in a hushed voice.

Yana instantly knew. She didn't know why or how, she just knew. "Male power," she replied with wonder.

"Is it willing to share its gift, or not?"

Yana felt a tingling in her palm. The shrub was so alive, vital. She could feel its youthful vigor, willing to sacrifice itself to become a part of the adventures of life.

"It wants to go with us," Yana said, opening her eyes wide to stare in disbelief at the leaf in her hand.

Ninka watched Yana's face. Smile lines crinkled the corners of her eyes at the sight of Yana's obvious delight. "You are good, Yana. Someday I will bring you harvesting when the full belly of the Moon lights the night. The plants are very loud at that time."

Now Yana's eyes followed the ground as she walked, passing clumps of field peas, wild vetch, and thickets of sumac. They were suddenly new to her, wonderfully strange. She couldn't help thinking how different her former homeland was with its flat, humorless terrain and one muddy river on which the life of the whole region depended. There, summer scorched the heart out of everything, turning the world brown and dull. The people of that place had been just as harsh as the land. They had cast her out because her son had been born with a twisted foot. But here the yolk of the Sun Goddess was gentle with her children, birthing a more compassionate people. They had helped her straighten Atum's foot with a wooden splint.

Yana lifted her head, surveying the hillside. The higher elevation brought coolness to the evening breezes. The days were warm and hot, but not unbearable. Although the grasses were beginning to pale as summer approached fullness, the surrounding hills of juniper, oak, chestnut, and pine were still green with life, the trees losing only a few leaves to summer dryness. Yana wondered about the transforming power of the Goddess. This place, this land was changing her. The world had become larger. Here the expression of the Goddess was complicated, wonderful. She felt like a child groping to understand the meaning in everything.

The two women left the grassy incline and began to follow a thin trail cut through the sparse undergrowth at the edge of the wood. Ninka maneuvered between this tree and that until she found the one she was looking for. The giant oak stood in a small clearing. They had passed other trees on the way, but none this big. The healer waved a painted arm upward toward its notch-tipped leaves. "This is the mother tree," she said quietly on the verge of reverence. "If Galea sends you for acorns, gather them here."

Yana noticed a few saplings struggling to grow in the great tree's shadow. Ninka plucked them up and tossed them aside. "Sometimes too many children can sap a mother's strength," the older woman explained. "We take care of this tree."

The ground was littered with bits of twig, last year's decayed leaves, and acorns—more acorns than she'd ever seen in one place. Ninka knelt and began to sift through the debris, gathering the cupped nuts in her basket. Yana squatted to do the same. The older woman's hands worked quickly as she spoke.

"When the leaves put on colors and begin to drop from the trees, the children will herd the pigs up here to be fattened on the acorns before winter. But the young ones are told to keep the animals away from this tree."

Yana looked up through the canopy of leaves. "The tree is so sacred?"

An amused smile twitched the older woman's lips. "Yes, of course, but that is not the reason. This mother oak not only yields the largest harvest, but her acorns are the least bitter. The pigs do not mind feasting on the sour kernels of the younger trees. We save these for ourselves."

Yana shook her head. There was so much to learn, so much more to understand about this place that was now her home.

13

Henne stood awkwardly in the doorway of Shem's mother's house. Leme looked harried as she bounced her youngest son on her hip, making Henne think of a hopping mother bird. The thin woman even had birdlike features, darting black eyes and a sharp nose. Henne couldn't help smiling as one of her fledglings, Ryle, winged past, stopping to hug her leg before bolting out the door.

"Be careful of your arm," Leme called after him. She cocked her head toward Henne. "His arm is still not strong enough to be of any use with the sheep," she explained. "Jozer said he could help design the pots today. I think he was more than ready to escape the chores I had planned for him. How I wish the Goddess had blessed me with a daughter," she lamented, not for the first time.

"Four strong boys—" Henne's voice faltered, thinking of how close they had come to losing Ryle.

"Yes." Leme's face brightened, remembering also. "Luck was with Ryle that day . . . but my second son is always getting into trouble. I hope the womb walk will teach him more sense.

Henne didn't comment on this. The sacred initiation of adoption was taboo to speak of, a symbolic ritual of death and rebirth. At the age of seven harvest seasons, every child of the village had to face the small death of the womb walk through the cave of darkness to be reborn as part of the communal group. It was the first of many such rituals of death and rebirth, learning to let go, and one became aware that the womb center of the Goddess was in everything and everywhere.

Henne smiled at Leme. "So Ryle is approaching his time."

"Yes." Leme's eyes misted. "It doesn't seem long ago that Shem was reborn to the people. And now my oldest is almost a man, and Ryle is—"

Leme's words reminded Henne of the reason for her visit. The High Priestess had given her permission to teach Shem to ride. "I suppose Shem is herding the sheep," she interrupted, the tone of her voice inquiring. "I haven't seen him in the village."

Leme shook her head and bounced the baby boy one more time before setting him on the floor. She stood up and frowned. "Shem's not with the sheep. My sister's sons are taking care of them until Ryle's arm is better. No. Shem left three days ago to seek the Goddess. Before he left he spoke of a dream. . . ."

Henne's brows pulled together in concern, her face attentive. The people believed dreams were sacred if they were strong enough to push into the light of day. "What kind of dream?"

"My grandfather came to him in his sleep, asking Shem to accompany him on a hunt. I told my son to inform the priestesses. After all, Grandfather hasn't bothered with anyone in my household since he went to the unseen world. Shem returned from the Goddess's shrine only to say he was going on a short journey."

"That was three days ago."

"I'm not worried," Leme said a little too forcefully. "I'm sure Grandfather wouldn't have asked for Shem if it wasn't important."

Henne remembered a large bear of a man who wore a vulture skull on a thong about his neck. The man had been a great Hunting Priest.

"Grandfather used to complain that people no longer respected the hunt," Leme continued. " 'Too much grain and pig fat,' he'd complain. I imagine Roan wanted to teach Shem a few things. Grandfather will guide my son."

Henne laughed. "I remember Roan. He trained me in the bull games. Used to tweak my ear when I held my net wrong."

Leme shuddered. "I know the games are sacred, but I've never understood the young women who want to take part. There is enough bravery in birth for any woman."

For a moment Henne remembered the domestication games of her youth when she stood with others as young and spry as herself, a net in her hand, trusting her life to another. Those most brave tried to ride the bull. There was nothing more binding, more fulfilling, as one let go of the net and the other flipped over the wild animal. The only thing that came close was the memory of Shem's arms around her as they raced to save Ryle. She thought of his dark eyes locked with hers, the touch of his hand as he thanked her. After all the pain she had gone through at the hands of the people of the Herd, Shem's innocent manhood called to her.

But he's just a boy, her heart whispered.

Shem observed the waking landscape with detached awareness, his body numbed to nothingness as black night softened to the misty grays of morning. The dark, hunkered-down hills of the highlands regained their edges, becoming rock-studded limestone, tufts of grass, prickly shrubs, and sparse trees. His nostrils flared. He breathed in thin mountain air nipped with the scent of dew-sodden earth. Slowly the yolk of the Sun Goddess smiled above the horizon, fingering golden warmth into his clothes. Firstborn light entered his pupils, filling his body like satisfying food, food he had not allowed himself to eat for three days now. But his fast would soon be over. The vision had finally come. Today the hunt would begin in earnest.

The leopard was a young male probably chased from its territory by another, larger male. For days he had followed the cat's padded prints, putting his hands and feet where the leopard had been, imitating the big-shouldered walk of the predator. He found the cat's scat and left his own. He climbed the claw-raked trunks of its favorite sleeping trees, dreaming in the nest of branches while the leopard hunted at night. Strangely, Shem began to feel connected to the young leopard. He knew the cat was aware of him, circling him in its mind like a foreign thought.

Men no longer hunted this way. This was the old way of the Hunting Priests. Grandfather explained it all. In the dream Shem had been a little boy again sitting at the old man's knee while he told of the hunt that made one a priest. "The man must become the animal and the animal the man," he said. "When both stalk as one, the sacrifice of the Wild Goddess is understood and accepted."

The night before, when his head was light with the intensity of the stars, the spots of the leopard moved before his eyes and the cat came to him, showing him how it would be. He would not use his sling or bow. No, only the spear of the old ones would be acceptable.

Shem spent the day finding the right branch to fashion the spear. He hardened its green tip in the coals of a fire as the Sun Goddess lowered on the horizon. Now the spear was loose in his fingers as he waited near the edge of a clearing. Gazelle grazed in the dip of a highland meadow below. The cat breathed in a nearby thicket, and Shem dimly sensed its feline awareness, but the leopard was more intent on the prey, hunger, and a strange kind of desire.

One gazelle wandered from the herd. The hunched leopard started to move slowly, its head low, golden eyes fastened. In a burst of movement it leapt from hiding, flinging itself after the gazelle, ripping up clumps of dirt and grass as it raced in zigzag trails after the gazelle. The other animals scattered, bleating fear. With one great swipe, the leopard reached out, tripping its prey. The gazelle's last cry was cut short in a gurgle of its own blood.

Shem felt the young leopard's triumph as it tore its victim's throat. The graceful gazelle fed the magnificent leopard. He finally understood the great indifference of the Goddess, the fascinating interplay of addiction and desire. All his life he had protected flocks of goats and sheep from predators, and he realized that he had been like the gazelle, one of the herd. Now he thought like the cat, understanding the moment of fierce lust when life and death met.

His thinking became as sharp as the first stars beginning to blink on the horizon; suddenly everything made sense and he knew his place. He stood with the ancient spear of the hunt in his right hand. He stepped into the meadow and approached the young cat. The leopard lifted its head and snarled through crimson whiskers. Yes. This is how he had seen it in the vision—the cat wary, but knowing.

The leopard growled, a deep-throated sound, a warning. It stood over the gazelle like a jealous lover, muscles tense, tail twitching. Shem continued to advance. The leopard crouched. Shem dropped to one knee. The leopard pounced, giant claws reaching through the air. Shem reared his spear. An eternity passed. Shem felt the brush of wind-whipped paws and thrust with everything he had. He felt the bone crunch of a hundred leopards, a hundred gazelles, a hundred men—and it felt true, solid. Up through the chest, the head. The leopard sprawled on top of him, its heavy flesh quivering, its blood blanketing them both. Shem slowly lay back, letting tension drain from his muscles as the cat shuddered in death.

Shem absorbed the leopard's death, triumphant in his gratitude. All along he had been the gazelle, the leopard, and now a man. He knew the power of desire and addiction. Tonight he would honor the leopard that had given its life. Under the full moon he would dance in its skin, get drunk on its blood, satiate his hunger on its meat. Yes, the Wild Goddess was worthy. He closed his eyes as the sun sank deep into the mountains, leaving behind the ruddy streaked sky of the sun's afterglow.

14

Tern strode toward the holding corrals where many of the other young men of the village were gathered to build another sheep pen and attend to the repairs of the old ones. The flocks had increased the last couple of years, and in a few days the animals would be herded from the hills for shearing. This was done in the spring when the days began to grow hot and the wool hung from the animals in heavy clumps. For a handful of days the whole village turned out to groom the long-haired sheep, cutting as much wool from their coats as possible before turning them loose again in the surrounding hills. Everyone helped, even the smallest child.

Tern looked forward to the work and couldn't help thinking of it as a celebration. Often, if the herd was strong and healthy, one of the rams or perhaps a sow would be slaughtered and put over a spit, while the people worked with the enticing smells of meat juices swirling in their nostrils. There would be much bantering, laughter, and singing in the village.

As Tern headed for the corral, he thought of Yana and the awkwardness that had sprung up between them. Perhaps he could use the next few days to draw Yana close again. Maybe it was time to repair more than just the corrals. Head down, deep in thought, he didn't notice Tamuz waiting in the path before him, and he had to stop abruptly in order to avoid bumping into her.

Tamuz put her hands on her hips and gave him a
saucy grin. "Your thoughts must be very important,"
she said. "Perhaps you were thinking of Yana?"

Tern flushed.

She cleared her voice as if unsure how to continue,
and then a look of determination crossed her face as
she peered up at him through a fringe of lashes. "It
must be hard desiring one who is destined to join the
priestesses. Everyone in the village knows you two
have not been speaking since meeting with the elders.
That is why I wished to speak with you privately. I
may have the answer."

Tern looked into Tamuz's small, heart-shaped face.
She sounded earnest, but what was this woman talking
about? He frowned. "Yana and I are waiting until
next spring. We will be mated then. The elders wanted
us to wait so she could learn more about—"And then
it dawned on him. It was still possible that the High
Priestess hadn't given up her idea of making Yana her
successor. He put a hand to his head. Now everything
made sense.

Tamuz watched the surprise dawn on Tern's features. Her eyes dropped. "I'm sorry," she said genuinely. "I thought you knew."

"Does everyone know this?" Tern asked stiffly, his
sandy brows pulling together in concentration as he
tried to sort through his confused feelings and
thoughts. "Does Yana know?"

"I imagine so. The priestesses are training her in
the songs and dances. She is learning the healing secrets from Ninka. Jozer and Heth have been teaching
Yana the old stories of the Great Mother."

Tern's thoughts whirled. If Yana became a priestess,
she would give up her place as wife to become a
mother of the people. They could still be together, but
not live together as a couple. Deep inside he had
known this could happen, but the idea of going to
Yana to relieve his needs repelled him. He wanted to
build a life with her, have children with her. Had Yana

known all along? Had she deliberately misled him while trying to decide?

Tamuz saw the confusion on his face and reached out to comfort him. Her hand looked small and her touch was delicate on his arm. "As I said before," she said quietly, her pert mouth forming each word carefully so there could be no misunderstanding, "I think I have the answer."

Tern looked at her as if there was nothing she could say that could comfort him.

Tamuz spoke in a steady voice. "If Yana chooses to become one of the priestesses, the elders will urge you to take another mate. I know your heart is only for Yana. I can understand this. Appa is the only one I wish. I can't imagine my hearth home without him. But he does not fill my womb. You want a home, children. I want an infant at my breast." She hesitated, then plunged on hurriedly. "I'm sure the elders wouldn't mind if you became my second husband. You would never have to pretend with me, or try to make me happy. I am already content. You could go to Yana anytime you wished . . ."

Tern rubbed his brow. This was too much to think about right now. "Yana and I will be mated next spring," he said vehemently, pulling away, taking a step back. "If she becomes a priestess, it will only be after her childbearing years are over!"

He left Tamuz standing alone in the path. She watched Tern's stiff back as he strode away. She put a hand over her flat belly. Tears glittered in her eyes. She prayed to the Goddess to soften his heart. Somehow Tamuz knew that only he could fill her womb.

"She should be helping us," Niam complained, her small nose wrinkled in disgust as she lifted the palm-sized stone to pound the dirty water out of the wet wool in front of her.

Yana looked out over the courtyard where most of the women of the village were working over the wool

as the men wrestled and groomed the sheep. She secretly agreed, but she came to Henne's defense anyway. "Moon became skittish; the bleating of the sheep
being shaved frightened her." Yana lifted her gaze
past the bent heads of the women to the hills beyond,
where her sister had disappeared on the back of her
horse. "Henne thought a hard ride would help calm
Moon. She should be back soon."

Niam frowned, muttering derisively under her
breath about horses and sheep. Yana took a closer
look at her friend. It wasn't like Niam to be in ill
humor. The flesh about her eyes and fingers seemed
a little swollen, but that was normal considering her
condition. But Niam's face was a little too flushed with
exertion and sweat beaded her forehead.

"Why don't you rest awhile," Yana suggested as
Niam continued to beat the wool in front of her with
decisive strokes. "If you pound that section any
harder, it's going to end up as felt," she teased.

Niam was about to snap back when she thought
better of it. She let the rock slip from her hand and
her face crack into a tired smile. "Henne really should
be helping us. She spends entirely too much time on
that horse. I'm surprised Galea allows it."

"Henne is a woman of the people. She can do as
she pleases."

Niam leaned forward, whispering. "I heard she had
slaves when she was Priestess of the Herd. I believe
she has forgotten the ways of our people. She should
be here with us. You and Galea do all her work. And
you spend more time with her daughter than she
does."

"I enjoy Enyana." Yana glanced over at the basket
where the baby was curled sleeping in the shade near
the closest house, her dark head peaking above the
rim of the basket. She was sure that her sister loved
her daughter. Henne made sure Enyana was well fed
and clean. But Yana had to admit that she wasn't an
overly attentive mother—Henne seemed to take for

granted that either Yana or Galea would be there to watch the child when she was off riding or grooming her mare. *She really should be here helping us,* Yana thought as she put aside an armful of clean wool ready for drying and carding.

"Galea and I do handle most of the chores," Yana admitted. She lowered her voice, whispering. "I think my mother is so thankful that Henne returned to her unharmed, she is willing to grant her daughter anything."

"I still don't think it's right that she orders you around."

"She doesn't really order us, it's just that she expects things . . ." Yana's voice drifted off with her thoughts. Their household did seem to revolve around her sister, but she had never thought of herself as Henne's slave. The idea sent a shaft of anger through her belly. Yana hated the Herdsman. Everything they touched, they destroyed. Perhaps Niam was right and Henne was taking her subservience for granted.

Niam curled her shoulders forward then threw them back in a long, slow stretch. The mound of her belly protruded like a melon. Yana thought her friend unusually big for only four moonspans into pregnancy. Niam put both hands on the mound. "Dagron thinks it's a boy and I told him—"

The girl abruptly stopped talking. A look of wonder dawned on her face. Yana remembered the first flutterings of life when she had been pregnant with Atum. "I can see the little one has something to say about that," she laughed.

"I was hoping for a girl, but Dagron wants a boy so badly . . ." She paused and sighed. "I would love to please him by putting a son in his arms."

As if he had been summoned, Dagron seemed to appear from nowhere. He stood over the two young women, hands on his hips, casting a broad-shouldered shadow. He smelled rangy. Specks of grime clung to the sheen of sweat on his arms and chest, goat and

sheep hair covered his leggings. His large-boned face
was dirt-smudged and twigs of straw were caught in
his beard. "The men are almost done for the day," he
stated, leaning close. Niam wrinkled her nose in disgust. A teasing glimmer came into his eyes. "I thought
I'd come and give my lovely hearth mate a squeeze
before the elders find another job for me to do."

He bent as if to hug Niam. She squealed and slid
away. He laughed and moved closer. She swatted at
him. He grabbed her arm.

"Dagron, don't you dare. I'll take our marriage stick
to you," Niam threatened over her giggles.

He pouted and winked at Yana. "I thought you
liked my smell. Why just last night—"

"Stop it," Niam hissed, blushing and glancing sideways at Yana.

He planted a quick kiss on the top of her head.
"I'm going to find Mother," he said. "The men are
ready to eat. We will finish up tomorrow." His gaze
lingered for an instant on Niam's face. Briefly Yana
thought he would give Niam a hug anyway, but then
reluctantly let go of her and walked away. "I'll meet
you by the courtyard fires," he shot over his shoulder.

"After you wash up," Niam called after him in a
stern voice.

Niam turned to Yana, her young face eager. "Yana,
do you mind finishing up here? I want to help Mother
and Galea feed the men."

Yana looked at the small pile of wool left to be
pounded and rinsed.

"Please," Niam begged.

When Niam pleaded, she sounded much younger
than her age. Yana heard the yearning love in her
friend's voice and for a moment was wistful. The coming of their child had bound Niam and Dagron together in fierce devotion. When Dagron looked at
Niam, pride settled into his face, and something more;
it was as if no one else existed. She wished that Tern
would look at her that way. A stab of resentment

poked at her heart, but she pushed it away and tried to smile. "You go on ahead. There's not much left to do. Tell Galea I will be there to help soon."

Niam's face brightened as she scrambled to stand. She bent from the waist and caught Yana's neck in a bear hug. "I'm so glad you're my new sister," she said in a rushed whisper, then she was gone.

Yana sighed and set to work on the pile in front of her. One by one the other women finished and began to leave the courtyard. After removing a few burrs and rinsing the last bit of wool, Yana spread it on one of the grass mats to dry. Without Niam's company to distract her, she realized that she was hot and tired. Enyana started to fuss in her basket.

"Hold on, little girl," Yana called. "I'm almost done."

Yana stood and shook out her skirt. Out of the corner of her eye she saw someone approaching. She squinted against the glare of the late afternoon sun. It was Tern. Her heart jumped in her chest. He'd made an attempt to clean up a bit, but he still looked hot and dusty from the hard day's work. She plastered a smile on her face to cover her nervousness.

Tern's step slowed as he approached. What could he say to her that would ease the ache in his chest? All day he had worked with the words of Tamuz running through his head until they had become tangled in an emotional blur. He had been grateful for the work. The men had worked in pairs, one muscling the sheep into submission while the other rolled the long wool on a wooden rod, pulling it tight so the flint blade would cut evenly along the skin. As Tern worked he tried to take command of his thoughts. Initially he had been hurt, then angry, then hurt all over again. Now he wasn't quite sure how he felt.

Yana pushed away the damp hair at her forehead, her chest tight with anticipation. She had hoped that the days of communal work would bring them closer together. Perhaps this time he would stop and talk to her instead of just offering a perfunctory smile before moving on. As he came closer she couldn't quite read his expression, but certainly there was no smile there.

Tern stood in front of Yana, arms dangling awkwardly at his side. He took a deep breath and opened his mouth to speak, but Enyana began to wail. A look of distress crossed Yana's features. She put up a hand. "Please, let me get her," she said.

Yana felt a surge of resentment as she hurried to Enyana's basket. Niam was right, she fumed. *Henne should be caring for her daughter, not me. How can I get close to Tern again with a fussing baby between us?*

Enyana was wet. Yana dug around in the basket for a dry wrap and impatiently cleaned the little one up. Enyana sensed Yana's frustration and wailed louder. Yana sighed. "I'm sorry, little sister," she whispered. "Tern's and my problems aren't your fault." She lifted the naked baby up and cooed into her ear until she settled down. She slowly walked with the baby back to Tern.

Tern watched Yana cuddling Enyana with her lips close to the infant's cheek. Yana came toward him with a gentle sway to her gait, a mother's walk. This was the Yana he knew—the real Yana. Everything about her was nurturing, exuding warmth and motherhood. How could she consider leaving it all behind to become a priestess? Remorse clamped his heart.

Yana offered him a tentative smile. "She's quiet now," she said softly, "but I hope Henne gets back before she decides she's hungry."

"Where's Atum?" Tern asked.

Yana tossed her head and laughed lightly. "Galea offered to watch him while I worked with Niam. He follows Mother around like a puppy." Yana leaned forward and lowered her voice. "I think Atum is quite taken with his grandmother. She spoils him with sweet cakes. Since I stopped nursing, my son hardly seems to need me anymore."

There was humor in Yana's voice. Was she purposely taunting him? Anger coiled in his belly. His eyes narrowed accusingly. "Have you forgotten that Atum was the reason that you left your homeland?"

"I've always wanted a family for Atum," she agreed cautiously.

Tern's words came faster. "You wanted a family for Atum, but not for yourself, is that it? Over and over on our journey home you made me believe we could have a life together, but once we were here, you realized you didn't need me anymore. Everyone in the village must think I'm a fool."

Yana shook her head. Words were coming out of Tern's mouth but none of them made sense. And why was he so angry? She reached out to calm him.

He flinched away. Yana's touch reminded him of Tamuz's hand on his arm. No. He didn't want her pity. He didn't want to be second husband. He didn't want to be second anything. "I won't wait, Yana," he threatened. "Go ahead with the priestess training if you want. I'm sure the High Priestess has many plans for you."

"Priestess training?" Yana shook her head again, confused.

"Don't tell me that you didn't know. The High Priestess has always made it known that she would prefer it if you joined the priestesses. Wasn't your mother a priestess?"

Yana put a hand to her head. Yes. She had known. On a deep level she had understood that the High Priestess guided her training. She also knew the elder hoped she would someday join the priestesses. And she had allowed it. A part of her spirit craved the knowledge of the Goddess. Every day a new layer of meaning complicated the webs of life around her, sparkling like dew beads in the grass. She was transfixed by beauty. And this beautiful man, standing so defiantly in front of her, was part of it. Would he understand? Yana took Tern's hand. He did not squeeze it in return. She held on to it anyway.

"Tern, not long ago when I had the burning sickness, I almost died. I almost left for the unseen world." She groped for words. "In a way I think I did . . . something happened to me. I began to see the world differently. I couldn't talk." She shook her head, frustrated with words that could not explain her experience. How could she explain that she had begun to see the womb of the Goddess everywhere; in a blade of grass, in the ant crawling by, in the butterfly that landed on a pile of sheep dung. "Everything became *too* real," she continued hurriedly, "terrible and brilliant at the same time. Even now there is something wonderful in this anger between us. It's shaping us, changing us. This pain can draw us closer, or push us away from each other."

Tern dropped her hand. Yana's face was so earnest, but her words were the words of a priestess. "So you've chosen to be one of them," he said gruffly.

Enyana started to fuss. Yana adjusted the infant on her hip. It was obvious Tern hadn't understood what she had been trying to tell him. She wished Enyana would settle down. There had to be some way to explain it to him.

"No—I mean I don't know," she stammered. "I've changed, that's all. I need to know how you fit into that. I believe the High Priestess was right. We need more time."

Enyana began to cry in earnest. Yana tried to shush her.

Tern had heard enough. He stared past Yana at something behind her as if she weren't there. "You'd better take her to Henne," he said gruffly. "We'll talk later." He turned and strode away.

Yana's heart sank as she watched Tern go. There was something vulnerable about his movements, in the way he held his head, and the defensive clench of his jaw when he turned away. *I hurt him,* she thought. *He doesn't understand. If only my arms were free. I could*

*run after him, hold him, show him how much I still
need him.*

Enyana howled her hunger. Yana began to seethe
inside. Didn't Henne know her daughter would be
hungry by now? She walked toward the communal
cooking area with the crying baby in her arms. Henne
stood next to the fire laughing with Galea. Her sister
looked freshly washed and had a clean wrap on. Yana
looked down at her own soiled tunic. Something
snapped inside. She stalked over and angrily plopped
Enyana into Henne's arms. The frustrations of the day
escaped Yana's mouth in an explosive hiss.

"I am not your slave, Henne," she snarled. "I am
a woman of the people now, or have you forgotten.
I'm sure as Priestess of the Herd you had many
women to do your bidding, but I am not a servant to
be taken advantage of. I traveled a great distance to
find a people—a family of my own. I fought the darkness of the Goddess to be reborn to your people.
Galea is my mother now. You're my sister, and I expect to be treated as such!"

A moment of stillness descended as the people who
overheard sensed the impact of Yana's words. Usually
Yana was meek, soft-spoken. But this woman, standing tall, raging like a great mother bear was someone new.

Henne's mouth hung open in shock, then snapped
closed, quickly giving way to indignation. How dare
Yana attack her before others? Yana was determined
to make her look bad. Enyana bellowed in her arms,
but she ignored her daughter, raising her voice above
the din.

"Someone needs to teach you respect, second
daughter." Henne sneered, her face reddening with
anger. "It's clear you haven't learned the ways of our
people. No woman would open her mouth before others as you have."

Atum buried his face in Galea's skirt. She lifted him
and stepped forward, ashamed of her daughters. "Be

still! Both of you, into the shrine," she commanded.

Fear fluttered in Yana's chest. She wished she could bite back her words. Clearly Galea was displeased. Would she lose her place as a daughter of the people? She glanced sideways at Henne's smug face and steeled her heart with resolution. *No. I will not let her push me around anymore. She will take care of her own daughter. She will help around the house. She will begin to treat me as a sister!*

Henne and Yana waited in the dim room of the shrine for the elders to gather. Henne opened her shift to nurse Enyana. Galea didn't say a word to either of them. It appeared their mother was very, very angry. Henne was glad. This time it was not her fault. Yana had started the confrontation. It was time their mother put a stop to Yana's subtle manipulations.

Yana pulled Atum into her lap, a protection against Henne's baleful glare. For a moment she remembered the time when they had been friends. It seemed long ago now. *Henne has changed,* she thought. The influence of the Horse People must have been very strong. She lifted her head, returning Henne's unflinching stare. *I will fight that power, Sister,* she vowed with her eyes.

First Jozer the potter ducked his white head through the narrow entrance. He was soon followed by Heth, who shuffled in to sit beside him. Ninka and the High Priestess came in together. The blind man, Lezra, led in by his daughter settled next to the two women. Four elders Yana didn't know accompanied by the priestesses found their places as well. As each person came in, the tension in the room mounted. Yana tried not to let her resolve weaken as she nervously toyed with the end of her braid.

Finally they were all seated. The murmur of whispered greetings died down. The High Priestess dipped her head to Galea, inviting her to speak.

Galea sat up, her spine a rod of anger. "My daughters have allowed an evil spirit to grow between them," she spat, "and I have had enough. They use me as a buffer for their dissatisfaction with each other. If I am with one, the other is upset. They fight over me like dogs over a scrap of meat!"

Henne gasped, shocked at the vehemence in her mother's voice. "Mother, it's not as bad as all that. When have Yana and I ever fought?"

Galea turned to Henne. "Every time you ride off—every time I see the back end of your horse galloping away, your anger is felt, Daughter." She faced Yana. "And you—you're always there to take her place, showing me how much better you are than Henne, how your stitching is better, your cooking, how much kinder you are with the children. I will no longer live with this poison in my house."

"But, Mother," Yana objected, wild-eyed and hurt. "I thought we enjoyed the same things. I help you with the cooking and mending. You need me. Henne leaves us to do all the work. I know you missed her after her abduction, but she is taking advantage of you. Can't you see what she's doing? Henne's using us. The People of the Herd have poisoned her with their ways."

"How dare you!" Henne flared, jumping to a stand, ignoring Enyana's disturbed whimper. "You are the one who brought rottenness to our household. You are the stranger who eats at the heart of our womb house. I don't know how you wormed your way into our lives, but Galea was my mother first. You should never have been adopted!"

"Enough!" the High Priestess stormed. "Henne, sit down!"

Henne grudgingly sank to a seated position, anger still burning in her chest. Yana never complained about the amount of work she did. How was she supposed to know that her sister had been harboring anger in her heart? She had assumed Yana enjoyed her tasks, the way she whispered and laughed with

Galea. Never once had Henne commanded her as a slave. What nerve to suggest such a thing!

The High Priestess took a deep breath, glaring at Henne and Yana. "You both have brought shame to your mother's house this day. You have invited danger to our village by allowing this evil to grow between you. The evil seed must be uprooted." The rheumy eyes of the High Priestess rested on Galea. Her voice softened. "My spirit weeps for you, Sister. It is not easy for the mother when the children must be punished."

Galea's angry façade began to disintegrate. "I must take the blame, Honored One," her voice quavered. She looked at Henne. "I did not want to face the possibility that my daughter had changed. I wanted her to be the young woman who left on the trading journey. But she has changed, and I must admit, some of the changes I do not understand. Our relationship is not the same as it was before. I think we need time alone to get to know each other again."

Yana gasped.

Galea reached out, taking Yana's hand. "I have been torn, Daughter. I have not wanted to destroy the tender shoot of trust growing in your heart. You never had a mother's love. I understand how important our time together is, but you swallow me whole with your need. I cannot make up for a lifetime of loneliness, Daughter. You must give me time with Henne . . ."

Telna pulled on her chin. Ninka murmured something in her ear and the old one let her gaze travel over the other elders. "What suggestions do I hear? How shall these two young women be punished?"

The blind man rapped his walking stick on the floor. "Lezra, you may speak."

The whites of the old man's eyes rolled. "I have been listening closely. I have heard much anger in this room, but beneath the anger is something much stronger." He paused and cleared the phlegm from his throat. "I hear pain. In my darkness, I feel a deep wound close to festering. No more trauma should be added to this wound. I beg the priestesses to use caution in this decision."

Yana's eyes glittered with tears. The old man was right. She felt like her chest had been ripped open, left raw, exposed. Galea had made her choice. Henne would be her daughter now. No wonder these people kept their deformed and disabled ones. The spirits granted them powers of seeing the unseen.

Henne wasn't one to cry, but bit her lip to keep it from trembling. *Yes, I am wounded,* she thought. *A man raped me, loved me, married me, then destroyed me with his death. All the while, I fought. Only Moon understands the need I have to run from it all.*

The High Priestess scratched at her shrunken arm. Lezra was right, this problem needed to be handled very carefully. She was quiet a long while before breaking the silence. "I think I speak for the elders," she said slowly, "when I say that this decision should be Galea's. She is the mother of both women now. The Great Mother knows her children's hearts, just as I believe Galea knows the hearts of her daughters. Both Yana and Henne need a little pruning of spirit, but it is better if one who loves them does this. We will give you a few days to make your decision."

Galea tilted her head in acknowledgment. "Actually, there is no need to wait," she asserted. "I have been aware of the storm brewing between my daughters for many moonspans. I've had plenty of time to think of a solution. I believe it would be in the best interest of all if Yana returned to her house on the hill for a moonspan. Henne will stay in my house doing the tasks I ask of her"—she glanced sternly at Henne—"with no voice of complaint. We will learn of each other again. She will not ride her horse until her sister is again under our roof, and they have both made a peace offering to the Goddess."

The elders listened with respect to Galea's proclamation, one by one nodding their heads in agreement.

Yana felt as if someone had reached inside, slashing her heart with a jagged blade. She could not contain her sadness. Once again, she had no mother. She jumped to her feet, tears blearing her eyes as she ran from the Goddess's shrine. Galea stood to go after her, but the voice of the High Priestess held her.

"Let her go, Galea. She is not your child to fuss over."

"But . . . she is—"

"You adopted her. But she came to this village as a woman. She was adopted as a woman. She must learn to accept this. Her past is not for you to repair."

"But she should not feel so alone. She still has a home . . . her time away will be only for a short while . . ." Galea's voice fell to a disparaging whisper.

Telna shifted in her seat, adjusting her aching hip. "When Yana is ready, I will send Kara to comfort her, stay with her on the hill. Your daughter can work here in the shrine with the priestesses while you and Henne get reacquainted."

Galea took a relieved breath. "That would make me feel much better. I don't like the idea of Yana living alone again, that's the only reason I didn't suggest it earlier."

Henne stood beside her mother, waiting respectfully as the elders left the shrine. She glanced sideways at Galea's small frame. Now that she had what she wanted, she was suddenly unsure. There were sure to be changes. Galea had mentioned it was time for them to grow close again. And what about Moon? The horse needed to be ridden. What right did anyone have to take her riding privileges away? Wasn't she a priestess, a leader of the people? Henne frowned. *Not here,* she reminded herself.

Outside the shrine, the High Priestess stood blinking in the bright sunlight, looking for Yana. From her vantage she could see most of the village and the terraced hills beyond.

Ninka pointed. "She has run to the mound again," the healer whispered, leaning close to her friend's ear.

Telna squinted toward the small hill. Sure enough, Yana's crumpled form and dark head could be seen peaking through the tall grass. The elder sighed. So much sadness for one so young, but then remembered that each small death brought about rebirth for the one willing to grow. She rubbed her stunted arm absentmindedly. The mound was a holy ground, a gathering place for strong spirits. It was curious Yana seemed drawn to the place, and she wondered what it meant.

Someone shouted a surprised greeting. The High Priestess shifted her eyes to the youngster running toward the group of elders still gathered outside the shrine.

"Shem's coming," Ryle called excitedly, "and he's killed a leopard!"

A young man strode into the courtyard. He walked in a leopard skin. The muzzle of the cat capped his head and the rest of its fur hung like a long cape down his back. Shem was naked, his body streaked red-black with the drying blood of the leopard. In his hand, he carried a crude spear.

15

The sun pierced the horizon, bleeding red and gold over the land before sinking deeper into the mountains. The rays warmed the mound where Yana lay, but she was too distraught to notice the beauty of the sunset. She pressed her face into the earth, tears watering the wayward grasses of barley and wheat, wishing she could scratch a hole in the dirt, carving out a place large enough to bury the pain in her chest. Perhaps then her self-inflicted isolation wouldn't hurt so much. She gulped, her nose and eyes swollen, and found it was hard to breathe. Galea was right; she had been undermining Henne. Her greed for a mother's love had cost her the only mother she'd known. "I didn't mean to," she whispered over and over through her tears. "I didn't know."

The words sounded false, even to Yana. It was so easy not to see the stain of one's own guilt. She forced herself to look at it—look at all the ways she had betrayed Henne and Galea. It was ugly. Her simple gestures of helpfulness had been self-serving. Yana grieved the loss of the illusion of family she had created. More tears welled as something died inside. She closed her eyes, feeling hollow and empty.

The evening air became uncommonly still, holding its breath, waiting for another wave of self-pity, but the wave never came. Yana had found her truth, accepted it. She sat up wiping her nose and eyes on the grass, its musty smell was comforting. She took a shuddering breath and lay back down in a fetal curl, allowing the warmth of the earth to cradle her, and fell asleep.

Yana dreamed. In the dream a lone ear of barley swayed in the breeze. For some unexplained reason, Yana knew that this ear was precious, valuable beyond all others. She drew closer, examining it carefully. Instead of two rows of seeds, it had six. The plant's stalk was a column of jointed vertebrae, each brittle joint shaped like the head of a bull. The stalk held the seeds up to a cloudless sky. The plant turned golden, glorious in the sun. The husks cracked open. The stalk could no longer hold its burgeoning offspring. The stem bent until it broke. Yana sighed at the vain struggle of life, sadness weighing her heart.

Something caused Yana to lift her eyes. A woman stood beside her. She had never seen this woman before, but felt sure that she knew her. The woman wore a plain leather wrap. Her hair was tied in a bun knot. Deer teeth and white tubular beads hung from a thong about her neck. She had strange moon-shaped tattoos on her face, but her eyes were kind, inviting. The woman took Yana's hands, drawing her forward. Together they stooped over the barley plant. The woman crushed the ear of grain, letting the chaff filter away on the breeze. She took Yana's hand, dropping the seeds in her palm, forcing her fingers to close in a fist around the grain. She held Yana's hand a long time, conveying with her eyes the importance of the seeds, then pushed the fist to cover Yana's heart. The woman's image began to fade into the field of grass around her. Yana grasped at the illusion. "Don't go," she cried aloud.

Her own voice startled her awake.

"I won't go, Sister," Kara said softly.

Yana blinked. The sickle-shaped moon hovered above. Stars crowded the silky black sky. An owl hooted in the distance "A dream," she murmured. "It was just a dream."

She turned her head. Kara's whitened hair seemed ghostlike in the moonlight. Her knees were pulled to her chest, and the woman's bare toes peeked from beneath a wool blanket. How long had Kara been sitting, patiently waiting for her to wake? Yana sat up quickly. The blanket Kara had covered her with fell to her waist. She rubbed her eyes.

"How long?" she asked.

"I watched the moon rise." Kara smiled.

Although Kara's face was hidden in shadow, Yana heard kindness in the voice the young woman usually reserved for children. "Who sent you?"

"Your mother and the High Priestess. They agreed you should not be alone this next moonspan. I am to be your companion."

Yana lay back and gazed up at the stars. "I'm not a child for you to take care of, Kara," she said, sounding distant. "I can take care of myself . . . always have."

Kara shrugged. "That may be true, but you are adopted into our village now. We are a family. You're not alone, Yana."

"Tell the High Priestess I do not need a companion."

Kara didn't respond at first. Finally she did, but there was hesitation in her voice. "I lost my mother too, Yana,'" she said softly. "My mother died trying to give birth to my brother. I moved in with the priestesses when I was only five harvest seasons . . ."

Yana understood that Kara did not share herself easily. She waited quietly for Kara to continue, but the young woman remained silent.

"Then we have something in common." Yana sighed. "My mother died birthing me. I was raised by priestesses of my village, but in my homeland they were cold, unfeeling women."

"I used to think the priestesses here were cold," Kara responded, "especially when I was young. Then I realized they had to be indifferent to the needs of a single person when considering what is best for the group. I do not believe it is an easy thing for them. They must put their own desires aside. When a woman chooses to become a mother to all people, she must forget her cravings for a child of her own to cherish. She must close the door on those feelings, distance herself."

Yana had a flash of insight. Kara was not talking about others. She was speaking of her own needs. Kara gave to the children what she had not been given as a child. "But you are not indifferent to the young ones, Kara," she whispered.

Kara sniffed and lifted her sharp chin. "No, I am not," she said briskly, apparently regretting revealing herself. She cleared her throat in an effort to change the subject. "The High Priestess instructed me to teach you the sacred songs," she said, waving her hand toward the moon. "It is such a beautiful night. I have thought of one of my favorites. It is a love song to the Moon Goddess. Help me sing it, Yana."

Yana agreed to sing, sensing Kara's desire to avoid the subject of children. Besides, it had been a long time since she had sung the sacred songs. She missed her music. In the past she had been known for her compelling voice, a gift she had made no effort to exercise here. But tonight her elusive companion enticed her. They both had wounds. Perhaps praising the Goddess was just the healing salve they needed.

Kara began by lifting her soprano voice to the crescent moon. Yana's rich contralto followed. Kara's chest expanded with amazed elation. Yana's voice was so unexpected, so magical, like finding a crocus blooming in the snow or a wild rose encased in ice, a gift from the Goddess. Their voices and words twined together in perfect union.

Tonight She lifts the corner of Her veil
The curve of Her smile for me
I will plant my faith in Her

Tomorrow She'll lift Her skirt
The mystery of Her fruit for me

I will plant my faith in Her
Soon Her belly will be full for me
I will plant my faith in Her

When She's dark
Her seed buried in the soil of night
I know She waits, and I will wait
I will plant my faith in Her.

As the last haunting notes faded, Yana sensed the night was alive, listening. The stars glittered brighter. The rustling grass stood taller. The breath of wind grew more intimate. The hollow place in Yana's heart began to fill. She was amazed at how alive she felt when focused outward instead of inward. "Let's sing it again," she whispered, her face turned to the moon. "I want to learn all the words."

This time Kara sang slowly, letting the notes hang in the cool air. As Yana echoed her words, she remembered the woman in her dream. She saw again the crescent moons tattooed on her face, her kind eyes. She remembered the feel of the seeds in her hand. The dream suddenly seemed significant. The last notes of the song drifted on the breeze . . . *I will plant my faith in Her.*

"Kara," she breathed, "I must tell you about my dream."

16

Henne heard the crunch of gravel as Shem approached. She turned from grooming Moon to appraise the young man who came to stand beside her, his dog panting at his heels. In the last handspan of days, Shem had changed. He was thinner, his cheeks hollow from fasting. His hair was pulled away from his face and tied in a hunter's knot on the top of his head. He wore a short breechcloth of leopard skin, which left his hairless chest and well-muscled thighs exposed. Hanging from a red-stained thong about his neck swung the canine teeth of the leopard he had slain. But the greatest change was Shem's eyes. They were distant as if seeing into a different world.

Henne gave Shem a tantalizing smile. "So Rav decided to make you a Hunting Priest. I never thought I'd see the day when that old man would take one so young as apprentice."

Shem didn't return her smile. He cocked his head, eyeing her coolly. "At what age did you begin to learn the ways of the priestesses, Henne?"

Henne tilted her head in acknowledgement. "Younger than you, I suppose."

Shem straightened his shoulders. "You are only five harvest seasons older, Henne," he reminded her.

"Five hard seasons," Henne muttered.

Shem fell silent, waiting for her to explain, but Henne was not about to delve into her past, and steered the conversation in another direction. "I

wanted you to meet me here because I'm hoping you
will take care of Moon. She needs to be fed and ridden for the next moonspan and I will not have the
time." She flushed with embarrassment, sure that he
had heard the gossip of her fight will Yana. "Mother
needs help with the barley harvest," she explained,
avoiding his eyes.

Shem moved closer, reverently petting Moon's neck.
The heat from his body seemed to reach out to Henne,
tingling the surface of her skin. She stepped back, surprised at the sensations. *I have been too long without
a man,* she thought.

The horse nuzzled Shem's hand. "You didn't need
to ask, Henne," he said quietly, lifting his head, his
gaze locking with hers. Shem's eyes pulled her inward.
For the first time Henne realized he was almost as tall
as she was. He tore his gaze away. "I am training for
the bull games with Rav," he said. "Riding Moon will
help with my training." He lifted his chin. "When I'm
not riding a bull, I shall be on the back of a horse."

"But they are so different," Henne objected. "Riding a bull is nothing like riding a horse." She
frowned. Hopefully Shem would not confuse the two
when it actually came time to net the wild bull.

Shem saw her concern for him and reached for her
face. He carefully tucked a wayward lock of hair behind her ear. It was a bold, yet intimate gesture. His
eyes took on a glow that she had only seen when he
caressed a prize animal. He let his fingers graze her
cheek, then the faraway look returned to his eyes. He
turned to go. "This year I am a man," he called over
his shoulder as he walked away. "After the domestication games, a priestess and I will share the gift of the
Goddess." He whirled around, eyes challenging her
even from a distance. "I would choose you," he called.
The dog barked, adding emphasis to his words.

Henne's mouth opened in surprise. He turned on
his heel and strode away.

*   *   *

"So tell me," the High Priestess queried, passing the skein of softened hemp string across the loom to Kara, "you have been with Yana for almost a moon-span. Will she join the priestesses? Does she have the calling?"

Kara's hands hesitated over her weaving then picked up the rhythm again. She had been expecting the question. For days she had been formulating an answer, but now that the question had been asked, she was suddenly unsure. How could she make the High Priestess understand all the wonders and complications she'd discovered in her new friend? She frowned, keeping her gaze on her busy hands as she spoke.

"At times Yana makes me nervous," she began slowly, then rushed to explain. "Not in a bad way, but in a strange way. She sees into things. Often I've caught her staring at a tree or flower as if it had some profound message from the Goddess." Kara flushed. "It is the same when she looks at people." She paused, feeling slightly foolish, but the High Priestess was listening intently. "I hear the laughter, and tears of the Goddess in Yana's voice when she sings. And when she dreams . . ." Kara went on to relate the dream Yana had shared the night they had sat under the moon, describing the pulsing energy that surrounded them as she told the story of the woman of the mound. "Yana is not a leader like others," Kara concluded. "She is too detached, too distant. But I do believe she is destined to be a great priestess." Kara determinedly pushed the red-stained yarn through the weft of the loom.

The elder reached to stop Kara's hands. "Does Yana know this about herself?"

Kara's eyes met the unwavering gaze of the elder. "I think she is beginning to know," she answered softly.

"What's keeping her from embracing the Goddess?"

Kara returned to her work, not answering.

"Tern," the High Priestess said knowingly.

Kara's hands stopped. She sighed and let them drop into her lap, nodding. "If Yana had grown up in a caring family," she said, "her needs wouldn't be so great . . ."

The elder leaned back. "Yana is blinded by her desire. Perhaps if we allow her to become satisfied with Tern, she will be able to look over his shoulder—see beyond to the harvest the Goddess offers." A light came to the elder's eyes. "Give Yana the herb that stops children, Kara. Tell her that she has my blessing to couple with Tern as long as she lives in the house of the priestesses."

Kara's eyes widened. "But we may lose her to him."

"Yana is a priestess. The Goddess calls her. She will come to us soon," the old one said with confidence, but her mouth twitched with uncertainty.

"Nonsense," Niam stated stubbornly, hands on hips. "I'm going. There is no reason why I shouldn't help with the harvest this year. Ever since I started looking like the Fertile Mother, you two have been acting like I'm one of Jozer's precious pots. I cannot be broken like a pot!"

Tern and Dagron exchanged a grin over the top of Niam's head. Dagron pulled her close with a purposeful pout on his lips. "But you are my precious pot," he countered, rubbing a large hand over her stomach. He leaned close to her ear. "I certainly enjoy what goes in and I'm sure I'll love what comes out," he whispered.

Niam blushed furiously, pulling away. "I think I liked you better when you were shy!" she admonished.

Tern threw back his head, bellowing with laughter. Everyone thought Niam would take the upper hand once they were mated, but Dagron had surprised them all. His relentless teasing kept Niam off balance, and although the couple sparred often, the clashes were usually good-natured.

Dagron put a bearlike arm around Niam and steered her to the door. "I've already spoken to Mother and Henne," he said, his voice dropping to a serious tone. "They are working with us in the fields today and need help with Atum and Enyana." Niam started to object but Dagron covered her mouth with a thick finger, his eyes creased with concern. "I know you want to be with me today, little mother," he said tenderly. "Singing the harvest songs is fun, but it's hard work to wield a sickle. You know how tired you've been lately."

For the first time Tern noticed the shadows hollowing Niam's eyes.

Niam's eyes dropped to where Dagron's broad hand rested on her belly. It appeared her bull of a husband was in no mood to relent, but he was right, she was tired. Some mornings it hurt to move. She wasn't sure she liked the changes pregnancy inflicted on her body. Often she wished for the days when she could run and dance like a young girl. This was one of those days. She sighed in frustration.

"I'll miss all the fun," she spouted, sounding more like a child than she intended.

Dagron leaned close again. "Well then, I'll just have to make sure you have a little fun later on this evening." He leered.

Niam stomped her foot. Tern started laughing again. "Come on," he said, pulling Dagron away from his wife. "Your precious pot is going to boil if you keep this up much longer. We have work to do."

Yana straightened to rub the ache building in her back. She smiled tiredly in Kara's direction while absentmindedly running her hand along the smooth spine of her bone sickle. She resolutely bent to grasp a handful of coarse straw, carefully sawing through the stems until she had an armful of barley sheaves. As she walked to the place where the sheaves were piled, she remembered to be gentle with the stalks so

as not to shake the seeds loose, losing them in the
soil. Kara began singing a harvesting song and soon
those working close by picked up the chant.

> *Goddess of the Barley Harvest*
> *We harvest the stalk of your sons*
> *Your daughters we return to the earth*
> *All are cherished ones.*

Yana glanced yearningly across the blond fields to
another terraced hill where her family worked. She
spotted Henne's russet hair and her mother's gray
head bending over the barley in the field on the next
hill. Not far from them, Dagron and Tern were binding sheaves in preparation for threshing. A plump
woman approached the men with a water jug on her
shoulder. Her family stopped working and gathered
around the woman for refreshment. A lump formed
in Yana's throat. *I should be with them,* she thought—
singing with them.

Kara came to stand beside her, eyes following the
direction of Yana's gaze. She cupped a hand over her
brows to deflect the sun's glare. "I believe that's
Niam," she stated. "She must have gotten someone to
watch the children. She'll bring us fresh water if we
ask." She gestured toward the clay urn that sat next
to the cut pile of sheaves. "Ours is almost too hot
to drink."

Kara's lime-pasted hair was caught up in a gray
scarf to keep the heat off her neck, but the scarf didn't
help much with the trails of chalky sweat running
down her face and neck. The young priestess began
to jump up and down, waving both arms to get Niam's
attention. Yana almost laughed out loud. Kara looked
like a great pale bird that couldn't quite lift off. Somehow the image didn't quite fit the woman. As a priestess, Kara was reserved. When she put on the robes of
her station, it was almost as if she were putting on
another self, playing a role for the benefit of others.

But once in a while another person peeked out, playful, awkward, animated. No wonder Kara preferred the company of children; they did not expect perfection.

Kara cupped her hands around her mouth, hollering until she had Niam's attention. She picked up the water jug and indicated they needed more. Niam waved back and after a short conversation with the others began to trudge across the fields in their direction. Yana watched as the pregnant woman pushed through the grass, her body movements brisk and angry.

Niam cursed under her breath as she walked. After spending a boring morning with the children, she'd hoped Dagron would be happy to see her, but he had been angry, really angry this time. She explained that the infants were sleeping and another woman had taken over, releasing her to spend some time in the fields, but Dagron thought she should be sleeping with the infants. He commanded her like a child, embarrassing her in front of everybody, admonishing her to return to the womb house after she brought water to Kara and Yana. What was worse, Galea agreed with him.

In her haste, she stumbled over a rock. A baby grass snake slipped over the toe of her sandal. She jumped in surprise. The snake startled her out of her anger. Snakes were gifts from the Goddess. If one crossed your path it was considered a good omen. "Ho, little one." She laughed. "What luck do you bring me this day?"

Suddenly, pain sawed into her abdomen, burning through her left side, taking her wind. Her knees buckled. She fell on all fours gasping for breath. The pain reared again, gnawing, insistent. She tried to scream but nothing came out. Dagron watched the water jug crash to the ground. Yana yelled, and then they were all running.

Niam's eyes streamed, her legs were wet with birthing fluid. She writhed in pain. Dagron reached her first. She lifted her arms to him, her round eyes fearful, uncomprehending. He scooped her up and started across the field in long anxious strides toward Ninka's house. Yana had to run to stay up with him. Galea, Tern, and Henne trailed after.

"It's too early," Niam whimpered, her fingers digging into Dagron's neck as another contraction clutched her. "Goddess, it's too early!"

Dagron flung aside the hide covering Ninka's door. Niam arched her back. A scream tore from her throat. It was an awful sound—the insane howl of a wild animal in pain. She became hysterical, thrashing in Dagron's arms, flailing his chest with bunched fists. "Put me down," she screeched. "It's coming. Put me down!"

Ninka pulled Dagron to her sleeping blankets and he quickly set Niam down. The healer pushed him aside, shoving up Niam's skirt. The baby's tiny blue-veined head protruded already between her legs. It looked like it had been crushed. Dagron paled and stepped back. Galea, who had just come in behind him, saw the situation and drew him outside.

"You must stay here until this is over," she whispered, and then disappeared again behind the leather curtain covering the door.

Dagron stood in the shadow of the house, his great shoulders slumped, his face bewildered as if the pain and loss had not yet registered. Yana went to him, took his hand. Henne came to his other side and leaned her head on his shoulder. Tern brought a large bowl of barley beer. They each took sips, sharing sad eyes, saying nothing as they waited.

17

Henne checked the oven pit to make sure the fuel mixture of charcoal, vine cuttings, and dried sheep manure burned low enough, hot enough to ensure a crunchy yet pliable loaf of bread. She slapped flat cakes of dough on the inside wall of the domed oven, watching them puff before sealing the clay door, leaving the loaves to bake. A few moments later a wonderful aroma rose in the courtyard.

Other women scattered about the courtyard were also busy over the ovens, making enough bread for their families to last through the upcoming days of celebration and the rituals of the domestication games. Galea instructed Henne to make enough loaves to share with Niam's mother, who still had small children in her household. Niam was in no condition to help. She was still in a stupor of grief, pretending to work, but often her hands were slack as she gazed at odd shadows on the wall. Every time Dagron tried to comfort her, she cried out, pushing him away. Unable to stand the rejection any longer, he had moved his sleeping blankets back to Tern's house. Henne sighed, realizing she would be baking all day, beginning to understand just how much she had taken Yana's uncomplaining service for granted.

Henne removed the clay seal that covered the door of the oven. As expected, the loaves had fallen into the ashes; they were done. One by one she speared them with a sharpened stick and hauled them out, dusting the ashes off the crust before dropping the loaves into a basket, then she started the whole process over again.

Henne didn't know when the idea first came to her, but the last couple of days it had grown large in her mind. She had been Priestess of the People of the Herd, married to the headman, who worshiped the God of the Shining Sky. It had been his dream that her Goddess combine forces with his God; a stronger people would grow from their union. Ralic's dream became her own—but then their dream died with him. Since that time she had felt unsure of her purpose, that is until Shem had confronted her with his desire. Suddenly she could see herself again as the mate of a powerful man. She would hone Shem, nurture him. Someday he would be a great Hunting Priest and she, the High Priestess, at his side.

As the day wore on, Henne's thoughts kept returning to Shem's vibrant eyes and challenging smile, unlocking anticipation in her loins. She wished she could be his partner in the bull-dancing ceremonies, but it was against tradition for a nursing mother to take part in the games. Still, she could be a priestess again, meeting his passion with the passion of the Goddess. Soon it would be night of the bull when the moon curved into the shape of twin horns. Her woman's place became moist at the thought of him. She flushed, instinctively knowing Shem had found his manhood, and his body was now tense to explore it. She imagined his youthful passion between her legs, his dark head bent over her breasts. Desire thrummed through her veins. She closed her eyes, took a shuddering breath. A small spasm of want radiated from her woman's place. She flushed. Her hand went to her throat. She opened her eyes, covertly glancing around the courtyard, convinced others could see the desire on her face, but the women continued to work without giving her a second glance. She breathed a sigh of relief, and pasted another slab of dough on the inside oven wall.

Kara gave him the message just as the sun settled behind the mountains. Tern strode quickly up the hill in the dimming light, trying to control his excitement, but his manhood grew anyway. Soon he would be burying his face between Yana's breasts, running his palms along the curves of her thighs and abdomen, twining his hands in her hair. He glanced ahead to the small house on the hill, the place Yana lived before she was adopted. She was there, waiting for him, open for him. *Yana must have convinced the High Priestess we belong together,* he reasoned, exalting in the victory of his love. *She needs me, needs family. She never wanted to be a priestess. I should never have doubted her.*

In her house, Yana was mesmerized by thoughts of Tern as she stared into the coals of a low burning fire. She sat on her heels toasting barley seeds on a flat stone plate, watching them brown until they exploded with a tiny hop on the plate. Later she would grind them, creating a sweet, nutty-tasting flour. She wanted to make Tern's favorite flat cakes for their first morning meal together.

Tern tossed aside the curtain covering her door. Yana looked up with eyes like a startled doe. She quickly regained her composure and moved the plate from the coals, standing slowly. Tern filled his eyes with her. Yana's face was flushed from the heat. Her hair, freshly washed, hung loose down her back and gleamed in the firelight. She wore nothing but the string skirt she had worn on the Night of Waking Fields.

"It's a warm evening," Tern said huskily, holding her with his eyes. "I'm surprised to find you cooking."

"I thought you might like barley cakes . . . later." Yana's voice quavered, questioning, offering more than barley cakes.

Tern didn't say anything. He stood in the doorway, drinking in her presence. Her eyes seemed large, swallowing him. He moved forward. She moved to meet him, their bodies colliding in a desperate pressing of flesh. He lifted her. His lips traveled her neck and face. Yana arched her neck and moaned as his mouth found a breast. He lowered her to the sleeping blankets, his manhood already escaping the flap of his leggings. He didn't bother to take them off as he plunged past the strings of her skirt into the moisture between her legs. They squirmed to get closer, go deeper. Each time he plunged, she gasped. Each time she gasped he growled and plunged. Her fingers dug into his back. They kissed deeply, their mouths matching the probing rhythm of their connected bodies. A deep vibrating sound came from Tern's throat, a growl of possession and submission. She felt his pulsing release.

For a long time afterward they lay in silence, occasionally caressing. Tern thought of how connected they were. "I should never have doubted you," he said, breaking the silence, gazing up at the thatched grasses of the roof. He turned his head to look at her.

Yana reached to touch his face. "We're bound," she said, speaking his thoughts. Her eyes misted. "We will always return to each other."

Tern rolled over, elevating himself on one elbow to get a better look at her. "Next spring we will be mated. I'm glad the High Priestess has changed her mind about us." With a long finger, he traced the curve of her breast down to her hips, thinking of the wonders of the Goddess. Yana's body was made to nurture, made to share love and give life. He leaned close, breathing into her hair. "And now, sweet mother," he whispered, "it's your turn."

Yana felt the swell of his manhood against her thigh. He began to trace her nipples with his tongue, his fingers found her swollen and wet. The rhythm began again, much slower this time. Yana rocked against him, wanting him to enter, but he waited until a shudder began to ripple through her body, then he was there with her, prolonging it, moving with it.

Afterward they lay curled together, the heat of their lovemaking still binding them. Yana held his head to her chest, twirling her fingers through his fine hair. He took comfort in the steady thump of her heart, melting into the safety of her soft breasts. His breath slowed, his face grew slack, and then he was asleep.

Yana began to drift with him into slumber, but something nudged her mind awake. Oh yes, the instructions of the High Priestess. She grudgingly opened her eyes and eased away. Tern groaned in protest, but didn't wake. She rummaged around in a basket until she found the leaves Kara had given her. She walked across the room, dropped them in her boiling bag, and then rummaged around in the fire for a few hot rocks. She hung the bag on a tripod of sticks, then sat down to wait for the leaves to steep.

18

The priestesses and elders reclined in the shade of a tree overlooking the small ravine. Across the surrounding hillsides, makeshift shelters of tents and woven reeds dotted the landscape. Mothers sat with children in the shade of a few scattered trees or under temporary awnings. Although the ravine was only a day's journey south from the village, the drop in elevation made it a much dryer and warmer place. The rocky hillsides were studded with limestone, marble, thatches of drying grass, and wild grapevines. Below, in the cup of the valley, flocks of sheep and goats milled around stacks of hay and dumped grain.

The funnel-shaped ravine, wide at one end, narrowed to a nature-carved corral of rock. Years ago the people had added to the corral, building a fence of piled stones on either side. Although the village was only a day's travel away, it had taken two days to herd the flocks of goats and sheep through the hills. Only those too old to travel stayed behind to tend the village fires.

The High Priestess placed a pinch of powdered herb under her tongue before tucking the leather pouch back into her dress. The deep ache in her hip slowly began to fade as she gummed the bitter root. She sighed in relief. In a few short years she would be one of the old ones remaining behind. She nodded to Rav, the Hunting Priest, indicating that it was time to begin.

He stood, picked up his spear, and strode down the hill.

As she watched him go, Telna recalled the storytelling of the night before. She remembered the mesmerizing chant of Rav's voice and Shem's fascinated face as the young man listened. Rav told of a time when their ancestors had followed great migrating herds of animals, and of the glorious hunts that dominated their lives. He impressed upon them the importance of respecting the "wild heart" of the Goddess, who only grudgingly and with great ceremony gave Her offspring to the spears of men and women. His voice rose as he described how their people herded great flocks of onagers, gazelles, sheep, and goats into small ravines like this one, tossing wide nets over them to prevent escape, while men and women alike took part in the ritual slaying of the animals. Now Rav stood at the bottom of the ravine. Before him a small group waited holding rope nets in their arms. He shouted loudly so those sitting on the hillside could hear.

"We live in a time when many of the animals we take for food no longer fight us," he asserted. "In exchange for the food we provide, and the protection from predators we give to their young, they give us their lives. But the untamable heart of the Goddess still lives in some of them and deserves honor. We give those animals a chance to escape, a chance to fight." Rav raised his spear. "I challenge the Goddess to reawaken the wild hearts of her offspring."

A handful of young men and women dressed in leopard skin caps and tunics burst from the tents and jumped off the rock ledge into the flocks of goats and sheep. Their bodies were painted red and black. Their antics were clownish as they hopped up and down, grimacing, growling loudly, pulling tails and grabbing muzzles. The animals became agitated, bleating in fear at the smell of leopard. A ram began to charge. A couple of goats lowered their horns. Soon the herds were a frenzy of fear and anger.

The High Priestess stood with the elders, craning
her neck to see. Rav raised his spear again. The group
waiting with ropes and nets jumped into the foray,
trying to capture the most aggressive animals, separat-
ing them from the others. More than a few met bruising force as the animals rammed, kicked, and tossed
their heads, trying to fight free of the nets. Only one
ram escaped to the hillside. Rav snagged the arm of
a young man who was intent on going after the animal.
"Let him go," the old man shouted over the noise.

Soon the dust settled. The High Priestess, with the
help of one of her assistants, made her way down the
hill. She walked between the netted mounds, conferring with Rav, pointing out the ones to be marked
with black paint. Throughout the year, before the next
mating season, these animals would be culled from the
herd. Usually the males were the least cooperative.
Some would be sacrificed to the Goddess and eaten,
others would be harvested when the air became cold
enough to freeze the winter supply of meat, but all
lived on as strength in the people. She stood over a
ewe. It was very rare that a female was marked. Fe-
males ensured the rebirth of the herd, but this one
had been very aggressive. Its eyes were wild, glazed
in fear as it panted and struggled in the net. She instructed a young boy to mark her but Shem quickly
crossed the corral, interrupting him.

"Honored One," he said quickly, addressing the
High Priestess. "I know this animal. If she fought
today, it was only to protect her young. I believe the
herd needs her kind of strength," he explained. "She
is the first to come running when I call. The others
follow her lead which makes gathering the sheep
much easier."

The High Priestess rubbed her chin and exchanged
a glance with Rav, who nodded slowly. The boy had
insight, he worked closely with the animals, and Telna
knew personally the dangers of too much inbreeding.
She placed her good hand on Shem's arm. "I value

the judgment of our future Hunting Priest," she said, smiling at the relieved look on his face. Shem turned to go, but she restrained him. "I've been told you are going to be one of the young people taking part in the bull games."

"Yes, Rav has been training me," he said, tilting his head to the older man.

"I have also been told Henne is to be your priestess afterward."

Heat crawled up Shem's neck, but he stood straighter. His chest swelled slightly. "This year I am a man. Henne will dance for me after I dance with the bull."

The High Priestess released his arm. Shem's fiery spirit burned in his eyes. It was right that he should challenge the Wild Goddess, riding the bull of Her power. His youthful vigor seemed larger than the body encasing it, straining for release. Yes, it was time for Shem to mate, releasing his seed to live on as strength in the people. She was suddenly proud, as if he were her own son.

"Go with the Goddess." She smiled, prodding with her foot the ewe wrapped in the rope net. "Because of you, this one will live."

Shem squatted to untangle the sheep. A small cloud passed over the sun and for a brief instant his bent head was cast in shadow. Telna looked up and frowned. The cloud was an insignificant puff of white, no larger than a ball of fur. It passed as quickly as it came. Why then did she shiver?

A pleasant breeze rustled the leaves of the tree. Yana glanced down at her son dozing in her lap. Atum seemed to be growing fast these days. His hands and feet were still dimpled, his cheeks full, but his baby plumpness had begun to disappear. She ran her hand lovingly along the length of his shin. A son was such a wondrous gift from the Goddess.

She looked up and caught Niam staring at them

with hungry eyes. Yana smiled but the younger woman purposely looked away. She shuddered and put a hand on her still-swollen belly. A large silent tear rolled down her friend's cheek. Yana wondered if Niam would ever smile again. She was about to say something encouraging when a burst of laughter from the young people gathered at the bottom of the hill diverted her attention. Henne stood among the group preparing for the bull games. Her sister threw back her head and laughed again.

Yana noted that Henne had been acting differently the last couple of days, more animated, more playful. It was as if something had awakened in her spirit, something she had buried. Obviously Shem had something to do with it. She didn't know the boy well, but he was well respected in the village. Her sister seemed to light up when he was near. Once, Yana had seen Henne purposely flirt with someone else, an older man, causing displeasure to flash in Shem's eyes. Why would she purposely tease him? Yana squinted, peering closer at the young boy at Henne's side. She shrugged, realizing she might never understand her sister, the two of them were just too different.

A small dust cloud formed on the horizon. People sitting on the hillsides stood one by one as a wild bull, followed by a band of men with slings, tambourines, and spears, charged the length of the ravine.

Shem tensed, but Henne didn't look at him. She could only imagine how his blood raced, how his muscles must be coiled with anticipation. Only a couple of years earlier she had been one of the young people facing the threat of sharp horns and wild eyes, and she wished she could take part in the dance again. She remembered the shine in her partner's eyes as she vaulted over the bull, the danger connecting them, defying death as they danced with the Wild Goddess, teasing Her with their youth and vigor in great leaps of exaltation. It was a moment of escaping boundaries, reaching to the great mystery of life with the minds and hearts of the people supporting them, propelling them onward.

Henne glanced sideways at Kire, the slip of a girl who would work with Shem. Like Shem her body was painted red and white, the colors of life and death. They both wore netlike skirts with leopard skin loincloths underneath. Henne knew only too well how hard the Hunting Priest worked the bull dancers. Many nights she had come home, falling to her sleeping mat, too tired and sore to eat the food her mother had prepared. Most likely Kire was well trained.

The wild bull was close now. Men surrounded it, herding the massive animal into the neck of the corral. Two men sealed off the opening with rough-hewn timbers. People reached to help the men scramble up the rocky fence of the corral. Shem and the girl positioned themselves on the top of the wall.

The High Priestess stepped forward with the priestesses and began to chant. A couple of men pounded clay drums. The people joined the priestesses, turning the chant into a song.

> *She comes at the call of Her children*
> *Waiting for us to dance with Her*
> *The sacrifice of passion, birthing something more*
> *Making boundaries, escaping boundaries*
> *We live, eating death*
> *And always She waits for us to dance with Her.*

Henne received a strong whiff of the bull's pungent, musty smell—a scent of fear and anger. The bull's sides heaved as it paced. Its drab coat glistened with sweat. Outraged, the animal bellowed.

The people repeated the song, increasing the tempo. Rav nodded to Shem and Kire. In one smooth movement, both leapt from the wall into the corral. The couple began to dance. They twirled with cartwheels and handstands, jumping high into the air, matching the rhythm of the chant. Their dancing confused the

bull. The furious animal snorted, paced, and pawed
the earth, bellowing again in loud frustration. As if on
command, the couple stopped. The drums became
quiet. The two came together, and stood very, very
still. The only sound was the bull's snorting rage.

The bull lowered its horns. The girl reached to her
waist, removing the net fastened there. The short skirt
disappeared, revealing the spotted loincloth beneath.
Her sweating thighs were marble-hard, her lean torso,
a whip of strength. She handed one end of the net to
Shem. Now her life was in his hands.

The couple stood close together, eyes tied to the
bull, hands knotted in the cords of the net. The timing
had to be right. They had trained hard, but this bull
was wild, unpredictable. The bull pawed the earth,
scratching the dirt into fluffs of dust. The charge began
slow, then gained speed. The couple stared, transfixed,
not moving as the bull careened forward. The people
gasped. At the last possible instant, the two spun
apart, spreading the net between them.

The bull plowed ahead, hooking its horns into the
net. The girl, using the force of the charge, swung up
and over the bull's side and back. Shem let go of
the net, catching her. The people screamed, laughed,
cheered. The bull ran to the other side of the corral,
grunting, tossing its head in an effort to shake loose
the draping net.

The priestesses' throbbing voices picked up the
chant while the drums pounded out the rhythm. The
couple's dancing matched the elation of the crowd,
their limbs flaunting a whirl of red and white as they
purposely brandished their power over the bull. The
onlookers became intoxicated with wonder, watching
the two young bodies doing the impossible; this was
what it was to be truly alive, pitching oneself into the
turbulent fury of life with calculated control, embracing the consequences.

The exhilarated roar of the crowd was deafening.
The bull roared with them, its rage palpable. A stream

of foam escaped its mouth. Rocks tumbled as it rammed the side of the corral. Finally it tore the net loose and stood for a moment, dazed, sides heaving, neck muscles bulging. The crowd quieted. Once again, Shem and the girl stood close together, and very still.

This time Shem removed his belted net. Henne leaned forward, her fingers gripping the rock ledge as the girl grasped the other end of the net. She knew that Shem was going to attempt to ride the wild bull. If only she could be with him, flinging herself at the untamable power of the Goddess.

The red and white paint had begun to streak on Shem's arms and legs. Dust powdered his hair. His body became a sinewy spring waiting to be unleashed. The noisy crowd died down to breathless whispers. The great beast lowered its head, the spears of its deadly horns swinging back and forth. The bull found its target and launched into a run. Again, the couple stood immobilized until the animal was almost upon them, then whirled apart in a flurry of flashing limbs. The girl held taut her end of the net. Shem flipped up over the bull, grabbing the horns, landing on its back. The bull bucked, reared. The girl danced out of the way. The people of the village hopped up and down, clapping, screaming, urging Shem to hold on. The muscles in Shem's arms and legs corded like thick ropes. He seemed something more than human as he held to the power of the Goddess. Joy stirred the people to a turbulent frenzy. And then the girl tripped.

"No!" Henne screamed.

Kire stumbled over the stones that had been dislodged earlier by the bull. She fell hard, her leg twisting up behind her. Without thinking, Henne hurled herself over the fence, grabbing the girl beneath the arms, hoping to pull her to safety. Then, strangely, everything began to move slowly. The malevolent bull became a backdrop to the depths of Shem's eyes. His shocked concern embraced her. For an instant Henne saw into eternity of him, and she recognized her place there. The possibility of a life together unfolded before them like a magnificent blooming flower. She loved him. He saw it. The bull lowered its horns.

Shem threw his weight to one side, yanking the horns and head of the bull, steering it away from the cornered women. The bull rammed him into the stone wall, shaking him loose like an unwanted thought. The bull gored him, flipping his body like a plaything. Henne opened her mouth to scream, but nothing came out.

Men and women vaulted the wall, brandishing spears and clubs. The bull went down, heaving in a pool of its own blood. Shem's broken body lay crumpled near a stone wall. Henne scrambled on all fours to get to him, bloodying her hands as she put his head in her lap. She crouched over him, begging him to live. But his sacred breath wheezed once, then stopped. She inhaled the pain of his death, the ache in her chest expanding, pushing against her ribs. "Why, Goddess!" she wailed in an explosive burst of air. She bent over him, broken, rocking in her grief. "Why do they die? Why take them from me?"

The people gathered in a reverent circle. Some keened with Henne. Others were deeply silent. The High Priestess pushed her way through the crowd. She knelt, putting her gnarled arm around Henne, hoping to help contain the woman's grief. "Do not dishonor his sacrifice, Henne," she whispered, her own voice breaking with emotion. "The Goddess has claimed Shem as Her own."

Henne lay her head on the old woman's shoulder, hot tears scalding her cheeks. The elder's words reminded her of a saying from her childhood—only the best are sacrificed. *Why, Goddess,* she moaned silently, *why play this game?*

The High Priestess pulled Henne away while the Hunting Priest slashed Shem's neck with a flint knife, draining his blood into a ritual bowl. Next, he went to the bull and did the same. The people quickly dispersed, gathering their things to return to the village, leaving a handful of the young people to follow with the flocks.

The fingernail moon was high in the sky by the time the weary travelers arrived home. Without being told, the people went to their houses, dropped their things, stripped down to shifts and loincloths, and began to paint each other white with limestone paste—the color of bones and death. Inside the Goddess's shrine the elders stripped the flesh from the bull's bones, and Shem's bones. Tonight the people would dance, eating and drinking with the spirits of the ancestors.

A short while later everyone gathered in the shorn barley fields where a bonfire blazed. Kara and the priestesses were already waiting for them. Each priestess held a ceremonial bowl. The bowls were the craniums of bulls—the same shape as a womb crowned by fallopian tubes. The womb and the bull, male and female power combined. The vessels contained a mixture of Shem's blood, the bull's blood, barley beer, and something more intoxicating. Living close to the earth and the cycle of seasons, the people understood that all living things were sustained, nurtured by the death of other living things. Even a stalk of wheat had to die to be reborn as another living plant. The bowls were passed from person to person by horn handles. Each took a swallow as two men ceremoniously carved a trench with digging sticks. Kara held one of the bowls aloft and began to pour the dark liquid into the soil.

> *The bull and the boy,*
> *This is their blood*
> *Womb water falling as rain*
> *Our tears an offering*

> *He is most precious*
> *Culled from the flock*
> *The stalk of his manhood severed*

For food, for peace in the herd
Receive our offering, sweet Mother
He is the son You love, sustaining us, making us strong
The best returned to Your mysterious womb
The broken reed to be reborn.

The priestesses took up flutes, clay drums, tambourines, and clicking shells. The people danced and sang
in the fields under the moon. Seeking oblivion from
her grief, Henne drank deeply of the intoxicating mixture, gorging herself on Shem's blood, inviting him to
dance within her. The people around her were nothing
more than gossamer shadows on the fringe of con-
sciousness, moths flitting about a flame. Eventually
someone handed her a strip of fleshy meat. She ate it.
The meat gave her energy. She wantonly dipped and
whirled, touching her breasts and woman's place. This
was the dance she would have shared with Shem, the
dance of desire, fertility, and rebirth. But deep inside,
Henne knew she labored with her own will to live.

Henne was still stumbling, dancing with her ghosts
when the fire died and the ash gray light of morning
revealed the outline shapes of houses, trees, and
corrals.

Yana left with the others, numbly crawling into her
sleeping blankets, curling her body around her sleeping son. His sweet baby smell enveloped her senses;
her thoughts drifted toward the place of dreams. *A
son is such a wonderful gift.*

19

Yana bent over the shallow stream, rubbing old paint and grime out of the robes and shift of the High Priestess. She was careful not to rub too hard so as not to wear out the precious fabric made of woven hemp and linen. Later, after the cloth was thoroughly dried, she would decorate the robes again using clay stamp seals dipped in dyes of red, blue, and saffron, marking the cloth with the sacred geometric symbols of the Goddess. A couple of other women joined her at the stream. Yana, intent on her work, didn't even look up. Someone touched her back.

"Hello, Yana."

Startled, Yana dropped the cloth into the stream. She looked up. Niam stood silhouetted against the sun, a basket of wash under her arm. Yana regained her composure, wiping her hands on her dress as she stood. "Niam," she said, reaching out to embrace the younger woman, "I'm afraid the priestesses have been keeping me busy. I was going to stop by your mother's house to see you when I finished here today."

Niam smiled wanly. "It's all right, Yana. I haven't exactly made myself available since"— her face fell, but then she lifted her chin resolutely—"since I lost the baby," she finished.

Yana nodded sympathetically, taking in Niam's thinning features and her hollow cheeks. "There hasn't been much to be joyful about this moonspan," she agreed.

Niam's voice lowered to a whisper as both women

squatted to attend to their washing. "Mother didn't want anyone to know the sacred drink of the bull made me sick. She was afraid of evil spirits. I vomited all that night and the next day. I'm just now recovering enough to get a little work done. Poor Mother, she has had so much to do."

"I'm afraid Galea is overburdened with work also. Henne hasn't been much use since Shem returned to the Goddess's womb."

The women exchanged guilty looks, remembering their unflattering words about Henne, and Yana's subsequent tirade.

"I'm sure Henne will be herself again someday," Niam said quietly, sad resolve in her voice. "It is hard to lose someone before you even have them."

Yana darted a quick look at her friend's profile.

Niam flushed, bending over her work to hide her shame. "I know I've not been much good to anyone. I didn't mean to push you away. And I've hurt Dagron terribly. I realized the moment Shem's sacred breath escaped into the wind, I had been selfish in my grief."

"Everyone understands, Niam."

Niam faced Yana with wide, beseeching eyes. "Do you think Shem died because of me?" she asked. "Did I bring the bad luck with my sadness? Is that why I got so sick? I have to talk about this. Please don't tell anyone."

Yana sat back on her heels. Something about Niam's face, something about the way she held her body, caused her to pause, but Niam was waiting for an answer.

"When I was a little girl," Yana said carefully, "the priestesses of my village taught us that life must leave the village if new life was to grow. If no one died, there wouldn't be enough to feed all the people.

Niam nodded. "Yes. I was taught the same."

Yana took Niam's hand. "Death is sacred. Your child's death . . . Shem's death . . . both will bring life and prosperity to the people. Don't look for bad luck where there is none."

Niam winced and stopped to take a deep breath. A look of confused loss came to her eyes. Yana wondered where she had seen that look before. Suddenly, she had a flash of insight. Niam was thinner but . . . Yana reached out and placed her palm on Niam's belly. "Niam," she whispered breathlessly, "does life still move here?"

Niam's face crumpled. "I know my baby is gone," she said, fighting tears. "I saw his crushed body. They didn't want me to see it, but I did. Now his ghost tortures me. I should have stayed home that day." Her anguished voice rose hysterically. "I shouldn't have gone to the fields. Dagron was right!"

Yana took Niam by the shoulders and shook her. "Stop this," she said firmly. "Nobody is blaming you. You must stop this now!"

Niam looked at her with hurt surprise in her eyes, but she stopped crying.

"Listen to me very carefully. I want you to answer my question. Does life move here," she asked again, rubbing her hand across Niam's belly.

Suddenly the baby kicked. Yana felt it. Niam saw that Yana felt it. Her eyes grew wide.

"Your son slipped away into the Goddess," Yana whispered in awe, "to give his sister room to grow!" The baby kicked again as if to affirm Yana's words.

Niam gasped. "Sister . . . but how?" Her voice dropped in confusion.

"I don't know," Yana responded. "This one was conceived during the Night of Waking Fields. Maybe it's luck."

"The little grass snake," Niam said, her face lighting with joy. She clasped Yana's hand. "I should have known. It was a luck message from the Goddess."

It was Yana's turn to be confused.

"Never mind, Sister." Niam laughed, hugging her with gratitude before jumping to her feet. "Meet me

at the Goddess's shrine. I will tell you all about it
when we talk with the priestesses."

Yana's eyebrows peaked. "We?"

"Of course you must be there. My mother told me
that the elders are convinced you will be a great priestess
someday. I believe it now. My daughter speaks to you
with her kicks." Niam's eyes sparkled, "But before we
talk to the elders, I want to tell Dagron."

Yana stood and watched Niam scurry up the hill.
She almost called after her to slow down, but then
doubted it would do any good. Instinctively, she knew
Niam was her stubborn self again. She looked down
and snorted a laugh. Niam had left her basket of
clothes. She put her hands on her hips, shook her
head, and picked up her friend's basket, deciding it
wouldn't hurt to do a little more wash. As she worked
she wondered about Niam's words—a great priestess?

Henne leaned forward, stretching her body along
Moon's back, letting the horse run where it willed.
She pressed her face into Moon's mane, closed her
eyes, allowing the steady thud of hooves lull her into
mindlessness. But no matter how far she ran, no matter where she turned, the great maw of the Goddess
waited to consume her. Henne saw Her as a hideous
thing, dark and vile, a great chasm of emptiness swallowing everything beautiful. For the first time in her
life, Henne hated the Goddess and all she represented,
and in doing so found she hated herself more.

Moon slowed to a trot, stopping by a stream. Henne
slid off so the horse could drink. She sat with her
head propped on her knees, idly gazing at nothing in
particular. Spongy moss carpeted the rocks in the
stream. A fern frond rustled. A fingerling trout
jumped back into the shimmering water. A silver drag-
onfly hovered, then was gone. Henne knew the scene
was beautiful, but nothing touched her anymore.

She sat back to remove a leather bag at her waist.
Her tattered fingernails were rimmed with dirt; her

·hands shook as she impatiently plucked at the draw-
string. Finally, it fell open. Empty. Henne cursed and
threw the bag into the stream. She looked around,
anxious now. The poppy extract she had taken earlier
was beginning to wear off. Awareness pressed in with
crushing force. Her tongue was a wad of thick fleece.
She could feel the slick grime of unwashed hair and
dirt ground into the creases of her skin. Dark ghosts
hovered at the corners of her mind, waiting to descend, feeding on her fear.

"I know the secrets," Henne whispered, scanning the
grounds for poppies. "I can make more of the sacred
drink." But as her mind cleared, she realized that it was
the wrong time of year to bleed the sap from the pods,
and knew she would have to go back soon.

Henne began to shake at the thought of facing the
villagers again. Surely they all knew by now that she
had stolen Ninka's pouch, but it had only held a few
small brown grains of opium cut with another dried
herb. Most of the supply had been used in the sacrifi-
cial ritual. Anyway, she didn't exactly steal it. She left
Ninka her most prized boots and a rare amulet in
exchange, but she doubted the woman would be
pleased to see her. The drink was not to be used to
escape the Goddess, but to embrace Her. Everyone
knew the plant was a powerful gift from the Goddess,
not to be abused. The healer used it only to help
someone past suffering, the priestesses used it spar-
ingly during rituals, but Henne didn't care. She hadn't
eaten in days, hadn't slept, and had ridden Moon hard.
Her body screamed the injustice, but she didn't want
to listen. She needed, wanted more.

At the top of the ridge, standing apart in the harsh
sunlight, she saw her answer. Henne scrambled over
rocks and bushes, scraping her arms and legs until she
stood over the plant. It was in full bloom, its serrated
leaves a deep summer green. She rubbed her hand
along the small glandular hairs at the top of the plant

until a smooth film of oil covered her fingers. She
rubbed the oil into her gums.

Somewhere, a horse nickered. Henne turned her
head. At the bottom of the hill, near a stream in the
shade, lay a sad-looking animal. Henne wondered if it
was sick. The horse's coat was dull, ragged. Its ribs
pushed through the skin. A red ugly gash cut deeply
across its flank. The horse lifted its head, nickering to
her again. Henne put a hand to her mouth. Moon!
But it couldn't be! She stumbled down the hill, falling
in her haste. She tried to get up again, but her limbs
wouldn't cooperate. A languid stupor took over and
she began to wonder why she'd been in a hurry.
Slowly she lay back down, gazing up at the blue sky.
Yes, it was not exactly the same as before, but this
was what she wanted, needed.

The world began to gradually move. The grass
hissed with the rhythm of the breeze. High clouds
drifted in a whirl of fascinating patterns. A bee
hummed past, then returned. "Hello, Mother Bee."
Henne laughed, then laughed again at the thickness
of her voice. "Did the Goddess send you looking for
me? Tell her I'm not coming home." The bee
zipped away.

Henne let her eyes droop shut. The afternoon sun
pressed through her lids. Red, black, and yellow spirals danced in the film of her eyes—Goddess symbols.
Her lids flew open. "Leave me alone," she whispered.

She gazed again at the sky and mesmerizing clouds.
A black speck formed, gliding in long, lazy circles.
Another dark spot joined the dance, and another. The
descending specks grew large. *Something must be
dead,* Henne mused. Vultures were servants of the
Goddess who kept the earth clean of rottenness, releasing the spirit to fly. As the birds swung low, she
could see the sunlight through their glossy wingtips
and the wrinkled skin of their naked heads. These
were griffin vultures, larger than eagles with talons
and beaks made for plucking and tearing.

With a flap of wings, one landed, then the others dropped to the ground. The first one hopped onto Moon's back. Until that moment, it hadn't occurred to Henne that the vultures were waiting to feast on her flesh. Angry, she rolled over and pushed to her knees. "Tell the gluttonous Mother that she's just going to have to wait!" she yelled, grabbing a branch, lurching to her feet. She took a few tottering steps and swung. The bird on Moon's back spread its wings and with a little hop, sidestepped her harmless blow. The swing threw Henne off balance and she fell to her knees.

"Go away!" she screamed. "I am sick of staring at your death mask, Goddess!"

The vulture cocked its head. "Is that why you stole my breath, Henne?"

Henne gasped. The bird hadn't moved, but she clearly heard Ralic's voice.

"You took my breath, Henne. Was it because I was dying and you couldn't stand looking at me?"

Henne spun around, wild-eyed. "Ralic?" But no one was there. She faced the bird again. It eyed her coldly.

She put her hands to her face, hiding, covering her eyes. "You were dying. I had to lay the cushion on your face," she said through tears. "They were going to bury me in the dirt with you. I had to escape—save the child we made together."

"Have you saved her? Our daughter should be in the dust with us. She belongs to the People of the Herd."

"No!" Henne yelled, slapping a thigh with her fist. "I don't believe in your Underworld where nothing is reborn. I am a woman of the Goddess!"

The voice changed. Now it was Shem she heard. "Are you a woman of the Goddess?" he asked. "Or did I give my life for a woman who has no respect for sacrifice?"

"How dare you. I did not ask you to die for me!" Henne screeched.

The bird eyed her balefully. "Who is dead, Henne?"

Henne suddenly saw herself through the eyes of the bird. She was lying dead in the grass. Her face was a mask of white. Maggots crawled from her ears and eyes. Blue veins showed through her hands. She screamed.

The great bird flapped its wings and rose over Henne's head. It pushed her to the ground and started plucking at her mouth. She tasted salty blood on her lips.

"Return to me the breath you stole," Ralic's voice hissed malevolently. "Return to me my daughter."

Henne flailed at the monster with phantom arms. She screamed a curdling sound. The giant vulture reached into her open mouth, pulling at the scream. She thought the scream would never end. It went on and on, filling her head with red and black pain. In the agony she saw her rape, the abuse of her body. She saw herself using the powers of the Goddess to make Ralic fall in love with her, how she manipulated him, controlled him, and the sickness and self-hatred that followed. She saw his death, and the guilt she carried. And finally, her jealousy of Yana and anyone else who would threaten her power. The vulture pulled at the scream until it came out of her—a long and slimy thing, dead and putrefying. At the tail end was Shem.

"No," she cried out. "You were never part of any of this."

The vulture dropped the dead meat on the ground. Shem's voice echoed in her head. "Eventually, you would have controlled me, Henne. But I wasn't him, and I couldn't stay. I belong to the wild heart of the Goddess—that thing beyond reach or understanding. That is my choice, my sacrifice."

The giant bird tore at the sickly flesh, eating it until it was gone, then flapped its wings, disappearing into the sky.

20

The news spread quickly. The villagers crowded into the shrine after Niam and her mother. Niam stood before the High Priestess, her eyes dancing as she spoke.

"I didn't know my baby was alive!" she said excitedly, placing both hands on her belly. "Until Yana touched me and the baby kicked, I didn't know."

The High Priestess motioned to Ninka. "Is this true? Is a child growing, or is a spirit haunting her?"

Ninka stepped forward. "I examined her myself. Another child lives in her womb."

"How can this be? You were there when she lost the baby."

"Yana says it is luck," Niam interrupted.

"Yana. Where is Yana?" the High Priestess demanded.

"I'm here, Honored One," Yana said quietly, stepping out of the shadows.

The High Priestess motioned everyone to sit. A couple of priestesses brought cushions for Niam and her mother to recline on. After everyone was settled, the elder turned to Yana, her face gentle but inquiring. "Daughter, how did you know a child was growing in Niam's womb when her own mother and the healer did not?"

Yana bit her lip. How did she know these things? "I don't know, Honored One. I just saw her pregnant.

When I looked at her, I saw a young woman carrying a child.''

The High Priestess appraised Yana as if she'd like to embrace her. If only the young woman could see her own power. She would have to be careful phrasing her next question.

"Are you saying the rest of us saw one thing, and you allowed yourself to see another?"

Yana's eyes grew round. "Yes," she said in discovery. "That's it."

Niam leaned forward. "This child is lucky," she said, a smile playing on her lips. "I conceived on the Night of Waking Fields. And later, the moment my birthing pains started, the Goddess crossed my path as a baby grass snake. My son was sending a message. He left my womb to give his sister room to grow." She put up her hands. "Don't you see, the grass snake was my luck. I just didn't understand at the time."

"I've heard of this," Ninka added. "When I was a girl, the old healer told me of a woman carrying twins who gave birth to one child, and a moonspan later gave birth to the other."

The High Priestess nodded sagely. "The sacrifice of the bull is already living on as prosperity in the people. This child surely is a gift from the Goddess. Niam, you and your mother will move to the shrine tomorrow morning. From now on, Niam must rest. The child will need the prayers and protection of the priestesses until it is born."

"But my other children," Niam's mother objected.

"Your sisters will care for them," the High Priestess said kindly. "You may visit them anytime, but your eldest daughter needs you now." The old woman turned to the crowd. "Now I must ask all of you to leave. The priestesses and elders have many prayers to offer up to the Goddess."

Tern, who had come to stand behind Yana, gave her his hand. Yana smiled into his eyes as he helped her up.

"I would like you to stay, Yana," the High Priestess asserted.

Startled, Yana turned around. Tern frowned.

"Our prayers concern your sister. I believe you should join us," the old woman explained. "Henne has been gone for many days now, and I know Galea is very upset."

Yana nodded slowly, her eyes clouded with concern. "Ever since Mother had to find someone to nurse Enyana, she's been sick with worry. She hasn't slept in days, and already spirits from the unseen world are taunting her."

"That is why we need your help seeking the power of the Goddess. Galea is too distraught to help us."

Yana dropped Tern's hand. "Of course," she whispered.

Tern asked Yana to meet with him later that evening, then turned to leave.

The elders and priestesses gathered in a half-moon circle around the idol of the Goddess. Sage and herbs smoldered in a rock dish before the wooden statue. In a niche to the left of the idol rested Shem's plastered skull; its cowry eyes stared dispassionately over the gathering. Above the skull, the bucranium of the bull that had gored him was in the position of giving birth. The bull's head had been stripped to the bone and painted the color of the uterus and life-giving blood.

The High Priestess began humming in a deep, raspy voice, inviting the ancestors to take part in their prayers. The priestesses and elders joined her. After a while, the hair on Yana's neck began to crawl. She clenched her sweating palms. When communal power came together, something more was born. She could feel the seen and unseen worlds converging, sensed their forces in the wavering shadows. The air became charged with anticipation. Her heart beat rapidly. She found it hard to breathe. The tones of the chant seemed to pull her down. She was sinking into a chasm, until Jozer the potter's voice broke out of the drone, giving her something to hold on to.

"She is encased in clay," he said in heavy tones. "Her arms are tired. Her legs don't move. She wants to break free of the pattern engraved on her stomach and head . . . but doesn't know how . . ."

Another voice, timid but reaching, called out. "Her heart bleeds into the soil and she is trying to gather the blood in her fingers."

"Yes," Ninka rasped. "And a snake slithers from its old skin."

Yana began to tremble. She found words in her throat, words pressing for release. Her throat ached with them, but she was too frightened to speak. She didn't know the ancestors of this place and was sure her words would be an intrusion.

"She is learning a story," Heth said quietly.

"Yes, a story," another added excitedly, "an old story. The gift of the Goddess is unseen. She thinks it's a trick and this makes her angry."

A wave of sadness engulfed Yana. In the shadows she saw eyes, great compassionate eyes; the face of the tattooed woman formed in her mind. The woman's eyes pulled Yana, leading her toward a clay streambed. Yana wanted to go with her but couldn't move her legs. She was stiff, frozen, but everything in her yearned toward the woman. Her trembling became violent. Tears flowed from her eyes. She wanted to speak, but couldn't, didn't dare. Yana sensed the people in the room gathering close to her, whispering concern. The High Priestess moved to stand above her, placing her hands on Yana's head. "Daughter," she whispered, "say your words."

Relief flooded Yana's spirit like blinding light. Words tumbled out of her mouth like rocks in a swiftly moving stream. "Heavy clay," she gasped. "It is not the mold, but the power of what it holds. The vessel must be broken—released. The pain of form will fly with the sky birds, free to be reborn."

Yana's hands began to shake as she tried to make an image with her hands.

The High Priestess bent close to her ear. "What is it you need, Daughter?"

"Wet clay," Yana rasped. "And a hot fire."

Yana barely heard the bustling around her as she sat in the trance. Someone reached for her hand, uncurled her fingers, and placed a cold, slippery lump of clay in her hands. This was the substance of the earth, the Goddess of dark caves and rich soil. What was the message here? The woman of the dream squatted before her, patiently showing her how to make the object, holding Yana's hands in hers as they worked. It was a crude image, a woman with large spreading buttocks and drooping, heavy breasts. With trancelike precision, Yana carved slits for eyes and nose with the quill of a feather. Tears of suffering ran down its face.

"The pregnant Mother," someone whispered in awe.

The dream woman led Yana to the fire. She stooped over the blaze and placed the dripping wet image in the center. The people watched. Blue and red flames sizzled around the object, licking it dry. Hearts thudded in fascination as the lump hardened and darkened.

The cowry shells in Shem's skull glittered with reflected fire. Yana felt lost in the flames of his eyes. She swayed with them. A chant rose from her deep in her chest, ancient tones, forgotten words remembered. The High Priestess and others joined her. The chanting of the people grew loud as they called to the Goddess for release, and birth. And then it happened. A hiss of power's breath. A loud cracking explosion. The statue in the fire split, flying into a dozen small shards.

The people stepped back. Yana snapped out of her trance. She looked around, strangely aware of what had happened, but feeling separate from it. The elders and priestesses were staring at her. She paled. *Am I so different?* She stepped forward. They retreated. She put a hand to her mouth, realizing the elders were afraid of her. Her eyes fell to the fire and the scattered shards. *Oh no. I've destroyed her.*

Yana turned and fled from the shrine. Kara lifted her skirt to run after her. The High Priestess reached out with her good arm, restraining her.

"It is time I talked with Yana," the old one said gravely.

Henne woke to the sound of birds chirping to the morning sun. It had been a dream, sacred to be sure, but only a dream. She stood on shaky legs and stumbled toward the stream. She knelt, put her face in the water, and tried to drink, but her throat was raw, burning. She forced a few gulps down anyway. I must have been sick, she thought, very sick. The effort of drinking exhausted her. She crawled back up on the bank to lie down and closed her eyes to sleep again.

The next time she woke it was late afternoon. She felt amazingly refreshed, but light-headed with hunger. She lifted her head. A short distance away, Moon's neck was bowed to the earth, grazing. The horse looked rested, healthier than before, and Henne wondered how long she had been in the world of dreams. She stood, slowly regaining the confidence of her legs, and began to look for something to eat. She found a few starchy roots. After wiping off the dirt, she began to gnaw on them hungrily. She walked to the stream to wash them down with water. A couple of crawfish scuttled away from her shadow. She caught them with trembling fingers, broke their crusty bodies, and ate them raw. She quickly turned over stones in the stream, catching more, and threw them up on the bank to grill over a fire later.

The food gave her strength. With the strength came the memories, memories of her anger and the haze of pain that followed. Now she could hardly stand the stink of her flesh and the grease in her hair. It was time to get clean. She stripped off her tunic, worn to a rag, and sat in the shallow water, using the rocks and sand in the bottom of the stream to scrub the oil and grime away. Soon her skin was pink and her hair was shining, but Henne was dismayed to find her body bruised, emaciated. Ribs like rolling hills protruded through her skin, her stomach was a hollow cave, and her breasts were now shrunken and useless. Henne's eyes misted, her head drooped in shame. She would never nurse Enyana again. *What did I do, little girl?* her heart whispered. She wondered who in the village was suckling her daughter now. *How could I have left you?*

She remembered the words of the vulture in her dream. *Our daughter should be in the dust with us.* "Never," she hissed through teeth that chattered more from fatigue than cold. "I will always fight you."

Henne rose from her bath and began to wash her tunic. As she worked, her mind mulled over the dream. The dream of the vulture seemed to be seared into her memory like an imprint. She had seen herself dead, but she wasn't dead, she was still in the seen world. The more she thought about it, the more fascinating the dream became. The Goddess had shown her secrets, and in many ways had saved her life over and over again. To what purpose? Then she remembered Shem's words. *I belong to the wild heart of the Goddess—that thing beyond meaning or understanding.*

Henne stepped from the stream, laying the wet tunic on a limestone boulder to dry. She walked a short distance, gathering kindling to build a fire. A bee buzzed past her, then circled back. Henne followed the insect with her eyes. It landed on a yellow poppy. Near the flower, a blue-black feather glistened, reflecting the light of the late day sun. She walked over and picked it up. A vulture feather. "So you were here, Goddess," she whispered. She glanced at the bee. "Tell them I will be home soon," she said quietly, then lifted her chin. "But tell them there is something I must do first."

21

Yana lay on her old sleeping mat in the abandoned house on the hill, an outsider once more. She stared at the plaster walls, seeing nothing but a future of emptiness. She'd destroyed the Goddess. The elders would surely force her to leave now. She closed her eyes against the threat of tears, but they blinked open again at the sound of someone at the door.

Telna entered, ignoring Yana at first, and placed her walking stick against an inside wall. Climbing the hill had been harder than she anticipated, even with her walking stick. Her heart hammered. Her chest was heavy with the effort of breathing, but without hesitating she crossed the room and went about building a fire, using clumps of dry dung left in a basket near the hearth.

Yana quickly sat up, wiping her eyes and face with the heels of her palms. She offered to help, but the priestess waved her away, suggesting she light an oil lamp instead. Yana reached for a green-veined limestone lamp set in a niche of the wall. She pulled out the wick and deftly separated its braided fibers so they would easily catch the flame. She placed a wad of moss next to the wick in the oil. She cupped her hands, striking a piece of flint against a scraper. Her hands shook nervously, but the spark caught the moss, the oily strings quickly blackened and curled. She watched the tiny flame dance, wondering why the High Priestess had come, and come alone. If the old

one wanted her to leave the village, wouldn't she do
it with the support of the elders?

The dung fire was small, but large enough to fend off
the cold. The oil lamp added light. Telna settled her
large, shapeless body on a mat near the hearth and motioned Yana to join her. Outwardly Yana was calm, but
inside she was quaking, her nails biting into her palms
as she waited respectfully for the elder to speak.

"I would have enjoyed a place like this when I was
young," the High Priestess said, her watery eyes encompassing the room. "Living with the priestesses is
rewarding, but being alone also has value."

Yana chewed the inside of her check. *The elders
want to isolate me,* she thought. *They want me to live
here again, alone, so my bad luck will not spread to
the village. The Honored One is trying to be kind—
but I'm sorry, old woman. I've lived too many years
without a family of my own, too many years alone.
There is nothing you can say that will ease my heart.*

The elder cleared her throat. "I see you still haven't
moved your things to Galea's house," she said, flipping a
hand toward a pile of baskets, various mats and blankets,
and a few wooden bowls stacked neatly against the wall.

Yana took a steadying breath, hoping to sound confi-
dent. "Galea's house is already crowded," she replied.
"After Henne returned, I thought it best to wait until
Tern and I had a house of our own before I moved
my things."

Telna noted the flicker of anguish in Yana's eyes at the
mention of Tern, but thought it wise to ignore it. She
grunted and changed the subject, eyeing Yana specula-
tively. "I'm sure you are wondering why I'm here, Yana."

Yana's gaze fell to her hands. She ran a finger along
the uneven weave of her skirt. "I have an idea," she
murmured.

The elder's face softened. "I have news," she said
quietly. "Late this afternoon a trader, a man of the
Leopard People, passed through the village, bringing
with him a message from Henne."

Yana looked up.

"Your sister is all right." The High Priestess smiled, showing the gaps between her teeth. "She told the trader to tell everyone she's hunting furs for a new winter cloak."

Yana cocked her head. *What an odd message,* she thought.

The elder smiled at Yana's perplexed look. "If Henne wants to hunt, that's her choice," she said. "She was very upset when Shem left for the Goddess's womb. Even as a child, Henne did not show her sadness like other children." The High Priestess fell silent. She didn't think it necessary to tell Yana that her sister had left with Ninka's opium bag. If Henne was all right, that was all that mattered.

Yana lifted her eyes to the leathery face of the old one. "I am glad my sister is well," she said truthfully.

Telna nodded. "Galea is relieved also." She hesitated. "But now she worries about you." The old woman's voice dropped. "I can understand why Henne ran away, but why did you leave us, Yana?" she asked.

Yana swallowed hard. Heat rushed to her cheeks as she avoided the old one's eyes. Was the elder trifling with her feelings? She peered through her lashes, but there was no mockery in Telna's face. Yana's eyes grew moist. "It always happens," she said quietly. "I try to be like others . . . but then I do or say something . . . I didn't mean to destroy the power of the Goddess."

An amused smile touched the old one's lips. "How could you destroy the Goddess?"

"The talisman exploded."

"And you thought you destroyed Her?" The elder leaned back, folding her hands across her belly. "Yana," she chided gently, "you didn't break the power of the Goddess, you released it. A dirt clod must be broken by the plow if the plant is to grow—a seed breaks open when sprouting. A mother's body is often torn when a child is born. All people know this. Birth and death are woven together in mystery, just as Henne must push her way through pain to come back to us. The Goddess was just reminding us of this."

Yana's voice trembled with surprise. "The elders aren't angry? They want me to stay?"

Telna laughed. "We need your gifts, Yana."

Yana looked at the old one as if she didn't understand.

The elder leaned forward. "Kara brings gifts from the loom as an offering to the Goddess," Telna said patiently. "Galea is a good mother to the children of the village—this is her offering. Others find joy in the patterns of the Goddess, making with their hands pots, ropes, mats, and baskets." The priestess lowered her chin. "In what way do you belong, Yana?"

Yana wondered what she could say to convince the High Priestess of her value. She rubbed damp palms on her dress. "I enjoy being a mother," she began, "and I cherish the time Galea and I work together. I am fairly good at weaving . . . and cooking—"

The old one looked at her expectantly, waiting for her to go on.

Yana's gaze lowered. "I could be a healer," she whispered hopefully.

"Where is your happiness, Yana?"

Yana lifted her chin, eyes glittering in the firelight. She suspected the old one knew the answer already. She loved learning. She loved looking into the patterns of the Goddess and finding the wonder there. When one listened closely, the Goddess sang the wisdom of the ancestors in rustling trees and the sounds of frogs croaking in the shadows; all told a story. If Yana could, she would spend her whole life listening, learning. But experience had taught her that unusual ideas or dreams had the power to separate one from others, and she needed closeness to keep her thoughts happy. How could she live and learn without having someone hold her close to the Earth Goddess? "I don't want to be separate—I don't want people afraid of me like they were in my birth village," Yana rasped, her throat tightening at the memory of that time.

The old woman sat for a moment in silence. She could feel Yana struggling. She had never known anybody who fought so hard against the birth of belonging, when it was the one thing the young woman desired most. How could she convince the girl that she would always be alone if she didn't embrace the gifts the Goddess had given her? Impulsively, the aged one reached out her shrunken hand, palm up.

Yana stared down at the deformed hand, then up into the priestess's eyes. The old one didn't have to say anything; the gesture spoke the elder's words. *We are all molded into form, scarred by differences, but choice makes that mold a gift to explore, or a burden to escape.* Yana's eyes filled with tears. She saw herself in the cracked lines of the woman's wrinkled palm. She had broken one mold to travel to this place where differences were embraced, but had she embraced herself? It was time to face what she really wanted, even if that meant letting other dreams go. She reached out and placed her palm on the palm of the High Priestess. The old one's stunted fingers curled around her hand.

"We share the priestess touch, Daughter," the elder said gently, reaching with her other hand to cup Yana's cheek. Yana leaned into the large breasts of the elder, allowing the old woman's arms to enfold her.

"Yes, Mother," she whispered, salty tears slipping into her mouth. "We do."

A moonspan had passed since Henne rode out of the village, taking only her anger and the opium that dulled it. Now she was sober, clear-eyed, strong. At her side hung the bow she had fashioned from a thick branch of a yew tree.

Living in the wild came easily to Henne. She had to scrounge for food, but there was plenty if one knew where to look. Luckily, it was the time of year when the fruits of the meadows and the deciduous forests were beginning to ripen, and it didn't take long to gather the food she needed: wild grain, crab apples, grapes, figs, almonds, pistachios, and a variety of berries. She substituted grubs, snakes, and snails for meat. In her spare time she fashioned a magnificent bow made from the branch of a yew tree.

The day Henne strung her bow with a length of sinew, the hunt for the wild heart of the Goddess began in earnest. At night she dreamed of Her animals, throughout the day and evening she stalked them. She prowled the haunts of high country herbivores: antelope, deer, wild sheep, goats, and gazelles. Occasionally she'd take a lynx or a fox for its beautifully furred autumn pelt. She followed the prints of leopards, hares, and wolves, learning their ways. The days melded in a haze of the mystery in the Goddess. Her instincts became sharper, sensitivity to light and sound increased. And always after a successful hunt she left part of the carcass as a gift for the vultures. But today, Henne received a message from the Goddess—a dead vulture near one of her old kills. It was time to go home.

Over the course of the time spent in the wilderness, Henne came to realize her place in the Goddess; she would be people's protector, purging them of self-satisfaction and rottenness. She would spend the rest of her life trying to understand the wild heart of the Goddess. Shem had said it was a place beyond meaning, beyond understanding, and although Henne knew she wasn't worthy, she was driven to serve his memory until she too returned to the Goddess's womb. If Rav accepted her, she would become the Hunting Priest of the people.

Usually a man held this position, but there were stroies, legends of women who preferred the wilderness and the hunt to home life and children. She found she no longer desired to be Mother of the People, never wanted that kind of control again, reminding her of her time with the People of the Herd. She would always question her use of power; it was too seductive, and she was weak. She shook her head in revulsion. No. Let others lead. She would protect and cleanse.

22

Tern unfolded the leather wrapping protecting the marriage stick he had carved the winter before. It was the femur of a red deer, a doe he had chased out of the bush and brought down with an arrow through the ribs and heart. He picked it up, feeling the smoothness of the polished bone. He turned it over in his hands, tracing with a finger the lines he had carved, remembering his whispered prayers and hopes as he created the sacred symbols. It all seemed so long ago. Now Yana was slipping from his grasp and there was nothing he could do. Dreams of a home and family were escaping him. He thought about dropping the marriage stick in the fire, but couldn't bring himself to do it.

All morning the villagers had spoken in hushed whispers about Yana's power. Most were convinced it wasn't a coincidence that news of Henne reached them soon after Yana released the power of the Goddess. Even Dagron's eyes glowed when he talked of his sister. After all, hadn't Niam's child jumped in her belly at Yana's touch, and didn't Yana bring the life back to his young wife's eyes? Tern could not deny the truth of her gifts, the strength of her songs and stories. Now everyone seemed to accept that Yana was born to be a priestess, but Yana was so much more than a priestess to him. He carefully placed the marriage stick back in its leather wrapping. No. He wouldn't destroy it, but he would no longer torture himself by looking at it.

"Tern, are you in there?" Dagron called loudly from outside.

Tern shoved the marriage stick under his sleeping blankets.

Dagron entered the room, bringing the fresh smell of the outdoors. He held two crab apples in his hand. "I've been looking all over for you," he said, leaning against the door frame, taking a bite from one of the apples, chewing as he spoke. "The trader from the Leopard People is about to leave. He's invited us along. Why don't you come?" He paused, took another bite of apple, and began again. "I thought I'd go, since Niam is staying with the priestesses until her birthing time. I have furs to trade, and I know you do too. Heth gave me knives. He wants obsidian and flint in exchange. The village needs more salt. We'll be back long before the dark days of snow, and I could use your help carrying supplies."

Tern looked into his friend's eyes. Dagron had kindly avoided the real reason of his invitation, but it was there in the lines of his sun-browned face. Would everyone pity his loss of Yana? Tern thought of the people of the village, their whispers, and stares. Perhaps a journey would be best right now. He wasn't ready to face Yana. The pain of his wounded pride wouldn't let him. Hopefully in time the ache in his breast would dull, and he could look into her eyes again, let her go, but not now.

Tern forced himself to smile while rubbing the back of his neck thoughtfully. "I have a few extra furs to trade," he said, thinking of all the hunting he'd done to prepare for his marriage, furs he no longer needed. "It won't take long to gather my things."

Dagron grinned, tossing one of the apples for Tern to catch. "The trader and I will wait for you by the big oak," he said, speaking of the tree at the edge of the village. "He wants to leave before the yolk of the Goddess is midway through the sky."

Tern smiled and waved the big man away, sensing Dagron was the one anxious to be off in a hurry. His friend's wandering spirit had been cooped up in the village for too long now, and the trader's stories of the night before had obviously awakened his appetite for adventure.

A short while later a small group of people gathered to wish the men a safe and profitable journey. Heth and Jozer slapped their backs and joked with the three men about the women they would meet in neighboring settlements. Niam's family, along with Henne and Galea came with extra travel food. Kara offered prayers and a priestess blessing. There were hugs and kisses, a few tears. After the good-byes were said, the men shouldered their packs and called the dogs that were to pull the heavy furs on a travois. A cluster of children escorted the men down the valley, through the harvested fields, chattering gaily, dropping off one by one the farther the traders walked.

By the time the men were specks on a distant knoll, the village had returned to its daily bustle, the traders forgotten. Still, two women stood in their doorways, both yearning, both continuing to watch. Tamuz with a hand over her womb and hope in her heart, and Yana, tears blearing her eyes, and a silent good-bye on her lips.

PART 3

The Harvest

23

Nine Harvest Seasons Later

"We will be back soon, Mother," Yana said quietly, bending over the High Priestess to tuck a shawl around her shoulders.

Yana sat back on her haunches, smiling tenderly and a little sadly into the time-worn features of the woman who had taught her so much about serving others, and what it was to be a true priestess of the Goddess. She had learned to live the life of small deaths, giving one's spirit so others might grow and change. This came easily to Yana's nurturing heart, still at times being a priestess of the Goddess was draining. The villagers' demands reminded her of small children. When fearful or in pain, they craved her dreams, prayers, and visions from the Goddess. She was at every birth, and every death. She was called in the night to comfort the sick with songs and offerings. Surprisingly, each time she gave of herself, her spirit seemed to grow more attached to those she served as if the umbilical cord of the Goddess bound them as family. When she explained this to the High Priestess, the old one smiled. "It is in tending the garden," the elder said with wise eyes, "that one comes to love the garden." Yana had to agree. She began to understand that every time she reached out in service, her heart confirmed the decision to walk the priestess path, and she was changed somehow.

Unfortunately, the last year had seen a slow decline
in her mentor's health. The High Priestess had withered to half her size. Skin hung in wrinkled folds from
her body; her arms had become fragile sticks. Now
Telna spent her days resting on blankets and cushions,
only getting up to move about when necessary. Unfortunately, with the old woman's waning strength,
Yana's old fears began to surface; fears she had
thought long buried. Telna had been a constant source
of strength, never allowing Yana to slip into uncertainty. Could she really lead the people without the
old woman's guidance?

"We'll be back soon," Yana repeated, noting the
elder's troubled eyes.

Telna grasped her hand. "You're going?" she asked,
sounding childlike, unsure. "But I don't want you to
go, Daughter. You must stay and serve the people."

Yana sighed. It was going to be one of those mornings. "Yes, Honored One," she replied with gentle
patience. "I will stay. But remember, the women must
harvest the gifts of the Mountain Goddess—sing
thanks to Her trees. We have to leave the womb of
our valley for a short while. Did you forget?"

Doubt darkened the old woman's face. "But the
wheat hasn't been threshed," she countered. "And the
grain must be spread out on the roofs to dry. And
what of the domestication games?"

Yana squeezed the frail fingers of the elder. "All
has been done, Mother," she said quietly. "The domestication ritual is over. Remember? Ryle twisted his
ankle and Henne rescued him by using her vulture
cloak to distract the bull. Surely you must remember
the celebration that came afterward. Rav gave Henne
his staff—"

The elder's eyes cleared, the doubt disappeared.
"Forgive an old woman," she said, patting Yana's
hand. "I was dreaming of another time." She sighed
and leaned back into her cushions. "The Mother's
womb calls. Soon I will return to the place of dreams.

Her eyes became distant, moist. "Last night my brother came . . ."

Yana's brow creased. "Did he have a message?"

She shook her white head. "No . . . but I know he waits . . ." Her voice drifted off.

"Perhaps I should stay," Yana said in concern. "One of the other priestesses can oversee the mountain harvest ritual."

The elder set her jaw. "You must go, especially now. The people need to see the strength of your spirit. It is what we've worked for."

Yana made a motion to object.

The elder snorted. "I'm not quite ready join the ancestors, Daughter. They will have to wait a little longer. You go. I will still be here when you return."

Yana nodded reluctantly. Ninka had promised to take good care of her old friend while Yana was gone. And the High Priestess had been close to death before, each time pushing Death's white mask away. "All right, Mother," she conceded. "I will go. But you must promise not to trouble Ninka when she brings your tea."

The old woman's face twisted in a sullen frown. "Old Mother Willow is too bitter," she complained.

Yana rolled her eyes. "Of course Mother Willow is bitter. She is strong medicine. Dagron traveled all the way to the city of the Leopard People to get it, and yet you complain, though you know you feel better." Yana patted the old woman's hand as if the elder were a small child. "But I will have Ninka stew dates into the tea the way you like," she continued in a voice of mock patience. She laughed and made a wry face. "Only I'll never understand how you can swallow that syrup."

The elder snorted and waved the younger woman away.

"I will miss you, Mother," Yana said seriously, planting a kiss of blessing on the old woman's brow. She unfolded her body to stand. She stopped just in-

side the door and reached for the priestess's walking
staff. She turned and smiled once more at the woman
she had come to think of as her mother before stepping outside into the bright light of morning.

The courtyard was a bustle of activity. Conversation
was spirited, animated. Children old enough to take
part in the foraging expedition were put in charge of
the dogs that would carry most of the supplies to the
autumn campground, a northern highland meadow
surrounded by forested hills. Mothers made sure their
children donned traveling clothes, sleeveless fleece tunics belted at the waist and worn as overcoats. The
tunics were made to slip off at the shoulder during
the heat of day, draping around the hips and waist.
As evening approached, bringing autumn's chill, the
garments were pulled back over the arms and used as
an added layer under sleeping skins.

Yana could see that most of the traveling food was
packed, loaded in bags, and lashed to the dogs and
travois. Large empty baskets with carrying straps were
stacked neatly at the edge of the courtyard for everyone to pick up as they left the village. Here and there
a dog pulled a travois with a baby bound to it, evidence that the infant's young mother was not willing
to be left behind. The autumn ritual was considered
an exciting adventure, a chance to get away from village chores before winter trapped the people in their
houses.

Galea was in the process of cinching the belt on
Atum's tunic when the boy caught sight of Yana. The
youngster whooped with delight, escaping his grandmother's grasp. "Mother," he called, bounding toward
her. "Did the High Priestess give her blessing? Are
we leaving now? Is it time to go?"

Yana knelt to finish the job that Galea had started.
There would not be time on the trail to make him
another belt, and although the boy was old enough to
secure the knot himself, he was her only child and
she enjoyed mothering him. She smiled into his honey

brown eyes while yanking the cord of twisted goat hair, pulling it tight. "I have a few things to take care of yet, but we'll leave soon," she replied.

Yana pushed a lank of wavy dark hair out of Atum's eyes, wishing she'd thought to braid it; it would be hot on his neck today. She glanced up at the burning sun. It was one of those fall days when summer refused to give up its strength. She would have to make sure they had enough water skins for the first leg of the journey.

Isha, a small-boned girl the same age as Atum ran past on coltlike legs, hesitating only a moment. "Grandmother says you left your sling in our house," she called over her shoulder to the boy. "If you want it, it's near the hearth."

Galea called to Atum. The youngster looked up at Yana with pleading eyes. "You may get the sling." She laughed, but then frowned, adding quickly, "Hurry. I will tell Grandmother where you've gone, but she's not going to be happy if she has to wait for you."

Yana crossed the courtyard as Atum ran off, her linen robe gracefully flowing about her. She stopped to talk with Galea and then moved on. She held the walking stick of the High Priestess, a wooden staff topped with the carving of a knobby pinecone. The pinecone was packed with seeds, symbolizing the abundance of the Goddess. The villagers parted respectfully as Yana passed. Even after years of acceptance, Yana was still surprised, humbled when this happened. She didn't realize it was her unassuming style of leadership and the way she had nurtured the High Priestess during the old woman's long illness that had won the hearts of the people.

Yana spied Enyana a short distant away, a lively child with curly obsidian black hair and Henne's vibrant green eyes. As always, the girl was in the middle of a clutch of children. The youngsters were feeding the dogs scraps from the morning meal. Some were busy binding their mothers' supplies to the travois, but even from a distance Yana could see that Enyana was doing little of the work.

Yana leaned on her staff, her eyes hooded with disapproval. Henne had given the child far too much freedom over the years, and it was sure to be a problem in the future. The girl rode her mother's horse, hunted, and took part in the sporting games, spending very little time learning the domestic skills important to village life. Most troubling, she had the tendency to be defiant when challenged. If the confrontation became heated, Enyana usually found a way to charm herself out of trouble. It wasn't as if Enyana was purposefully manipulative. She was a natural leader, quick-witted, and always had an interesting comment or humorous retort on her lips, but Yana's small moon sister needed to learn to use her leadership skills in ways that would benefit *all* the people. Yana straightened her back and lifted her head to call to the girl.

Enyana separated herself from the group and did a half skip in Yana's direction. "What is it, Honored One?" she asked brightly, excitedly hopping from one foot to the other while she spoke. "Are we ready to go? Should we gather the little ones?"

Yana smiled. Today the children were squirming bundles of anticipation. The sooner they left for the harvesting journey, the better.

"The yolk of the Sun Goddess is going to be very hot today," Yana warned. "It would be wise if we had more water skins." Yana raised her eyebrows and ducked her chin, making her voice firm. "I want each of the older children, including you, to take turns carrying extra water."

Enyana stopped fidgeting and wrinkled her nose. Her mouth dipped in a thoughtful frown older than her years. "How will we be able to take care of the dogs and children?" she responded, implying the added burden of carrying water would interfere with the task of controlling them. The girl hesitated and

Yana could see the youngster's thoughts were churning as her green eyes began to glow with a solution. "Moon can carry the water," Enyana said excitedly. "Mother will be riding ahead with the scouts. I'm sure she will agree to help."

Enyana shot her a hopeful glance, just submissive enough to ease Yana's growing irritation. Yana sighed. The girl refused to be guided, and was always ready with her own solutions. Still, there was nothing wrong with the young one's reasoning—the children would have to work hard to keep the younger children and animals under control. She licked her lips and nodded slowly, making an effort to keep her voice neutral. "Your idea is good, Enyana," she said. "I think you should fill the water skins and load them on Moon. We need at least six more. And hurry. It's almost time to leave."

Enyana laughed gaily. "Atum will help."

Yana eyed her sternly. "Atum is busy. Everyone is making preparations. This was your idea, now it is your responsibility."

Enyana nodded glumly. "Yes, Honored One," she said, shuffling off at a slow pace.

"You don't want to be left behind, Enyana," Yana called after the girl.

Enyana acknowledged her with a slightly insolent shrug, but began to walk faster. Yana dismissed the child from her thoughts, turning to other, more important things needing her attention.

The traveling baskets, wool bags, leather packs, and carrying straps were checked once more. Extra water was loaded while the women gave last-minute instructions to those remaining behind. Henne, wearing her vulture cape and carrying the spear of the Hunting Priest, sat on her mount toward the back of the crowd. A few men stood alongside, joining her as scouts and protectors of the women.

Yana made her way to the front of the throng. She turned around to face the crowd. The people stopped milling about and gathered around her. She lifted her long tanned arms, tattooed with the marks of a priestess, and raised the pinecone staff. Her hopeful voice called to the Goddess.

> *Lead us to your abundance, Sweet Mother*
> *As we are pushed from Your sacred womb*
> *We go to gather Your children,*
> *Into our caves, our querns, our storehouses*
> *So they may sleep with us, keeping us strong*
> *When the days are dark and long.*

Yana was the first to step ceremoniously over the shallow trench encircling the village, and the people followed one by one. Throughout their lives, the villagers learned that life was a series of letting go experiences as they stepped from one womb circle to another. Each morning the child woke from the dream sleep of the small deaths, moving through the door of his mother's house into the brightness of the sun. Once in the courtyard, near the Goddess's shrine, the youngster knew he or she stood in the womb center of the village. Later, when old enough to herd livestock or tend the fields, the child had to cross a shallow trench that circled the village, into the womb ring of the valley. Then as the eyes traveled to the hills beyond, one would recognize that the valley and everything beyond was also the transforming center of the Goddess.

This was especially true today for the women who were usually tied to the hearths of the village. Today they stepped eagerly away from their tethers. The long walk was a great renewing time of spirit. Autumn was a time when the plants bent close to the earth laden with the fruit of the Mother, and the women celebrated their own abundance. It was a time of reflection, a time of realizing that all mothers had to let go of their children, just as the Goddess gave so freely of her own.

Once the valley was left behind, the walk up the foothills became pleasantly languid, and slow. Along the way the women stopped in areas known for particular crops, filling their baskets with wild onion, turnip, garlic, bitter vetch, mustard, and caraway seeds, always leaving enough shrubs untouched to ensure a good harvest the following year. Occasionally a woman would burst out in song, her voice trilling in praise, singing thanks to the Goddess for Her gifts.

Henne and the men followed behind, circling areas to make sure bears and other predators were not lurking about. Wild animals were also gorging on the Mother's harvest, putting on a thick layer of fat before winter snows. Some were in rut, making them more unpredictable, and dangerous.

Henne returned to the clearing in time to see Yana stoop over Tamuz and Tern's youngest son, instructing him on the proper use of a digging stick, showing him how to remove a starchy tuber from the soil. Henne let the reins go slack in her hands. She wondered if she would ever understand her adopted sister.

Yana had been heartbroken when Tern became second husband to Tamuz, yet over the years she remained civil toward the other woman and her children. Each year Tern stayed only long enough in the village to get Tamuz with child. He would then leave on another trading journey, avoiding Yana altogether, and each year Yana became a little sadder. Henne didn't understand why her sister didn't go to Tern, work out their differences somehow. The flame of love was too precious to leave untended. She sighed. Her own heart had become a dead coal since Shem's death, and it was apparent that nothing would ever wake it again.

Henne thought about her relationship with Yana and how it had changed over the years. There had been an uneasy truce between them since Yana moved in with the priestesses, and Henne had observed her training with interest. Admittedly, Yana was blessed

by the Goddess. The people were continually inspired
by her songs and visions. Yet her sister was a mystery.
She was distant, unassuming. Yana did not face life's
obstacles in a headlong challenge; she stepped back,
observed. Could her sister really become the backbone
of the people, did she have that kind of strength?
Telna treated her as a daughter, making it known that
Yana was her chosen successor, but in the end, it was
the people who would decide.

Henne tossed her head. A toddler had escaped his
older sister's eye and was wandering too far from the
group. Henne pulled on her reins, steering Moon in
the child's direction, thinking to herself that the decision of a successor would have to be made soon. The
High Priestess would probably not last the winter.

On the third day of walking, the women reached
the highland meadow. The pale grasses were already
bending, breaking in preparation for winter's sleep.
The clearing was partially encircled by a deciduous
forest flaming with autumn hues. Leaves toasted
brown, honey gold, and persimmon drifted to the forest floor in lazy whorls. Some were as wide as a man's
hand, others, no more than thumbnails of color. A
large savannah oak stood in the middle of the
meadow. The women set up camp under the tree,
sweeping away the newly fallen leaves to uncover the
rock-lined cooking hearths that had been built by their
ancestors. The children unloaded the dogs, then were
sent to gather kindling for the fires.

The first few days the foragers spent their time
working the scruffy underbrush at the forest edge
where mushrooms, grapes, and pistachios grew. After
these were harvested, they moved deeper into the
wood. The trees yielded acorns, almonds, walnuts, and
crab apples. The children spent the afternoons scrambling up and down tree trunks, laughing in the
branches as they shook the harvest to rain on their
playmates below. The younger dogs jumped and

chased the leaves as they scuttled along the ground. By nightfall, baskets were full. Everyone was exhausted, content, and sleep came swiftly.

Now Yana wondered what woke her. She turned her head to gaze at the huddled, sleeping mounds. It was early yet. The waning moon had only partially risen. Except for the chirps of crickets and the scuffle of wind through drying leaves, all was quiet. She lay back, enjoying the view of stars whisking in and out of sight as the leaves moved.

Henne's horse snorted. Startled, Yana sat up. Her sleeping skins fell to her waist, and she hurriedly caught them up again to ward off the cold. A dog barked then was quiet, too quiet. Her heart suddenly hammered in her chest. Something was wrong, she could feel it.

Yana stood, pulling her sleeping blankets around her like a long winter coat. She gazed around, then breathed a sigh of relief. The men were already up and moving about. Henne stood next to Moon, spear ready. Yana made her way toward Henne, her bare feet making prints in the dew-sodden grass.

"Is it a bear?" she rasped when she got close enough.

Henne shook her head no and kept her voice low. "We don't know, but it's gone now." She frowned adding, "It came last night too."

Yana's brows shot up. "You didn't tell me?"

"We didn't know what it was." Henne rolled her shoulders forward and hissed in a frustrated whisper. "We thought we could track it today, but we didn't find anything. Whatever it is, it's very clever. Apparently even the dogs are under its spell."

Yana gripped her blankets tighter about her shoulders. "The dogs?"

Henne nodded curtly. "We sent them out last night. They never once barked. Later they returned, only to curl up next to the fire and go to sleep. Today they seemed uninterested in the hunt."

Yana chewed on the inside of her cheek. "What can it be?" she whispered. "The spirits of this place have always been kind to our people. Have we angered them somehow?"

Henne shrugged. "Perhaps winter's breath is going to come early this year and the spirits are warning us." Henne looked away. She didn't really think that it would snow before they could get off the mountain, but she did believe that remaining any longer was a mistake. Whatever was slinking in the shadows didn't want to be discovered, making it all the more sinister. She would rest easier if the people were safely back in the village. She faced Yana again.

"Most of the baskets are heavy with the gifts of the Goddess. We have enough supplies for winter. Perhaps we should leave tomorrow," she suggested. "We can use the extra baskets to gather medicine plants on the way back, which is sure to make Ninka happy."

"But we can't," Yana responded in a terse whisper. "We still haven't thanked the Goddess. It would be bad luck to leave without performing the songs and dances under the waning moon."

Henne looked up at the star-bright sky. "It is still early," she suggested.

"Tonight!?"

Henne smoothed Moon's mane with her hand. "Whatever was lurking out there is gone," she replied patiently, hoping that Yana would warm to the idea. "It is safe now. I can have the men make the bonfire. The children will enjoy the break in routine. They'll think it's fun."

"But what will the women think?"

"Tell them you've had a dream."

Yana frowned and Henne rolled her eyes. "All right," she said impatiently, "you don't need to lie. You can say the spirits sent a message in the night shadows, telling you it was time to sing our thanks because tomorrow we must leave. That is close to the truth. Something woke you, didn't it? Anyway, they

will believe you." As Henne said the words, she realized how true they were. The people were so accus-
tomed to Yana's dreams and visions, they would
believe anything she said. Perhaps Yana would make
a good leader after all, if only she were more decisive.

"I will go wake a few of the women to help prepare
the warming tea," Henne continued firmly. "You prepare for the ritual. By the time you're done, the people will be awake and ready to dance."

Yana stood for an unsure moment, then nodded
slowly. "Perhaps we should leave early," she agreed,
thinking that it would be nice to see how Telna was
faring. She had never really stopped worrying. She
froze with a thought. What if it was the old woman
who haunted the night shadows? Perhaps the High
Priestess needed them to come home so the rituals
could be said that would lead her safely to the spirits
of the ancestors. Yana lifted her chin. "Yes," she said
decisively. "The dances must take place tonight."

Henne let out her breath slowly as she watched
Yana depart. "That's right, go, Sister," she murmured
silently. "Lead our people back to the village so I can
come back alone, sniff out this evil, draw it from the
lair. I have fought the spirits before, and I will again."

Like a furtive animal, the man crouched in the darkness, watching in fascination as the women whirled
and danced in a figure eight pattern around the bonfire and the big oak. He could not hear the words they
sang, he was too far away, but the flames illuminating
their bronze faces and uplifted arms made him think
that it must be something wonderful. At the cross
where the two dancing circles met, women hugged and
twirled, before continuing around. Their joy suggested
the force of life connecting things, and even though
he didn't understand the meaning behind the dance,
his heart was warmed with the beauty of it. Briefly,
he wondered if his Mern had ever danced this way,
but then closed his eyes. He must not think of her.

When he opened them again, he saw Henne. She was standing apart with her horse at the rim of the forest, guarding her people. Days earlier, he had been shocked when he saw her leading the troop of women up the hill toward the meadow, riding the mare she had stolen so many years before. Like the others of his tribe, he had thought Henne was dead. But here she was, alive, thriving. He'd even seen the little girl that looked so much like Ralic. Deep in his breast, the man found it comforting to know that his old chief still lived on in his daughter.

The dog nuzzled the man's hand. He promptly reached inside his traveling bag for another strip of dried venison. "That's all you get, dog," the man said gruffly, his unused voice grating his throat. The man sighed. He was going to miss the dogs when the women left, especially this one. He kneaded the animal's ears. "If you eat more, you'll get sick. Your belly already sweeps the dirt from the ground."

The mongrel looked up at him, not understanding the words, but hearing the affection in the man's voice. The dog's tail thumped the ground, knowing it would soon be gnawing on another chewy morsel of dried meat.

24

The High Priestess dreamed.

An exquisitely shaped oil lamp, made of white-and-green-veined limestone, sat in the niche of a wall. It was oval-shaped, with a birdlike beak for pouring, and in the lamp a small blue-green flame flickered. The flame grew weaker and weaker, then fluttered one last time.

Yana entered. Her priestess robes were trimmed with shells that clicked about her feet as she crossed to the lamp. The young woman seemed unaware that anyone else was in the room. She picked up the wick, separated its fibers into curls of string, then dropped it back into the oil with a small clump of moss. She used a flint scraper to make an igniting spark. Briefly, she sat back on her heels observing the flame, an unguarded look of satisfaction on her face, then pushed to stand and walked out the door.

The High Priestess watched the mesmerizing flame. It flared to the size of a wavering finger. As Telna drew close, she saw the faces of the people in the fire: her brother, Roan, Ninka, Niam, and others of the village, generations of the old and young all living in the continual flame. The fire constantly changed, sometimes burning red, blue, green, and white—the colors of the Goddess. She leaned toward the lamp, her heart large with wonder, but then inhaled sharply. The oil—it was almost gone. The flame would surely die without fuel! Something must be done. The elder looked around, but there was no oil anywhere. The flame began to dwindle.

The spark sputtered in the bowl just as Henne entered the room. She was wearing her vulture cape and priestly robes. Like Yana, her face was blank, as if she were alone and no one watched. She carried a large crudely shaped clay urn, spouted for pouring. Henne knelt, slowly pouring oil into the lamp so as not to destroy the flame. The oil was pure, rich, and fell from the urn in a translucent arc. The flame leapt in response, licking at the new oil, and the High Priestess sensed joy in the fire's dance. Henne smiled, filling the lamp until it was full, almost overflowing, then set the jug down beside her feet.

Telna woke from her dream, her old heart fluttering in her chest—*a spirit dream, I've had a spirit dream*, she thought. She had had many night visions during her lifetime. Over the years she had learned to discern spirit dreams from the normal muddled dreams of sleep. One woke from a spirit dream with clarity, a sense that ends were being tied, and something elusive was clear. That is how she felt now. The Goddess had given her a message. Now she knew she could leave the people; they would be safe. There was only one thing more to do.

Yana entered the Goddess's shrine. She was relieved to see the High Priestess sitting up in her blankets. The wizened woman's eyes were brighter than they had been in months, and there was color in her face. Yana brought with her a bowl of gruel. Usually she had to coax the old woman to eat, but not today. Today the priestess ate heartily, scooping up the last few bites with her fingers, then surprised everyone by asking for more, demanding extra honey and dates mixed in.

Yana leaned next to Ninka and whispered in her ear. "You are a great healer, Ninka. When we left for the long walk, I was afraid I would return home to

find the Mother of the People much worse. But I can
see she has gained strength while I was gone."

Ninka forced a smile, but averted her eyes. There
was no reason to tell Yana the truth, she would find
out soon enough. The healer had seen this many times
before. Often when a person was closest to death, they
rallied for a day or two, as if their spirit wished to
squander all the reserves left in the body, becoming
drunk on life for the last time before swiftly disinte-
grating in death. Ninka sadly realized her old friend
had finally mustered the strength to say good-bye.
Soon Telna would join the ancestors, living in the
womb cave of dreams, until a portion of her spirit was
reborn in the people.

After the High Priestess had eaten, she called for
the priestesses to wash, comb, and rebraid her hair.
She dressed in her best ceremonial robes and commanded those around her to do the same. They were
all to prepare for a feast and celebration. The women
of the village made a stew of mutton and bread. Nuts
and fruit from the recent trek to the surrounding hills
were cracked and peeled, then tossed into large communal wooden bowls.

It was late afternoon when everything was finally
ready. The High Priestess asked the people to gather
at the sacred pool. The elder walked among them
toward the pool with only the pinecone staff and Yana
supporting her elbow. This was something the villagers
had not seen since the last harvest season, and the
sight lightened their hearts. Near the sacred water, the
old one bent awkwardly to sit on a large, flat-hewn
marble boulder. Yana sat on the ground beside her.
A sheen of exertion glowed on the elder's face, matching the wetness of the spring water behind her. A few
butter-colored and persimmon leaves floated down,
settling to glide like small boats on a great pond. The
old one lifted her good arm, signaling the people to
be seated.

Henne remained standing in the back with some of

the younger men. The High Priestess called her forward. As Henne maneuvered through the throng, the vulture feathers of her cape fluttered in the breeze. The people saw strength in Henne's features, purpose in her stride. Over the years they had come to understand how seriously she took the task of Hunting Priest. She was like a mother eagle or a great hawk protecting her young, and this was comforting. The High Priestess nodded, indicating that Henne should sit on the opposite side of the boulder. The two women, flanking the High Priestess on either side, lent support to the old woman's words.

The elder spoke for a long time. She retold the story of Yana's journey to their homeland, her adoption, and her surprising rebirth from the sacred womb water of the Goddess. She told of the sacrifices Yana made to become one of the people. She reminded them of Yana's gifts, her insights and songs, her dreams and visions, and reiterated what a wonderful daughter Yana had become to an old, enfeebled woman.

The villagers nodded, murmuring their agreement. Most had expected the High Priestess would someday ask them to accept Yana as their next High Priestess, and now it appeared she was doing just that. But then the elder surprised them.

She began to talk about Henne. She talked of Henne's bravery and her abilities as a leader. She reminded them of the time when Henne first returned to their village—the same instant Yana emerged from the underground river to be reborn to the people. She suggested the two women were more than sisters—their fates were entwined, tied together with the birth cord of the Goddess.

The High Priestess sat quietly for a moment, allowing the people to swallow the meaning of her speech. She could see their questioning eyes, feel their intense attention as they waited for her to say more, knowing their own fates were also entwined in her words. Finally the old one cleared her throat. Her eyes blinked with emotion as she told the last part of her story—the spirit dream.

"This is why I am asking you to take both Henne and Yana as High Priestess," the elder continued. "Yana is the wisdom of the people. She will keep the fire of the Goddess burning in your hearts. Henne brings sustenance. She will bind you in strength when I go to the Womb in death."

It started quietly at first. A delighted laugh, a relieved sigh, a cheer of joy. Soon all the people were reveling in the words of the High Priestess. One man backslapped another. A woman kissed the cheek of a friend. The young people whooped and hollered. Of course they all loved Yana. Of course they would have accepted her as High Priestess. But this was better, much better, and the Goddess had made the choice for them. The High Priestess smiled toothlessly at their exuberance. Yes, the Goddess would live on in the people.

Henne's mouth fell open at the reaction of the crowd. *But I don't want to be High Priestess,* she wanted to shout at them. *I am Hunting Priest, protector of the people, defender of the wild heart of the Goddess.* She stood slowly. The cheering increased. She couldn't refuse them if this is what the spirits wanted, what the people wanted, but she could not allow herself to be their leader. She raised her staff to quiet the crowd.

"I will accept this responsibility on one condition," she stated loudly, her voice grave. She stepped over to Yana, who had risen also. Henne took her sister's hand, lifting it above both of their heads.

"In all things, Yana's voice will be heard first," Henne shouted, then her voice dropped. "Remember the dream? Yana is the heart, the wisdom of the people. She lights the flame—I follow to keep the flame strong."

The people shrieked, clapping their acceptance and excitement. Only Yana and Henne were unsure. They exchanged troubled glances, but kept their fists clasped and smiles plastered on their faces as the feasting and dancing began.

Late that night, while the people danced, the old priestess sighed contentedly in her sleep. Her aged heart sputtered one last time as she slipped into the realm of unending dreams.

25

Tern hurried toward his homeland. He shifted the pack on his back, and yelled at the dog pulling his travois, cursing under his breath. The gangly mutt misjudged the path again and the travois tipped precariously. Tern repeated his curse, louder this time. He was in a hurry and couldn't afford to stop if the dog dumped everything. Dark Nose had been nothing but trouble for the moonspan since his lead dog Stone Paws's gut was ripped opened by a boar. The boar had burst from a thicket of sumac, grunting outrage when the dogs came too close to its mate's nesting place, killing Stone Paws with its large tusks. Unfortunately, with only one unruly dog to help him, Tern found the endeavor of transporting his goods almost an impossible task, and the effort had slowed him considerably. He should have been home two handfuls of days earlier. He pulled his felt-lined tunic close for warmth. The days were getting too cold to be traveling. Just that morning he had found a dusting of snow on his sleeping skins. It was time to settle in for the winter.

Traveling became easier as Tern approached his home village; he found the old sheep trails and other well-worn paths to follow. The landscape began to take on familiar curves. He passed through the wood where he often hunted with Dagron. He came to a small stream where he'd played as a child and stopped for a moment to rest on its grassy bank and to eat a ball of toasted grain packed in fat. Afterward he washed in the trickle of water then crossed the stream to the fields where the women harvested bulbs of wild onion and garlic. Soon he was greeted by the faint smell of dung smoke and family fires. His pace quickened as he crested the hill overlooking his valley home. A winter mist hung in the valley, leaving a flat, dull sheen to the landscape. His eyes took in the cropped fields, the holding pens, and the little whitewashed houses with smoke curling above them. Tern pushed the hair out of his eyes and inhaled deeply in gratitude. He was home. The sight warmed his spirit; he had been gone too long this time. But then he frowned and his step slowed. The news he brought was not good.

His first priority would be to tell the elders and the High Priestess what he had learned on his travels; rumors concerning the Herdsmen and Henne. It was said they had settled on a distant plain, but some of them were on the move again. Apparently their leader had learned of a woman who lived in the mountains, a woman with russet hair who rode a white horse, a woman who served the Goddess of Death.

Being a trader, Tern understood how easily rumors of Henne could have spread. Many traders had passed through his home village over the years, and often men traded more on the strength of their stories than their actual goods. If a man's tales kept the people of a village fascinated deep into the night, usually he was welcomed into the best lodge and given the choicest food—even his trade goods were more valued. He also knew, the sight of a woman carrying the spear of the Hunting Priest, riding a pale horse and wearing vulture feathers would make for an interesting story to tell on dark nights around communal fires. Unfortunately, the word had spread to the Herdsmen, who were now determined to find Henne and kill her and her people.

The children and dogs of the village were the first

to notice Tern as he approached the terraced fields. Many stopped what they were doing and raced to greet him. Tern's two sons led the pack. Isha, his daughter, ran close behind. The youngsters bounced around him like young rabbits, begging for trinkets and sweets. Tern's oldest son, Jem, offered to carry one of his packs. Tern gave him the lightest one, smiling affectionately at the boy, who had his mother's eyes and his own long limbs. He wondered if his youngest daughter was talking yet. He sighed. The little one had probably changed considerably in the year he'd been gone, and the boys were getting big, old enough to learn to hunt and trap. Perhaps this year he'd stay awhile, get to know them better.

As they walked toward the village, Tern asked the children about their mother and news from the village. His younger son, Rel, was always the first to talk. Rel had his mother's small features and bright smile. At first the boy chatted about the squirrel he'd killed with his sling, then he went on to talk about a nanny goat that birthed three kids earlier in the spring. Rel proudly puffed out his chest, explaining that he'd helped Tamuz feed the baby goats until they were strong enough to graze. Tern nodded, only half listening to the jabber until something the boy said pricked his ears. He stopped, carefully placing both hands on his son's shoulders, gazing directly into the youngster's eyes.

"You say the High Priestess went to the womb of the Goddess?" he asked urgently.

"Mother said it was all right." The boy frowned, not understanding Tern's concern. "The Honored One was tired. Everyone said she was ready to go to the Sacred Womb. Mother told us not to worry—the old one probably wouldn't disturb our sleep with her demands."

Tern looked to his older son. "Is this true?"

Jem nodded. "Yana and Henne are High Priestess now."

"Yana and Henne?!"

Jem rushed to explain. "The old one was sick for a long time, but before she died, she had a spirit dream. She told us that Yana would be our spiritual teacher, and Henne would teach us to be strong in other ways."

Tern's hand went to his forehead. This was too much to absorb at once.

"It's all right, Father," Rel said. "The people are happy about it. The elders say it is wise when the Goddess gives the power to lead to more than one person."

"Yes," another child chimed in. "My mother says the Leopard People have twin priestesses who oversee their city, and they are a strong people."

The children gathering around nodded in agreement. Apparently their mothers had told them the same thing. Tern was about to ask another question when he heard someone bellowing his name. He looked up to see Dagron striding across the fields toward him. The big man's face was split in a huge smile. His daughter, Ashra, attempted to keep up with her father's long strides.

At once Dagron's beefy arms circled him in a squeezing embrace, lifting Tern from the ground before letting him go, slapping him on the back in welcome. He then took Tern's heaviest pack and hoisted it on his own back. The men talked as they strode across the field toward the village. Dagron noted that one of Tern's dogs was missing. Tern's face sobered as he told Dagron how Stone Paws had protected him from the boar. Dagron shook his head in sympathy and suggested that he talk with Niam's mother. Apparently, the last time Tern was in the village, Stone Paws had mated with one of her bitches. The dog's pups had Stone Paws's pale markings. He thought Niam's mother would be willing to negotiate a trade.

Tern nodded, keeping the conversation lighthearted. There were too many ears around to delve into the questions he really wanted to ask, questions about the High Priestess and Yana. He also wondered how Niam was faring. When he'd left the village she'd been pregnant again, but since Dagron had said nothing, he guessed Niam had probably lost the child, like all the others. His heart went out to his friend. At least the couple had Ashra, a sweet-tempered girl with her mother's bubbly laugh and her father's large bones.

A small group of people gathered by the great oak, waiting for Tern and Dagron. Tern ceremoniously stepped over the shallow trench that encircled his village. The people laughed and clapped. His eyes misted as he stood inside the womb ring of his village. He was getting older. Although the trader's life had brought him wealth and prestige, traveling had never been foremost in his heart, and each time he came home, it was harder to leave. Perhaps it was time he made peace with Yana, but first there were more urgent things to discuss with the elders and Henne.

Tern spied Enyana in a group of curious youngsters hovering near his travois. "Enyana," he called, "where is Henne? I need to speak with your mother."

Enyana shrugged and yelled back, "Mother left a handspan of days ago—said she was going hunting!"

Tern turned to Dagron with raised eyebrows. It was late fall. The skills of the Hunting Priest were needed in the village. Soon after the first freeze, the butchering of the sheep began. The Hunting Priest had to read the omens, say the prayers of apology and thanks to the Goddess's children. Why would Henne leave the village now?

Dagron read his bewildered expression and shrugged. "Henne said she'd be back before the killing time," he said, his mouth twisting in a wry smile. "I don't know why my sister thought she needed to hunt right now, but Yana seemed to think it was important enough not to dissuade her." Dagron scratched the length of his face and grizzled beard. He laughed, changing the subject. "Niam will take our marriage stick to me if I don't ask you to come to our hearth tonight. We're all anxious to hear about your travels. Bring Tamuz and the children. Niam always makes extra sweet cakes for her mother's brood, and we will have more than enough to go around."

Tern nodded slowly. Yes, he would enjoy an evening with Dagron and Niam. And he was sure most of the rest of the village would show up. Everyone would bring something to eat or drink, something to share, or objects to trade. After the long walks alone, he found these gatherings stimulating, enjoyable, and he had become a competent storyteller over the years. But first he had to talk with the elders and the High Priestess—tell them of the rumors he'd heard.

His heart skipped a beat. He frowned. Yana was now High Priestess. He knew how deeply she hated, feared the Herdsmen. He wished he didn't have to be the one to tell her what he'd learned.

26

Henne lay asleep curled next to her horse for warmth, using Moon's neck as a pillow. Morning light tried to nudge her awake, but Henne resisted, pulling the wolf fur hood of her winter coat over her face. She did not want to leave her blankets. Outside it was freezing. Frost covered the buckskin tarp blanketing her. Fortunately the tarp was well oiled, keeping out dampness while creating a cavern of snug warmth inside, but her nose was cold, and her body ached from the long ride of the day before, so she burrowed deeper into the cave. Sadly, at that moment Moon decided to wake up. The horse snorted, prodding her snug nest with its wet nose.

Resolutely Henne threw off the tarp covering them. She was greeted by a blast of cool air, bringing clarity to her sleep-hazed mind. Walking a short distance away, she relieved herself, then set about building a small fire for her morning tea. She tied a boiling bag on a small tripod over the fire, added a few hot rocks, and while the tea steeped fed Moon a portion of the grain she'd brought with her. After the horse was fed she returned to the fire, reaching to warm her hands over the small blaze. The water was hot. She made a bowl of gruel from barley, flour, wheat, and a few wild seeds. While she ate she gazed up at the mountains, wondering what she'd find there. She said a silent prayer to her ancestors and the Goddess, asking for strength and guidance. The minty tea warmed her nostrils, the gruel left a comforting bulge in her stomach, and she could almost feel the strength of the ancestors pulsing through her veins, pushing her onward.

When finished eating, she brushed the frost from her tarp and folded it, strapping it once again on Moon's back as a riding blanket. She walked back to the dying fire, picked up her bowl of tea, and took a sip, but it had become tepid. She tossed the remaining liquid on the fire, watched the embers sizzle and smoke, and kicked out the rest with her boot. She glanced one more time at the mountain, then determinedly pulled on her felt-lined gloves before climbing on Moon's back.

As the horse carefully made its way toward the highland meadow, Henne's thoughts drifted to her last conversation with Yana. Yana had not wanted her to come alone on this trek, but she had insisted, arguing that the sacred leopard hunted alone. The spirits could be very elusive, tricky. Henne needed stillness to listen to the breath of the trees and the whispers of the land. It took a singleness of mind, a focus of spirit to purge rottenness from the earth, and whatever was hiding in the hills was shrewd, cunning. All her senses needed to be sharp. She didn't need others who would jump at every shadow, distracting her from her purpose. She didn't bring the dogs for the same reason.

By midday, Henne reached the highland meadow where the harvesting dances had been. She was slightly surprised at how quickly she reached it without the women and children plodding along in front of her. The frost of morning had melted. Mud oozed up through the grasses. Henne decided it would be best if she went the rest of the way on foot. She slid off her horse and tied her supplies in the limbs of the big oak. She left Moon to graze on the stubs of dying grass, reasoning her horse would be safe from predators if allowed to run free. Only a starving leopard or mountain lion would attack a healthy horse, and it was too early in the season for that.

She started her search by traipsing along the edge of the wood, looking for disturbances of any kind: broken twigs, torn leaves, paw prints. Searching was difficult. Most of the leaves had fallen into large drifts, covering everything. The leaves had lost their vivid hues, turning the slick color of bracken and rot. Trunks and branches were dark skeletons reaching in worship to the dying vegetation Goddess. Henne found nothing. She pressed deeper into the wood. After walking a short distance, she stopped, inhaling sharply. There. The heel of a man's boot print between the leaves in the mud. And it was fresh!

Instinctively she crouched, but soon realized the foolishness of this; there was very little cover among the naked trees. Besides, it was probably just the print of a trader passing through. But she wondered what he was doing in these hills and not on the main trails. Perhaps he was lost, she thought, or hurt. She looked again, taking off a glove to trace the print with a finger, and then she had another thought. Could an angry spirit be playing tricks? She put on her glove and stood. The heel of the print seemed to point deeper into the woods. She decided to follow, see if she could find more.

It didn't take Henne long to realize she was following an old deer trail that skirted the mountain. Occasionally she'd find a boot print, and it soon became apparent that whoever now lived in the forest was no longer hiding. Still, to be safe, she would use caution. She crept among the brittle branches of the trees without breaking them, trying not to push too hard as she walked. It wouldn't be wise to sweat inside her clothes, especially if she had to sleep out in the night air without a fire to warm her. No. It was best to go slowly.

It was late day when she first inhaled the smoke of a cedar fire. The smoke came on puffs of breeze from the north. The temperature had dropped and vapor escaped her mouth as she breathed. Luckily the higher elevations produced more pine and fir, clumps of green where she could hide.

The smell of burning cedar grew stronger. Up ahead, blue curls of smoke rose above the treetops. Henne squatted on all fours, creeping forward as she neared a clearing. Thoughts that had been worrying her mind raced through her head once more. Whoever was living up here should have left for a better place by now; the winters in these mountains were harsh. She gripped her spear, slowly parting the boughs of a juniper tree, peering between the branches, heart thumping. Henne's eyes grew wide with her discovery.

At first she thought it was a spirit—something part man, part animal. The creature's eyes were closed. It was leaning against a large boulder near the fire, apparently asleep, not more than five body lengths away. She inhaled sharply, smelling the wild sickness of him even from her hiding place. The creature was big, covered from head to toe with molting fur. She looked closer, realizing the fur was a patchwork of hides, so dirty, matted, and haphazardly put together so as not to resemble any garment she'd ever seen. Twigs and leaves were caught in the creature's hair and beard, blending with his mangy overcoat of fur. Henne rubbed a palm on her legging. Something about the creature was familiar, but she couldn't put her finger on it. Perhaps she'd met this rottenness in a dream. Whatever it was, it would be better to catch it off guard than to wait for the creature to wake and find her.

Henne slowly removed the bow slung over her shoulder, took an arrow from her quiver, and notched it. She half stood, taking careful aim at the creature's large chest. And then she heard a voice—a rough scratchy sound coming from the mound of fur.

"Would you really kill me, Henne?"

Henne almost dropped her bow. The voice was familiar, someone from her past, but who? The creature spoke the language of the Goddess, but the accent was foreign, heavy. Its blue eyes were open now, star-ing into her hiding place. Where had she seen those eyes before? She slowly straightened, stepping care-fully over a rotting log into the clearing, the arrow still taut in her bow. "Who are you?" she snarled. "What spirit calls my name?"

The creature eyed her impassively then turned to gaze at the fire.

"Answer me!" she growled, raising the bow to her shoulder.

The creature spoke in dead tones, dull eyes fastened on the flames. "There were those of us who would have fought for you, Henne. I watched you sneak off in the dark. I did not call out an alarm. You should have stayed, but you didn't. The Goddess left us when you ran away . . ."

Henne lowered her bow slightly. That voice. She knew that voice! "Gath?" she asked in wonder. "Gath, is that you?"

The man remained silent.

Henne's arms fell to her sides. She stepped hesi-tantly forward. "But how," she said, sounding con-fused. "How did you keep our dogs from finding you?"

Gath made a strange sound deep in his throat and Henne wondered if it was supposed to be a laugh. "Your dogs do not hunt people, Henne. All I had to do was feed them."

Henne's thoughts spun with disbelief. Obviously Gath was alone, banished, but how could this be? He should have been the next headman. He was the big-gest, the strongest. He had been Ralic's closest com-panion, his most trusted friend. What happened?

"Why, Gath?" she whispered. "What did you do? Why did they cast you out?"

For a long time the big man didn't say anything. The air about him seemed charged with unfathomable pain, and he appeared to retreat to some hiding place deep inside. She moved closer. His eyes flew to her

face, warning her to stay away, but he just as quickly
averted them, but not before she saw his inner wound.
Gath had not been cast out—he'd run away. He was
grieving! It was the same wild grief she'd experienced
when Shem died; only this was worse, much worse.

"Go away, Henne," he growled. "I will leave these
mountains in the spring. Your people have nothing to
fear from me." His voice became tight. "I only wanted
to see the dances of the Goddess."

Henne crouched close enough to see the mites
crawling in his beard. She stayed there, though his
unwashed smell repulsed her. "What happened,
Gath?" she whispered. "You were to be the leader of
the Herd. Why are you here?"

He looked at her then. She saw it in his eyes and
remembered. Even when she had lived with the People of the Herd, she'd known that Gath would resist
being leader. He did not have the heart, or the desire
for it.

"Enak is headman now," the big man said simply.

"Enak? But he's so young . . . barely a man,"
Henne countered, the vivid image of Ralic's firstborn
son coming suddenly to the forefront of her mind.
"Surely the men of the Herd wouldn't let a child
lead them."

Gath didn't respond. His eyes were lost in the
flames again, oblivious of her presence. For the first
time Henne noticed wrinkles encasing the big man's
eyes, lines filled with dirt and grease, and she wondered at the years passing since her time with the
People of the Herd. Enak had been a gangly boy on
the brink of manhood, and even then he had been a
formidable enemy; he hated Henne, she'd won Ralic's
affection away from his mother. The boy had made it
clear he would never forgive her offense. Henne
hoped Enak, the man, was far from this place and her
village, instinctively knowing he'd be driven to kill her
if he knew she was alive.

Henne leaned forward, her eyes boring into Gath's

disheveled face, forcing him to look at her. "How did you find me? Where are your people?" she asked urgently. "How did you come to these mountains?"

Gath grunted in irritation and clumsily stood, using the boulder for support, towering over her. Henne stepped back. He eyed her balefully, then looked past her into the trees, his words slurred. "I didn't see what was happening before it was too late." He sighed heavily. "I wasn't looking for you, Henne . . . not for you." His words fell away, and there was something sad in his face. Henne wanted to ask him what he was searching for, but knew he wouldn't answer, and probably didn't know.

Without saying more, the big man turned and lumbered away, and Henne couldn't help thinking of a large, tired bear as he disappeared into the trees.

27

Tern stepped quickly into the Goddess's shrine. Everything was as he remembered. The sacred loom still hung close to the entrance for best use of daylight. Kara worked with another priestess, weaving a red strand of wool through the weft weighed down with balls of clay. She smiled as he passed. The large wooden idol of the Goddess stood at the far end of the room, the elders' sheepskin cushions surrounding it. The room was painted burnish red, the color of life and the Goddess's womb. A couple of the old ones sat in a corner gambling with the knucklebones of gazelles.

The only thing different in the room was Yana. She had changed in the time he had been gone. The uncertainties of youth had left her face. Her hair was now braided and piled high on top of her head in the manner of the High Priestess. A single copper spiral swung from her left ear. She wore a simple short robe stained black, the color of fertility. It did little to hide the sensuous shape of a woman who had borne few children.

Yana slowly put down the tunic she was mending for Atum and stood. She motioned him to join her, then turned and walked toward the elders' cushions. As Tern followed, his eyes were drawn to her long legs and the flap of woven wool riding above the back of her knees.

Yana sat, folded her hands in her lap, and calmly asked him about his travels. Tern began his story casu-

ally, telling her of the people of the east who mined
and smelted copper, making rings, small bowls, orna-
ments, and other household items. He told of the Sea
People to the south, who carved and painted their
long boats to look like colorful serpents.

As Tern spoke, Yana examined his face, hoping to
memorize each feature before he left again on another
long journey. She noticed the lines around his mouth
were tighter, as if he frowned more. His face was
wind-beaten and some of the boyish humor had left
his eyes. But in other ways, Yana considered Tern
more handsome. He was lean from walking mountain
trails and had the self-reliant air of a traveler who had
been to foreign places. Two tightly braided ropes of
sandy hair hung to his shoulder from the left side of
his head. The braids were woven with the early silver
streaks of age. He wore the garb of a wealthy trader;
tusk-shaped dentalia shells about his neck, boots of
cowhide with red fox fur linings were tied to his feet,
cut beads of rare stones decorated his tunic. Yana's
chest expanded with feelings for him. They were both
getting older, wiser. They had both changed so much.
Still, when she looked in his eyes, the rest of the world
faded into shadows, and she wondered if she would
ever stop loving him.

Tern paused, wondering how he was going to
broach the subject of the Herders. Yana opened her
mouth to fill in the void, asking more about the Sea
People when she noticed the gravity of his eyes. Something was wrong. "What is it?" she asked carefully.
"You did not just come here to tell the High Priestess
of your travels."

Tern looked directly into her eyes. "I have news of
the Herders."

The room stilled. Kara's hands stopped weaving.
The elders left their game pieces where they lay. Yana
paled but quickly regained her composure, lifting her
chin. She was High Priestess now. It was important

she stay strong for the people. She nodded for him to go on.

"I had hoped to speak with Henne also," Tern continued. "This concerns her, but I have just learned that she is gone from the village."

"She is hunting," Yana said, "but she will be back soon. If it is important, then I must know."

Tern shifted uneasily in his seat. Yana seemed much stronger than he remembered, but he also knew how much she hated the Herders. He cleared his throat, then went on to explain all he'd learned from the Sea People, and how news of Henne had spread to the People of the Herd. As he spoke he watched the color drain from Yana's face. Her eyes darted to the door as if she expected one of the barbarians to come bursting through. He wanted to reach out a hand, comfort her, but this was not the place. The other priestesses and elders gathered, listening to what he had to say.

"The Herders live far away on a great plain," he continued. "They have made a tenuous peace with nearby villagers who live on the shores of a great lake. The two peoples have intermarried. It is said that some of the Herders have given up their nomad way of life and are herding cattle instead of horses. They exchanged meat for wool, grain, and other luxury items.

"But you said they are coming here," Yana interrupted tersely, struggling to keep her voice steady. "They are looking for Henne."

"Only a few of them, the ones who have decided to remain warriors. It is said that the headman of the Herders has vowed to destroy Henne. He believes it was her power that killed his father and divided his people."

Yana's mouth went dry. "How long do we have?"

Tern's lips pursed in a grim line. "The headman knows Henne lives in these mountains, but he won't attempt to cross the passes in the winter. I sent another trader to the lakeside dwellers, a man I trust, a man I traveled with for many seasons. He will spread rumors that Henne lives in the eastern ranges where the land is harsh and there are very few villages. Hopefully they will go there first and we will have time to prepare."

"How long?" Yana repeated, the words thick in her mouth.

Tern sat straighter, inhaled deeply, and locked gazes with Yana. "Late spring," he answered. "It could be longer, but we should be ready by spring."

Yana briefly closed her eyes. So little time. How could they possibly be ready to fend off the barbarians, a people who had no reverence for the Goddess? She opened her eyes, the muscles of her face stiffening with resolve. She eyed each person in the room. "Hide these words in your hearts," she said severely. "Tell no one of the Herders. This knowledge must remain hidden until Henne returns. We do not need fear to breed in the village until a plan has been made to overcome it. I will send a tracker after Henne. In the meanwhile, the priestesses and I will seek the guidance of the Goddess."

One by one the people in the room nodded solemnly. She faced Tern. "Act as if you know nothing," she said. "Tonight when you entertain the people with your stories, keep your voice light. They know you have been talking with me and they will be curious. Tell them that you felt the need to greet the new High Priestess."

Yana sat erect, and her voice was strong, but she chewed the inside of her cheek, and Tern knew she was nervous.

"I will tell the people I brought the new High Priestess a gift," he said with warmth, taking her hand and opening her palm. I found something on the trail. It was partially buried in stone. I chipped it out with my knife."

Yana turned the object over in her hand. It was a perfectly shaped cowry shell. Everyone knew the shell was sacred. One side was humped like the abundant belly of the Goddess. Turning it over, the cleft ridge of the Goddess's birthing place was exposed, leading to Her mysterious center. The shell itself was rare, but amazingly, this image was made of stone! Her mouth fell open in disbelief, yet she could feel the truth of ancient power in the heaviness of the rock in her palm. Her questioning eyes went to Tern's face.

"I know it is a message from the Goddess," he stated with confidence. "It is a birthing stone of water and the soil. The moment I found it, I knew I had to give it to the High Priestess. I believe there is hope for us—for all of us." He reached out to squeeze her hand, wanting to pass some of his strength in a gesture that said he would help protect the people.

Yana's fist closed around the stone. She nodded and smiled briefly, but the smile didn't reach her eyes. "Go to the people," she said. "Trade with them, tell them the stories of your journey. I must spend time alone with the Goddess. Seek her wisdom in this."

Tern unfolded his limbs and stood to leave. Yana's eyes followed his lithe body to the door. *He has changed,* she thought. There seemed to be less need in him, more strength. His words rang in her spirit. *There is hope for us—all of us.* She glanced down at the stone in her hand, wondering at the message it contained.

28

Enyana ducked behind the boulder overlooking the ravine, turned around, and slid down to sit on the dry grass, "Is the net ready?" she asked in a rough whisper. "This won't work unless we can separate the stallion from the other horses."

The young man beside her growled with disapproval. He should never have allowed the children along. He glanced sideways at Enyana's profile, her firm jaw and the soft curve of her cheek, and remembered how convincing she'd been. Though still a child, the woman she would be someday enticed him. Already her breasts were small buds of promise, and her face held the mysterious curve of the barbarians. Her eyes sparkled intensely as if everything in life were a challenge to overcome. He wasn't the only young man in the village drawn to the power of her smile; there were many who hoped Enyana would choose them someday as a lover or hearth mate.

"You will do nothing unless I give the signal," he said with concern. "Stay hidden until I tell you it is time to bang the tambourine. Your mother may be Hunting Priest, but you still haven't learned all there is to know about riding the wild heart of the Goddess."

"I ride my mother's horse better than you do," Enyana shot back.

Ryle snorted annoyance. Sometimes Enyana's childishness pushed through her mature guise. "Moon is not wild," he said with controlled patience. "Besides, she is a mare. You and the other children better stay well away from that stallion."

"Someday I'm going to ride a stallion," Enyana boasted, her green eyes flashing dangerously.

The square-faced young man took a deep breath, hoping to quell his growing irritation. He had told Enyana repeatedly that the children were along only to chase the herd down the ravine, but she refused to listen. She had been the first to spot the small herd grazing in a meadow not far from the village. The plan to capture them had been Enyana's idea, but she needed to learn respect for those who were older, letting more experienced hunters take the lead. He opened his mouth to say so then closed it again, realizing that he could not allow too much anger to build between them; he needed Enyana's help convincing Henne to support their efforts.

Ryle had wanted to go to the elders with the plan, but Enyana warned against it. Why ask, she reasoned, and give them a chance to say no. Everyone knew Yana would object. Yana despised the ways of the Herders, and let it be known she didn't like Moon, yet she never confronted Henne. Enyana believed her mother was their only hope, convinced Henne would help persuade the elders, but only if the animals were already captured. Henne would never purposely go against the wishes of the Honored Ones.

Ryle's head jerked up as the enraged whinnying of a stallion echoed down the ravine.

"They're coming," Enyana whispered excitedly.

Ryle gripped his spear. He stood and cupped a hand around his mouth, cawing like a raven. The dark head of a young woman appeared across the ravine and answered the call. Ryle turned to Enyana, his heavy brows drawn in determination. "Go back to the children. After the horses pass they can follow with the tambourines and drums. We need the noise, but don't follow too closely."

Enyana pouted her displeasure but when the horse

neighed loudly again, she decided against arguing and ran to the handful of children hiding in the brush close by.

Ryle watched her go, sighing in relief. The elders would hold him responsible if anything happened, but the possibility and excitement of having a horse of his own was too compelling to turn back now. As a boy he remembered seeing Shem gliding through their valley on the back of Moon. His brother was gone now, but his memory never faded and remained close to the people's hearts. The elders of the village still spoke with reverence of Shem's sacrifice, and because of him, many of the young people were drawn to Henne's mare, eager to learn how to ride.

Ryle gazed down on two large evergreen oaks that stood side by side in the heart of the ravine. They planned to capture the lead stallion, then force the other horses into the distant corral. A large net, blending with the dirt on the ground, was strung between the two trees, waiting to be pulled on by men hidden in the branches. They would force the stallion to run between the trees, tripping him, allowing them time for the capture.

He heard the shouting first, then saw three men and a woman chasing the herd into the ravine, trilling loudly, brandishing raised spears and bows. His heart beat in anticipation as the lead horse charged into the gully, kicking up dust and rocks. Ryle tried to count the horses but they were too far away, but even from a distance he could tell Enyana was right; the small size of the herd was perfect. There couldn't be more than three handfuls of horses, and any more would have been too many to manage.

Ryle jumped from hiding to the sound of thundering hooves, throwing himself down the hill, focusing his will on the lead stallion. He ran, yelling loudly, brandishing his arms. Others lunged down the slopes, joining him in the effort to discourage the horses from climbing the foothills and doubling back out of the

ravine. It looked as if the lead horse was going to take
the obvious path through the large trees, but at the
last moment swerved. Ryle cursed. He bellowed at his
followers, lifting his spear, indicating that they should
continue pursuit. Hopefully the horses would continue
down the gully, and once corralled, they could try to
net the stallion again.

Hooves beat a clattering rhythm into the ground,
and he could barely hear the tambourines and the clay
drums of the children behind him. His legs churned
to keep up, but the horses were no more than brown
blurs in a cloud of dirt. Ryle's mouth was dry with
dust, and then he saw the sharp rise of the cliff
blocking the end of the ravine. His chest expanded
with excitement and the need for air as the horses
streamed into the narrow neck of the canyon toward
the corral.

"Now!" he yelled.

Four men, waiting near the corral opening, fenced
the horses inside by sliding three logs into the carved
notches of two limestone boulders. Ryle whooped with
joy, joining his friends in a gleeful dance outside the
corral. They did it! They got all of them! He scrambled up the rock wall near the fenced opening to get
a better look.

The horses were shorter than Henne's mare, a
stockier breed, with mushroom-colored coats and
dusty brown manes. Eight mares, their foals, and another seven yearlings were huddled away from the excited spectators at the far end of the corral. The
younger animals were darker and Ryle guessed their
tawny coats would lighten over time. The lead stallion
was almost white. It raced the rim of the enclosure,
looking for a way out, tossing its head and neighing
in frustration.

Enyana climbed up beside Ryle, her face open with
fascination. She inclined her head toward the stallion.
"He'll tire soon," she said with confidence. "Do you
have the nets?"

Ryle looked over her shoulder and nodded. Enyana whirled around. Two young men were trotting down the corridor of the ravine, carrying between them the large net that had been strung between the oak trees. She recognized them as Gelb and Reb. Within a few moments, the men were climbing up alongside Enyana and Ryle, dragging the heavy net behind them. Both were breathless and dusty. Ryle and Enyana helped pull the net up over the top of the rocks.

Briefly, they all watched the stallion pacing in the corral, transfixed by its furious power. Gelb broke the silence, still breathing hard from his run. "We'll capture him the next time he runs by," he gasped.

"But we'll need help throwing the net," Reb added.

"No," Ryle responded, frowning thoughtfully. "Let's wait until the stallion settles down. We may only get one chance to do this right." The stallion pawed the earth as if to underscore Ryle's words, then suddenly reared, screaming fury. Hooves flashed in the air then crashed down on the gate; there was the sound of splintering wood, but the gate held. All at once legs and arms were in motion as weapons and nets were grabbed up again.

"Don't let him break it down!" someone yelled.

"Use your spears!"

"Unfold the nets!" Ryle shouted.

The net was unfurled. Ryle helped Gelb and Reb swing it back and forth. The three men let it go all at once. The net billowed, settling over the horse like a loosely woven shroud. A spear arched through the air, making dull thumping sounds when it hit flesh.

"No!" Enyana wailed. "Let him go!" She jumped from the wall and started running.

No one saw her; their eyes were focused on the shrieking horse as spear after spear found its target. The stallion buckled, falling sideways. Then Ryle saw something moving at the corner of his eye. He turned his head. Enyana was already down, already hurt, by the time he found his voice.

"Keep your spears!" he hollered.

Enyana's huddled form was dangerously close to the thrashing hooves of the stallion. A spear was imbedded in her upper thigh. She grimaced in pain. Her hands pressed the flesh of her leg, trying to stanch the blood flow.

The other horses saw their leader down. They smelled blood and shook their manes, whinnying fear. Their agitated pacing turned to nipping and kicking.

"Get her out of there," Ryle growled to the men beside him. "They're going to stampede."

Reb and Gelb jumped down, sprinting the short distance to Enyana. One deftly pulled out the spear. The other gathered her to his chest and raced for the walls. Arms reached down, helping the men pull Enyana up and over the rock enclosure just as the horses charged past.

They gently laid Enyana on the grass outside the corral. She sat up, holding her leg. Dust and tears streaked her face. At first Ryle thought it was the wound causing her tears, then she glared at him accusingly and began to shout. "That stallion was mine!" she screamed. "I saw him first. How dare you kill him!"

Ryle stood over her, anger and something more smoldering in his eyes. A young woman approached and untied the cloth belt girdling her waist. Ryle took it and squatted next to Enyana. The spear cut deeply into the muscle. He had to stop the blood flow before Enyana's life waters escaped her body. He reached to bind the wound, but Enyana pushed his hands away.

"You will not touch me," she said, hissing, spitting like an angry cat. "I will do it myself." She tried to grab the cloth away from him, but he was too fast for her.

Ryle's face darkened to an angry mask, hiding his fear. This stupid child had almost cost them the lives of two men, and her own life was in jeopardy now.

He would not listen to more of her foolishness. He loomed over her.

"Your wound must be bound with a firm hand," he snarled, eyes glaring. "If you fight me, angry spirits may find their way into your body, creating rottenness. Is that what you want, Enyana? Do you want streaks of evil running up your leg and the smell of dying flesh in your nostrils?"

Fear flickered in her eyes. She had never seen Ryle so angry. She remained quiet as he deftly wrapped the wound, but he was not gentle. Enyana bit her lip, her eyes filling with hot tears. When finished, Ryle barked instructions to the young people standing around, telling them to make a litter with the extra nets and wooden poles.

Enyana sat up, mustering her courage. "Is the stallion dead?" she asked, grinding her teeth against the pain in her leg."

"Of course he's dead," Ryle growled heartlessly. "His own herd trampled him. They would have trampled you too if we hadn't gotten you out in time."

"You said nothing about killing," she wailed. "We were only going to separate the lead horse from the others."

Ryle threw up his hands in frustration. Was she blind? Hadn't she seen the horse's rage? "That stallion would never have let us keep his mares," he responded caustically, mocking her ignorance. "He'd have found a way to break out of any pen we built; the wild heart of the Goddess was too strong to tame in him. I can't believe you jumped into the corral."

Enyana drew herself together to look into Ryle's eyes. "All right," she said in slightly defensive tones. "I may have been foolish, but I wasn't wrong. We need all the horses. I want a stallion of my own!"

"We'll make do with one less," he growled. "Your mother may be Hunting Priest, she may have a mare of her own, but these animals belong to the Goddess, they belong to all of us! Even your mother shares

Moon freely with those of the village." His voice became indignant. "And I doubt Henne will allow you to ride at all once she learns how foolish you've been today." He turned, stalking away, afraid of losing total control of his anger.

Enyana watched him leave, sullen and silent. Part of her knew that Ryle was right, another part argued. She wondered if it was her nomad blood that insisted she have a horse of her own. As much as she loved Moon, and rode her, the horse always came quickest to Henne's call. There was a special bond between Moon and Henne, and Enyana wanted that kind of relationship with one of the magnificent animals. She just had to have a horse of her own.

Ryle stopped to talk to two young women. Enyana realized by his gestures, he was telling the women to run ahead, inform the village of what had happened. Her temper calmed, and for the first time she began to regret her impulsive behavior. She wondered how the elders would react to her injury. Enyana looked down at her leg and bit her lip with worry. The blood was already soaking the bandage. Would they think her idea had brought bad luck?

At that moment, four young men approached with the litter between them. They put it on the ground and lifted her, settling her onto the double strung nets. Ryle strode toward them.

"You need to get her to Ninka as soon as possible," he asserted, giving Enyana a dismissive glance. "But don't stumble. We can't risk opening the wound again." The men nodded and started off at a fast trot.

The ride seemed to take forever. The only way Enyana could stay comfortable in the litter was to lie flat, but still the coarse ropes rubbed the backs of her legs and arms raw. Halfway to the village she begged the runners to stop. Luckily they were near a swampy area. The men cut marsh grass, making a cool nest for her to ride in. Afterward, traveling became easier and the steady swaying of the litter lulled Enyana to sleep.

She jerked awake as her body was lowered to the hard ground. Hot pain surged through her leg. She struggled to sit up, pushing the hair from her eyes.

The sun was just beginning to duck behind the mountains, but there was still enough light to see. The people of the village had gathered around her with varying degrees of concern and disapproval on their faces. They parted as Henne led Ninka to Enyana's side.

Henne had just returned to the settlement. She was unloading Moon when a runner approached with the news of her daughter's injury. After hearing how it had happened, Henne's heart stilled with fear, then she became furious. What were the young people thinking! Such a daring enterprise needed the approval of the elders, the ancestors, and the spirits of the Goddess. Omens had to be read. But then she remembered how often Enyana had begged for a horse, and became angrier still, cursing her daughter, realizing the whole unfortunate incident had probably been brought on by her own stubborn will. By the time she reached Ninka's house, fear and rage were hot in her mouth. She didn't trust herself to speak, and motioned Ninka to join her. One look at Henne's face and the old woman rushed to get her things.

Now Ninka sat on her heels and unwound the crusty cloth, already drying black with blood. Enyana swallowed a yelp of pain. Fresh blood spurted from the wound. Ninka probed the tender area then turned to her granddaughter, Plera. "I need you to grind wheat seeds—at least ten handfuls. Make sure no sand gets into the flour." The young woman nodded and scurried away.

The healer turned to the men who had brought Enyana. "Reb, take her to the sacred pool," she rasped. "She must sit in the pool until the flow of blood slows, then she must drink some of the water. Perhaps the Wild Goddess will be satisfied with her offering. Afterward, bring Enyana to the shrine."

The young man lifted Enyana, carrying her through the heart of the village to the spring near the shrine. He carefully descended the steps, lowering her until she was waist deep in water. Enyana inhaled sharply. The water was shockingly cold. She shivered, then slowly released her breath against the penetrating chill that only added more pain to the ache in her leg. She watched as the blood from her thigh swirled and disappeared into the glimmering wetness, praying that the Goddess would accept her offering. Someone handed her a pink-veined marble bowl. With trembling fingers she dipped it in the water above the wound. This was her life water and the sacred water of the Goddess, mingled. She drank deeply, reverently, then wiped her mouth and nose with the back of her hand.

Reb lifted her once more and carried her to the shrine. Her teeth chattered with cold, but she wasn't bleeding as badly. Once inside the shrine she sighed with relief. The fire crackling in the hearth and the press of body heat covered her like a warm blanket. Her mother was there, the elders, and Yana.

Ninka pointed to a cushion near the hearth and the young man gently set her down. She examined Enyana's wound then nodded with satisfaction. She sprinkled a dusty-looking herb over it and began to chant.

> *Goddess of the Harvest*
> *Accept Your broken children*
> *Into the furrow of this flesh*
> *Protect Enyana from angry spirits*
> *She has been disrespectful*
> *But she is young and has much to learn*
> *Do not let the rottenness of death swallow her*
> *Allow this flesh to be reborn.*

Ninka stopped chanting and took a handful of flour from a nearby bowl. She began to pack the flour into Enyana's wound. The flour turned to a bloody paste. She added more until the wound was dry and powdery, then wrapped Enyana's leg once more in a linen cloth. She leaned back, placing her tattooed hands on her knees. "All we can do is wait," she said. "Hopefully the Goddess and the ancestors will hear our prayers."

Henne stepped forward, her green eyes flashing. "If Enyana had sought counsel with the elders, if she would have waited for her mother's approval, we would not have to call on the powers of the ancestors and this would have never happened," she hissed.

The people in the room murmured their agreement.

Enyana lifted her chin. "That's right, Mother," she said bravely, although her eyes shone with tears. "Nothing would have happened. Now we have over two hands of horses."

"Horses to return to the Wild Goddess," Henne spat. "How are we supposed to care for them, Enyana? Have you forgotten that the days grow dark? The horses will need food through the winter moons."

Enyana's face fell. In her excitement over discovering the small herd, she hadn't thought of feeding them. None of them had. "I'm sorry, Mother," she mumbled. "We should have sought the wisdom of the elders. But we were afraid Yana would disapprove . . ."

"Yana is your High Priestess now," Henne growled, unable to contain her anger any longer. "You must seek her counsel in everything!"

Henne turned to Yana, who was standing nearby. "She is my daughter, but I give her over to you and the elders to discipline. But first I will say this—Enyana will never ride again!"

Enyana gasped. Her eyes flew to her mother's face. She couldn't mean it.

Yana stepped between Enyana and Henne, looking directly into her adoptive sister's eyes. "No," she said firmly. For the second time in her life Yana felt shadows shift, worlds converge. Once more, the patterns of life hinged on her words. "Enyana and the young people of the village will ride again," she said. "We will keep the horses. We will find a way to feed them."

Henne was shocked out of her anger. She glanced down at her daughter, then up again at Yana. "Why?" she gasped. "Why would you risk our supplies? We need that grain!"

Yana took her arm, steering Henne away from listening ears. "Tern brought news from the Sea People," she said in a barely audible voice. "I need your help, and the prayers of the elders. There is much to do before spring."

29

It was the killing time of year, late enough in the fall for carcasses to freeze, yet early enough that fat from summer's abundance still thickened the flesh. Hundreds of sheep, mostly gelded rams and barren ewes were harvested at this time. The carcasses were stacked outside under tarps on top of the houses to slowly dry out and freeze. The women stuffed sheep stomachs with viscera—hearts, livers, kidneys, abdominal fat, and guts—to be frozen for later use. Both men and women worked to scrape the undersides of the hides and to carefully cut sinew from the legs. It was a busy time. Hardly anyone noticed that Henne and Yana were subdued. Only those closest to them saw the change.

It was late. Tern's arms ached from a long day of butchering and scraping, but it was over now, at least until tomorrow. His belly was full of Galea's blood stew and Niam's sweet cakes. His body was freshly washed. An unspoken agreement had grown between Tamuz and himself; she was content with her three children and Appa held her heart. She no longer needed Tern. Nowadays he spent most of his time with Dagron and Niam, and they had happily welcomed him in their house.

Tern exhaled contentedly as he leaned against the door frame and gazed up at the stars. He had been many places in his life, but his spirit always longed for this place of highland meadows, terraced fields, and forested glades. His eyes traveled past the white-washed houses to the darkening hills. Light came from the doorway of Yana's house. Idly, he wondered if she was standing there too, gazing at the stars. Galea came and stood near his elbow.

"She is always sad when you come home." The older woman sighed. "But something more worries her now. Henne too. I know being leaders of the people is difficult. I wish there was something I could do or say to ease their hearts."

Tern clearly heard the hint in her words. Galea wanted him to go to Yana, find out what was wrong. Unfortunately, he already knew what was troubling her.

Galea put her hand on Tern's arm. "She still waits for you. You know this, don't you?"

Galea's words squeezed his heart. He looked down into her worried eyes, realizing for the first time that Galea was getting older. Her shoulders were stooped, the lines of her face had deepened, and her hair was almost white. A few years ago she would never have approached him like this, but old people had a way of seeing the important things, speaking their mind. Yes, he knew Yana waited for him. He had always known, and he'd always stayed away. But over the years his anger had mellowed, and he'd found peace in the Goddess. Perhaps it was time to make peace with Yana. He pushed away from the door frame and smiled down into her worried eyes. "I will go to her," he said. "It is time."

Galea's face cracked into a smile. She patted his arm as if to say he was doing the right thing, then turned to reenter the warmth of the house.

Tern walked out of the village, pondering the things he wanted to say to Yana. He had hurt her deeply, had hurt both of them. All these years he should have loved her, but instead he'd run away, wasting years searching foreign villages, distant peoples, looking for that one woman to care for, but no one held his heart like Yana. He had come to learn that his perfect woman was not perfect at all. Yana would never meet all his needs, she would never fulfill him completely, but perhaps this was not her responsibility. Now he wondered if the wound was too deep, the chasm they had created too far to cross. Could she forgive him?

Tern's step slowed as he approached her house. This was his and Yana's real home—separate, set aside from others. He remembered the many times they had shared the Mother's gift in its warmth. He could see the outline of light around the flap of hide covering the door and reached toward it, pushing the covering away. Yana sat before the fire with her legs crossed, her eyes closed, humming a husky chant. Her face was serene. She opened her eyes and looked at him. He was surprised to find no question in her face, no objection, only an endless kind of relief. She stood slowly and came to him, placing her long brown arms around his waist. He buried his cheek in her neck, inhaling her smell. Tears burned his eyes, a lump formed in his throat. Words would come later. He was home now.

30

Henne had gone over and over it in her mind. The only way to protect the people was to leave, go to the people of the Herd, offering herself to them. She'd never escape her past; no matter where she went, and she knew that now. The Herders lived inside her, breathed in the very core of her being, but so did the Goddess. She could feel the pull of opposites—the unswerving purpose of the Sky God and his horse, and the mysterious womb of potential life in the Goddess. She was both of those things. For years she had fought it, but when she had faced Enyana, telling her daughter that she couldn't ride, Henne saw her own reflection in her daughter's disbelieving eyes. The power of the horse ran in Enyana's veins. She was the offspring between the Herders and the people of the Goddess. She was the marriage between opposites that strained the boundaries of things. She was vibrant, strong, something new. Someday Enyana would lead the people, lead them to change, but now Henne had to give her daughter time to grow and become stronger.

Henne packed the last of her traveling food in her sack and stood. She rummaged around for her sewing pouch and water skins, but suddenly felt eyes on her back. She whirled around. Yana stepped through the doorway. She wore her winter robes and held the staff of High Priestess.

"It won't work, Henne," she said quietly. "The dark

days are coming. You do not know the trader's trails. You will die in the mountains—and they will still come."

Henne cursed her sister's intuitiveness. She returned to packing.

Yana came to stand in front of her. "You must stay with us. The young people need to learn how to ride the horses. Can't you see the Goddess's plan?"

Henne's shoulders slumped. She had been afraid of this. She felt strange since the horses were caught, uncertain yet excited. She knew the seductive power of the horse, and also knew what it was like to be tainted with the ways of the Herd. Could the people remain pure in the Goddess after learning the ways of the Horse People? Henne's throat tightened as she spoke.

"I am too much a woman of the Goddess. I cannot lead the people in the ways of the Herd. I cannot teach our children to kill."

"The mother leopard teaches her children the ways of the hunt," Yana challenged. "You are our Hunting Priest."

"Animals do not hunt their own kind."

"They are nothing like us," Yana said with deadly calm, lifting her chin.

Henne looked into Yana's determined face. When had her sister become so strong? Yana hated the ways of the people of the Herd, but now she was willing to go to any lengths to protect the people, even if that meant going against her beliefs. Yana had become a true mother of the people. Henne shook her head at the mystery of the Goddess who brought a stranger to lead them.

"The Herders are people," Henne stated, her voice low and insistent. "Their children cry out in the night, and their mothers comfort them." She put up her hands. "The women care for their men, sew for them, cook for them. But unlike us, the man is the center of the family. If we kill even one man, his whole fam-

ily risks death and starvation. Do you want women
and children to starve?"

Yana whirled around and began to pace, her hands
clenching and unclenching in frustration. "I cannot believe they are anything like us. What mother would
let her son kill women and children, permit him to
take the Mother's gift without a woman's consent?
It's madness!"

Henne didn't respond, allowing Yana to hear her
own words. Yana stopped pacing and dropped her
hands, but her shoulders and back remained rigid.
"Our children will learn only to protect," she said
roughly. "They will not kill ruthlessly."

Henne briefly challenged Yana with her eyes, then
returned to packing. Yana strode across the room and
took Henne firmly by the arm, pulling her around,
forcing her sister to face her. "You cannot leave. You
are the added oil—our sustenance. The people need
your strength to keep the flame of hope in their spirits.
The Honored One's dream . . ." Yana's stopped talking, her mouth parted, and her eyes grew round. Why
hadn't she thought of it before?

"Sister," she gasped, clutching Henne's arm tighter,
"the cave of the ancestors! Telna had a dream. Perhaps our answer will be in a dream." She paused as
if the thoughts were coming too fast, then spoke again
with rushed enthusiasm. "The people will accompany
us. We will go the womb of the Mother. They will
pray. Both of us will eat the belly-shaped mushrooms
that bring dreams."

Henne tilted her head, a wary look in her eyes.
"How can dreams save the people?"

Yana took a deep breath. "Don't you see, the
Dreaming Cave is a place of death, rebirth, change.
Our answer is there," she said confidently.

Henne thought of Enyana, of the changes her
daughter would face someday. Perhaps there was a
way to stay true to the Goddess while learning the
ways of the Horse. She nodded slowly, but her voice

sounded doubtful. "And if the dreams tell us that I am to go, what then?" she asked.

Yana lifted her chin. "Then you will go."

Later that evening, the people solemnly followed the torches of the priestesses up the mountain path leading to the cave of the ancestors. Most had been in the cave only once or twice in their lifetimes, now they were going into the womb of the Goddess, into the cavity of Her belly where life and death were inseparable. It was considered a place of power and magic, only to be approached in times of dire need, or rebirth. The people exchanged nervous whispers. Obviously their new High Priestess and Hunting Priest believed the power of the cave was needed, but why? The storage houses were full of meat and grain. Sickness had not visited the village. What harmful thing warranted the need of their prayers?

Yana was the first at the cave. She had been inside three times, initially as part of her adoption ritual, then twice more to enact ceremonies with the High Priestesses and the elders. Each time, the cave inspired wonder. The entrance was a narrow fissure in a cleft of gray limestone, hidden by ropy vines and a scraggly juniper tree. She had to go around the tree, push away the vines, lifting her torch high so those following could see. A strong draft came from deep within, bringing the odor of wet clay, and Yana couldn't help thinking of the breath of the Goddess. The opening, not much wider than her shoulders, went on and on, twisting and turning in the darkness. The tunnel narrowed and she had to stoop slightly. The earth walls seemed to press inward in all directions, urging her feet deeper into the silence of the mountain. Then, without warning, the pass widened. Yana heard the sharp inhalation of those behind as they stepped into the expansive cavern.

The womb of the Goddess struck fear and awe into the hearts of those who revered Her. It was a beautiful

place, yet unworldly. Everything glittered and twisted
in the torch-lit shadows. Calcite draped from the ceiling in long white folds trimmed in orange and red,
reminding the people of the linen robes of the priestesses. A great stalagmite pillar stood to one side like
a spirit guardian, demanding honor. Everywhere odd
formations hinted at unresolved shapes. Here potential life waited in the eternal dark for the cast of light,
bringing form into being. Heads craned to see them,
murmuring their reverence, a silent prayer to the Goddess on their lips.

Eventually they passed a place where bear bones
scattered the ground. The bears were long gone now,
but had left behind carved pockets, nests in the
earthen floor where they once hibernated. The people
carefully stepped around the places of dreams without
disturbing the bones. Yana's torch swept the wall of
another cavern. To the left were handprints, spirit
hands outlined into a halo of red ochre. The silhouette
of a cave bear hunkered over the prints as if to protect
them. Many closed their eyes as they passed under
the bear's watchful gaze. They rounded another bend
and were met by musty smells and dripping water.
Before them glistened a dark pool made by a small
river disappearing beneath the rocky floor. Yana
stopped. This was her sacred place; the place she had
entered to be reborn to the people. Henne and Kara
came to stand beside her.

Henne held her torch aloft, noting her sister's solemn face. "Shall I tell the men to put the wood here?"
she asked.

"There should be enough room on this ledge for
everyone," Kara added. "And it's dry enough for a
fire."

Yana shook her head, clearing her thoughts of the
past. "No. We will go to the birthing chamber of the
Goddess. The power is strongest there." Her face became speculative. "But have the people wait here. I
will go on ahead to prepare the fire."

Henne nodded, knowing how important it was to sanctify the chamber, preparing the place so the observers would feel the greatest impact of the ritual. "I will stay with the others until you send for us," she agreed. "We will contemplate the waters of rebirth."

Yana glanced around. On a nearby wall, the painting of a great bull glared down on those below. A bulge of rugged stone became the forward thrust of a shoulder, the beginning of a charge. It was almost as if the bull were living in the rock, waiting for that moment when it would break free. Yes. This would be a good place for the people to contemplate rebirth, a place for Henne to prepare their hearts for the ritual to come.

Yana went on ahead, the men carrying wood following close behind. Tern was one of these. He had only been in this cave once before as a child. Here, in the oppressive darkness it seemed time had disappeared and he was that child again. His palms sweated into the coarse ropes bundling the firewood. The blood in his temple sounded loud in his ears. He felt disoriented, odd. He had no frame of reference for this moist, dark place. This was not the darkness of night. At night, when looking at the stars, he had a sense of an emptiness so vast it could never be filled. But this seamless black was full, packed with every conceivable thought, every dream, as if spirits of the past as well as the future were breathing close by, pushing for release, for understanding. And here, Tern's own thoughts and fears found form, raising to tower over him.

Concern for Yana churned in his belly as Tern set about building the fire with the other men. Those he loved died. He knew the mushroom she was about to take was powerful. He had heard stories of those who had stayed far too long in world of dreams, only to drift off into the endless sleep of death. Now that he'd given in to his love for her, now that she completely consumed his soul, would Yana die, taking his hopes with her? He discreetly watched as she sprinkled the area with a purifying herb.

The glowing fire and the torches lit up the walls of the sacred chamber. For a moment they all stood, transfixed by the charcoal paintings of bison, deer, ibex, and horses. The animals were running in herds, flowing in and out of a large niche in the far wall. The niche itself was unusual. Large rippling arches, rolling rock spread from the niche to the ceiling and walls, and one had the impression of the ridges in a great open mouth, or the undulating lips of a woman's birthing place in the last stages of labor. Here the consuming power and the birthing power of the Goddess appeared to be one, and Her power was absolute.

Yana took sage, igniting it on her torch, and walked around the chamber, waving a whorl of blue smoke until a woodsy smell filled the cavern. She passed Tern. He was frowning, his eyes alive with fear for her. She placed a reassuring hand on his arm. "I need your hopeful prayers," she said gently, "not your fearful ones."

Tern heard the wisdom of her words. He remembered what she had said earlier in the privacy of an embrace. She suggested creative power took many forms, but he had a choice of where to look. Would he gaze into the great maw of death, or would he see the potential of rebirth in the Goddess? He stiffened his resolve. He would not let his most negative imaginings control him.

Yana saw Tern's eyes clear. His love for her was strong, a great power, and she was thankful. "Go tell Henne I am ready," she said quietly. "Have the people come."

A short while later the villagers filed into the chamber led by Tern and Henne. They settled themselves on the dry dirt floor, necks craning to look at the magnificent paintings. The animals fluttered to life in the firelight, their muscles moving in the shadows. The people waited expectantly for Yana to speak, but were surprised when Ninka stood, supported by her grand-daughter.

The old woman held her head rigidly, waiting for the people to settle until there was only the sound of the snapping fire. Ninka nodded once she knew she had their full attention. "Many of you have heard the stories," her old voice quavered. "Stories of how our ancestors came to this land and found the living spring water of the Goddess. But it was a place filled with ancient spirits foreign to us. We discovered this cave. We found evidence of another people—their tools, their grinding stones for paint." She waved her tattooed arm to the lifelike murals.

"They were a great people who seemed to understand the powers of the Goddess. Our priests and priestesses made peace with the ancestors of this place . . . they allowed us to stay. In return, we have guarded the secret of the dreaming cave of the Goddess, only coming here in times of great need. Now our ancestors mingle with the ancient ones of this land and we ask them all to acknowledge us. We will sing to the most ancient spirits, asking guidance and wisdom.

Henne stood, lifting her vulture staff. Its shadow seemed to make a grimacing face on the wall. "When I left the people of the Herd, I ran away with their power." She paused, then her voice rose. "It was power they gave me. I was their priestess, nursing them on the knowledge of the Goddess. I became equal with their headman. But when he was injured, I learned I was to follow him in death—accompanying him in the underworld as his mate. I refused. Instead, I escaped to return home." Henne faltered, but quickly regained her composure. "Unfortunately, I have just received news that death has followed me here." Henne leveled her eyes on Tern.

Tern stood, meeting Henne's gaze before turning to address the people. "Yes, I brought the news of the Herders to the elders," he responded in answer to the alarmed eyes of the villagers. "I have learned from

the Sea People that the Herdsmen are looking for
Henne. They want her power. They believe the Goddess has stolen the strength of their spirits, and they
wish to purge themselves of Her ways. They have
sworn to come here and kill Henne—kill all her
people."

The crowd sat in shocked silence, then began to stir.
Fearful eyes darted to the faces of loved ones. Men
instinctively clutched at phantom spears, wishing they
were in their fingers.

"We will fight the barbarians," Dagron growled,
putting his arm around Niam.

"We will use the horses," a young man called,
"chase them from our homeland."

Henne stepped forward, her eyes flashing a warning.
"If we kill the Herdsmen, their women and children
will starve. They do not live off the land in the same
way we do. The men depend on hunting and managing
large herds of cattle and horses. Their women are not
trained to do this."

"What do we care if their women and children
starve!" someone shouted.

The shout echoed in the chamber, the walls rever-
berating with the words of sacrilege. The people's eyes
darted to the paintings, scenes suggestive of the hunt
displayed beautifully, reverently. Here life and death
were woven together, both a sacrifice to be carefully
pondered. Many sensed the disapproval of the ancients who had gone on before them.

Yana raised her pinecone staff before stepping close
to the fire and gazing into its depths. Her voice was
less forceful than the others, more contemplative. She
seemed to be talking to herself rather than to the
villagers.

"I hear fear for your families in these words," she
said slowly. "If we allow this fear to fill our minds,
we may only see the pain of death and not the laboring pains of rebirth." She lifted her head. "Tonight
Henne and I will dream in the Goddess's womb"—

she pointed to the two bear-carved indentations in the floor—"and we need your prayers." She extended both arms to the panel of horses as if in worship. "Pray not out of despair . . . but of the wonder of this place. The Goddess allows all to move from one womb ring to the next. The horse is magnificent. Beautiful. I see that now. We must pray for guidance. How shall we use this new tool to protect our people, how shall we harness this power our children have brought us?" She smiled down at Enyana, who was sitting at her feet.

The people heard the wisdom of the Goddess in Yana's words. A man nodded. Another grunted his approval. A woman trilled her satisfaction; her lilting voice seemed to dance from wall to wall. Yana lifted her staff to quiet them.

"Henne and I will sleep now," she said humbly. "Tonight we will be your children, not your leaders. You will sing us into dreams, just as a mother sings a lullaby to her child." Yana's eyes became moist. "We step timidly toward that dark place with the safety of your hearts and the power of your prayers as our nesting place."

Yana stopped talking and stepped back.

Kara began to sing. Her soft soprano voice fluttered around the chamber like a young bird learning to fly. Others joined her. It was lullaby everyone knew; even the children sang the song recalling the soft breasts of the Mother, the sweetness of Her milk, the flowery perfume of Her body on a summer day.

Yana handed Henne a wedge of mushroom, impulsively grasping her sister's hand. Henne shared with her a long look. When had this change come? When had they become so bound together? Reluctantly Henne let go, imitating Yana as she placed the fleshy mushroom in her mouth.

Yana stepped toward the earthen pocket in the floor, her eyes resting one last time on her people: Atum, Ninka and her grandchildren, Galea, Enyana,

Dagron, and Niam. Ashra was leaning against her mother's shoulder. Yana's gaze traveled beyond her womb family to all the others in her village who had become precious to her over the years. Finally her eyes found Tern. She held tightly the sacred shell he had given her, hiding it in her palm. He smiled, nodding his approval. She knew he was worried, sensed it, but tonight he was strong for her. She thanked him with her smile.

Yana took off her robe and curled naked into the indentation in the earth, already feeling the numbing affect of the mushroom. Her limbs became languid, loose; her eyes drooped. She barely felt the dusting of ochre Kara sprinkled over her body, the color of birth. Kara covered her with a wool blanket.

Yana lay for a moment bemused, listening to the singing voices. If she listened carefully, she could hear each one separately. A child's warble sang of the newness of things, a song of discovery. It was accented with the deep-sounding cords of a young man's determination and pride. She listened to the squawk of wisdom in an old woman's voice, superimposed on a mother's tireless devotion. Each was rich, full of possibility. All were precious, deserving meticulous observation. The unity of their voices was almost too powerful to contemplate. Most humbling of all, they were singing for her.

She opened her eyes one last time to the murals on the walls. Images swam around her—running horses, stalking lions, herds of deer and bison. They swirled together, blurring, becoming a whirling pool in the darkness. The pool slowed, stopped, and Yana realized she was looking into a dark well. The hazy images that had been vibrant animals were merely reflected light in water. She leaned over the pool, expecting to see her own distorted reflection. Instead she saw the tattooed face of the woman in the mound. The woman was trying to tell her something, but the sounds were garbled and Yana didn't understand her words. She leaned close, drawn to the woman's mouth and eyes. Suddenly a great power tugged at her spirit, pulling her downward. She fell sinking into darkness. Something large swam upward to devour her. She screamed but no sound came from her throat. Her chest tightened, she lost air, and couldn't breathe.

Suddenly Yana felt detached, strangely calm. She recognized this place between life and death; she'd been here before. Her arms and legs were paralyzed, but this time she had no desire to struggle. Deep inside, she was tired of the precarious squabble between life and death, and it was as if she were already outside of herself, watching, bemused. But as she saw the flame of her spirit dim, a great sadness overcame her. It had been a struggle, but there was so much wonder in the ever-changing Goddess. Life and death were intertwined, painfully, beautifully. She realized the struggle had been precious, worth every moment.

"If my life must fade, sweet Goddess," she whispered, "my last breath will be a song of praise, a song of thanks for this life You give."

Yana's mind filled with a child's song. It was simple, pure. The melody gently rocked her as she slid deeper into numbing death, singing her faith in the Goddess. She floated gently on the waves of the lullaby. In her mind's eye, the flame of her life turned into a red-gold leaf drifting on a pond and in the pond were all the faces of the people, their lives supporting her, singing with her. She turned her head. The face of old man Heth surfaced. He had been dead for many years now, but here his eyes were alive. A memory came, one she had long forgotten. It was the night of her adoption. His gnarled hand was wrapped around a cowry shell. He told the story of his childhood, his father's wish that he take the shell to an island, offer it in trade. She heard his words again. *I often dream of that island,* he said. *Sometimes, when the morning mist settles in the valley and the distant hills peak above, I can almost see it. I always thought I'd make the journey someday. . . .*

Yana abruptly woke from her dream. She blinked her eyes.

"She's awake," someone whispered.

Henne hovered near. Encircling her were the concerned faces of the elders. She looked up. Tern, Galea, and Kara were crouched near her head. She sat up slowly, putting a hand to her forehead in an effort to hold back the throbbing pain behind her eyes. Her mind felt like it was shifting in her skull. "How long?" she asked in a ragged breath.

Henne gestured to the low-burning coals. "We ran out of wood," she said gravely. "I had to send for more."

Yana dropped her hand and looked at her sister. "But we had enough to last a day and a night."

Ninka leaned forward. "Henne has been awake for many fingers of time, leading the people in chants and prayers. We were worried. You were moaning, then stopped breathing for a short while. Your dreams must have been—"

Yana's brow furrowed. She raised her hand, interrupting Ninka. She rubbed her forehead again. "Don't speak," she whispered. "I must hold on to this dream. I must remember."

The people waited quietly. Yana's headache began to dissipate as she went over the images still vivid in her mind. Surely it had been a spirit dream. The scenes were clear, sharp, but they made no sense. She turned the cowry shell over in her hand, then looked up at Henne. "Did you dream, Sister?" she asked quietly.

Henne shrugged. "Yes, but not long. I have already told my dream to the people."

"I wish to hear it," Yana said.

Henne sat down next to her. The elders squatted close by and the villagers crowded to hear the story once more.

"There was no color in my dream," Henne began, "only the black, white, and grays of night shadows. I was riding Moon when we approached a large body of water. The moon was full and glistened in a long path across the water. For some reason I wanted to follow the path, but Moon wouldn't go past the water's edge. She reared, stomping and neighing. A snake slithered out of the shadows, into the water, frightened by the stomping hooves. It swam in the dark, following the lighted path to the center of the moon." Henne shrugged and sat back. "And then I woke."

Yana felt her heart begin to beat rapidly in her chest. Henne had had a water dream also. "The water, the moon," she gasped, "and a snake! Your dream was surely a gift from the Goddess, but what does it mean?"

Lolim cleared her throat. "Perhaps if you told us your dream, Yana."

Yana pulled her wool blanket around her shoulders, clutching the shell that was still in her hand. She glanced toward Tern, who stood not far behind the elders. He still seemed uneasy, but when he caught her looking at him, he straightened and nodded his encouragement. Yana took a deep breath.

"The Goddess also came to me in a spirit dream," she began, her voice low, solemn.

Yana did her best to retell the story of her dream. It frustrated her that words could not seem to capture the images in her head. She didn't realize that her husky voice and the wonder in her tones held the people spellbound. Mouths dropped. Eyes widened as she told of the dark pool of running animals and the woman who drew her downward. When she came to the part where she was drowning Niam interrupted. "But you *were* dying," she said. "We thought you were lost forever in the place of dreams, and you were very—"

"Quiet," Ninka snapped. "Yana must finish the telling."

Yana offered Niam a conciliatory glance before going on. She spoke of floating on the songs of the people, resting in the sounds of their lullaby. She smiled wistfully. It had been such a lovely place, so peaceful. She sighed as she came to the end of her story, telling them of Heth's wish to go to the island to trade his cowry shell to buy a gift for his new mother.

A couple of the elders exchanged knowing glances. Those who knew Heth remembered the shell that hung about his neck. Many of the old ones recalled the faraway look that came to the old man's eyes when he told of his childhood journey. That look was in Yana's eyes now.

Jozer rubbed his chin. "So . . . Heth still longs for his island," the elder mused.

She nodded. "But I still don't know why he showed me this."

Galea's words were rushing with excitement. "My daughters have had water dreams. Water brings change! Isn't the liquid of the Goddess expelled from the womb in birth? Doesn't it fall to the earth and the land is reborn in the spring."

"Yes," Ninka added. "Water makes the woman moist to receive the man, and the soil soft to receive the seed."

"But Henne's horse was afraid of the water. Moon wouldn't go in," Ryle's voice boomed from the back of the chamber.

A hush of realization descended on the people. The villagers held their breath, straining hard to understand. This was their answer, if they could only grasp it. They gazed at the paintings of horses on the walls, frozen, yet seemingly living in endless motion in the womb of the Goddess. They sensed the ancient spirits trying to tell them something, something about movement and change.

Henne rose slowly, her green eyes surveying the

walls before they dropped to the upturned faces of the villagers. "The Herdsmen cannot cross the great waters of the Goddess with the horses," she breathed in discovery. "Their horses are too large to be carried in boats."

Tern pushed his way through the crowd, heart drumming with excitement. "The Sea People have sailing vessels. I'm sure they will help us. Their ships are painted"—he paused with the profound implication of his next words—"and they are painted to resemble serpents!"

Yana began to tremble. She reached for Tern. He helped her stand, steadying her. She slowly extended an arm, fist clenched. She turned the hand over. Now she understood. It was time the people understood the meaning of the cowry shell, time to show them the message Tern had brought from his travels, the message of water and rebirth living forever in stone. She uncurled her fingers, opening her palm.

Ninka leaned forward to examine the shell. "But will the islanders trade?" she whispered in awe.

Many of the elders decided to take their evening meal with Galea and her family. Important decisions had to be made before winter's white blanket covered everything, and life snuggled deep into Mother Earth for the long sleep. Henne paced the central room of her mother's house, bouncing a fist against her thigh in frustration. Going to the islands had seemed the obvious solution in the magic of the cave, but in the light of day, the idea did not seem as plausible. *I can't do this,* she thought. *I can't allow my people to pull up roots, leave this valley because of me.* She stopped by the loom near the door and stared out at the hills beyond the village.

"I should leave now," she said to no one in particular, "before the snows fall."

Ninka's aged voice cracked as she spoke. "You will

disregard the signs, the messages of the Goddess and the ancestors?"

"Signs?" Henne spun around. "Signs can be interpreted many ways." She threw up her hands. "Yana thought she was dying in her dream, drowning, yet we are seriously contemplating crossing the waters. It's madness!"

Galea stepped close to Henne, grabbing and shaking her daughter's arm. "Who are we to question the ways of the Goddess?"

"I won't run screeching like a frightened mouse from a owl. I will face the Herders myself!"

"Mother Mouse is small, humble, and hard to find," Jozer said, smiling at his own wit. He tore off a hunk of bread and put it in his mouth. "Often she thrives when others perish."

"Perhaps this way no one will die," Galea added, desperate fear for Henne in her voice.

Henne shook her head in frustration. "This is our home."

"A home we will soon outgrow," Yana said, stepping out of the shadows. "Telna and I spoke of this before she left to join the ancestors. Each year more children are born. In a handspan of harvest seasons there won't be enough land in our valley to grow the crops we will need. Already our flocks are so large the young men must go farther and farther away from the village to graze them.

Some of the elders nodded.

Yana looked directly into her sister's eyes. "Change is coming, Henne. The Herders have just forced us to make these decisions earlier than we anticipated."

Ninka's old eyes flashed. "The ancient ones have shared their valley for many harvest seasons. The woman in Yana's dream showed us that we would be drawn into death if we stay. Our own ancestor, Heth, gave us the answer. We will go where the horse cannot. We will cross the Great Waters of the Goddess to be reborn to another life."

Henne looked around the room. The faces of the elders were sober, yet determined. "So the decision has been made." One by one they nodded. Henne began pacing again, thinking out loud. "I will go with Dagron and Tern to the Sea People, making sure our people will be provided for. One of us will return early in the spring when everything has been prepared."

"No," Yana said quietly. "You must stay and train the horses."

"The horses!" Henne snorted in exasperation. "We can't keep the horses, not if we want to save enough grain to last through the winter, and we will need planting seed when we get to—" Henne threw up her hands, unable to bring herself to say "island." It just didn't seem real.

"We need the horses to pack the tents and grain," Tern interjected, "and to carry the elders."

"We will use the grain reserves held back in case of drought for planting in our new homeland," Yana added, "but we will have to slaughter most of the sheep. The hay we've stored for them will go to the horses. We will keep only the best ewes and a few rams as breeder stock."

"A few horses must be trained for the scouts to ride. The people will need protectors on the long walk." Tern continued, nodding to Henne.

"But I've never trained a horse," Henne objected.

Yana's glance slid over Enyana and Atum, who were sitting near the hearth. "I'm sure the young people of the village will be willing to help," she said, unable to stop the smile playing on her lips.

31

Tern traced Yana's lower lip with his finger. She flinched in her sleep, and he smiled.

Over the years, Tern had become an adept lover. Often the women of foreign villages were eager to share their sleeping mats with someone new. He had explored many of them, all with different tastes and ideas about the Mother's gift, but here in Yana's blankets, he did not need to prove his worth. If he touched her lips, traced a nipple with an exploring tongue, or combed his fingers through the fluff of hair below her navel, it was because every detail of Yana was compelling, mysterious, deserving the full focus of desire. He was entranced with the way Yana's eyelashes lay on her cheeks as she slept, and the way her chest rose and fell with her breath. He bent over and licked the small mole at the rise of the breast over her heart.

Yana woke to find Tern examining her chest, wide-awake hunger in his face and eyes. She smiled sleepily and reached for his manhood pressed hard against her thigh. His eyes flared. Her caress deepened. He closed his eyes and lay back, savoring the feel of her sliding fingers. Yana rolled her naked body on top of his. She was determined. This morning there would be no tender good-byes. The connection of their bodies would be vigorous, warm, loving, with no drawn-out promises, no half-hopeful whispers. Now that they were together, the confidence of their love would bind them, no matter how far he traveled.

Tern ran a rough hand over her smooth hips and thighs, cupping a buttock. Yana offered her breasts to his mouth and he engulfed them with urgent kisses. She inhaled sharply at the passion radiating from her breasts, pooling as a wet core in her woman's place. He opened his mouth to consume her entire nipple, sucking deeply. She winced, gasping at the pain accompanied by desire; lately her breasts were swollen, tender, and she was reminded once again of the ever-changing body of the Goddess. She yearned to tell Tern about the child growing in her womb, but acknowledged that if he knew, he would probably find some excuse to stay, sending another in his place to the Sea People. As Mother of the people, Yana couldn't allow that. Tern knew the Sea People; they trusted him. Everything depended on his negotiations with them.

Tern interrupted her musings by reaching to pull her head and ear next to his mouth. He whispered passion with a wet, breathy probe of his tongue. Yana shivered, all thoughts of the Sea People fleeing her mind. Eagerly, she grasped his manhood, guiding him to the wet cavern of her warmth. He plunged with a moan of abandonment, and Yana met him there.

Afterward, Yana snuggled next to Tern in a cocoon of satisfied warmth. She breathed into his neck, letting her hands linger on thighs made hard by years of walking the mountain passes, passes he would soon walk again. She would miss him.

Later that day, the heat of their lovemaking was still with Yana as she stood under the oak tree at the edge of the village. She felt strong standing among those gathering to say good-bye to Tern and Dagron. She smiled. Not for the first time she thought how handsome her lover looked in his beaded traveling tunic, but this time her heart was not heavy with sadness at seeing him go; he was coming back to her.

She cleared her throat and lifted the pinecone staff,

chanting a prayer and blessing. The people joined her, singing loudly, understanding that their future depended on these two men.

Tern's dog jumped up, placing his paws on Tern's belly. "No, you're not going this time." He laughed, ruffling the dog's fur playfully.

Dagron and Tern smiled, nodding gratefully at the villagers' boisterous enthusiasm before stepping over the womb ring encompassing the village, signaling their departure.

They had not gone far when Yana changed her mind. Anything could happen on the mountain trails, and she wanted Tern to know the secret hiding in her womb. She pulled up her skirt and ran after him, snagging his arm.

Tern stopped, his brows arched in confused surprise. They had already said their good-byes. What could Yana want?

Yana laced her long fingers in his, and placed them over her belly. "Come home soon," she whispered, her eyes glowing. "Our child sleeps. We will both dream of you during the dark nights of winter."

32

Enak scratched at the scar raking his left cheek. With the other hand he pulled on his horse's reins. He cursed the low-slung clouds scraping the tops of the surrounding mountains. The purple and gray horizon looked sullen, as sallow as the faces of the men accompanying him. He slowed to an easy canter, scratching the scar once more as he waited for them to catch up.

The scar always itched in the extreme cold. Frigid air pulled the skin tighter across his nose, irritating the old wound, reminding him of the time long ago when another man had challenged his right to lead the people. The man who slashed his cheek was dead, traipsing in the dust of the Underworld for over two hands of winter seasons now. His challenger had suggested that Enak was too young. Enak had proved him wrong. He yanked once more on the reins, slowing the animal to a walk.

The sharp breath of winter always brought back the vivid memories of the past. It had been winter when his father had lost power to that witch of the Goddess, Henne, who transfixed him with her seductive spells. It had been winter when his mother followed Ralic in death and Henne disappeared on the back of her horse into the blinding snow. Enak knew his people still whispered about Henne and the strength of her Goddess. Many had been lured to Her ways, settling on the outskirts of villages, eating sweet cakes, learning the customs of farmers. Oh yes, they still listened to him. He could still get them to do his bidding. Enak looked back at the ragged group of men following him. Unfortunately, they only did it grudgingly and with promises of great reward.

Enak lifted his eyes once more to the bruised underbellies of clouds holding the certainty of snow. He knew the men would not want to continue the search once the first flakes began to cover the ground. He began to suspect that the trader who had come to his camps had not been entirely truthful. These mountains were harsh, inhospitable. The only people he had come across were small and skittish, hiding in shadows and caves. They had nothing of Henne's spirit. Enak pulled on the reins of his horse, slowing the animal to a walk, cursing as the first snowflakes drifted downward.

33

Enyana filled the last water skin, cinched it onto a carrying strap fastened to Moon's back, and climbed up, kicking the mare into a fast trot. She frowned as she approached the small canyon where the wild horses were corralled.

Nothing had gone as she'd expected. Ryle's anger was like an irritating burr in a fur-lined boot. He wouldn't look at her, and only spoke in short grunts when she asked something of him. But it wasn't Ryle's dissatisfaction that concerned her most; it was the disgruntled glances of her friends when she passed by, and the tiredness in her bones when she woke each morning.

The horses were more work than the young people of the village could have imagined, and Henne had been a ruthless taskmaster. First they had to extend the corral, building a large fence so the horses could roam, grazing on what was left of the valley grasses. They had to erect a large lean-to, a place to shelter the animals from winter's onslaught. They had to haul hay and fodder from the village before the first snows. With no water nearby, daily trips needed to be made to a mountain stream, ensuring enough water for the animals as well as the people residing in the work camp. Enyana gazed across the canyon to the hastily erected tents on the lower hills. *It's more like a small village,* she thought derisively, *and I have to supply them all.*

Henne had given Enyana the task of keeping track of the food and water supplies while her leg was healing. The work was exhausting. Worse, Enyana was bored with it, and impatiently waited for the day when the horse training would begin. A whole moon cycle had passed since their capture, and there had been no attempt to train them. Enyana couldn't understand what her mother was waiting for. Already some of the yearlings were becoming tame, taking food from the hands of the young people. She envied Atum and Isha, who spent their days feeding and watering the herd, but acknowledged she was not likely to escape the drudgery of her work. Henne was still very angry with her.

Enyana pulled Moon to a walk as she approached the extended fence made of stacked lengths of wood woven with berry brambles. She straightened her back and lifted her head, stretching to see the horse she had secretly chosen for herself, a dun-colored young stallion, easy to spot. He had taken to prancing the perimeter of the herd, tail high, dark mane lifting in the breeze. Enyana's breath caught at the sight of him. He was magnificent.

Henne whistled; three sharp bursts came on the breeze. Enyana tore her eyes from the horses, brushing the hair from her eyes as she gazed toward the camp. Her mother was watching from the hill, hands on her hips in a stance of irritation. Enyana frowned. Henne probably wanted to send her back to the village for more supplies. She shifted on her seat, urging Moon with her knees, eyes sweeping wistfully one last time over the herd. Someday soon she was going to win that stallion for herself, and she would learn to ride him. Her leg was almost healed. Hadn't she been trained to dance with the bull? How much harder could it be?

Yana listened to Henne's request, but informed her sister it was for the elders to decide. Henne sent a priestess to call the Honored Ones of the village together.

It was late morning by the time the elders trudged through the snow, assembling in the Goddess's shrine. Henne sat beside Yana, combing a thumb across the tip of a vulture feather, waiting for their answer while trying not to let her impatience show. She was not one to sit in silence for long periods of time. Finally, Jozer lifted a hand, shaking slightly with the tremors of age.

"But how will you find this man?" he asked Henne. "His tracks will have disappeared in the snow now that the white face of the Death Goddess covers everything."

"I will bring the dogs," Henne repeated once again, making an effort to keep the strain out of her voice. "Gath hid in the forest when the women were gathering the mountain harvest. He fed the dogs to keep them quiet. The dogs know his smell."

"Can he be trusted?" Nachen asked nervously.

"No man of the Herd can be trusted," snarled Dak, a trader who had witnessed the fierce attack on the women of the Leopard People.

"Gath was one of the kinder men I knew during my time with the people of the Herd," Henne responded soothingly. "He was good to his wives, an affectionate father. I do not believe he enjoyed the raids, especially the killings."

"Why can't we train the horses ourselves?" another man objected, discomfort at having a stranger in their village evident in his voice. He looked squarely at Henne. "Your horse is gentle. I should think it would be much easier to ride a horse than a bull."

Henne stood and started pacing. Had they heard anything she said? She stopped and whirled around, the vulture cape billowing about her. "You must understand," she responded, exasperation beginning to show in her face. "The horse is different than a bull. It is unpredictable, skittish, and would rather run than face a challenge." She paused then began again. "I don't know how to train horses; the women of the Herd do not take part in these things. Moon was already tame when she was given to me. I do know the training has to be done right, or the horse will never allow a rider on its back."

"I say we forget about the horses," Lolim interjected. "I say we go to the Sea People without them."

Yana tilted her head, her tone contemplative. "Remember the dream? The horse went to the water's edge. Only then did the snake leave the safety of the shore."

"And Tern has promised the horses in exchange for the cooperation of the Sea People," Ninka piped.

Henne tossed her head. "There is only one person who can help, one person who can teach the young people the proper way to handle the horses before spring. Right now that man is living in our mountains. I'm not even sure he will be willing to help, but Gath has abandoned his people . . . and he is alone."

"It is strange," Galea mused, pulling thoughtfully at the corners of her mouth with a finger and thumb. "The Goddess brought us this man now, at a time when we need him most . . ."

The elders contemplated Galea's words, finally nodding one by one. Henne gave her mother a sideways glance. Galea had just recently joined the circle of elders. When had her mother's hair grown so white, when had she become so wise?

"It is decided then," Yana said resolutely, interrupting Henne's thoughts. "Henne will go to the mountains taking scouts and dogs with her. The young people will tend the horses until she returns." She nodded formally to dismiss the gathering.

Henne spun toward the entrance, already thinking of what she must do to prepare for the journey. She almost ran into Jozer sitting near the door. He stood in front of her, leaning close.

"How do you know this man Gath will not betray us to the Herders?" he asked in a low voice.

Henne kept her voice low also, steeling her eyes. "If I sense any deception in Gath's heart, I will kill him with my own hands," she hissed, pushing past the old man toward the open door.

Enyana saw her mother striding purposefully across camp with the hunting dogs bounding about her feet. Obviously the elders had granted Henne's request; the dogs always seemed to sense the promise of a hunt. Enyana bent to load more grain and frozen meat on the travois. Henne had told her to pack extra supplies in anticipation of the elder's decision. This time Enyana did not mind the extra work. It would be her last trip from the village; Henne was taking Moon and the travois with her to the mountains. Enyana would remain behind, helping with the horses while Henne and her companions traveled on. As the girl stacked another sheep stomach packed with butter, a plan formed in her mind. Atum worked closely with the horses. They trusted him, came to his whistle. She had to convince him to help her.

34

Gath ate his last strip of dried venison. Chewing hurt his mouth, but swallowing was worse. His chapped lips were bleeding again. His mouth and throat were spotted with round, yellow sores. He knew he needed food, something besides meat, but he was too weary to contemplate the search. He pressed himself deeper into the cold crevice that barely passed for a cave, absentmindedly watching the white flurries outside, then let his eyes drift closed.

The dreams called again, pulling him inward. He no longer resisted them. Instead, he stepped gladly toward the offered warmth—Mern's smile, her plump arms about his neck. His infant daughter was there too, laughing, giggling, crawling to get into the middle of all that warmth. He hoped the dreams would go on forever. A part of him knew he was dying. He wondered if he would go to the Underworld where his ancestors roamed, or if somehow his love for Mern would take him on into the womb of dreams and rebirth. The thought was foreign, yet when he dreamed, Mern came to him, made love to him, and the joy of their love danced in her eyes. He could almost believe.

An icy blast of wind invaded his cramped chamber. Gath's dream twisted, turning nightmarish. The warmth of Mern's embrace was replaced by cold rocks cutting into his knees as he knelt in a shallow current near the bank of an angry, swirling river. Upriver, foaming rapids whipped around jagged boulders. His arms felt heavy. He looked down. Mern's broken body lay lifeless in his arms, her eyes cold, unseeing. He bellowed like a wild thing, sorrow and anger slashing his heart. He raged at the gods, at the injustice of Mern's death. She was the one good thing in his life. How could she have thrown her life away? And then from the corner of his eye he saw her—his first wife—a mask of compassion on her face, a look he knew was not real, or felt.

He growled a warning deep in his throat. He hunched over Mern as if to say this is mine, don't come near. The woman continued to advance.

Mern had told him that his first wife smothered their daughter, sending the little one to the Goddess's womb, but he hadn't believed her, hadn't listened. The life in Mern's eyes died when he'd scoffed, refusing to see the poison brewing in his own tent. But Gath saw it now. He saw it in the smug sympathy of his first wife's face. She approached, reaching to place the shroud over Mern's glassy eyes. Gath clawed the blanket away. The woman smiled patiently, placing a hand on his shoulder, admonishing him like a child. She reached for Mern again, and something within Gath rose up, roaring in anger.

"You will not touch her!"

He lunged for the older woman's throat. His wife's eyes bulged with surprise as Gath's large hands squeezed, then snapped her neck like a branch he'd break over the fire. Both wives lay dead at his feet.

The world turned dark, a place of shadows. Gath started running, his feet pounding the earth, sending shock waves through his body. He ran for days, until he could not run, but still he stumbled on, the knives of grief tearing his sanity until he was nothing more than a wild thing, wandering in disbelief.

Large wet flakes spun in urgent flurries around her. Henne let the reins in her hand go slack, reaching to pull the fur-lined hood around her face. She adjusted the wool muff covering her nose, scraping beads of ice where the warm vapor of her breath had frozen so she could breathe easier. She twisted on her mount to see how the two men accompanying her were faring. Both were falling behind; the dogs were trailing even more. Henne stopped and slid off Moon, peering through the white haze at the two mounds of fur walking toward her through the dark trees.

As they drew close, she recognized the diamond cut markings of Ryle's parka, and stepped in his direction. "We'd better stop here," she shouted through the flurries. "We're almost there, but it's getting too hard to see!"

Ryle silently nodded into his hood. Most men considered Henne a strange woman. In the years he'd known her, she'd never taken a lover. When she wasn't doing her duties as Hunting Priestess, she spent her time alone, hunting. Ryle had the impression Henne didn't quite see him when she looked at him; her eyes went past him as if seeing into a distant place. It was disconcerting. She looked past him now. So instead of responding, he just nodded and turned toward the travois.

Before leaving the village, the men had fashioned runners so the travois slid easily on the snow. Henne unloaded an oilskin and went to search for a flat piece of ground. When she found a likely place, she scraped away as much snow as she could before unfolding it. The two men approached with the tarp and tent poles. The heavy tent material was specially made to resist dampness and cold; the lanolin from the sheep was not cleaned from the wool, but left in the fabric so the natural oils would seal out moisture. The coarse hair was then pressed into long strips of felt, and sewed tightly together into one large blanket.

Henne tethered Moon to a tree and poured water from a water skin into a large wooden bowl. She waited for Moon to drink, then filled the bowl with peas, lentils, and other fodder. She left the horse to eat, joining the others as they finished erecting the tent. She retrieved another oilskin designed to cover Moon, and tossed it over the horse's back, tying it in the appropriate places. By the time she finished, the tent was up.

Henne helped pull the travois close to the tent entrance to block out the wind and snow. Moments later, Henne, the men, and dogs were snug inside. One by one they removed their parkas, shaking them out, sweeping away the snow. Afterward they placed the heavy furs over their bodies again as blankets. Henne took grain cakes and fat balls from her pack, handing the travel food to the others. They ate in weary silence, then burrowed under their blankets to sleep.

Deep in the night, Henne jerked awake. The tent flap was askew. Outside, a dog was barking. Instantly, she recognized Jagged Ear's sharp yip. Rabbit Dancer, the dog nestled next to Henne, perked her ears and started whining. Henne reached to ruffle the prickling fur on the dog's back. "What is it, Dancer?"

The dog ignored Henne's calming hand and scrambled to a stand, nosing her way through the tent flap, darting away in the dark. Ryle elevated himself on an elbow, rubbing the sleep from his eyes. "It could be a wolf drawn to Moon's smell," he suggested.

Henne frowned. "The barking would be closer," she responded, pulling on her oilskin leggings and knee-high boots. She shrugged on her parka and crawled to the opening, peering through. The travois blocked the view, but she could see that it had stopped snowing. The dogs had already dislodged the large stone holding the door flaps, so she stepped outside.

The clouds were gone. Trees stood in shrouded, white silence. The wind tossed small handfuls of icy powder near the ground. Luckily, the full moon illuminated the wintry landscape, clearly exposing the blue holes of paw prints leading away from camp, disappearing beyond the trees. Moon was tethered under the nearby tree, head down, unperturbed. Everything seemed eerily peaceful, if not for the urgent barking of the dogs.

The dogs did not sound like they were a great distance away. Henne instructed Gelb to stay behind with their supplies and motioned Ryle to accompany her. She followed the trail of prints through the trees up the gradual incline of the mountain. The cold air cut deeply into her lungs as she walked, and the warm vapor of her breathing hung about her face like a small cloud.

Henne hardly needed the torch in her hand; the white moon overhead brought everything to glittering life. Her feet sank in the snow, but only to her ankles, and she realized that it must have stopped snowing soon after they made camp. The barking sounds grew louder, urging her feet on. Most likely the dogs had cornered fox or mountain cat, but deep inside Henne knew there was something more disturbing in Jagged Ear's bark. She quickened her pace.

Henne and Ryle entered a clearing near an outcropping of rocks. The dogs were at the far end of the clearing. Jagged Ear's hindquarters poked from a narrow fissure in the boulders. The dog was crouched, paws forward, rump high, barking excitedly, and Henne felt a quick rush of disappointment. Apparently it was only a cornered animal after all. She was about to turn around, head toward camp, when Rabbit Dancer darted across the clearing, hopping around Henne with expressive yips as if begging her to stay.

Henne laughed. "All right, Dancer," she said, rubbing the scruff of the dog's neck. "I'll take a look."

Henne crossed the clearing, calling Jagged Ear to her side. The dog refused to come, and Henne had to pull him away from the narrow opening, admonishing him in dark tones. Ryle followed close behind, reminding Henne not to get too close; there was no telling what might burst from the low opening. Henne squatted, restraining the dog, holding the torch aloft with the other hand. She peered into the darkness, expecting to see the red glow of an animal's eyes. Instead, she had to stifle a scream. A face. A man's face. His lips were painted black with dried blood crusting into his yellow beard. His eyes were closed, swollen, his thin face pale, the white mask of the Death Goddess. Henne sat on her heels, dismayed. "It's him," she said over her shoulder. "We're too late."

Ryle squatted close, peering inside. Henne wondered how long Gath had lain there curled against the cold. She pulled off a mitten, reaching into the shallow cavern, feeling for warmth. His breath tickled her hand, and she pulled it back as if stung. Gath was alive!

Henne jumped to her feet. "He breathes," she croaked in disbelief. She turned to Ryle. "Get Gelb and the travois. We have to get him out of there."

Ryle stood slowly, disbelief on his face also.

Henne stomped her foot impatiently. "Run," she commanded.

Ryle snapped to attention, turning to leave the clearing at a fast trot. The dogs followed close at his heels.

Henne paced to keep warm, thoughts spinning in her head. Gath needed heat and sustenance, fast. It would take too long to find wood dry enough to build a fire, and their tent was too small to accommodate one anyway. She stopped pacing. The cave, the steaming womb water of the Goddess, a place of rebirth! It was not far. Surely she could fight the rottenness of death there.

Ryle and Gelb entered the clearing, riding double. The men jumped off Moon and joined Henne. "We have to get him out of the cold," she said hurriedly, taking Ryle by the arm, guiding him toward the crevice.

The dogs barked wildly again as Ryle bent down and crawled forward into the dark cubby. The light of Henne's torch guided him as he reached to grab one

of Gath's arms. Ryle pulled. The man did not budge.
He adjusted his grip and pulled harder. Little by little
the big man's torso emerged from the opening, and
with it, the smell. He must have soiled himself, Henne
thought. Rotting, greasy cloth came away in Ryle's
hand. He grimaced and threw the cloth away before
reaching to pull again. Finally Gath was completely
out of the cave.

Henne inhaled sharply. Old strips of wool were
wrapped around his hands, offering very little protection from the cold. Gath's boots were no more than
pieces of leather tied around his feet with a strip of
sinew, his robe, a haphazard patchwork of fur. The
big man's beard was stained yellow with spittle, sores
chapped his face.

Ryle made a triangle sign over his heart, a symbol
of the womb and the protection of the Goddess. He
did not believe that the man, if it was a man, could
live much longer. Perhaps his spirit was already lingering in the blue shadows of the trees. Ryle exchanged
a fearful glance with Gelb as he stepped away from
the rangy body.

Henne had no time for the younger men's foolishness. She bent to lift Gath, gripping him under the
arms. "Help me get him on the travois," she barked.

Grudgingly Ryle and Gelb grabbed Gath's trunk
and feet. The man swung awkwardly between them as
they carried him to the travois and heavily set him
down. Gelb placed an oilskin tarp over the body then
they each took turns lashing Gath down, stretching
the ropes back and forth across the travois. When finished, they all stepped back, pulling a deep breath of
fresh air into their lungs. A moment of silence fell
between them.

Ryle looked into Henne's eyes, wondering at her
intentions. They brought only one tent. Surely she
didn't expect them to share it with this foul-smelling
creature. Henne read his look, and gave him a wry
smile that was also sympathetic.

"Not far from here is a cave," she explained, "a small cave, not large enough for all of us, but two can easily fit inside. I stayed there once when I was hunting. It is warmed with the womb water of the Goddess. We will take Gath there."

Ryle and Gelb exhaled an audible sound of relief. Henne eyed them sternly. "But we must work fast if we are to save Gath from the spirits," she continued. "As soon as we reach the cave, the two of you must take Moon and return to our camp, gather our things and bring them to me."

Both men nodded resolutely. Henne turned and threw a leg up and over Moon's back. Once seated she murmured to the horse, prodding her knees into the Moon's sides. The travois lurched forward. The men followed behind, but not too closely.

35

The horse stood above Enyana trembling with indignation, wide nostrils flaring, heaving a vapory fog into the dark night air. His feet did not trample her. Something held him back from hurting the girl with the mane that curled and twisted like dark water, the one with eyes that spoke the language of the horse. Why did she wish to do this thing to him? Why did she wish to subdue him, mount him, as he would mount a mare?

He stood rigidly, waiting for her response to his indignation and anger. No, he would not trample her, but neither would he allow her on his back.

Enyana lay in the snowdrift, the wind knocked out of her. Atum called frantically from the rock fence, asking if she was hurt, afraid that if he jumped down and ran toward her the stallion would become more aggressive. He was suddenly angry with himself for allowing Enyana to talk him into this. They should be sleeping in their huts, huddled in warm blankets, instead of sneaking out in the dark under the cold moon, trying to overcome the wild power of the horse. But Enyana had assured him that the Goddess would bless their efforts. Hadn't the stallion been following her around for many nights now, allowing her to tie sacks of grain on his back? It had seemed so plausible when she explained it, but his misgivings had grown stronger each night. They had been foolish to try this alone. He was about to jump down, run, and get help, when

Enyana elevated herself on her elbows. "I'm all right," she gasped. "Just give me . . . a moment."

Atum sat tensely on the fence, ready to run at the first sign of trouble. Enyana breathed deeply for a few moments, then stood. She walked slowly toward the stallion, talking in soothing tones. The horse visibly calmed, surmising the strange girl creature had given up her domination game, and he was in control again. He tossed his head as she lifted a hand to stroke his sleek flank, leaning against him. He leaned back. She put her cool forehead on his hot neck, cooing lowly. He snorted, nuzzling her hand for food.

Enyana looked around, desperate now, her mind grasping for something, anything to help her tame the animal. She was determined to do this tonight, before someone tried to stop her. She suspected that others in the encampment had guessed her intentions since the discovery of the missing grain bags behind the water trough. She gazed past the horse's back, beyond the inner corral to the outer fenced area. After the heaviest snows, the young people had to clear the corral so the horses could move around. As she gazed at the mounds piled outside, a memory came to her, a terrifying experience she'd had as a small child.

It had been a bright day. The sun was sparkling off the snow. She recalled being bored, tired of being cooped up in the house after a long handspan of gray days. She wandered from the village, heading for her favorite hiding place in an attempt to escape the chores that Grandmother Galea would surely to make her do. She strayed off the path, falling into the snowdrift, a deep hole of white terror. It had been hard to fight her way out. Over and over again she struggled in the snow, trying to climb her way through the deceptively soft-looking mounds with no support, nothing to grasp. She almost gave up, but even as a child she had known that if she didn't continue fighting, she would die. It was late afternoon when she finally worked her way out. She returned to the village, exhausted. She never told anyone, but she often suspected that Galea knew. The old woman hadn't said a word when she walked past her and fell into her sleeping blankets. Now that she was older, she understood that no child left the village without a watchful eye following them, and realized that her grandmother had probably been observing from a distance. One thing for sure, she never wandered away from the village in winter again.

Enyana's thoughts returned to the present and the horse standing in front of her. The answer to her dilemma worked its way to the surface of her mind. Of course. The snow!

She turned to Atum, hissing a whisper. "Open the gate."

Atum looked at her as if she were crazy.

Enyana's eyes became stormy, insistent. "I know what I'm doing," she said, flipping her head toward the stallion. "He can't fight me in the snow."

For a moment Atum thought he saw Henne's commanding presence in Enyana's features. But there was something more, something in the arrogant lift of her chin that he'd never seen before. Perhaps it was the possessive way she gazed at the stallion. Innately, he knew there would be no arguing with her. His impulse was to turn, leave, but he knew she would go on with her plan, and he was too deeply involved to turn back now, so he slowly made his way along the fence. It took longer than expected to slide the heavy wood poles away from the gate. Meanwhile, Enyana distracted the horse by feeding him handfuls of lentils, talking in gentle tones.

The stallion stepped aside nervously. There was something unsettling in the brush of the girl's fingers. Her voice became firmer; she moved closer. He was about to nip her arm when she vaulted, landing on his back, grasping the reins as she jumped.

The stallion whinnied outrage. The test for dominance was not over. He reared, attempting to toss her off, but she held tight. She was light as a feather, no more irritating than a black fly, but how dare she mount him. He turned to bite her leg, but she kicked at his head, jarring his jaw while slapping him with the reins. And then he saw it, the opening to freedom.

The stallion galloped for the gate, plunging into the snow. He pushed deeper, trying to reach the expanse beyond.

"Close the gate!" Enyana screamed.

Atum quickly closed the gate. Others heard the commotion and were awake, running toward the corral. The stallion bucked and kicked at the snow, floundering deeper and deeper. His flanks glistened with sweat, froth lined his muzzle. He reared again, bellowing rage, but the girl's hands wound tighter in his mane, her words were loud and hard. The moon rose high in the sky, and still she held on.

On an instinctual level, the horse understood. His body remembered the fight with the other stallion, the one with all the mares. This was like that. It was not so much strength, but determination that he had battled, and lost. Deeply, he understood the girl creature on his back wanted this more than anything and he knew she would never give it up; it was in her eyes, in her smell. She had mounted him, taken him. He slowed, sides heaving, and stopped kicking. He allowed her to steer him toward the gate again.

Yes, this strange girl creature would ride him, but no one else. After all, she was the leader of the herd.

36

Steam rose from the ground in front of them and the air was heavy with the smell of sulfur. The clearing was an eerie place, as if the Earth Goddess were breathing a vapory fog into the dark night air. The snow-covered earth stopped abruptly, melting into a ragged edge of cold and hot. The hot water seeping from the soil had discouraged plant life; there were no shrubs anywhere.

Henne dismounted, taking the horse by the reins, steering Moon carefully across oozing mud and clay. The small cave was not far now. She lifted her torch and glanced back at the men following her, giving them a look of caution, nodding toward the mud. It was slippery and they couldn't afford an accident right now, especially in the dark. Most people would have avoided the place, following the deer trails farther down the mountain. She was sure this was the reason Gath had not discovered the cave.

Henne resisted the urge to stop and check for Gath's breath, telling herself that if he was dead it was the Goddess's will, but her heart stilled at the thought. She didn't know why this foul man was suddenly so important to her, but she desperately wanted him to live.

After crossing the slick of mud and clay, the small group found themselves in the snow again. Henne led them around a few giant pines to a narrow but deep stream of steaming water. The stream cut through the snow, pooling in places where trees had fallen and boulders formed natural dams. She pointed upstream to a gashlike crevice in the hill. Water flowed from its opening.

"The cave is there," Henne said. "It is warm, but damp inside, and there's not much room to move around. We will have to remove his clothes here."

Ryle and Gelb nodded, turning to unhitch the travois, laying it flat. They helped Henne untie the ropes strapping Gath down. Henne squatted to remove his boots and robe, but everything from the legs down clung to his skin. Henne fought the bile rising in her throat. Gath's clothes were crusted with excrement and vomit; he must have been sick for a very long time. She planted the torch in the snow and took a deep breath, steeling her senses from the sight and odor of sickness. She removed her knife from its sheath and began to saw through the tangle of furs and cloth. The skin underneath was pale like the underbelly of a fish, and slick with grime.

Gath was thin, too thin. The hard edges of his bones protruded in places through skin. Scabs tore away in her hands as she removed the rotting cloth. Henne felt tears stinging her eyes. She wasn't one to cry, but she couldn't help remembering her own emaciated shape and the abuse she had put her body through in her grief over Shem, and wondered what torture churned in Gath's spirit.

Finally she was finished. Gath lay naked on the travois, his body exposed to the cold. She grabbed the torch and quickly motioned her companions to lift him, carrying him to the cave. The opening was low and narrow. Henne went in first, stooping, lighting the way. She slipped. One of her boots landed in the stream and hot water soaked through the leather. She regained her footing, cursing. She pressed herself against the cave wall, carefully avoiding another slip into the stream.

The tunnel bulged to her right, then opened to a

wider cavern. She sighed in relief. "We're here," she whispered, standing aside so the men could lay Gath down.

There was barely enough room for all of them to stand. The air was slightly steamy, warm from the hot spring gurgling near the far wall. Henne turned, hurrying to lead the men from the cramped enclosure. Once outside, she grabbed Moon's riding blanket and the water bag.

"You two go back and get our things," she said, waving the men away. "I'll stay. Hopefully he'll be awake by the time you return and we will know what spirits must be fought to save him."

Ryle shifted uneasily on his feet. "What if he tries to hurt you?"

Henne snorted. "He's too sick and weak. Besides, we've taken his knife and spear." She didn't add that Gath was not one to harm a woman. They wouldn't understand. Most of the villagers believed that all the Herders were evil and violent, but she knew this was not true.

As the men led Moon away, Henne turned quickly toward the entrance of the cave. She was about to go inside when she realized how foolish this would be. The air in the cave was steamy, moist, and soon she'd be sweating profusely in her wool wrap and furs. The slightest amount of dampness would turn her clothes into a frozen death when she stepped back out into the night air. She stood at the cave opening, thinking, and then once more planted her torch in the snow. She stripped down to her loincloth and boots, wrapping the other garments in her long fur cloak. Shivering, she found a deep fissure in the rocks and shoved the bundle inside so it would stay dry. She picked up the torch, the water skin, and the riding blanket and entered the cave.

The torch she carried did not like the dampness of the cave. It hissed and sputtered, but grudgingly continued to burn. Yellow light fell over Gath's naked body. Henne squatted to get a closer look.

He was a big man; dark-haired, pale-eyed. His abundant chest and arm hair lay flat against his ashen skin. Jutting bones and gaunt features seemed at odds with the robust figure she had once known. She reached out to touch him, hoping to find life in his skin, but he was cool. Henne sat back on her heals, dismayed. She wasn't a healer like Yana or Ninka. It was not easy for her to stay at the bedside of the ill or injured. The weak seemed to swallow her strength, requiring more than she could give, and Henne couldn't wait to get away from them. But this was Gath, someone who understood the ways of the Horse People. This time she was the hungry one, wanting his strength, a taste of the male power of the People of the Herd, and she was confused by these feelings. Deep inside she knew that Gath shared her confusion. She would never forget his accusing eyes and the words he had said when her arrow was aimed at his heart. *Would you really kill me, Henne?*

Henne bent to cover him with her riding blanket. If only she could warm him faster. Perhaps if she rubbed his skin, but then she realized his skin was too fragile, the sores too raw. Instead she stood and rubbed the sides of her arms, a nervous gesture as she tried to think. She wracked her brain, trying to remember the charms and prayers Ninka uttered when fighting death. She thought of the time Yana had been dying, how Galea had covered her sister's fevered body with cool cloths while Ninka chanted a song about the womb water of the Goddess.

Henne's eyes flew to the hot stream. She grabbed the blanket off Gath, scrambling for the water. Gath wasn't hot, he was cold! She dipped the heavy blanket in the water, wrinkling her nose against the smell of horse sweat and wet wool. She dipped it again. The water scalded her hands, but she didn't care. Her own sweat trickled down her face, under her arms, mingling with the damp air of the cave. The thoroughly soaked blanket was too heavy to lift, so she dragged it across the rock floor, letting it cool for a moment before carefully covering Gath's body.

She waited. There was no response. She sat on her haunches, trying to sing like Ninka. She sang of the life-giving waters of the Goddess, but the effort felt awkward, false. Her voice sounded harsh, lonely in the cave. Gath was not a man of the Goddess, just as she was not a woman of the Herd.

A great sadness engulfed her. She remembered the first time she'd seen the Herders wielding their spears of destruction. She looked down on Gath. She had heard rumors; more barbarians from the north were coming to the lands of the Goddess. Many people would not survive; others would become slaves, conforming in order to live. But there would be many on both sides, good people like Gath, who would become lost in the destruction. She hung her head and began to weep, realizing she was weeping for the futures of their clashing tribes. She remembered Gath's words. *The Goddess left us when you ran away, Henne.*

Henne doubled over, feeling her heart tear with guilt. Only once had she cried like this; the night she'd smothered Ralic, killing the man she had come to love and admire. Now she knew why it was so important that Gath survive. His spirit held the seed of hope. He had been willing to reach out in his confusion, open his heart to a new understanding of the Goddess, but it was too hard to be alone, and he'd gone half wild in the effort. She knew this, because she knew herself.

Henne curled up next to Gath, wrapping her arms around him, holding him as if holding the innocent child she'd once been. She whispered and sang between her tears, begging him to live. She even prayed to his Sky God, realizing the Goddess and the Sky God had already seeded a child—a child of suffering. She wondered who would nurture this infant born of rape who bawled so lustily its confusion? Who would wrap it in a blanket, smoothing the tears away? *The Goddess left us when you ran away, Henne.*

Gath stirred. He moaned a woman's name, and something that Henne didn't understand. She gulped back her sobs, bending over him, straining to hear, but he slipped once more into silent dreams. Henne's heart pounded with hope. Something she had said, something she had done momentarily brought him back from the spirit world. She jumped up, dragging the blanket off Gath's body to the stream. She dipped it again in the hot water. Suddenly, the light of her torch sputtered and died.

"No, Goddess," she said through clenched teeth. "I will not let him go."

Henne worked all night. She crawled across the cave floor, the rocks bruising her knees, returning again and again with soft words and the warm blanket. The silky black air of the cave accompanied her in the blind touching, and the believing. Somewhere in the nothingness, the fear she had been harboring since her time with the Herders fell away. She was creating something new in this dark, moist place. She could feel it forming. Sweetness returned to her heart. Henne came to understand what it truly meant to be a woman of the Goddess—a magical channel of transformation, leading to birth and change. Over and over again she felt for Gath's face and his breath, whispering words of comfort. She sensed he was growing stronger, choosing life over death. He began to breathe deeper, and then she heard a wonderful sound; Gath snored. Relieved, she laughed out loud, collapsing against his warm body and blanket. Moments later she was also breathing deeply, and snoring softly.

Later that morning, Ryle and Gelb entered the cave and found Henne asleep, draped over Gath. The sight of their Hunting Priest, nearly naked, and wrapped around the dark stranger was disturbing, but Henne was obviously exhausted. The two men silently backed out of the cave, allowing the two of them to rest.

The sky was indigo blue, and the sun glittered off the snow. Ryle found dry wood at the base of a large fir protected from the weather by the large, low-lying limbs of the tree. It had been days since he'd had a warm bowl of juniper tea, so he decided to build a fire. The flames were just beginning to crackle when he noticed Henne standing at the mouth of the cave, rubbing the sleep from her face. She shivered. Ryle grabbed one of the tarps from the travois and took it to her, placing the heavy cloth around her shoulders. Henne turned to him, smiling gratefully.

"I'm heating water," he said. "Would you like a morning meal of warm grain?"

Henne's eyes clouded with worry. "No, not yet. I need to feed Gath first. He is very weak, and I believe he hasn't had water in days."

Henne reached into a fissure in the rocks, retrieving her fur parka. She handed the tarp back to Ryle, putting the cloak on. She quickly crossed to the travois, rummaging around until she found her traveling pack. She retrieved a small bundle, a repair kit every traveler carried. She pulled out a bone needle large enough to puncture through thick leather. She rummaged deeper until she found a wooden cup.

Ryle perceived that there was something different about Henne this morning. She was obviously concerned about Gath, but her movements were less tense, more relaxed. Nervousness was gone from her face, and there was softness in her eyes. When he had covered Henne with the thick wool blanket, she had smiled gratefully, as if really seeing him. Ryle watched her curiously, wondering at the change.

Henne walked away from the travois toward Moon. She talked in soothing tones while combing the mare's mane and neck with her fingers, examining the horse closely. She lifted the needle and Ryle's heart jumped in surprise as she pricked a small bulging vein in Moon's neck, catching the stream of blood in the cup until it was half full. The horse snorted, but calmed quickly with Henne's reassuring touch. Ryle quickly crossed the clearing. He didn't have to question her.

"I saw this done while living with the Herders," she explained, bending to scoop a handful of snow. She packed the snow against the injury until it stopped bleeding. Ryle could see that the hole was actually a very small intrusion, something that would heal within a few days. "The Herders do this only during the starving moons, when food is scarce," she continued. "This way they do not have to kill their horses."

"But we don't need food," Ryle said, sounding confused. "There is plenty in our packs and on the travois."

"A sick man cannot eat balls of fat, or chew dried meat," Henne explained patiently, walking across the clearing. Ryle followed her to the fire. She dribbled warm water from the boiling bag into the cup, mixing the water and blood. "Gath is a man of the Horse People. This will give him strength," she said with confidence.

Ryle frowned with disgust. How could Henne give Gath the blood of a live horse? If this was a custom of the Herders, it explained why they were wild, uncivilized. The horse's essence coursed through their veins, tying them to animal ways. No wonder they fought like stallions, trampling those who did not follow their customs. "How can you give him the blood of a living spirit," he said, a hint of disdain in his voice. "It is not done."

Henne noted the repulsion in Ryle's eyes. "We drink the blood of the bull," Henne challenged, "We accept the bull's sacrifice as the blood of the womb, death as potential life. The Herders find our ways just as unacceptable." Henne looked down at the cup, realizing she was wasting precious time. Gath needed her help now, and it would take too long to explain the ways of the Herders to Ryle.

Henne turned away and walked up the incline of the hill, carefully carrying the drink so as not to spill it. She set the cup down on a rocky niche near the mouth of the cave, removed her cloak, and picked up the cup again before entering. Once inside, Henne stopped for a moment to let her eyes adjust. Daylight from the entrance diffused the dark. Light played off the steamy air in a fuzzy warm haze; it felt thick in her lungs as she breathed. Her eyes went to Gath's pale body stretched out on the stone floor. Earlier that morning she had removed the blanket so he would not become overheated. She quickly crossed the slick floor, kneeling to feel his forehead.

Gath's body heat felt right, and he wasn't sweating profusely, but he couldn't continue without liquids. She sat down, pulling his head onto her lap. She forced a finger between his lips, making a pocket in his cheek, then carefully poured a mouthful of the blood mixture into the pocket. He spluttered half of it out, but Henne was pleased to see him swallow. Gath moaned, talking in his sleep, but didn't rouse completely from his dreams. She continued until the liquid was gone, then took water from the water skin and repeated the process. Once satisfied, Henne stood and made her way out of the cave, pulling on her winter parka at the entrance, walking purposely toward the fire.

This time, when Ryle offered her warmed grain and juniper tea, Henne accepted gladly, responding with a genuine smile of thanks. She squatted with the two men near the small fire. While she ate they talked of the village and the captured horses. They avoided the subject of the stranger asleep in cave. Eventually their conversation dwindled to things that didn't matter, and the avoidance became obvious. They fell silent.

Henne sighed and put her bowl of tea down. First she looked into Ryle's eyes, then into Gelb's. "I want both of you to leave," she said, her voice dropping. "Gath is sick, very sick. I must fight the rottenness of death alone." Ryle looked like he was about to object, but Henne's voice rose over his protests. "The People of the Herd worship a foreign god," she continued. "After death, their ancestors remain forever in the Underworld. I know Gath dreams of them. They are calling him to join them. I'm afraid he has already started the journey, and I must bring him back. I know the rituals of the Herders, and perhaps I can appease Gath's ancestors, but not if they smell confusion and fear. The two of you do not understand these things. I am afraid your fear will draw angry spirits."

Ryle rubbed his square jaw with the back of his hand, baffled. The people of the Goddess understood that death was the womb of life. The spirit of a loved one lived on in the people. Of course a portion of the spirit stayed with the ancestors, but sacred breath continued to live in the wind, lifting the wings of sky birds. How could anyone believe that one remained forever in the Underworld?

Henne knew she wasn't being completely truthful with her companions. She was almost sure that Gath was over the threat of death, but he was weak, and it would take days for him to recover completely. During this time she needed to be alone with him. She needed time to gentle his spirit without interference from Ryle and Gelb. The men of the Herd were different from the men of her homeland. They competed for wives, food, and the admiration of the headman. When Gath became strong again, the presence of Gelb and Ryle would only make him wary. And if Gath were to live with her people, she would have to find a way past the horrible thing that haunted him.

Ryle stood. "You can't expect us to leave you here with that creature," he scowled, flipping his head contemptuously toward the cave. "He's not a man. He has the stench of a wild animal, but even a beast would take better care than that one."

Henne nodded her agreement, but something in Ryle's words gave her the answer she needed. She stood slowly, meeting his gaze. "You are right," she said evenly. "Gath is not a man of the Goddess. Perhaps he is no longer a man at all. But I've been trained in the ways of the priestesses, and I know what brings life to a man. I will initiate him in Her ways." She stepped closer, eyes narrowing, and a bit of the old Henne showed through. "But you forget," she added coolly. "I am also the Hunting Priest of the people, purging rottenness from the earth. Either Gath will become one of us . . . or he will die." She stepped back.

Ryle grumbled. Gelb stood at Ryle's elbow. The younger man darted anxious glances at the cave. "Perhaps it is better that we leave now," he said quickly. "If we are lucky, the weather will hold and we'll make it back to the village before nightfall tomorrow."

Ryle turned to Henne. "But what about food? In a handful of days your dried meat and fat balls will be gone. The weather may take a turn for the worse. You could get stranded here." He nodded toward the cave. "And he will want to eat once his strength returns."

Henne put her hands on her hips, eyes flashing. "I am your Hunting Priest. I will find food."

Ryle did not back down. He returned her challenge with a frustrated glare. He wanted to go, pack up and leave without a backward glance, but he was a man, protector of his clan. Henne may be his Hunting Priest, but how could he leave a woman alone in the wilderness with a dangerous enemy?

Henne examined Ryle's face, and for a strange instant another young man glared at her through his eyes. She saw Shem in his younger brother's features, Shem's determination and possessiveness. She suddenly understood his frustration. She smiled grudgingly, her mouth twisting in a grin. "If Gath and I have not returned to the village in two hands of days, the men of the village may come to my rescue."

Ryle, brows raised at her sudden submissiveness, had to smile. Henne's words made him realize his foolishness. Henne was a strong woman. She had faced a whole tribe of the Herders, and had lived to escape them. She could most certainly care for herself and a sick man for a handspan of days. He ducked his chin. "I will inform Yana and the elders you will be home soon," he said with grudging admiration.

Henne watched the men gathering their things. It didn't take long. In order to travel quickly they would leave most of the supplies behind, but Henne insisted they take the dogs. She didn't want to have to worry about them. She kept Moon and the travois with her, reasoning that she might need them to transport Gath.

It felt strange watching Ryle and Gelb disappear down the hill into a grove of trees. They were men of the Goddess—good, strong men, and she had to restrain an impulse to call them back. Henne took a deep breath as her eyes strayed up the incline toward the cave. She was alone once more with the power of the Horse People, but this time she was not hoping for escape. This time she would dance with the bull, mount it, wrestling with forces beyond her understanding.

37

Enyana, her dark hair loose and wild, raced through the heart of their small valley mounted on a large stallion, carving a dark path through the shallow snow, obviously showing off her riding skills to the village. She rode with ease, as if the horse and girl were one.

Yana put a hand on the tiny mound of her belly as if to protect the life growing there. She had been hiding her pregnancy under the long robes of winter. The people were so unsettled now, so unsure. She didn't want to trouble them more. Her thoughts returned to Enyana. How had she done it? How had Enyana tamed the wild heart of the horse so quickly? But even as the question formed in Yana's mind, she knew the answer: Enyana had found her power. The blood of the girl's ancestors galloped in her veins. Already, the People of the Horse had come to their valley; the invasion had begun with the determination of one young girl. Yana inhaled sharply as the life in her womb kicked an objection. "No, young one," she whispered. "There is no going back."

On the other side of the mountains, near a salty lake at the edge of a large plateau, stood another leader, dreaming of conquest while observing his son, Gilash, glide across the grassy plain on the back of his favorite gelding. The headman's heart swelled with pride at the sight of his tawny-haired boy on the magnificent steed. Gilash was almost a man now. Next spring they would ride together, conquering Henne and her people, destroying forever the power of the Goddess. The People of the Herd would soon wake from a lazy slumber, leave off suckling the breasts of the Goddess of this land. They would seek other lands, other peoples to possess. He would leave his son a legacy of strong people, and a powerful herd of horses.

Far to the west and south of the Herders, in the homeland of the Sea People, Tern stood on a beach near the Great Waters of the Goddess. The briny water advanced toward his feet, a front of foam that crisscrossed then fell back, leaving bubbles and lacquered sand behind. He lifted his chin, gazing across the ocean to a handful of purple smudges on the horizon, the beginning of a chain of islands. Above them, under charcoal clouds, a thin string of birds wavered, heading south for the winter. He watched until they became obscure, blending with the gray clouds. His lip dipped to a worried frown.

A trader had come from the land of grasses with rumors in his mouth. It was said that Enak was very angry. The headman's trek to find Henne in the eastern ranges had failed, but he was more determined than ever to destroy her. He was offering precious stones, knives, obsidian, salt, slaves, anything in trade for information of her whereabouts. Tern turned around. The western passes were covered in snow, dangerous now. He couldn't get back to Yana, yet, but he had to warn her, help her prepare the people, convincing the elders that they must cross the mountains at the earliest opportunity. He would leave at the first snowmelt, regardless of the threat of avalanches. He shifted his gaze to the village situated on a hill overlooking the bay. Dagron would not know he was gone until it was too late, but he would quickly realize it was for the best. There was no use in risking both their lives. Besides, someone had to stay behind, making sure the Sea People worked diligently, repairing and readying the boats to ferry their people to the islands. He turned once again to look out over the angry swells. A wave crashed over a boulder, sending a spray of fine mist into the air. The dark islands were no longer distinguishable, having merged with low clouds and the heaving sea. He found himself beseeching the Goddess. In the stark face of winter, the excursion to the islands seemed daunting, but the idea of facing the barbarians, far worse.

38

Gath did not wake until the third day. Henne began to wonder if he would ever open his eyes and see her. A couple of times he had, but she quickly realized that he was still in the place of dreams. He looked right at her, speaking in his guttural tongue, calling her another woman's name, Mern. His foreign words were fog in her brain, hazy and hard to recall, but after a few days the language came back to her.

It was apparent that Gath cared a great deal for Mern. The first time Henne washed him, running a warm cloth over what was left of his wasted muscles, he responded by pulling her to him, burying his face in her breasts, kissing her, begging for forgiveness. Shocked, Henne struggled to escape, but he started crying. Gath seemed so distraught she couldn't help smoothing the lines of his forehead with a caress, comforting him like a child, until he drifted into a mindless sleep in her arms. As he calmed, she realized that she really had forgiven Gath, forgiven all those who had once enslaved her.

While Gath slept, she fashioned a tunic and leggings using fabric from one of the tarps. The clothes were certain to be bulky, uncomfortable, but they would be warm, and the lanolin in the wool would keep the cloth from irritating Gath's healing skin. She returned to the cave to take another measurement for his sleeve. She found him sitting up, leaning against a boulder, a look of speculation on his face. Henne stopped in her tracks, holding the measuring string in one hand and an oil lamp in the other, wondering if he was seeing her, or Mern.

"I was told death was a dark place, dry and dusty." He paused. "But it is moist here . . . comfortable." He looked around the cave then directly at Henne. "And I never expected to be cared for by a servant of the Goddess."

There was no reprisal in his voice, just curiosity. Still, Henne was suddenly uneasy. The last few days she had come to feel safe with Gath, in tune with his needs and emotions. Now that he was fully awake, she realized many harvest seasons had passed since her days with the Herders, and she hardly knew Gath at all. She caught him grazing her breasts with his eyes, and realized that he obviously wasn't the same young man she'd once known; the old Gath would never have looked at his headman's woman in such a way. She looked down, dismayed. She wore only her loin-cloth and the temporary boots she'd fashioned. The women of the Herd were never seen unclad outside their husband's tents. Gath was sure to get the wrong impression if she didn't explain.

"You are not dead," she said, speaking as clearly as she could in his language. "But you have been wrestling with spirits." She cocked her head. "Apparently they have decided to let you live." She briskly crossed the room, squatting to measure the length of his arm with the string. "I am making you a tunic and leggings," she said quickly to hide her discomfort at being close to him. "Those you were wearing were not acceptable. You have noticed that we both are not wearing clothes. I had to remove my clothes to take care of you; it is too damp to wear anything in here. If you recall, the white hair of the Death Goddess blankets the land. Everything is frozen. The land is asleep, just as you have been." She started to stand, but he grabbed her arm.

"Mern was here with me in the Underworld," he

said, searching her eyes. "So was our little girl, Ree. My women were not dead . . ." Hope quivered in Gath's voice. Henne's heart went out to him. What words of comfort could she say?

She smiled sadly, placing a hand over the one gripping her arm. "This is not your Underworld," she repeated quietly. "We are in a cave. My people believe caves are sacred, places of dreams." She looked around. "Here the womb of the Goddess is understood. Obviously the Goddess gave you a sweet dream of your wife and child. Perhaps She was trying to show you that they are not in your Underworld . . . but someplace else."

Gath let go of her. His head fell backward against the boulder. He threw an arm over his face, his voice grating over a sob. "Why did you bring me to this place, Henne," he asked, taking a deep breath, squeezing the words past the pain in his chest. "I would have stayed in that world of dreams."

Henne swallowed hard. She knew he would ask this question. She had been rehearsing an answer for days, but now that it had been asked, she was suddenly unsure. Would she be able to convince him? Could she make him believe in her, believe in the Goddess again? She decided to be honest, asking what was in her heart. She had to know if Gath truly wished to embrace the Goddess.

"I know you cared deeply for Ree and Mern," she said. "You spoke to Mern often in your dreams." Henne hesitated, and a hint of speculation crept into her voice. "Sometimes you used the language of the Goddess, so I guessed she was one of your slaves."

Gath dropped his arm, a look of reproach on his face. "She was my wife, Henne," he said, anger in his face. "She came to me of her own free will. We met while I was bartering with the men of her village." Gath closed his eyes and leaned his head back again, suddenly weary of the painful memories haunting him. He would never forget the first time he saw Mern's

plump cheeks and lively smile. She walked around
him, arms crossed as if inspecting a fine gelding. Her
eyes danced at his discomfort. She loudly informed
her father that she would take him, crude as he was.
Everyone laughed. They settled in his tent not far
from her village along a swift river. At first Mern did
not seem to mind being second wife.

Gath opened his eyes, glaring balefully at Henne.
"I know it may be hard for you to believe that a
women of the Goddess might choose to be with one
of us, but not all men of the Herd are brutes. Many
have come to enjoy the life offered by those who re-
vere your Goddess. We've stopped wandering. We
sleep with sacks of grain in our tents. We are content
to know the bellies of our children are full. We trade
cattle and horses for barley, wheat, and other useful
items. Many of my people have come to believe that
Ralic was right when he said a greater Herd would
grow from the union of our peoples." Gath looked
away. "He should never have died . . . and you should
never have left," he said bitterly.

Henne's sighed. There was so much hurt and anger
between them. She lifted her eyes to his so he might
see the truth of her words. "I would have been
killed—sacrificed to your Sky God so Ralic would not
have to go the Underworld alone. You know this,
Gath. You would not have fought for me; the love of
the Goddess had not taken root in your people. Yes,
your lives since then have changed, but try to remember how it was then."

Gath avoided her eyes. Henne was right. He probably wouldn't have fought for her, just as he had not
fought for Mern. Part of him still believed the Sky
God was stronger than the Goddess of this land, but
he had half expected, hoped that Henne would prove
herself, fighting, showing the people she was favored
by the gods. Wasn't that how the scepter of leadership
was won, by proving strength? But Henne ran away.
Her defection had seemed cowardly, as if the Goddess

abandoned their Sky God with no thought of the consequences. He turned his head away.

Henne could see that Gath was done talking. She put her palms on her knees and pushed to a stand. "You must be hungry," she said. "A stew is cooking over the fire outside. I will see if it is ready."

Henne left the cave without a backward glance. Actually, she was anxious to leave. She needed to gather her thoughts. Gath was still very despondent, his willingness to live fragile. She understood this. She had to help him find a way past his anger. She dipped a boxwood bowl into the rabbit stew. While it cooled, she took a strip of cloth and bound her breasts. She cut another strip for Gath, reasoning they would both be more comfortable covered.

Henne entered the cave. She dropped the strip of felt in Gath's lap. "When you are finished eating," she said trying to sound casual, "I will help you tie the loincloth."

Gath nodded stiffly, and spread the cloth over his waist and thighs. Henne knelt beside him, holding the bowl to his lips. He took sips of the meaty broth laced with an herb he'd never tasted before. Some dribbled into his beard, but he was too disinterested and weak to wipe it away, so Henne did it for him.

They didn't talk. Henne sensed that Gath needed time to think, time to trust her again. She concentrated on nursing him. Soon the broth was gone, leaving chunks of meat and herb in the bottom of the bowl. She tore the meat with her teeth into smaller pieces, placing them one at a time into his sore mouth. He chewed slowly, painfully. He pointed to the water skin in the corner and Henne crossed the cave to fetch it, pouring a splash into the bowl. When he was done drinking, she helped him urinate into the empty bowl, then set it aside.

"I will help you with your loincloth now," Henne offered.

Gath watched Henne from the corners of his eyes,

observing the intimate way she went about caring for
him. He realized how much she had gone through,
how much she was willing to go through to keep him
alive, and for a moment his defenses fell. He reached
out and touched her cheek. "Why do you do this,
Henne?" he asked.

Henne's eyes dropped to the cloth in her hands.
Amazingly, by nurturing Gath something inside her
had begun to heal. How could she explain this to him?
Each time she put salve on his wounds, gave him
water, cleaned his excrement, she was tending her own
wounds. She hardly understood it herself. She looked
up, a much simpler answer to his question on her lips.
"It is the way of the Goddess to nurture the sick and
injured,"she said.

Gath thought he saw tears glitter behind Henne's
eyes. He knew something more burdened her heart,
but he was too tired to pursue it. There would be time
to talk later. He leaned against the boulder once
again. "We can tie the loincloth tomorrow," he said
to her through closed eyes. "I will sleep now."

39

Yana dreamed of Tern. She looked down from the peak of a high mountain. He was far below, struggling to get to her, but his feet were caught in sticky mud, and he couldn't lift them. He seemed so far away, desperate. He cupped his hands around his mouth, calling for her to come to him, but the wind blew his words away. She yelled back, told him to stay there, she was coming, she'd bring help. She made an attempt to move toward him, but couldn't; her feet were encased in ice. Her heart began to pound in panic. How could she go to him when she was trapped also? She started to call out when one word came to her on the breeze. "Hurry."

Yana woke with a start. Her feet had somehow slipped out of her sleeping furs. She quickly pulled them in, rubbing them together for warmth. The dream had been a spirit dream, she was sure of it. Her mind groped with the images. Didn't mud come with the spring rains? But the ice encasing her feet suggested it was still winter in the mountains.

Hurry, he had said.

"We will come," she whispered to the night shadows.

"Your people are evil!" Gath yelled, knocking the bowl Henne offered from her hands.

He stood, anger giving him strength. He gripped her arms, shaking her. "You with your soft words and

gentle ways." He sneered. "You tease a man with
your fingers and tongue, your kisses suck the power
from his veins like a blood-tapped horse, until he is
too weak to fight you."

Henne's first instinct was to escape, run, but then
she realized this was exactly what Gath wanted. Two
days had passed since he'd awakened, and under her
care, he was growing stronger. His initial despondency
gave way to the real cause of his illness—anger; the
pain between them finally surfaced like a boil that
needed lancing. She had felt the heat of his anger
smoldering, and understood that this also must pass
before the real healing could begin. Now was not the
time to pull away.

He leered, his face close to hers, his fingers pinching
her flesh. "Your Goddess does not fight with honor
like a strong man," he said, his voice heavy with sar-
casm. "She presents herself as a harmless serpent, saying she is only there to keep the tent clean of rodents.
All the while she invades his spirit like an evil wind,
taking a man's breath!"

Henne closed her eyes against his tirade. He shook
her once more and she let him, knowing he would
demand a response; Gath wanted answers. She opened
her eyes, gazing directly into his fury. "Mern did not
take your power, just as I did not take Ralic's power.
She was a woman of the Goddess . . . that is all."
Henne hesitated, then continued. "A woman of the
Goddess who loved you."

Gath threw her against the wall of the cave. "No,"
he bellowed, his eyes crazed. "She did not love me."
He put his face in his hands. "She threw herself into
the river, killing herself to escape me."

Henne stumbled but regained her footing. She put
a hand to her head where it had hit the wall. "Why?"
she whispered more to herself than to Gath.

Gath laughed harshly. "I didn't believe her. I told
her that many sons would suckle her breasts. I told
her to forget our daughter. Later I found Mern's body,

and saw in my first wife's eyes Ree's death. Mern was right. My first wife had stolen Ree's breath, and now Mern was dead. I killed her with my disbelief." He looked at his shaking hands as if he detested them. He choked on his words. "And then I killed my first woman in anger, the mother of my sons," he said haltingly. "I killed her . . . with these hands."

Henne moaned. A hand went to her mouth. She remembered the jealous fights between the women of the Herd. A wife's status depended on the pleasure she gave and the amount of sons she provided her husband. As a woman of the Goddess, Mern must have been brokenhearted when Gath dismissed her accusations, believing he thought their daughter nothing compared to the wife who had provided him sons. But Henne suspected that Gath was just as devastated by the death of their daughter, too distraught to understand how his words of future sons, words only meant as comfort, had destroyed the hope in Mern's spirit. It was obvious he knew this now. Henne's heart ached for him, for the sorrow of misunderstandings between their peoples.

"Mern was in pain over the death of your daughter," Henne whispered over the lump in her throat. "She didn't know what she was doing. Just as you didn't when you attacked your first wife."

Gath was silent for a moment. "It is not that easy, Henne," he said bitterly.

Henne pinned him with her eyes. They stood and stared at each other. An unspoken understanding passed between them; she had loved a man of the Herd, he, a woman of the Goddess. They had wrestled with the gods, and lost. Henne couldn't help thinking of Shem's battle with the bull.

"No, it isn't easy," she agreed.

After that day, something changed between Gath and Henne. They found a mutual respect, treating each other gently. Gath tried to be more pleasant. He agreed to return home with her, help her train the horses, but said that once done, he would move on. Henne noted with satisfaction that Gath seemed to have come to terms with the deaths of his wives and the part he had played. The deep despondency left his eyes, replaced by a more mature wisdom, a wistful sadness, but the terrible anger was gone. One morning she found him standing at the cave entrance in only his loincloth.

"I'm ready to leave this dark, wet place," he stated. "You said you have clothes for me?"

Henne shook her head. "First you must do something for me," she answered mysteriously.

Gath raised his brows.

"It will be pleasant," she promised, walking toward him with a blanket in her arm and pair of roughly stitched leather boots dangling from a thong. She handed the boots to him. He noted that they were stuffed with hay to absorb the dampness of his feet. He squatted, shivering, jerking the tying strings awkwardly as he put them on.

"Now may I have my clothes?"

"Not yet," she smiled, throwing the blanket over his shoulders.

Henne gave him her arm for support. He was still weak so he allowed her to lead him down the hill through the snow. They came to a steaming pool fed by a hot spring. A cold mountain stream also fed the pool, cooling the water's temperature just enough to make it pleasing. Henne removed the blanket from his shoulders and motioned him to sit down in the warm water between the boulders that dammed the stream. He looked at her as if she were crazy.

"You will enjoy it," she insisted.

Gath decided to humor her. How else was he going to get the clothes he wanted. He grappled with his boots and set them aside. He sank into the water and his face registered instant pleasure. The water's soothing touch calmed him like a woman's caress. The

water fizzed about him in little bubbles that prickled
his skin, stripping away aches in his muscles. He inhaled a long deep breath and let it out slowly, sinking
deeper before glancing up at Henne.

She smiled a self-satisfied smirk. "I will be back
shortly with your clothes," she said.

Gath leaned back into the water, slitting his eyes in
her direction. "Humm. No hurry," he responded in a
noncommittal voice. She turned away, and as he
watched her trudge determinedly up the hill toward
their camp, the memory of the conversation they'd
had the night before returned. Once again he was
amazed at how complicated and interesting these
women of the Goddess seemed to be. It had been a
small argument, but Henne had certainly gotten the
best of him.

He had been reprimanding her for leaving the People of the Herd. "You should have fought death,
Henne," he had scolded. "You were the Goddess to
my people. They expected you to fight for your right
to lead."

Henne stood, exasperated. "I had a child in my
womb—Ralic's daughter. I couldn't fight. Even if I
had wanted to, my people do not battle each other."

His jaw jutted forward. "A leader must prove his
strength, how else can he protect his people?"

Henne began to pace like a caged cat, but there was
not enough space in the cramped cave. She stopped.
She crossed her legs and sank to the floor, elbows on
her knees, chin in her palms. Although she had dis-
tanced herself from him, she seemed determined to
make him understand. She stared into his eyes, thinking, then straightened her spine and dropped her
hands. This time she spoke slowly, quietly, as if explaining something to a child.

"I could never have killed another to gain the position of your headman; it never occurred to me." She
shook her head at the foreign thought. "Our high
priestess—or priest," she corrected, seeing Gath

frown, "is chosen by the elders. One who shows promise is chosen, a dreamer, or seer who has been trained
for many harvest seasons. He or she must be one who
listens carefully to the wisdom of the elders. After the
elders choose, the villagers gather to agree or disagree.
No decision is made without the consent of all.

Gath's brows pulled together in concentration. He
recalled a conversation long ago, a discussion he'd had
with Mern. She tried to explain this concept of
agreement, but it made no more sense now than it did
then. His people never agreed on anything; fights
often broke out over cattle, wives, and other goods.
The people needed a strong man, a man feared and
respected to settle disputes. No one dared challenge
the word of the Headman, unless he wanted a fight
to the death, taking the headman's place as leader.
Gath pulled on his long beard. This idea of agreement
had no strength in it.

Henne watched Gath toy with his beard and knew
his doubts. "Our leaders have knowledge," she stated,
lifting her head proudly. "Knowledge that insures the
strength of leadership."

Gath quirked an eyebrow, she had his attention
now.

"Tell me," she asked, eyes challenging. "Do the
People of the Herd know when a filly or colt is going
to be the strongest mare or stallion?"

Gath snorted. "The men of the Herd know more
about their horses than their children.

Henne rolled her eyes. She knew he exaggerated,
but not by much. "So you agree that it is easy to spot
the stallion that shines beyond the rest," she continued. "Your people groom the animal, train it, feed it
well. If done right, the animal is a great asset to the
herd, and its dominance goes unchallenged until one
greater comes along."

Gath nodded his head. He could see what Henne
was getting at; the comparison was a good one. The
strongest and smartest ruled the herd, just as the

strongest man ruled the tribe. It was apparent Henne understood.

Henne inhaled deeply. "You may be surprised to know that our ideas about leadership are very similar," she continued. "Our elders watch for that one special person who stands out among the others. They spend many years grooming the individual, training them, watching them grow. All the people come to admire the person's beauty, inner strength, and power in the Goddess. By the time the individual is ready to take his or her place among the elders, the people have accepted them already—trusting their power. This person has great influence over the community."

Henne's voice dropped and she spoke her words carefully so he would understand. "I knew this. I was trained as a child, taught the secrets of the priestesses, given the knowledge of chants and songs to influence people. Why do you think your people accepted me so readily as a consort to your headman, and as priestess of the Goddess."

Gath's lips parted, surprised. Henne was right. His people had accepted her almost immediately, without a question of her strength. She overtook them with her beauty, her regal power, like a lead mare in a herd of horses. Now that he thought of it, the wild mare controlled the actions of the herd, nipping or isolating wayward colts and fillies, teaching them the rules of the group by example. The stallion only protected his herd from other stallions, or warned of predators lurking nearby. He had gazed at Henne, amazement on his face. Maybe there was some merit to this idea of "agreement" after all; he would have to think on it further.

His thoughts were interrupted by Henne's approach. Her arms were piled high with the drying blanket and his clothes. She dropped them on a flat boulder where the wind had blown away the snow. She held a flint knife and a stick in her hand.

Henne's face and tone were slightly apologetic.

"There is one more thing that you must allow me," she said, dropping her fur coat on top of the pile of clothes.

Gath eyed her warily as she squatted to remove her boots. Was Henne about to initiate him in some strange ritual? He had heard rumors of blood sacrifices, wanton dancing. Henne looked up and caught his worried frown. Her eyes dropped to the knife, then returned to Gath's face. She smiled reassuringly.

"We will be leaving tomorrow," she explained. "My people do not wear long beards. They are already nervous about you. It might be easier for them if you looked more like one of us."

Gath fingered his beard, an ugly tangled mess that hung to the middle of his chest. He was more than ready to let it go. He nodded, and she exhaled with relief.

Henne stepped into the pool, holding the knife and stick, wearing only her loincloth and the sash binding her breasts. She would shear his beard the same way her people sheared sheep. She tentatively reached for him and he smiled encouragement. She wound one end of the long beard around the stick, rolling the hair, pulling it tight until she saw the pink skin underneath. She sliced as close to the skin as possible without cutting him.

Gath held very, very still. Their bodies were close. The steam rose up around them. Her sweet breath brushed his face. Her touch was gentle, inquisitive. He felt his manhood stir. The beard was almost gone now. His hand bumped her inner thigh, and stayed there like an unanswered question. Henne looked down into his eyes, her fingers on his face. He let her look into him. She inhaled a small gasp of air. He arched his back to kiss her. The kiss was long, lingering, full of lonely pain, understanding, and terrible yearning. She moved over him, adjusting her loincloth to accommodate him. He put his hands under her binding strap, loosening it, feeling the fullness of her breasts, and the weight of her body on his. He looked down into the water, to the place where they were connected. She looked with him. A tenderness came to his face. They kissed again. Slowly, their bodies discovered the rhythm of each other. Henne closed her eyes and leaned close. This was so different from her experience with Ralic; sweeter, more honest. Tears blurred her eyes, blending with the wetness around them. Once again, she loved a man of the Herd.

"We will not leave tomorrow," Gath whispered huskily into her neck. "I want one more day with you."

40

Yana sat in her house on the hill, trying to hum a chant, but she couldn't concentrate. She opened her eyes and looked around.

She always came here when something worried her. It seemed hard to believe she once felt confined in this house. Now the plaster walls encased old memories and friendly spirits that comforted her. She remembered Atum as a baby playing near the hearth, covering himself with gruel, and Galea's laugh. She remembered the moonspan she stayed here with Kara, a time of isolation that turned out to be a time of joy as they both discovered their mutual love for song. Here, Telna had come to her, forcing her to face her calling, embracing her as a priestess. But most importantly, this was her place with Tern, where they'd loved, and fought, laughed, and despaired. She had conceived the precious child in her womb here. This was home.

Yana stood and went to stand at the door. She hadn't placed the heavy wood door used in winter over the entrance. The bright day had no wind. She pushed away the door flap and leaned against the door frame, looking out over the village below. The small whitewashed houses reminded her of cut blocks of ice stacked in the snow. Dark trails meandered between them where people were coming and going. Dogs and goats milled about, trying to sneak into the warmth of the houses.

From where she stood it all looked peaceful, but Yana knew only too well the turmoil brewing in the village. How she wished Henne or Tern were here. They'd know what to do. The young people were getting tired of caring for the horses. None of them except Enyana had learned to ride, and the novelty of caring for them was beginning to wear off. The fear of the barbarians was also beginning to wear off. Some of the women were mumbling against her strict rationing of food. But most worrisome was the disapproval of the elders. Yana was almost sure a couple of them suspected her pregnancy. Why else would they question her leadership. Two had come to her privately, telling her that they would not leave their homeland. Yana couldn't blame them. How could one trust a leader with a child in her womb? How could she care for all the people when her love centered on one?

Yana's hand went to her breast. "I have fed you with my heart for many years," she whispered to the small village, her hand sliding down to her growing womb. "Please accept this."

Yana looked out over the terraced valley, noting that Enyana was riding her stallion again along the muddy slopes of the river. The snow was shallowest there, allowing the horse more leeway. This time one of the younger children of the village rode with her, arms wrapped around Enyana's waist, clinging to her for dear life. Yana's heart froze with fear and anger. The child wasn't a rider! What was Enyana thinking?

Suddenly she heard a shrill whistle. Yana looked to the far hills where the sound had come from. She recognized Henne and her horse, but not the man with her. Yana noticed that Enyana had pulled her stallion to a slow canter at her mother's sharp call. *Good,* she thought. *This time Henne can be the one to reprimand her daughter.*

*   *   *

Gath had agreed Henne should be the one to hold the reins since Moon knew her commands. Secretly, Henne was glad. She didn't need the villagers thinking Gath controlled her, at least not yet. So he rode behind, nuzzling her ear, occasionally caressing a breast, talking to her as they rode.

"First we must weaken them," he said, speaking of the horses, "feed them only hay for a few days. No more lentils and grain. Then we will geld them; the yearlings will be impossible to harness if we don't."

The couple crested a hill overlooking Henne's village. Before them stretched the terraced fields, the corrals, the houses, and the forest beyond. Henne inhaled sharply, pulling Moon up short. Below, in the very heart of the valley, Enyana raced on a stallion, her wild mane flying behind her. How dare she, Henne thought, her temper rising. How dare she train the horse without my instruction, and she has a child with her!

Gath slid off Moon and she followed, standing next to him. Henne let out an angry whistle. She now understood the outrage of the elders when she had blatantly ridden through their valley so many years ago, and her mouth twisted at the irony of the Goddess. Enyana slowed her horse to a trot and then a walk, eyes searching the hills for her mother. Furious, Henne turned back to Moon and grabbed the reins, ready to go after her daughter. Gath caught her arm, stopping her before she could mount the horse. Henne looked back at him, but he wasn't looking at her. She followed his gaze down the hill to Enyana. His lips were parted in surprise, and there was a look of astonishment on his face.

"She has harnessed the wild one," he mumbled in disbelief, "and the stallion is not gelded."

Henne shook her head as if she didn't understand.

"Look at her, Henne," he said. "Enyana is more than Ralic's daughter; she is Priestess of the Herd, the lead mare." He turned to her, eyes shining. "Don't you remember our talk in the cave?"

Henne looked at her daughter. Even from a distance, Henne could tell that Enyana was bracing herself for a confrontation. She sat proudly on her mount, her arrogant chin lifted, reminding her of herself at that age. Barely two hands of harvest seasons, and her daughter already carried herself like a woman. Henne wondered where the time had gone. When had Enyana escaped her mother's grasp?

"Yes," Henne sighed heavily. "She will be leader of her people, but she still has much to learn."

41

Enak listened carefully to the trader. He understood most words of the Goddess, but he had one of his female slaves interpret in case he misunderstood. The man's eyes shifted beneath his dark bushy brows, and Enak had the distinct impression he was lying. The trader told him that a woman with hair the color of burning embers, riding the white horse of the Moon Goddess, lived far to the north in the western ranges. He informed Enak that the easiest way to get there was to follow the Taru River north, a river Enak knew was treacherous, hard to navigate.

Enak pulled on the braids of his beard, asking what the man wanted for this information. The trader shuffled his feet, then settled on a price: a yearling colt, and perhaps some salt, not much. Enak sat for a moment as if he were considering this, then reached between the folds of his robe to the hidden knife, lunging at the man, burying the blade in the other's heart. Enak stood over the man shaking in outrage. How many more men with false tongues would he have to contend with? He gestured to his men to drag the body out into the courtyard. Perhaps these traders would now think twice before crossing him.

He stalked out after the body, calling Gilash to his side. "Where is this man from?" he demanded.

Gilash, proud his father had asked him a man's question, squared his shoulders. "He is one of the Sea People," he responded, anxious to tell his father all he had learned. "They live far to the west along the coast. I understand they are very wealthy, prosperous traders."

"I knew he was lying when he asked for so little," Enak snarled. "Obviously these Sea People know more than they are willing to share. I think we will go there first after the spring storms. I'm sure that if we take enough of their women and children, they will be more than willing to trade for the information we need."

A slave woman stepped away from the door flap inside the tent. Her hands trembled as she wrapped traveling food, a small knife, flint, and a scraper into the little girl's pack. She wiped the blood up off the tent floor with some of the girl's old clothes and hid these in a bag. She had been planning this for a long while, but after seeing the death of her cousin, she knew it could no longer wait.

"Amara," she said in a furtive whisper, "follow the river south. I have hidden more food and supplies in the old log I showed you, remember?"

The girl nodded, her face struggling against tears.

"I will tell the men you have gone to gather wood near the lakeshore. They will only find your bloodied clothes, a few locks of hair and the tooth I pulled. They will think a leopard dragged you away. I do not believe they will waste too much time looking for one little girl."

Amara threw her arms around her mother's neck. "I don't want to leave you, Mammar."

The slave woman pulled the little one to her chest in a tight squeeze, then inhaled a deep breath and peeled her arms away. She took the girl's hands, gazing directly into her eyes. "You must follow the river south until you come to the sea. Tell the people that live there that you are kin of Shanra and Roc, the High Priestess and Priest of the Sea People living in the west. Ask them to ferry you there. My sister will reward them handsomely for their efforts. Tell Roc what you have seen here, and that the Horse People are coming to take their women and children."

"I can't leave you," the little girl repeated, her chin quivering.

The slave woman had not wanted to frighten her daughter, but could think of no other way to convince her. The woman's face became stern, her voice lowered. "You must go now and never return," she said harshly. "I overheard the men joking. Raydag is going to ask for you as a gift for accompanying the headman and his son on the raid to the western mountains."

Amara's eyes widened with horror. Raydag, the most brutal of Enak's men, wanted her. The swarthy man frequently drank until he passed out. He beat his wives and it was said that he took pleasure with his young daughters as if they were his women. She had caught him looking at her with lust in his eyes, even though she still wore her child's beads.

"I will go, Mother," she said quietly.

The slave woman pulled the dear child to her breast. They held each other heart to heart, but at the sound of someone approaching the tent, they quickly pulled apart. "Now go," the mother hissed, hiding Amara's pack in the carrying sling used for hauling wood.

Amara fled the tent, tears streaming from her eyes just as Enak's first wife stepped inside. The girl almost ran into the big woman, but swerved out the opening at the last moment.

"What's wrong with her?" the older woman snapped.

The slave woman hardened her face to cover her emotions. "I punished her—told her she was lazy and needed to bring more wood for the fire. Tonight she will not eat."

The elder woman nodded, grunting her approval, glad that the woman was finally taking a hand in disciplining her daughter.

42

The people of the village observed winter solstice with much less enthusiasm this year than years past. No one knew just what the New Year would bring, and none of them were looking forward to spring, when they would leave their homeland forever. The festivities that usually lasted deep into the night dwindled early; many were weary and wanted nothing more than to hibernate in the darkness.

Yana had been driving the people hard, determined everyone would be ready to leave by the first snow melt. She wouldn't let up on the preparations for the journey across the mountains. Everyone worked from dawn to dusk making extra clothing, hard cheeses, travel food, and trade items for the Sea People. She went from house to house, helping the women decide what to take and what to leave behind. Henne was worse. She forced the young people to spend long days in the cold, working with Gath to domesticate the horses. Most of them were nervous around the Herdsman, who stood a head taller than any other man of the village, and who had eyes the color of the sky. Many thought he was a strange spirit who had bewitched their Hunting Priest. Henne certainly acted differently around the man, and everyone knew he shared her sleeping blankets. Nothing was right anymore.

It was night, another long, hard day finished. The

elders returned to their huts. Yana sat alone in the Goddess's shrine, contemplating these things. A rush of cold air interrupted her thoughts.

Henne burst into the shrine, tossing her feather-lined hunting cloak to the floor, plopping down next to Yana on the cushions before the idol of the Goddess. "Why, Goddess?" she asked, looking up at the statue, real frustration in her face. "Why is this so hard?"

Luckily Yana was the only one in the shrine. It wouldn't be wise for others to see Henne so agitated, especially now with tensions the way they were. Yana slowly lowered her spinning stick.

"Gath says only a handful of the horses will be ready to ride," Henne complained, slapping her hands on her knees. "The others are too young. He says we may be able to use a few of them to haul the tents and grain, but we are going to have to let four of them go."

Yana nodded but kept quiet, suspecting her sister's frustration had nothing to do with the horses. Henne sat in silence then began again, turning her whole body to face Yana. "Did you know Mother is considering staying behind?"

Yana took a deep breath. "I suspected as much," she said quietly.

Henne rose and began to pace. "Is it because of me?"

"You?"

"I brought this death to our village," Henne said angrily. "Everything changed when I returned home . . . and I see how our mother looks at me when I am with Gath. She doesn't approve. She doesn't understand how I can care for a man of the Herd." Henne stopped pacing and faced Yana. "And then of course there is Enyana to consider. Gath thinks I should continue to let her ride, but I know Galea thinks I should be more firm with her. I believe our mother is afraid I'm allowing her granddaughter to become too much like the Herdsmen. I know she loves Enyana dearly, but she no more understands her than she understands me." Henne collapsed again on the cushions, gazing directly into Yana's eyes. "Do you think our mother is disappointed in me? Is that why she is willing to stay behind?"

Yana contemplated her words, then nodded slowly. "Yes she is disappointed . . . disappointed in both of us."

Henne snorted. "You? You have always been able to make our mother smile."

Yana dropped her eyes and was silent.

Henne sat up, suddenly aware of Yana's discomfort. "What did I say, Yana?"

Yana's voice became hushed. "Do you think if I had removed the child in my womb, our mother would join us on the journey?"

Henne moved closer. Hesitantly she reached out and put her hand on Yana's belly in an intimate gesture the two women rarely shared. "Tern?" she asked quietly.

Yana looked up, her eyes glittering. "I already care for this child too much," she said in a rushed whisper. "I know I should have taken the herb that releases the womb as soon as I discovered life had taken root. It's not proper for the Mother of the People to give her heart to one child, but I'm getting old, Henne. This may be my last chance. I . . . couldn't do it."

Henne never desired another child after Enyana, but she knew that many women longed for children even after their children were grown and their wombs stopped giving blood to the fields. Such women were meant to have many children. Yana was one of these. She started to say so when she heard a loud commotion coming from the courtyard.

The dogs began to bark. Somebody screamed for help. Henne bolted to her feet, grabbed her spear, and ran for the door. Yana followed on her heels, but before they could exit, three men entered carrying a man bundled in furs.

"Lolim was checking one of her ewes and found him heaped near the corrals," Gelb rasped.

"Move aside," Henne commanded the young men.

"Who is it?" someone whispered.

Yana's hand went to her throat. She knew who it was even before Henne pushed back the parka hood—he hadn't stopped trying to get to her. "Tern," she said loudly. "It is Tern."

Henne gazed up at her sister, a question in her eyes. Yana came to squat beside her. With shaking hands she folded back the wolverine fur lining of his hood. Tern's closed face stared up at them, cheeks burned with frostbite.

Yana paled. Henne bent to close to listen for his breath, then jerked up her head. "He's alive," she whispered.

Tern slept for two days while the priestesses prayed and chanted for his recovery. On the third day he woke to find Yana sitting beside him. He was still very tired. He asked for water, then without speaking further asked that she gather everyone in the shrine. He had something to tell them, and he wasn't sure he had the strength to repeat his story over again. Yana quickly did as he requested, instructing the priestesses to bring the people. It wasn't hard to pull them away from their tasks; most had been anxiously awaiting Tern's awakening, curious as to why he crossed the mountains when winter storms were at their worst.

Tern waited, resting his reddened eyes that had seen too much snow. Yana sat at his head, a hand on his shoulder, trying to reassure herself that he was alive and would soon recover fully. Finally everyone was gathered. Tern opened his eyes, asked for more water, and began his story.

He told of a little girl. The girl had been a slave of the Herdsmen. She escaped, and after many hardships found her way to the mouth of a river where a small family group, people of the Goddess, lived. She begged them to take her to her mother's people far to the west. The men of the river were boatmen, and although the seas of winter were harsh, they agreed to take her up the coastline, fearing the wrath of the Herdsmen if the girl was discovered among them. Tern went on to tell the girl's story and of her warning to the Sea People.

"The Sea People have decided to escape with us to the islands," he said. "They are building more long boats, working day and night, even in the storms. On mornings when the sea is calm, they are risking transport, taking their wives and goods to the islands. The women are setting up camps in island caves. They tell of other islands, larger ones to the west with better lands, but for now they just want their people safe."

The people started to mumble their concern and Yana had to raise her arm to quiet them.

Tern paused, took a deep breath, and began again. "The Sea People sent me over the mountains to urge our people to come quickly; they don't want to lose any of their boats to the Herdsmen when they come. Spring advances sooner in the lowlands, so we must leave while winter is still in our mountains. Dagron stayed behind to make sure the link between our peoples is not severed." Tern closed his eyes tiredly.

Yana squeezed his shoulder. She had only one question. "How long will it take for us to travel through the passes?"

Tern reluctantly opened his eyes and gazed at the worried faces in the room. "A man alone with only his bow and carrying pack can make it in three hands of days. A whole village carrying all their supplies"— he shrugged—"six hands of days, maybe more. And that is only if there are no storms to hamper us."

Tern's head fell back on his sleeping mat. He was too exhausted to speak more.

Yana stood up. She called Henne and the elders

forward. They stood together in a group, sharing thoughts and ideas, conferring while the people watched. Finally Yana and Henne stood apart, addressing the people.

"It has been decided," Yana stated. "We will leave during the next waxing moon."

"If the weather permits," Henne added.

For a moment the people sat in silence, digesting these words, then the objections began.

"But that is only four handfuls of days away," Ninka's granddaughter, Plera, groaned. "I have more herbs to dry and salves to make. I can't possibly be done in time."

"My ewes won't have given birth by then," said another.

Henne's voice became firm. She lifted her vulture staff. "We are going to have to sacrifice most of the herd." Loud moans of dismay erupted around the room. Henne raised her other hand. "I know we originally said that we would take seed stock with us," she continued, planting her staff once again at her side, "but the pregnant ewes will not be able to travel, and the soft skins of their unborn lambs will be very useful in trade."

Everyone knew the short-curl lambskins were of considerable value, but rarely were they taken. The continuity of the flock was far too important for this. The destruction of the very seed of the herd, their livelihood, brought fear to the people's hearts.

Yana stepped forward, sensing the people's fear and reluctance. "We have been given a new seed," she said, reaching for the shell Tern had given her tied to a thong hanging from her neck. She lifted it as a reminder. "We will learn a new way with a new people. We will discover the ways of the sea, traveling the great womb waters of the Goddess to a place where the men of the Herd cannot find us."

The people fell silent. Yana's words held the ring

of power, strength in the Goddess. Who were they to question her? Most of them nodded, convinced that what she said was true, but a few held their heads stiffly, reluctant stubbornness remaining in their eyes.

43

The next few days were torturous for everyone as women and men slaughtered their favorite animals, curing the hides as quickly as possible, softening them with rancid butter. More than one woman cried as she held the precious pelt of an unborn lamb in her hands. Some of the bloody meat was dried in ovens, the rest carried to the top of the houses, left to freeze in the night air.

Not everyone was preparing to leave. Many of the women refused to kill their prize ewes and rams, and Yana was shocked to discover that at least a third of the village had chosen to stay behind. Most had aged parents who refused to leave the home of their ancestors. Yana worried about them. Who would counsel them as Mother of the People when she was gone? Guilt gnawed in her belly until a solution presented itself a few days before their departure.

It was morning. A hint of spring warmth teased the air. Kara entered the shrine, carrying a heavy armful of beautiful tapestries, and presented them to Yana. Yana received them, her mouth open in amazement and surprise. Kara was the best weaver in the village, making beautiful cloth for the robes of the priestesses, but these rugs were of magnificent quality. She'd never seen anything like them and wondered when Kara had found the time to make them. They would bring a fortune in trade goods, but Yana instantly knew she could never trade them.

Kara's eyes glowed at Yana's obvious delight. "These were the pleasure I kept for myself," she admitted. "I worked late in the night to make them. Each one tells a story." She pulled one from the pile. "This one represents the time you and I spent in your house on the hill." Yana's eyes dropped to the weave where the light-colored geometric patters made her think of birds. The pattern seemed to dance, and she remembered how they used to sing together. Kara pointed to another. "And this is of the time Shem saved Henne and Kire from the bull, remember?" The black-and-red weave charged into Yana's eyes, and the day came back clearly. Kara went on and on with the stories and Yana realized that the rugs represented the years of Kara's life, the years of the village.

"Why are you giving these to me, Kara?"

Kara reached for Yana's hand. "My mother died when I was young, taking my infant brother with her. Her sisters died in childbirth also. I've always known that if I was to have a child, I would also go to the Mother's womb. All my ancestors sleep in this valley. Someday my bone seeds will rest here with them." She paused, then plunged on. "I know you worry about the people remaining behind, I will stay with them, comforting them in the ways of the Mother. We will hide in the caves of the mountains until the seeds of summer have hidden in the ground. Hopefully the Herders will leave once they find our abandoned village. It is right that you and the others are going. Our valley was getting too small to accommodate all of us and the whole village could never hide safely in the mountain caves. The cave of the Goddess's womb is too sacred to invade. That is why the Goddess gave you and Henne another answer." She rested her hand on the rugs. "I want you to take these stories with you, so that when you are an old woman, the patterns in these tapestries will remind you of our stories, our ways, so we will find each other again in the place of dreams.

Yana nodded, reaching to pull Kara in a fierce embrace, letting go quickly, briskly wiping her eyes. "Now tell me the stories one more time," she said. "I want to remember them all.

It was just before dawn. Yana stood on the mound where she'd dreamed of the tattooed woman and the stalk of barley. Over the years she had felt the woman's presence and guiding wisdom. Although she still didn't know who she was, she felt tied to her in many ways, and couldn't leave without saying good-bye. As she stood watching the last stars of night fade, it came to her how richly she'd been blessed. She had always wanted a mother and had been given three: Galea, Telna, and this mysterious woman of the mound. She thanked the woman silently, bending to return the shard of pottery she'd found so many years earlier, and thought she felt the brush of fingers on her cheek.

Down in the village, Henne left her mother's womb house, head down, tears burning her eyes. Galea still refused to come. Henne had gone to her secretly, inquiring if her own failures were the reason her mother had chosen to remain in the village. Galea gave Henne the same answer she had given others. She was too old to follow the wandering womb of the Goddess. Her place was in this land among her mother's people. She didn't have the heart to tell Henne all the reasons she wished to stay behind.

Galea was not comfortable with her daughters and their new ways. Admittedly, she was somewhat disappointed in Yana; no Mother of the People ever put her own needs above the needs of the group. Yana should have done away with the child the moment she suspected it lived in her womb. And Henne. How could she love that strange man with his gruff ways? Sometimes he commanded her as if she were no more than a domesticated sheep or dog. Galea had to admit that Henne often objected when his requests were ridiculous, a man should get his own water, but she complied just as often. Galea shook her white head in frustration. She believed in the Goddess of growth and change, but this was too much.

Galea took her winter cloak from a peg and stuffed her arms in the sleeves, and as she did so, the real reason for her discomfort came to her mind. She had let Henne go once. The person who returned was not the same girl as the one who left. Deep inside, she was terrified of losing Henne once again. In some strange way, by staying here in the old ways, she was holding on to her daughters instead of letting them go. Here, memories of them were safe. Galea nodded curtly, and gazed around her house, thanking the spirits who had given her this insight. Now when her daughters said good-bye, they would find unguarded love in their mother's eyes.

The sun had just risen, casting a pink-and-gold blessing on the snowy horizon. It was a crisp, clear morning as Yana walked back to the village. She thanked the yolk of the Sun Goddess for smiling on their day of departure. Her eyes fell on the travois where Kara's precious tapestries were packed and her heart warmed, grateful to be carrying with her the memories of this place. Two travois carried fodder and grain for the horses, the other three hauled tents and heavy blankets. Her eyes scanned the crowd. Everyone going appeared to be present and dressed in traveling clothes, everyone carried something. Even the children had small packs strapped to their backs. But there were fewer people leaving with them; more families chose to stay behind once they learned of Kara's plan. The group had dwindled to half of the village.

There was a strange mixture of emotions present. Those going were excited and slightly nervous about the adventure, those staying wondered if they were making the right decision. All were a little sad. Yana and Henne made their way through the crowd as friends around them said their last farewells. The two women took turns embracing Galea, whose faith in them shone in her eyes. Tern came to stand beside Yana. Gath stood at Henne's side.

The two women stepped ahead of the group. The day before they had rehearsed the departure ritual, modifying the words usually said at the time of the Mountain Harvest. Yana began, lifting her staff and voice with words of hope.

Lead us to Your abundance, sweet Mother
As we are pushed from Your sacred womb
We carry with us the seeds of Your children.

Henne stepped forward, raising her hunting spear, speaking loudly.

Protect us, Wild Goddess
As the lioness, her kittens
The bear, her cubs
Protect Your offspring
Wandering from the den.

Yana formally handed Kara the pinecone walking staff. "The heart seed of the people is now yours to carry, Sister. It shall be a comfort to you in your old age, just as your woven memories will comfort me."

Kara nodded solemnly and took the staff.

Henne and Yana, followed by their men and children, stepped across the womb ring of the village, leaving its circle forever, but looking back and waving over and over again until they crossed the foothills and the village was out of sight.

44

The first four days of the trip were tiring but un-
eventful. On the fifth day a child slipped into a
crevice, breaking his leg. The people stopped early
while Plera set the limb. It was decided the child
would ride with the scouts the rest of the way, and
Enyana was given the task of caring for him. Enyana
started to complain, but one look at her mother's face,
and she snapped her mouth closed. Henne only allowed her to ride because of the strength of her stallion, and Enyana didn't want her mother to change
her mind. Gath gave her a sympathetic wink when
Henne was not looking. Enyana smiled. She liked this
new man of her mother's.

The people traveled for many days in the shadow
of a great cliff. They came to a place of deep snow.
Camp was set up, the travois unloaded, and for two
days the horses trampled the chest-high drifts, pushing
a trail through. As they followed the ancient trade
route up through the mountains, it became hard for
many to breathe the thin air. Again the group had to
stop and rest a few days, allowing their bodies to adjust to the higher elevations. By the time the people
passed through the highest ranges, most were exhausted, and with the exhaustion, anxiety grew. Children cried easily. Parents were less patient. Anger
broke out between friends. Yana shared her concerns
with Tern, and was surprised when he responded with
a solution.

"We need a few days of play," he said, tweaking her nose like a child.

Yana's brows furrowed into a frown. "We don't have time to stop and play," she admonished. "You said yourself that the boats will leave."

"Trust me," Tern replied, a twinkle in his eyes.

The next morning, Tern gathered the men, informing them that they would each be in charge of a group of women and children. Everyone laughed agreeably as he tied an oilskin about his waist, sat in the snow, and began sliding down the hill. After the men carved the safest route, the children, and even some of the older women took part in the sliding, sometimes coming to a stop in the middle of a snowbank, spitting puffs of white out of their noses and eyes. They traveled long distances this way. Yana could not remember a time when she'd laughed so hard. Even the dogs seemed to want to take part in the adventure, stumbling and rolling down the hills after the children. Tern was right, she thought, this is exactly what the people needed.

The people soon left the snow line of the mountains, descending into an environment different from their homeland. The air was warmer, dryer; the sandy soil the same gray and white color of the pockmarked limestone cliffs around them. The green boxtrees, junipers, and evergreen oaks contrasted starkly against the pale backdrop of cliffs, and it was apparent spring had come to this strange land; budding wild roses, honeysuckle, and the odor of thyme was everywhere. One day they crossed a shallow riverbed and thousands of tiny mud-colored frogs accompanied them on their journey, bouncing everywhere they stepped, and Yana couldn't help musing on the changes of spring and the wandering womb of the Frog Goddess.

Finally, after a moonspan of travel, the people stood on a bluff overlooking the ocean. They had heard stories of the Great Waters of the Goddess, but nothing in their experience could have prepared them for the sight before their eyes. Many sat down in numbed shock, fear on their faces as they watched the incessant waves throw rocks and sand again and again on the shore.

Tern pointed to two dark mounds on the horizon, barely discernable from the low clouds and the heaving sea. "Those hills are the beginning of a string of islands," he said. "The first one is a day's sailing from here."

"We are going to cross that?" a woman gasped as a wave crashed over a boulder, sending a spray of fine mist into the air.

Tern gestured to nine colorful boats, overturned and pulled high up on the sand, away from the tide. "The men here are competent sailors," he responded, putting confidence in his voice. "The Sea People will get us to the islands safely."

Henne threw a leg over Moon's neck and dropped to the ground, striding to where Tern stood. "Where are these Sea People you speak of?" she demanded. "I see only an abandoned village."

Startled, Tern shifted his eyes past Henne to the huddled group of houses on a distant rise below. Life did not seem to stir in the village. There were no signs of sheep or pigs in the corrals. The fields hadn't been tilled. Dogs did not bark a warning at their presence. A few tendrils of weak smoke escaped a large house in the center of the village, but nothing more.

Henne turned to her scouts. "I will go down first," she growled. "If the Herdsmen are hiding in the houses, I will whistle a warning." She gave Enyana and Ryle a hard look. "You must lead the people back to the mountains, no matter what happens to me."

Gath stepped beside her. "I will go also," he asserted, addressing the worried faces gathering around Henne. "I was Enak's advisor after Ralic's death. He will not expect me to be with your Hunting Priest.

Hopefully he will listen before coming at us with raised spears, and you will have time to escape."

Henne nodded soberly at Gath's words. The plan was not perfect, but it would have to do. She turned to mount Moon when suddenly her eyes caught movement in the village. A man stepped out of the central house, automatically turning his face toward the mountains, searching the passes, and Henne had the distinct impression he had done this many times. She inadvertently stepped forward, noting something familiar about the cut of his winter parka and the broadness of his shoulders. The man let out a whoop of delight, waving his arms in a wide arch.

"Dagron!" Niam shrieked, recognizing him first. She dropped her pack and lifted her skirt, already running down the hill toward the village with Ashera close on her mother's heels.

Another man joined Dagron in the courtyard, and another, all waving a welcome. The people surged down the hill after Niam and her daughter like sheep returning from pasture, relieved that soon they would be resting in dry houses next to warm hearths, reliving the adventures of crossing the mountains in their storytelling.

Only Henne and Gath hung back, both frowning in apprehension, noting the village was not situated well for defense. It had been built to take in the beauty of the sea and surrounding fields of grain. Henne's eyes searched the terrain for strategic places to hide and defend if need be. She conferred with Gath, pointing out likely places, and then both decided that it would not be wise if the scouts remained in the village. They needed every extra person on guard, watching for the Herders.

"Gelb and some of the others are sure to complain," Gath hedged, not mentioning Enyana, the one most likely to object. "We have been pushing them hard, and they will expect at least one night of rest and refreshment."

Henne flipped a braid over her shoulder, hearing the hint and warning in his voice. "Our men will protect the people," she said firmly. Her eyes narrowed. "As for Enyana and the other women who have chosen to serve the wild heart of the Goddess, I will hear no murmuring of protest from their mouths. Our people's safety is too important."

Gath pointed out over the ocean. "The scouts will be raising their tents in the mud if we wait much longer. There's no telling how long that storm is going to last."

Henne followed his gaze out to sea. Distant clouds began to charge inland, bringing the scent of rain. The water churned angrily, tossing pewter dark limbs to the sky then slamming them down again on the shore. A gust of wind lifted the flap of her skirt. Henne nodded curtly and without another word, mounted Moon, pulled the reins toward the village, and kicked the horse into a trot.

It rained incessantly for three days and nights. The third night, near dawn, the Hunting Priest of the Sea People suddenly woke from his dreams, unsure of what caused his eyes to flutter open. Roc listened. Distantly he heard the comforting lullaby of the Great Waters, but all else was silent. He quickly realized it was silence that roused him—the endless drumming rain had stopped. He threw off his sleeping blankets, donned his leggings and cloak, and stepped outside to find the last stars of night still struggling against pre-dawn light. Clouds no longer marred the sky. He stretched. It smelled and felt like a good sailing day, but there was much work yet to do to prepare.

Taking long strides, Roc quickly walked toward the outcropping of rocks where he knew Henne and Gath were camped. He missed Rana's laughter and their new daughter Senra's smile. All he needed was one full day of rowing and he would be with them again.

He wondered how they fared in the cave that had recently become their home.

Roc was surprised to find Henne and Gath already up and moving about. Henne waved him over, inviting him to sit and share their morning meal of gruel and nuts. Roc declined, indicating he would eat later.

"I came to tell you that we must start loading the boats now," he said urgently. "It takes a full day to sail out to the islands, and that is only if the wind is right. I am sure by now you understand how dangerous the spring storms are here. We cannot afford to wait."

Henne stood slowly, remembering the heavy, pelting rain and driving wind of the last few days. "Have you told the others?"

"I will. I thought you might want to get word to your scouts. We will have to leave before midmorning."

Henne nodded curtly. Gath stood beside her. "We will be prepared to go," Gath said, his voice dropping gravely, "but we must remain hidden until the last boats are ready to depart."

They all shared a look of concern, not needing to share what was on their minds. It was certain the Herders would be on the move again now that the storm had passed.

A smile crept into Roc's face and eyes. "It will be good to feel the sea breeze on my face again." He laughed, eagerness for the adventure in his voice. "And as soon as my Rana sees our boats coming, she will begin preparing a great feast. Tonight our bellies will bulge with food. All our people will sleep warm, safe in the arms of the Goddess this night."

Henne smiled at Roc's enthusiasm. Gath, seeing the tension leave Henne's face, reached to caress her neck with his large hand. Roc averted his eyes, apparently uncomfortable with Gath's affectionate display.

Henne sighed, wondering if the men of the Goddess would ever completely trust this blue-eyed giant beside her, the man who had come to share her heart so completely. She turned and faced him, resting a hand on Gath's arm.

"I will gather our things," she said quietly. "Take one of the horses. Make sure everyone knows to wait for my signal before descending to the beach. They are to stay alert for any signs of the Herders."

Enak walked around the gritty ashes of the cold fire, growling at the men still sleeping after drinking themselves to a stupor the night before. He detested this group of lazy complainers, the worst of his men. The good ones had stayed behind with long excuses on their lips; it was the calving time of year, some wanted to move their herds to better pasture, the family tent needed mending, but Enak knew the real reason.

Most no longer wanted to quarrel with the Goddess of this land, were no longer interested in the glories of conquest. Why take something and run when you could have a steady supply of grain, blankets, seasonal vegetables, baskets, and pottery? They were happy with the trade relationship with the farmers. The villages of the Goddess were hungry for meat and leather, the big game of their lands having been hunted down to nothing over the countless years of settled life. The boon of grassland-fed cattle was rewarded richly in trade. Enak shook his head, having to admit that his people lived richer today than they had in his father's day, that is everyone except this ragged group of men who took everything and gave nothing in return. Enak kicked Raydag's foot.

"Get up," he snarled. "The God of the Shining Sky has been spitting in your face all morning. I won't wait any longer."

Raydag grumbled, elevating himself on his elbows. He lifted a hand to ward off the glare coming from the tent opening, bleary eyes surveying the makeshift shelter to see if any of the other men were getting the same treatment. Most were in varying stages of waking up, disgruntled as he was.

Enak put his hands on his hips, elbows out. A scout had just returned, saying he had spotted a large village near the Great Waters a short ride to the west. Enak was sure it was the village of the Sea People. Finally he would learn the whereabouts of that traitorous woman, Henne. Secretly, he missed the comforts of his home tent. The glories of conquest, especially with this disgusting group, were not the same as they had been in his youth, and he had grown tired of it all. He realized he just wanted this raid over and his honor returned.

"The storm is over," Enak bellowed to his men. "Pack your things. Today we ride. Today we take women and slaves!"

45

It was a bright day, the air calm. Sun glared off ocean stretching as far as the eye could see, the expansiveness of it diminishing all else. Henne sat rigidly on her mount overlooking the bay, gazing down on the white sandy beach scattered with people working hard to fill the boats with essential items they would need to survive in the islands. Many of the serpentine-shaped vessels were already packed, bobbing in the surf like colorful flowers of indigo blue, spring green, yellow, and amethyst red.

Henne began to relax as the last of the children climbed into the boats. After months of worrying, soon her people would be safe. Her only regret was that she'd have to leave Moon and the other horses behind.

It was hard for Henne to imagine life without her precious mare, and it saddened her to think that Moon probably wouldn't last long in the wild. Moon had been a constant companion, a friend over the years, and she knew she was going to miss her terribly. Henne let her thoughts wander. Perhaps their domesticated horses would form a small herd. Later in the summer, when the threat of the invaders passed, she could return with her scouts and recapture them. Maybe the Sea People would help them figure a way to transport the horses to the islands. Henne shook her head, upbraiding herself for foolish thoughts. It would take many seasons to reestablish the villages.

Houses needed to be built, fields tilled and prepared for planting. There would be no time to pursue the dream of horses. She reached sadly to pet Moon's neck, comforting herself with the knowledge that Gath had decided to come with her to the islands. At least she would not have to leave him behind. They both would make a new life for themselves away from the conflicts of their opposing peoples.

Henne sat up. She had been daydreaming, not paying attention. Her eyes nervously swept the landscape but did not find anything unusual. She could not see Gath or her men in the surrounding hills, but knew they were hiding, awaiting her signal to join those on the beach. Roc waved at her from below. Tern and Yana waved vigorously also, and Henne suddenly realized that the time was now. Only two boats waited near the shore, the others had pushed out to sea. She was about to lift the large conch shell, send the signal, when a shrill whistle from the east came to her ears, lifting the hair on the nape of her neck. Henne's head jerked toward the sound, her belly roiling in fear. Enyana, mounted on her stallion, raced along the top of a nearby ridge, a pack of men on horseback close behind.

"Oh, Goddess, no," she whispered.

Henne kicked Moon into a gallop. Somehow she had to intercept them, get between Enyana and the Herders before they killed her daughter.

The people on the beach also heard Enyana's sharp whistle. Tern's head lifted abruptly, finding the scene he feared most. Men. Strangers on horseback. He watched Henne's scouts spill out of hiding, racing to save Enyana. He turned around, picked up Yana, almost tossing her into the boat. "Get to deep water!" he shouted to Roc.

Yana grabbed his tunic, refusing to let go, screaming, "You're coming with me!"

Tern tried to shake her off but she held fast, desperation in her eyes.

"We will go a short way out and wait," one of the men yelled. "If any escape they can swim to us."

"There is nothing you can do," Yana insisted. "They have horses and we don't know how many more are waiting in the hills."

Tern looked back toward the bluff. Yana was right. The barbarians were too far away. He would never be able to make it in time to be of any use to the others. He quickly helped push the boat away from shore and jumped on board.

Henne careened down the hill, barely aware of her men around her. Dimly she sensed Gath nearby, but her entire focus centered on saving her daughter. Enak's angry scarred face flashed before her as he reined close. He lunged with his spear, missing, but grazing Moon's flank. Henne slashed outward with her knife, nicking his arm, tearing the cloth. Behind her, Gelb screamed as a man stabbed him with a spear, flicking him from his horse, trampling him. Ryle leaned from his mount, grabbing the Herdsman and they both tumbled off their horses. Henne jerked her reins. Moon sidestepped to avoid the wrestling men.

Suddenly, Henne felt the heavy thump of a spear butt in her side. Someone had hit her from behind. She found herself on the ground, the wind knocked from her lungs, the right side of her body screaming in pain. Enak dove on top of her, blade raised. She tried to reach up to stop him, but her arm would not move; it lay twisted and broken beneath her. The world seemed to slow as she looked into Enak's crazed eyes. She felt his hatred descend with the knife. She lurched. The knife missed its mark, but penetrated below the ribs. Enak fought to hold her down, raising the red-stained knife.

Suddenly Gath was there, bellowing like a wild ox, ripping Enak from his deathlike embrace. The knife went flying. The two men struggled in the dirt, fists plowing into ribs and faces, both screaming outrage.

Ryle crawled to Henne on all fours.

"Go after Enyana," Henne gasped.

Ryle nodded and whistled for his horse, mounting it only to discover that he was too late. Three men approached on horseback, leading Enyana's stallion. She struggled in the arms of one of them, hands tied behind her back. It was evident the girl had put up a fight. Her legs were bruised and bloodied, her braids loose. Flyaway hair clung to her sweaty torso and face. Ryle knew he couldn't fight all three men so he hid in the shadow of a boulder, deciding to retreat to the safety of the hills, rallying the others with a plan of rescue.

Gath and Enak continued to roll in the dirt. The men of the Herd stood around watching, faces blank with confusion. They knew Gath. He had been their former leader's advisor. It was obvious he was challenging Enak's right to lead, but why now?

Gath's breath came in quick, hurtful gasps, his arms aching and heavy, but he would not give up. He would fight until death for this dream of a new life burning in his heart, the hope Henne had brought him.

Enak rolled over, spitting out a tooth. It had been a long time since a man had challenged him in battle, and the man panting beside him was stronger than a bull. He lifted to lunge again, rolling on top, looking into the other man's face. Enak's heart skipped a beat. Blue eyes stared up into his. Gath! His father's old friend, his best advisor. He struggled to stand, pulling Gath up with him.

"Why is a man of the Herd fighting me?" he gasped.

Gath leaned over, panting hard, then stood and wiped the blood from his lip. "I believe," he gasped, "Ralic would have wanted it."

Enak shook his head as if he heard wrong.

"Ralic wanted his children to live and grow strong in this land," Gath insisted.

Gath heard Henne groan, and all interest in the fight fled his face. He jerked away and stumbled toward Henne, dropping to his knees, pulling her head onto his lap. He moaned at the red stain spreading under her ribs.

Henne's eyes fluttered open. She felt weightless, almost the same feeling as riding Moon across a grassy plain. Gath's torn and bleeding face hovered over her. She wanted to reach out and touch him, but found her weightless arms were really very heavy.

"Is Enyana safe?" she choked.

"What?" Gath asked, bending closer.

"Enyana. Is she all right?"

Gath's face struggled against the truth. "Enak's men have her," he whispered.

Henne tried to elevate herself on her elbows, but fell back again. "Tell the headman I wish to speak to him."

Enak, standing close by, watched the curious scene, wondering why Gath held his enemy as if she were a precious wife. He stepped into Henne's view.

"What do you want, woman?" He spat.

"You have captured my daughter."

Enak laughed harshly. This was even better than he planned. He motioned Gilash and the others to bring Enyana forward. "Mother and daughter will die together!" he snarled.

"Mother!" Enyana screamed, seeing Henne's blood-splattered tunic. She struggled in the younger man's arms, trying to break away.

"Stop, Enyana," Henne barked, forcing as much strength into her voice as she could muster. Henne closed her eyes, the sense of euphoria slipping away. Pain returned with her determined thoughts, her chest felt heavy and she couldn't breathe. "Goddess," she whispered. "I must do something."

Ralic's face rose before her closed lids, his body black as the vulture cape she wore. Kindness stood in his eyes. *Return to me the breath you stole,* he whispered. *Return to me my daughter.*

She blinked. Henne had her answer. If only Enak would understand.

Henne challenged Enak by hardening her eyes and lifting her chin. "Look at your sister," she said quietly, using the language of the Herdsman. "Tell me who you see."

Enak snorted but he couldn't help doing as Henne requested. Sister? He remembered being amazed at the way the child had sped across the cliffs on her fabulous stallion. No woman of his tribe would dare approach such a horse. He stepped closer. Enyana's eyes sparked with belligerent anger. Where had he seen that look before? Looking past her tousled hair and dirty shift, he found features that suddenly spoke to him. Ralic stared back at him, proud, defiant, indestructible. His father was in every curve of her face, in the shape of her mouth and eyes, the flare of her nostrils. This was his younger sister!

Enak turned back to Henne, questions and bewilderment in his eyes.

"Would you really destroy Ralic's blood?" Henne asked, grinding her teeth against the pain ripping her side. "I had to save your father's seed growing in my womb," Henne gasped. "I was right to save her!"

Enak wiped the sweat dripping from his brow, peering once again at Enyana held tightly in the arms of his son. Both young people sat proud, defiant, determined. Deeply, he knew Enyana and Gilash were the best of his people, and he was strangely humbled by the strength in their faces. This was the new seed his father had spoken of so many years before. No wonder the best of his men had stayed behind, choosing not to fight. They still remembered Ralic's words, his vision. Enak realized he had let his anger blind him for too many years. No. He would not kill this small sister who had the face of his father.

Enak turned to Gath, cocking his head toward Henne. "Will you come or stay with this woman," he asked cautiously, knowing the men around him were waiting for an end to the challenge.

Gath stood slowly. "My women are dead, my sons

grown to manhood by now. I will stay with Henne, protect her." He paused, adding emphasis. "I believe your father would have wanted it."

Enak glared at Henne. "It appears you still have the power to bewitch your men, woman." He sneered.

Gath took a threatening step forward.

Enak waved him away. "Take your woman, Gath. Leave this land. I do not want to hear rumors of your presence. I will live with the belief that Henne has died from her wounds."

Henne lifted her head weakly. "Enyana?" she gasped.

Enak paused, his brows pinched in concentration. Perhaps there was still time to mend the rift that had grown between himself and the other men of his tribe. He would be a hero if he brought Ralic's daughter back to the people; his conquest regarded a victory. But he had to make sure there would be no attempt of rescue or escape.

"It has been ordered by the gods," Enak said loudly, lifting his horse-headed scepter. "Ralic's child will live as a daughter in my tent, given wealth and prestige, but if I hear of any attempt to rescue her, her life will be forfeited." He turned to Gilash. "Let the child go to her mother." He glared at Henne. "I would advise you to urge your daughter not to try to escape me," he said in threatening tones. "You know what happens to our slaves." The headman turned to walk away, but tossed words of caution over his shoulder to his son. "Watch her closely," he growled.

Henne closed her eyes in relief. Enyana would be a daughter, not a slave.

Gilash untied Enyana's hands. She jumped from the horse and ran, throwing herself on her knees beside Henne. "Mother, this is all wrong," she whispered. Tears began to flow down her face. "We have to get to the boats."

Henne dragged her eyes open. This time it was much harder to keep them open. She gasped at the tightness in her chest. "You must go with your father's people. Learn all you can about the People of the Herd, then teach them about the Goddess in ways that their hearts will understand." Henne wheezed. "Promise me you will never forget you are a woman of the Goddess, Enyana."

The girl nodded through her sniffles, throwing her arms around her mother.

Henne began to feel euphoric again, floating on a drift of air. A breeze sprang up, and she noticed how it teased her daughter's hair, caressed it in a way she wished she could. She tilted her head to Gath's face, her eyes shimmering with love for both of them. "I want to see the boats," she said.

Enyana sat back. Gath hauled Henne to his chest so she was almost sitting in his lap. She gazed out at the water and the two boats bobbing in the surf. It seemed appropriate that the snake of the Goddess who continually sheds her skin in rebirth was taking her people to a new land.

Enak barked something and Gilash strode over, standing over Enyana, indicating it was time to leave. Wild desperation filled Enyana's eyes.

Henne's voice became firm. "Now is the time to prove your strength, Daughter. The blood of the headman runs in your veins. Let them see how you ride, how tears do not keep you from your purpose. Someday, your time of power will be handed back to you."

"Mother . . ."

Gilash tugged on Enyana's arm. Henne looked into the young man's face. The boy was almost the same age as her daughter, yet hard lines cornered his eyes.

"She is your sister now," Henne told him in the language of the Herdsman.

The young man's chest puffed out. Raw intelligence smoldered in his eyes. He understood the message behind Henne's words. "The women of my father's tent are always protected—well provided for," he said proudly.

Henne's eyes extracted his promise. She nodded slowly.

Gath reached to squeeze Henne's hand as Gilash led Enyana away. He whispered love in her ear, begging her to live. Henne leaned deeply into his chest, the sobs of her daughter dwindling as the Herdsmen rode off. The grief of losing Enyana tore at her heart. She prayed the girl's strong spirit and quick mind would save her. She looked once more out at the small boats lifting their sails to the wind, sad to see her people go, but glad they would remain true to the Goddess. Someday perhaps, a kinder people would live on these shores, and her people would be able to return.

"Go with the Goddess, Sister," Henne urged, closing her eyes. "Keep the heart of the Goddess alive for all of us."

Roc pointed to clouds gathering on the horizon. "Another storm. We can't wait any longer!"

Yana chewed her lip at the dark threat.

"If we leave now, we can outrun it," Roc insisted.

Tern grasped an oar. "We must make the islands," he said roughly, determined to save Yana and their unborn child.

In the distance, Yana could see the sun shimmering off the red highlights of Henne's hair. Her sister was down, wounded. She had seen Enyana ride off with the Herders. Deeply, Yana understood Henne's spirit would remain behind, living on in her daughter, as would the wild spirit of the Horse People. She felt the rise of a breeze, her stomach lurching as a wave rocked the boat. She put one hand over the child in her womb.

"We will always remember your sacrifice, Sister," Yana breathed, her heart swollen with love. "We will sing for you, dance with the blood of the bull. Your wild heart will never be forgotten."

Yana squeezed Tern's thigh. A memory, and words

came to her mind as she lost sight of her sister on the shore.

> *As wheat fills the belly in times of abundance*
> *May your life be abundant and long*
> *May your seed spread on the wind,*
> *Finding rich soil until the Mother Goddess holds you*
>   *again*
> *In Her sacred Womb.*

Epilogue

Gath shot the young buck, but his hands shook badly and he missed the heart. Fortunately, other arrows helped down the animal. After thanking the wild heart of the Goddess for Her sacrifice, Gath found he no longer had the strength to carry his own meat, and the younger men of the hunting party had to haul it to their temporary camp. Later, he found butchering and preparing the hide was difficult for his knobby fingers, and Gath sadly realized this would be his last hunt.

Benel squatted next to him. "Why don't you let me do that, Honored One," he said, reaching for Gath's knife. "Tonight the men would enjoy the wisdom of your stories as we work."

"Benel, I can still . . ."

"Tell the one about the serpent and the sea," the youngest man in the group interrupted, pleading. "Tell how the men of the horse wanted the seeds of rebirth so they could be as strong as the Goddess, but the Snake Goddess rose out of the great waters, swallowing the seeds, and carried them out to sea."

"You tell the story better than I do, Chirack." Gath laughed at the youngster's enthusiasm. He leaned back as if in thought, and scratched his nose. "No. I will tell another story, one you have not heard," he said slowly, tilting his head to one side, a hint of mystery in his words.

Gath was well known for his storytelling and the

tone in the old man's voice promised a very entertaining evening. The young men of the hunting camp eagerly leaned forward. A smile twitched the corners of Gath's mouth. He had been working on the new story for a moonspan now, and the ending had come to him earlier in the day.

Gath placed his hands on his knees. "This is the story of a man who forgot he was a man, one who grew up on the steppes," he said loudly, "running with the People of the Horse, lost in his mind and heart."

Gath went on to chant the story of a man who could no longer live with the wrongs he found in himself and others. The man ran away from his clan, becoming wild like the animals, wearing only fur, living in caves and holes, running with the gazelle and deer. One day he drew close to a village and saw women dancing to the Goddess. The dancing reminded him that he was a man, but he did not want to remember, so he ran and hid once more.

Gath shifted in his seat, his voice dropping. "Rumors came to the village of a strange creature living in the hills. The Hunting Priestess wanted to see this animal for herself. She hunted it down, only to find a sick man fighting evil spirits. She called on her Goddess. She danced for him, prayed for him. She removed his furs and bathed his body in womb water, washing away his pain, feeding him fruit and grain. She told him to leave the animal man behind, open his heart again to the gods. She placed her wondrous body next to his and treated him to a woman's task. The man woke from his sad dream, embracing the priestess and her Goddess, leaving his wild life behind forever."

Gath cleared his throat, letting his eyes rove the captive audience. "The priestess led the man to her people," he continued. "She taught him of the Goddess, he taught her the ways of the horse, until one day a message came to the village. The horsemen of the steppe were coming to steal the strength of the Goddess."

Gath's voice rose. "The Goddess hid some of Her strength in the caves, some of Her strength in the sea. When the horsemen came they found only the priestess and her daughter." He hesitated, seeing smiles glint in the eyes of some of the older men who were beginning to recognize the story.

"Don't stop now, Honored One," Chirack begged, not realizing childlike insistence had replaced the manliness in his voice.

Gath sat for a while mulling the words in his mind. Words were a powerful force, and he wanted to end this story just right. "As I was saying," he said slowly, "the priestess and her daughter stayed behind as a diversion, allowing the strength of the Goddess to hide. The men of the Herd thought that if they killed the priestess, her power would die. But when the headman attacked, the wild man burst from hiding, charging like an angry bull. The Herders did not expect a man who had lived on the steppes to fight for the priestess. The two men wrestled in the dust until blood ran down their faces, until the headman recognized that he was not fighting an enemy, he was fighting one of his own. They stopped fighting and leaned together as brothers.

"In exchange for the life of the Hunting Priestess it was agreed that her daughter was to return with the Herders to teach them the ways of the Goddess. Eventually, the Hunting Priestess recovered from her wounds and left with her horses and scouts, traveling far to the west and north, away from the Herdsmen. There she began a new people."

"But what happened to the daughter?" the boy breathed.

Gath's smile added wrinkles to his face. "For a while it was rumored that the girl traveled to the Herdsmen's Underworld," he paused. "Then we heard that the young woman returned to become a great priestess over a vast city." Gath was handed a chunk of roasted venison. He took a bite. He waved his hand in a dismissive gesture, blue eyes twinkling. "But that is more words . . . for another time." He laughed. "Now we eat."